TWISTED FREEDOM

First edition. March 10, 2024.

Copyright © 2024 J.Grayland.

ISBN: 979-8224181834

Written by J.Grayland.

I'm lucky to have so many special people in my life to thank in their unconditional love and support in my endeavour to follow my dream.

Besides the ever present love of my husband and children, I would like to thank my brother, sister, their families, and my mum with a special thank you .

Twisted Freedom

By

J.Grayland

Prologue

Pulling my body closer into the wall, I try to absorb as much warmth from it as I can. With chattering teeth and dry lips and mouth I wrap my arms around my legs and try to make myself as small as possible. I roll my tongue around in my mouth trying to moisten it...but there's nothing. Rubbing my hands against the dirty flesh of my legs I can feel my bones. They ache so much. Every part of my body hurts, and the smell in the room is a mixture of human waste and death. Time is non-existent. I used to count every hour, every minute, and every second until the pain made my head feel fuzzy, and then all the numbers just blurred into one.

I hear a noise at the door, and I look up to the small hole that was made in it some time ago. The tiny little spot of hope that sometimes gives me a small glimpse of light through it reminding me of a star, until it flickers, and I know he is there watching, and while he's watching, he's not hurting me. That particular pain stopped when that tiny hole appeared in the door. Around the same time, he ceased his morning ritual of throwing me a bottle of water and scraps of bread. Then he would walk away laughing as I greedily stuffed them into my mouth to soothe the pain in my belly. Now that pain is a constant reminder of how desperately hungry and thirsty I am.

I know it won't be long now before sleep overtakes my body, and I won't wake up. I keep hoping that this time when I close my eyes it will be over, no more pain, no more hunger, no more...him. Just peace.

Chapter one

C*asey*

Leaning my head back against the top of the chair, I gazed out the walls of glass that look outside onto the tarmac of the PDX airport. The sun was just going down, and I stared at the different planes lining up in rows, some waiting to take off on their journey, and some waiting for passengers to board. I watched as people shuffled and dragged their bags and cases through the departure lounge to their designated area before they flopped down into the rows of plastic seats.

Looking down at the passport held tightly in my hand, I saw the word "Sydney" printed on the top of my boarding pass that was wedged between its pages. *"Home....I'm going home, so why am I not as excited at that prospect as I expected to be?"* I let out a deep sigh, releasing that thought. Suddenly, I felt warm fingers entwine with mine as he brought my hand up to his mouth to place a kiss against my skin. I look up into those beautiful, steel grey eyes that never ceased to make me smile.

"Stop," Nate said in a low grumble.

"Stop what?"

"Overthinking. I can hear your brain ticking over," he said, one brow arching.

"Sorry," I murmured. "I'll try to keep the noise level down."

"No, you'll tell me what's going on in that crazy mind of yours," he said with a quirk of his lips.

I slowly shook my head and said, "Well, apart from the obvious, I thought this would feel different. Going home, you know?"

"And it doesn't?"

"Yes...no, I don't know. It feels strange. I mean, I'm excited to see Flynn, but it feels like I'm leaving home. Does that sound weird to you?"

"No, baby, it sounds great to me," he said smiling.

"You're not being very helpful here," I said, giving him a playful scowl.

"I'm sorry, it just sounds good to hear you say that you don't want to leave. I know you have Flynn in Sydney, but here, you have a new family that you've bonded with, so it's understandable that you're apprehensive."

"I guess," I said, nodding.

He placed a finger under my chin, tilting it up so I was looking into his eyes. "Hey, everything is going to be okay. I promise you."

Looking at Nate, I saw the strength he put behind his words, and I felt it as his lips lightly brushed over mine before the intimate moment was broken by a sudden loudspeaker announcement. "Attention all passengers, Qantas Flight 112 leaving at 7:40 a.m. for Sydney, Australia is now boarding. Will all first and business class passengers please make your way to the check-in counter."

Nate leaned his forehead against mine. "That's us, baby." He stood, pulling me up with him.

"No, wait, they said first and business class," I started to say, but my words were instantly stopped by the smile tugging at the corner of his mouth. "Wait. What? Please, tell me you didn't book us first class seats." Still smiling, he shook his head and led me to the check-in desk.

"Okay, I won't tell you that, and I won't tell you we're in business class, either," I stopped walking, causing him to stop, as well, and look at me.

"What?" he said, amused. "Look, if you think I am going to squash all six foot three inches of me into one of those tiny seats for nineteen plus hours, you've got another think coming. Besides, the first class seats were too far apart, and when I sleep, I like to be able to touch you."

I gave him a playful slap on the chest. "If you think I am having sex in our seats, *you* have another think coming, mate."

"Not in the seats, but maybe..."

"Not happening, don't even think about it," I said as I pulled him toward the check-in desk. We handed the hostess our boarding passes, and then made our way down the gangway and onto the plane. He was right, the seats were much more comfortable, and there was much more leg room, but I didn't feel comfortable about the cost. Yes, I knew he could afford it, but I liked to pay my own way, and I would never pay that amount of money for a plane ticket.

"Stop," I heard him say in a low growl.

"Stop what?"

"Stop overthinking about how much the tickets cost. I don't give a damn, and besides, Paxton will have some sneaky way to write it off as a business trip or something."

I gave him a weak smile, wondering how the hell he knew what I was thinking, then let out a defeated sigh. "Okay, I'll stop."

"Good, now buckle up," he said, motioning to my seat belt.

With a smooth lift off, it wasn't too long before we were served our evening meal, and I had to admit this business class seating was pretty good. A flight attendant with roving eyes came to clear away our trays, grabbing mine first so she had to lean over Nate, her boobs almost rubbing against his face. Looking at her through narrowed eyes and giving her a primal bitch look, her eyes widened when she saw my stare, and she pulled back quickly to offer Nate a huge smile.

"Would you care for a drink, sir?" she asked sweetly.

"Just some more water, please," Nate said, smiling back at her.

"And a baseball bat," I whispered under my breath as I turned to look out the window, making Nate cough to cover a laugh.

"What the hell, Casey, a baseball bat?" he said once the flight attendant left.

"Yeah, well I might need it to subdue her when she tries to molest you in your sleep."

"Most flight attendants are over friendly. She's just doing her job," he said, making me turn my head sharply to look at him.

"Are you fucking kidding me? If she's not standing around eye fucking you, she's over here trying to rub her chest over you, Nate. She practically has drool on her chin," I said, crossing my arms over my chest like an insolent child.

He stared at me for a moment, and then his lips twitched into a wide grin before he reached over the console that divided our seats and easily lifted me over it and onto his lap. "Nate," I started to protest, but he stopped me with a soft touch of his thumb over my lips, then tucked my head under his chin. "What are you doing?" I hissed.

"Calming your jealous ass," he said in a low tone.

"I'm not jealous," I pouted as he kissed the top of my head.

"Okay, then I am going to keep you here on my lap so that she can plainly see that I only have eyes for you, and she doesn't stand a hope in hell's chance."

"Now you're just mocking me."

"No, I just needed an excuse to touch you, and you gave it to me," he said, running his hand up and down my back. His touch felt so good that I snuggled in closer to his warmth as he tilted his seat back a little, continuing to hold me against him.

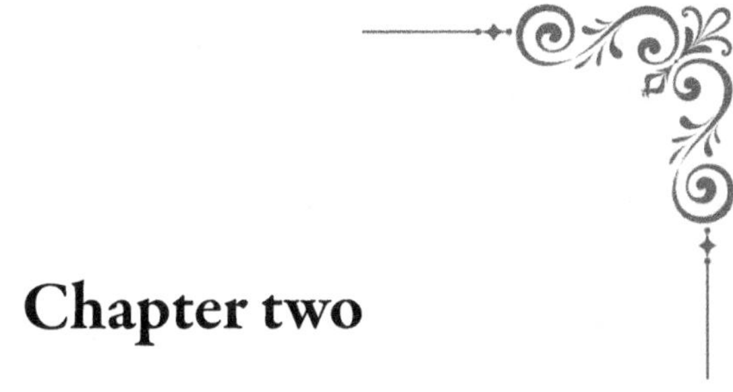

Chapter two

N*ate*
I felt the moment her body relaxed against mine and her breathing slowed to an even rhythm. She had fallen asleep, and she was exactly where I wanted her to be. I knew we had the fancy seats that lay flat into a bed, but I also knew that I would sleep perfectly fine with her in my arms. When the flight attendant walked past, I caught her attention, asked for a blanket, and covered Casey with it.

I wanted her warmth against me and for her to feel safe. I knew that over the past week, she had been putting on a brave front, shrugging off any talk of this trip, covering her anxiety with over-exaggerated excitement about seeing Flynn. I knew she was excited about seeing him - Flynn means a lot to her - but her actions felt almost scripted and animated with what she thinks will keep me pacified about this whole situation. And I had to admit that with everything that she had waiting for her over the coming week, the thought of her trying to protect and cushion me from it all just made me love her more...if that was even possible.

Stroking a hand down her back, I noticed the serene look she had on her face; one that was so different to the past few nights in bed. She had no idea that I had been watching her toss and turn as she was visited by her demons in her sleep, or how I tried to calm her without waking her by pulling her tightly into my body while whispering calming words into her hair. This past week was challenging, to say the least, so I was glad to see that she was finally getting some sleep.

I, on the other hand, had been doing some research on Max Sullivan – well, what little I could find on the prick - and also putting up with constant lectures from Paxton on how I needed to keep my temper in check and control myself, or how I am there for support, not vengeance.

"Yeah, yeah, I know, Paxton," I said with exasperation, recalling the conversation we'd had over the phone on the way to the airport this morning.

"Look, I know you think I'm nagging you, Nate, but I know how you feel about Max Sullivan, and I also know what kind of trouble that could get you into."

"Paxton, I don't intend on getting into anything, okay? I promise I will behave myself. You just look after your girls, and I will take care of mine."

"Fine, just call me when you get there," he got out between what sounded like clenched teeth.

"I will. Talk to you later, Paxton," I said before ending the call.

"Is he alright?" Casey asked.

"Yeah, he just likes to think he's the older brother sometimes."

"He cares about you, Nate."

"I know, but damn. He's been relentless this week," I sighed in annoyance.

"That's because he knows how much of a hot head you are."

"Me? Hot Head?" I looked at her with a raised brow, making her smile.

"He'll relax...eventually," Casey said.

"Yeah, when we're back in the States, he will."

The last thought before I closed my eyes was of a frustrated looking Paxton, pacing the floor, waiting for me to call him as soon as we landed in Sydney.

Soft fingers ran over the rough stubble on my jaw, and when I opened my eyes, they were greeted by a pair of wide, but sleepy-looking, perfect blue ones.

"Hey," she said in a whisper.

"Hey, yourself."

"I was thinking that maybe I need to get into my own seat."

I wrapped my arms around her a little tighter and said, "Nope, not happening."

"Nate, it has to be uncomfortable for you, and besides, we keep getting funny looks from others."

"Don't care," I grumbled into the top of her head. "And I can assure you, baby, I am very comfortable."

"You are a stubborn man."

"I know, but it always gets me what I want...right?"

I couldn't see her face, but I knew that she was rolling those damn pretty eyes of hers as she finally relented, saying, "Okay, as long as you're not cramped."

"I told you before, I am perfectly fine. Now, go back to sleep and stop wiggling your ass against my groin or I will be taking you back to the bathroom so we can join the mile high club," I chuckled and she groaned.

I had been teasing her all week about how I could not go for eighteen hours without being inside of her, and we would have to test out the size of the bathroom. This caused her to blush and make me promise not to even think about it or she was leaving me at home, and that was never going to happen, so I dropped the subject...for now.

Smoothing my hand up and down her back, she relaxed back into sleep, and I closed my eyes and went with her. She had been the only person in my life for so many years that I was able to relax and fall asleep with so fast. Fuck, she is the only person in my life besides my family that I love more than life itself, and I just want to get this shit over and done with, take her back to our paradise by the ocean, and keep her in bed permanently. I never thought I would ever be able to say this before, but she is my life...she is my everything.

I must have slept really soundly because the next time my eyes opened, I had to squint from the brightness of the light and quickly became aware that Casey was no longer in my arms, just the blanket. Pulling my chair into an upright position, I stood and stretched out the kinks in my back while looking toward the bathroom at the back of the cabin. The smell of hot food permeated my nose, making my stomach grumble as I walked toward the bathroom on the other side. I needed to clean myself up and take care of business before I ate.

When I returned to our seats, Casey was sitting back on her side, with her face looking freshly washed and her hair pulled into a ponytail. Before dropping into the seat next to her, I leaned down across the console between us and cupped her cheek in my palm, placing a gentle kiss against her lips.

"Morning," I whispered against her mouth.

"Good morning to you," she whispered back.

"Did you sleep okay?"

"Yes, very well, and you?"

"Perfect," I said as I smiled at her.

We spent the rest of the flight talking about our plans for the beach house when we got back and watching the in-flight movies. It was a long flight with only a three-hour layover at San Francisco at the beginning of the journey, and even then, I found that my muscles were starting to protest from being inactive for so long. I did try and stretch whenever I got up to use the bathroom, and I was starting to think that the people I passed by each time I went there must have thought I had some kind of bladder problem from the frequency, but what the hell, I am a big guy and I need my space. Well, except when I have Casey on me, that is.

While I was trying to get interested in the movie on the screen in front of me, I found myself watching her. She had her head leaned back into the headrest with earbuds in, listening to her iPod, and that had me a little worried because I knew that she used that thing as her stress relief, and even though she kept reassuring me that she's fine...she's not.

A tightening feeling in the pit of my stomach reminded me of how much I wanted – no, needed, - to protect her from anything and everything no matter what the cost. The reality portion of my brain also reminded me that there were some things I wouldn't be able to protect her from, but what I could do is be here for her and with her.

I was lost in my thoughts when she waved her hand in front of my face, "Earth to Nate. Come in, Nate."

Shaking my head, I slipped the headphones off my ears, "Sorry, did you say something?"

"Yes, I said, 'look we're getting closer,'" she said, and I followed to where her finger was pointing at the screen in front of us that showed our flight path. "Another couple of hours, big guy, and you can have all the exercise you want."

"Really?" I asked with a wiggle of my eyebrows.

"You are a dirty, dirty man, Mr. King. Get your mind out of the gutter."

"Ha, with you, baby, my mind is always in the gutter."

Chapter three

Casey

Once the "fasten seatbelts" sign illuminated with a ding, and we slowly started to descend, I looked out the window and watched as the thick, white clouds moved past until they finally broke, and I could see land. And with that, the butterflies started to make their presence known in my lower belly. When I leaned back into my seat, Nate took my hand and threaded his fingers through mine.

"You okay?" he asked. Closing my eyes, I just nodded. There was nothing more I could give him. I mean, I was excited to be home and to see Flynn, and I was even more excited that Nate was with me, but the prospect of having to re-hash my past again was emotionally overwhelming and debilitating. Although Nate and I had spent some time talking about what had happened, there was a big difference between hearing it from me and experiencing the truthful, raw facts.

I continued to stare out of the small window, watching as the outline of Sydney Harbor slowly came into view. The continual descent of the plane made my ears pop. We hit the ground with a bump and the loud sound of the thrusting engines as they powered down into a taxiing speed, and the Captain's voice interrupted my thoughts.

"This is your Captain speaking. On behalf of myself and the crew of Qantas Flight QF112, we hope you enjoy your stay in Sydney, Australia, and thank you for flying with us. Please remain in your seats until we have come to a full stop and the crew gives you instructions to disembark. Once again, thank you for traveling with Qantas."

Once we were able to get up and leave the plane, I was pretty sure I heard some cracking sounds coming from Nate's joints as he walked down the gangway on our way up to customs with his hand holding onto mine. The poor guy. Even with the extra room in business class, his six-foot-three frame was still cramped, although it didn't help that he insisted that I slept on top of him throughout the trip, either.

As usual, customs was a pain in the arse, but we eventually made it through and located our bags on the baggage carousel before continuing our way down toward the arrivals lounge.

It didn't take long to see a familiar figure walking toward us, his lean body dressed in jeans and a black t-shirt, his messy brown hair a little longer since the last time I had seen him, but still with that eye-catching wide, beautiful smile spread across his face - Flynn. As soon as I saw him, I stepped up my pace and matched his smile with my own. It was the first time I had let go of Nate's hand as I dropped my bags and wrapped both arms around Flynn's neck as he scooped me up and spun me around, laughing.

"Fuck, sweets, it is so good to see you," he said, pulling back and looking into my face.

"I know, it feels like forever," I breathed out, a little winded by his crushing embrace.

Eventually letting me go and placing my feet back on the floor, he looked at Nate and held out his hand. "You must be the lucky guy that stole my girl's heart?" Flynn said as Nate shook his hand.

"And you must be Flynn. Well, I hope you are, or I might have to throat punch you for pawing my girl in the middle of the airport," Nate answered amiably.

"No need for violence, mate, I can assure you that I am indeed Flynn," he laughed, then turned back to me. "Come on, let's get you home. I have some beer in the fridge chilling," he said, picking up my bags. Flynn grabbed my hand and started toward the exit, pulling me behind him, so I quickly grabbed Nate's hand as we walked toward the doors.

Once outside, I was hit by the familiar smells of home, the beautiful, clear blue sky, and the heat of the early morning sun's warmth against my face. It's funny how different places that you travel to have their own unique smells, and as good as the air smelled right now, it had nothing on the smell of the ocean at Paxton and Lynda's beach house.

As usual, Flynn had parked in a "No parking zone" area, his huge, green Jeep taking up way too much room.

"I see you brought the toad?" I said, nodding toward the Jeep, making Flynn laugh and drawing a curious look from Nate.

"That," I said, pointing to the ugly green vehicle, "is the toad."

"Well, it was better than bringing your car because that man of yours would have never fit into Daisy," Flynn said, pressing the fob on his keys and unlocking the doors.

"What the hell is a Daisy?" Nate asked, perplexed, as we got into the Jeep.

"Daisy is Casey's Mini coupe. Her pride and joy. But for you, I have the feeling it would be a pain in the arse...and neck...and legs," Flynn told Nate.

"Great," Nate muttered under his breath.

"Don't worry, Nate, I'll use Casey's car while you guys are here and leave you the Jeep to get around in. Much more comfortable for a big guy like you," Flynn said, smiling as he slid into the car.

Nate opened my door for me, closed it, then got into the front seat next to Flynn. "Fuck, this is weird."

"What is?" Flynn asked, looking at Nate.

"Sitting on the wrong side."

"If you think that's weird, wait until we drive on the opposite side of the road to you. Now, that is really going to make your brain spin," Flynn chuckled as he pulled away from the curb and we started to make our way over the familiar road to home.

"We're about a twenty-minute drive down at Clovelly Beach," Flynn continued. "You guys must be tired after your trip."

"A little," I said.

"I'm just glad to be walking," Nate said.

Nate and Flynn made small talk as we drove. Well, it was more like sizing each other up, asking various questions about work and common interests as I looked out of the window and watched the familiar sights and buildings rush by in a haze. It was weird. I was home, but I wasn't. I felt a little lost here, even after being away for such a short period of time.

As we drove down Park Street, I started to feel a bit nervous. Flynn pulled into the driveway of the modern, two-story home that we had shared for so long. It should have felt comfortable being here, but it didn't. Getting out, Nate took a look around his surroundings. Looking at me, he said, "This is nice, and I can smell the ocean."

"Yes, it's pretty close. We'll go there while we're here," I said, and he pulled me into his arms.

"You okay?" he asked.

"Yeah, it just feels weird being here for some reason. It feels strange."

"Well, I'm not going to say I'm sad about that. I don't want you to get too comfortable," he said with a wicked grin on his lips.

"Don't worry, I am very much looking forward to moving into our beach house," I said with a pat against his chest.

"Good, just keep that in mind."

Flynn cleared his throat. "Come on, you guys, enough of the PDA. There's plenty of time for that later. Let's go in, shall we?"

Grabbing our bags, Flynn opened the front door, and I walked into what used to be my home, but now kind of looked like a bachelor pad. A video game console sat in front of the huge, flat screen TV with controls and games littering the floor. An old empty pizza box littered the coffee table, and dirty clothes cluttered the couch.

"Gee, Flynn, I'm glad you took the time to clean up for us," I said, giving him the stink eye.

"Sorry, I ran out of time, but believe me when I tell you it looks a lot better than it did."

Dropping our bags in front of the front door, I took Nate's hand, leading him into the kitchen, which actually looked pretty clean compared to the living room. Flynn passed me and opened the fridge door, "Do you want a beer, mate?" he asked Nate.

"No, thanks. Maybe later; it's a bit early for me," he said, shaking his head.

Reaching past Flynn, I grabbed two bottles of water and took them to the kitchen table, motioning for Nate to take a seat before passing him a bottle.

Flynn left the beer, grabbing a water for himself, and sat down at the table to join us. "So, how was your flight?" he asked as he popped the lid off the bottle and took a drink.

"It was okay," I said.

"It was too long and too cramped," Nate said almost at the same time.

I looked at Nate. "We were in business class! With all that extra space, how could you be cramped? There was plenty of leg room, even at your height."

Nate gave me a smile then looked at Flynn. "Like I said, it was cramped and it took way too long."

"It was twenty hours, Nate," I sighed.

"Yes, I remember it well, baby, which still doesn't change the fact that we left on Friday and got here on Sunday."

Flynn's head flitted between the two of us before he said, "Listen to you two. You sound like an old married couple already!"

Nate reached for my hand, bringing it to his mouth, placed a gentle kiss on my fingers, and smiled.

Flynn leaned back in his chair, "You look great, Casey. You really do."

"Thanks, I feel great," I said as I smiled.

"I don't know what you did to my girl, Nate, but I owe you my deepest gratitude from the bottom of my heart."

"I think it's more what she has done to me," Nate said, grinning.

I opened my water and took a long drink before asking Flynn the question I had been dreading the whole flight here. "So...has the date and time been set for the hearing?" Flynn's eyes dropped to the bottle of water he had in his hands before he gave me a quick nod.

"And?" I pushed.

"Thursday, 11 a.m."

"Flynn, I'm fine, alright? We knew it was going to happen one day."

Flynn ran a hand through his already messy hair. "I know, it's just the timing of the whole thing, you know? You were just starting to breathe and enjoy life, and it pisses me off that you have to go through it all again," he said with frustration.

"It's different this time," I told him.

"How?"

"I'm not the same, Flynn. I'm a stronger person now, and I can deal with it."

"Casey, you have always been strong. Hell, any normal person would have given up years ago, but not you," he said softly.

I placed my hand on his arm. "Flynn, you have been looking out for me for a long time, but this day was coming, and I promise you I am done with it all. He's been stealing from me for the last eighteen years, and it ends now."

Flynn stared into my eyes, and I saw the flicker of recognition in his own eyes when he realized my determination. Closing his eyes, he nodded.

Chapter Four

Nate

My legs were still aching from that fucking long plane ride to the other side of the world, and I almost lost my breakfast with not only sitting on the wrong side of Flynn's Jeep, but also driving on the wrong side of the god damned road. The thought of my girl going through the hell that robbed her of almost half her life all seemed to come into perspective with this, right here in front of me. The bond that I saw between Casey and Flynn was apparent, as a simple look conveyed hundreds of words without sound.

Yeah, I admit I knew I was not going to like seeing another guy with his arms around Casey, and it might have helped just a little if he was some skinny, nerdy looking guy, but I was surprised when I saw Flynn at the airport. He was taller than I expected with a pretty solid athletic build. When he wrapped his arms around Casey, I didn't have to rein in any ill feelings at all for this guy pawing her in public because I could feel the innocent and deep relationship they had with each other and the way he looked at her with a fierce protectiveness, but yet a somewhat disheartened look. Of what? Failure? For some reason, Flynn looked like he had failed Casey, and I wondered if it might just be because Paxton found a way to break through what I was guessing would have been years of constant hard work at keeping Casey's identity a secret. Fuck, I hoped I wasn't responsible for putting that look on his face. I realized that I might just have to make sure we had a chat about my brother's powers of untangling legalities.

The house was a comfortable double story, modern looking, tidy house, although it did have the tell-tale signs of a bachelor pad about it. In fact, the rooms that I had seen didn't seem to show any signs of a female presence living here at all. I mean, I knew Casey had been away for a while, but considering this was her home, I expected to see at least some feminine touches in this rather large space.

I felt a hand touch my forearm, and I blinked away my thoughts, turning to look into those beautiful blue eyes of hers.

"You're very quiet," she said, in almost a whisper. "Everything alright?"

I gave her a reassuring smile and took her hand in mine, threading my fingers through hers. "Yeah, I'm just tired," I said.

Flynn stood and tossed his empty water bottle into the garbage. "Listen, why don't you both go grab a shower and some sleep. It will help with the jet lag, and I have a few things to do today anyway."

"You don't have to go out, Flynn. I am pretty sure we'll be able to sleep through an earthquake right now," Casey reassured him.

"No, honestly, I have some things to catch up on today, and I need to do some grocery shopping. The cupboards are a little bare," he said, grinning.

Casey gave Flynn a hug. "If you're sure," she told him, and after giving her one last squeeze, he pulled car keys from his pocket, flipped them up into the air, and caught them before he took off out the front door.

"Come on, let's go upstairs to my bedroom," Casey said, grinning, with a seductive tone in her voice.

"Now you're talking my language," I said as I grabbed both of our bags and followed her up the polished wooden stairs, then down a slim hallway where she pushed open a door and stepped back for me to enter. It was a good-sized room with a large bay window that was covered by thick, black blinds that I was guessing came in handy when she pulled a night shift at the hospital. I dropped the bags as she walked over to the window and opened the blinds, instantly saturating the room with warm sunlight. In the middle of the room was a queen-sized, polished, wooden framed bed with matching bedside tables and a thick gray quilt covering the bed. As I looked around the room, it wasn't what I expected. It was pretty bare and cold. There were no fluffy pillows adorning the bed, no girly touches at all. Just a bed, side tables, a large set of drawers against one wall and a built-in closet on the other with nothing more. No pictures on the wall and no photos that I could see. For a moment, I felt a pang deep in my chest as it hit me hard just how alone Casey had been all these years.

"It's not as comfy as the penthouse, but it's okay," she said. Her words drew my attention to her solemn tone, and I realized that she was apologizing to me. I pulled her into my arms, lightly placing a kiss to the top of her head.

"It's perfect, baby," I breathed into her hair and felt the tension release from her body instantly. "Now, how about that shower," I said, letting out a low growl because damn, being this close to her was reminding my dick that it's been lonely.

She pulled back, smacking a hand against my chest. "I wondered how long you could last," she said, smiling wickedly at me.

"What can I say, you wouldn't let me initiate you into the mile high club, and do you know how torturous it was to have you sleeping on me with a hard-on for all those hours?"

"Your problem, you wanted me there," she sang as she pulled me behind her down the hall and into a large bathroom with a huge bathtub and shower. As she reached in and turned the water on, I closed the door, flicked the lock, and watched as she started to peel off her shirt, boots, jeans, and underwear. Then, she started to un-buckle my belt as I pulled my own shirt over my head, and between the both of us, we made quick work of getting naked and under the pulsing hot spray of the shower.

Pulling her naked body against my own, I just wanted to feel her...all of her. My hands smoothed up and down the soft skin of her back as the water cascaded over us. Placing my palms on either side of her face, I tilted it up to mine and took her mouth in a soft kiss, tasting the water as it ran over her lips. A small moan escaped from deep in her throat that made me want to take more from her. Breaking the kiss with a lustful pant, I smoothed the wet tendrils away from those beautiful, icy blue eyes.

"I want you so bad right now, but logic tells me that it's been a long trip, and we should get some sleep," I said. Her eyes searched mine for a moment before she closed them and gave me a slight nod.

I turned her around to face the shower wall and filled my hands with liquid soap. I washed every inch of her body. Every touch was driving me even more insane, but I knew that even though she was playing it cool at the moment, she was anything but cool. I knew she was wound as tight as a steel coil, just waiting to spring undone, so I decided to take a back seat with the act of fucking her senseless for the moment, but not the thought of it.

After drying off, Casey pulled the bedroom blinds closed, and we slipped in between the soft, cool sheets of her bed. Pulling her into my arms, I dropped a kiss against her temple before we both surrendered to the lull of sleep.

Waking, I rolled onto my stomach, running my hand over the empty space next to me, and, just for a moment, I had to think of where I was. Damn jet lag gave me brain fog until I smelled something delicious wafting from downstairs that instantly made my mouth water and my stomach growl in hungry protest. Getting up, I pulled on a clean pair of jeans and a t-shirt and headed downstairs, following the aroma that, if I wasn't mistaken, was a fat, juicy steak cooking. When I get to the kitchen, Casey was leaning against the kitchen counter, chopping salad vegetables. She stopped and looked up when I walked into the kitchen. Now, most normal people would just see a woman chopping and tossing salad into a bowl, but me? I saw a pair of smooth, long, tanned legs fitted sinfully into a pair of shorts and a tank top that clung to every delectable part of that body that I promised to leave alone for a few days.

"Hi, did you sleep well?" she asked, smiling as she continued chopping.

"Yeah, fine," I said, rubbing a hand over my face, trying to scrub the remnants of sleep away. Moving up behind her, I leaned down and nuzzled my nose against the soft skin of her neck, giving her a kiss just as the sliding door to the outside opened and Flynn walked in carrying a tray full of what looked like an assortment of barbequed meat that he placed on the kitchen counter. "Hey, Nate, just in time for some food! You hungry?" Flynn asked, passing me a plate.

"Starving," I said, taking it.

"Then dig in, mate. I cooked extra, I figured you could handle it on account of your size," he said with a grin.

After the meal, I gave Casey a hand with the dishes. Flynn handed me a beer and motioned for us both to sit on the couch in the living room. Taking a seat himself, he took a pull from his bottle before speaking.

"Okay, so the biggest decision that you have to make is how you want to present your victim statement," Flynn said, looking straight at Casey.

"So, what are our options? I mean, how does this all work?" she asked.

"Well, there are two ways it can be done. You can do a written statement and then it will be my job to read it on your behalf to the parole board. Or you can attend yourself and make an verbal statement."

Before Casey could answer, I said, "She'll be doing the written statement."

Casey's head whipped around to face me. "What?"

"There's no need for you to go anywhere near the hearing, and this way, you will have time to think long and hard about what you want to say."

Casey leaned back into the couch. "Well, thank you for making my mind up for me, Nate. I mean, it's not as though I have a perfectly good mind of my own," she said in the acidic tone of hers that I loved so much.

"Baby, listen. You have a beautiful mind, and I know that you're very capable of making your own decisions, but I also know how hard-headed you can be, and I think that facing the board is an unnecessary stress that you have the power to avoid."

"But what if I don't want to avoid it? What if I want to have my say, Nate?"

"If I thought it would help you in the way that you're thinking it's going to, I would say go for it, 100%. But a parole hearing is not going to get you the closure you're looking for, baby."

Casey stared at me hard, then turned to Flynn. "Flynn?" she asked, and Flynn nodded.

"He's right, babes. If it was an open court, and you could look right into the bastard's eyes and tell him everything you wanted to, then I would agree. But with a parole hearing, he's not going to be there. It will just be the judicial officer and a few others, like a corrections officer from the prison, a medical expert, and maybe a representative from the community, and as far as they're concerned, he's done his time, and he's kept his nose clean."

Casey stood quickly, her voice suddenly raised. "Fuck that! He hasn't done his time," she spat out.

"According to the law, he has, and that makes him eligible for parole." Flynn's voice was low, and Casey started to pace the room, chewing on a fingernail. I hated seeing her like this, her body so tense with pent-up anger. Then she turned, looking at Flynn.

"I want to speak at the hearing. I don't give a shit if it makes no difference on the outcome. I want to speak." She enunciated the last four words with such determination that I knew there was no stopping her. Flynn let out a weary sigh and ran a hand down his face.

"Fine, if that's what you want, then that's what we'll do, okay?" He stood and pulled her into his arms, rubbing a hand soothingly over her back for a few minutes. When he pulled away from her, she looked relieved at the choice she made. This woman had so much strength, that my chest swelled a little with pride.

"So what do you need me to do?" she asked Flynn.

"Nothing right now. Just relax, go enjoy some sights, and show Nate around Sydney. I've taken care of everything, I just need to take a run up to Gosford…" His words tapered off like he just realized he said something he shouldn't have, and by the way Casey was staring at him, I had a feeling this place called Gosford was not a good place for her.

"Why do you need to go there, Flynn?" she demanded.

"I…err…just need to pick something up."

"Flynn? This is me you're talking to. You do realize that, right?"

Flynn let out a curse under his breath and sat down on the couch, leaning his head forward in defeat.

"You remember the people who bought your parents' house, right?" Flynn asked. Casey nodded.

"Well, the same couple still owns it, only they're older now and have been doing some renovating. Well, they wanted to extend the ceilings, and they had some work done on the roof. Apparently, they found an old box up there that seems to have belonged to your parents."

Casey dropped onto the couch next to me. The look on her face at the mention of her parents was a mixture of shock and maybe...sadness?

"What kind of box?" she almost whispered.

"They didn't say. Just a box that feels like it has something in it, but it could be worth a look, Casey. I was just hoping to look at it myself before telling you," he said, grimacing at her.

"It's okay. We'll go pick it up," Casey said..

"No, no. I don't want you up that way, sweets. Just let me get it."

"It's okay, I think it's about time I put that place to rest, as well. Don't you?" she asked him.

Flynn shook his head before saying, "Fuck, you're a pain in my arse."

"Hey," I growled at Flynn, and he put both hands up, surrendering to my warning.

"Calm down, it's all in jest, big guy."

"I know, just watch your mouth," I told him. I know it was said in fun, but fuck if it didn't piss me off, and he needed to know exactly where I stood on protecting Casey from anyone including him.

Chapter five

Casey

C I placed a hand on Nate's thigh and looked at him. His eyes were full of turmoil, and I was hoping the calming stroke of my hand over his thigh would help to ease the wildness I could see growing in those deep, steely eyes of his. Since we arrived at the house, he'd been pretty quiet and taken a back seat to the relationship between Flynn and me. I understood how protective and dominant he was, and what was normal banter to Flynn would be a new experience for Nate. I knew that he was used to being in control and in charge of situations, and it was hard for him to see Flynn taking charge of my protection, physically or emotionally. I needed to reassure him that I was alright.

Smiling at him, I said, "It's okay. He's my annoying big brother, remember?" Nate sighed at my words, and I saw the storm in his eyes starting to retreat as he gave me a slight nod, and I leaned into his chest. "What do you say we get up in the morning, and I'll show you around Sydney? You know, to get in the tourist stuff, and take some photos to take back to Paxton and Lynda?" I asked, looking up at him as he reached out and slid a stray strand of hair away from my eye, tucking it behind my ear.

"Sure, baby. Whatever you want," he said, smiling at me.

"I want what you want."

"I want this over and you back in our home," he breathed into my ear.

"Soon, babe. That reminds me, I need to go through some of my things and pack what I want to take back with me."

"Just pack it all, we'll take it," he said.

"No, I need to go through it. There's probably a lot of useless rubbish in that room."

"So, what room should we start in?" he asked.

"It's just my room, upstairs," I said, and he shot me a puzzled look.

"Just your bedroom? That's all you own?"

"Yep, apart from maybe some stuff in the kitchen, but that can stay."

"So, none of the furniture?" he asked, sounding a little perplexed.

"Nope, it's all Flynn's."

Nate pulled me into his lap, wrapping his arms tightly around me. He just held me for a while, running his chin back and forth over the top of my head.

"Nate?"

"When we move into the beach house, the first thing I want to do is take you shopping, and I want you to buy anything and everything that you want, okay?" he said, his voice cracking a little with emotion that I recognized was Nate not coping with the fact that all I owned in this world was contained in that one small bedroom, so I gave him this one. I snuggled deeper into his hard chest and said, "Sure, you just try and stop me."

It seemed that while Nate and I were lost in our own little bubble, Flynn had left us alone, and that was exactly where we stayed until we decided to go up, get into bed, and try and recover from traveling. As soon as we slipped in between the sheets and into each other's arms, we were both out in a split second.

I awoke sometime in the middle of the night to fingers making soft swirling patterns against my thigh, and I felt a warm breath against the back of my neck that sent an instant shiver through my body. I buried myself deeper into Nate's arms, against his hard body, and felt his equally hard shaft pressing into my back. My movement caused a deep groan in his chest that vibrated through my own body. His hand snaked under my back and up between my breasts. Then, his fingers slowly slid up the front of my throat, gently pulling my head back, giving him access to the side of my neck. I felt the warm wetness of his tongue glide across my shoulder as he gently nipped and bit at the tender skin there before placing warm open mouthed kisses across my neck until he found that small area where I could feel my own pulse racing as his tongue glided over it.

"I need you," he breathed into my neck.

I placed a hand behind me, running it over the taut muscle in his thigh. "Good," I said, giving him the answer that I knew he wanted. His fingers gently circled the delicate flesh of my throat. He moved his hand up to stroke the pad of his thumb over my bottom lip, and I sucked it into my mouth, running my tongue over his calloused skin, making him growl. I felt his other hand as it slowly moved down my body, directly to the core of my sex. He ran his fingers through the wet folds, causing my body to arch into his palm with a desperate cry of frustration of needing more.

"You want more, baby?" he asked. I couldn't see his face, but I knew he had a wicked, sexy grin on it right now. He knew exactly what he was doing. I released his thumb from my mouth with a pop, and responded, "Do you?"

"So much more, sweetheart." His voice was tense with lust as he moved closer behind me, lifting my leg up slightly to give him just enough access to my slick entrance, where he rubbed the hard head of his shaft along my folds, coating it in my wetness. Then, in one thrust, he pushed inside of me, making me gasp with his palm still at my throat. His other palm splayed across my stomach, pulling me harder into his body as he whispered into my ear, "Okay?"

"Yes," was all I managed to say before he started to move in a slow rhythmic motion. Reaching behind me, I dug my fingers into his thigh, pulling him harder against me, encouraging the depth and speed of his thrusts.

My craving for him was palpable and fierce. I needed him to never stop possessing my body like he did when he was inside of me, causing me to get lost inside of myself, only wanting to be found by him. His thrusts started to ram forward with an urgency to match my own building climax, and as his palm slid from my stomach and back down to the apex between my legs, he pressed his finger against the sensitive flesh. I was completely lost in the heightened pleasure of my orgasm as he found his own release, flooding my body with his warmth as he let out a succession of curses as he bit into the tender flesh of my shoulder.

He held me tightly against him, breathing hard while gently kissing my shoulder, and that was where we stayed, still connected, until our breathing calmed and we dozed back off to sleep again.

Waking up early the next morning and pulling Nate out of bed was hard work. He had plans of his own that included spending most of the day in bed with me, but I had other plans for us today. Knowing just how shit this week was going to progressively get, I wanted to start it off by showing Nate around my city and doing the whole tourist thing today. After a shower and a quick breakfast, we took Flynn's Jeep into the hub of Sydney, the Circular Quay, where I was lucky enough to find somewhere to park. I watched as Nate's eyes widened with pure awe as he got his first close-up look at the Sydney Opera House and the vast expanse of Sydney Harbour with its iconic bridge standing strong and proud across it.

We strolled along the harbour, his fingers threaded through mine as we took in the wonderful sights. We snapped selfies on the stairs of the Opera House, and we made our way down to the ferry terminal and hopped on board a ferry across to the Taronga Zoo. As we crossed the water, I pointed out Kiribilli House, explaining that was where our Prime Minister resided. When we got to the zoo, I pulled him on board the sky cable cart as it took us over the top of the zoo for a bird's eye view. Placing his arm around me and pulling me close, he gave me a playful, child-like smile, and said, "I haven't been to the zoo since I was a kid." All I could do was smile at his enthusiasm as we looked down at the animals.

The day was magical, and it felt good being the one in charge for the day and leading him through an area that was all new to him. After we finished up at the zoo, we hopped onto another ferry, where we stood on the deck, his arm wrapped firmly around my waist as he pressed a kiss to my lips. Once back at the main ferry terminal, we walked back along the upper promenade to a sea of tables along the waterfront where we found somewhere to sit and grab something to eat. I even took the lead when I ordered him a typical Aussie Burger and watched as he dissected it to see what was on it before he took a huge bite and moaned with satisfaction.

"I would have never believed that beets could taste so good on a burger. This thing is phenomenal," Nate said before taking another bite. I leaned over and wiped the corner of his mouth with a napkin just in time to catch the drop of sauce that threatened his t-shirt and laughed.

"See, I told you the good old Aussie burger is the best," I said, smiling.

"Damn, baby, you're not kidding," he said through another muffled bite.

After lunch, I took him to an historic area of Sydney called The Rocks. We browsed around the open market stalls, and I managed to pick up some small gifts to take back to Paxton and Lynda, which included shirts bearing the Australian flag with the words "Awesome Australian Tourist" written across the back in bold letters, and a tiny, matching pink one for Emily.

We walked around, taking in Sydney's old buildings until it started to get late, so I took him down to one of my favorite Italian restaurants, which was tucked away beside a sandstone wall with its quaint little courtyard of small tables covered with red and white checkered table clothes and a tray filled with candles. Pulling out my chair for me to sit, then taking the one opposite from me, Nate let out a huge breath. "This place is great. In fact, the whole day has been an experience."

His words made me smile. "So, you had fun today?"

"That's an understatement. I've been to a lot of places around the world, but unfortunately, Australia was not one of them, so to actually see the things I've only ever seen in books and movies is fucking mind-blowing."

"I just wish we had more time. There's so much more for you to see, but with our limited time here, I at least wanted to show you something that you'll remember." He reached across the table and took my hand in his, running his thumb across my knuckles.

"Hey, we will be back. I promise you, okay?"

"Yeah, I know we will," I said, giving him a small smile.

A tiny knot formed in my stomach as I said those words. I would be leaving my home and Flynn for an unknown period this time. Nate must have seen through my wry look and into my thoughts.

"I mean it. I will bring you back here as often as you want, baby, and Flynn can come and stay with us whenever he likes." I smiled at him, glad that he understood how important Flynn was to me.

"Speaking of which, I'll need to book our return flight. Any idea what day we are looking at?" Nate asked, taking a drink from his bottle of water.

"Well, I guess once the parole hearing is over, it's pretty much open. I mean, I don't have much to take back with me, plus you need to get back to King Security. Otherwise, Paxton will be pulling his hair out."

He laughed. "Yeah, I guess, but I need you to decide when it's right for you, sweetheart."

Taking in a deep breath, I looked away from him for a moment before I spoke. "To be honest, I want to leave as soon as the hearing is over. I don't want to be anywhere near him once he's out."

"Hey, you don't know he's going to get out."

"Yeah, I do. I'm not sure what it is, I just have this feeling," I said, shaking my head.

I watched as that little muscle in his jaw twitched with tension. "If he gets paroled, I will have you on the next flight out of here, okay?" he said, bringing my hand to his mouth and placing a kiss on the top of it. Feeling the strength of his words and reassured by his presence, at that moment, I felt lighter.

Chapter Six

Nate

It was late by the time we got back to the house. Flynn wasn't around, so we just had a shower and got into bed. It had been a full day of activities, and one that I would remember for a long time, not just because I was getting a tour of such a huge and amazing city, but because of my tour guide. This woman amazed me every day with her strength. We had to make this trip under pretty terrible circumstances, and to be honest, getting a tour of her home city was not on my agenda at all. Yeah, it's cool being in Australia, but I didn't want her feeling obligated in any way to entertain me. I just wanted to be here for her, and once again, she blew me away with her unselfish personality. This woman was always giving...always strong.

Pulling her as close into my body as humanly possible, it wasn't long until her breathing changed into the calming, light, deep breaths of slumber. Having this woman in my bed next to me every night, I got a peaceful pleasure from watching her as she slept until I fell asleep myself. Except for tonight. My body was physically tired, but my mind was unsettled. I didn't like her being here, and I didn't like the thought of her having to stand up in front of a parole board, dragging up her painful past again. Casey was just starting to get a hold of it, get control of it, and I hated the way that she looked and felt out of place here.

Slowly sliding from the bed, trying hard not to wake Casey, I pulled on a pair of jeans and a t-shirt, grabbed my phone, and headed downstairs to the kitchen to grab a beer from the fridge. I opened the glass sliding door and went out onto the back patio, sitting down on the carved wooden bench leaning against the wall of the house as I flipped the lid off my beer. Searching my contact list, I brought up Paxton's number and pressed "dial." It took a few minutes for it to connect, and on the fourth ring, Paxton answered.

"Hey, Nate. How's it going there?"

"So far, so good. How are things there?"

"Smooth sailing, just working on the final touches on the West contract."

"That's great, it should be good to go as soon as I get back then?" I asked him.

"Absolutely. Any idea when that will be?" he asked after a strategically placed pause. I knew he didn't want to push, but really, he did.

"I'm going to call the airlines to try and get us on a plane on either Saturday or Sunday." I smiled into the phone, knowing that the news would make him happy.

"That's great. So, how's Casey doing?" he asked hesitantly.

"Surprisingly good. Better than I thought, although the house is a little weird."

"Weird? What do you mean?"

"Not so much the house, just the atmosphere of the place, you know? I mean, Casey has lived here for years, but there's none of her in the place. No photos of family or friends, and she looks kind of lost and uncomfortable in her own home. I don't know. It's pretty friggin sad, Paxton."

"Well, you can't blame her for no family photos, Nate. She doesn't really have any great memories that she would want to relive there," Paxton said matter-of-factly.

"Yeah, I know. I guess I thought in her home, I would see more of her in it. Does that make sense?"

"I guess, but isn't that a good thing? I mean you don't want her to become comfortable there and want to stay, do you?"

"Fuck no! I'd drag her ass back to Portland kicking and screaming, but believe me, that's not going to happen. She's made it clear that once the parole hearing is over, she wants to leave."

"Good, because Lynda is driving me nuts with all the constant questions and updates she insists on getting 24 hours a day," he said, laughing.

"Yeah, Casey is missing her, as well. She said she was going to call Lynda tomorrow night after we get back from picking up some mysterious box from her old family home."

"What do you mean?" he asked.

"I don't know, it's something to do with the people who bought her family home after her parents passed away. They were doing some renovations and found an old box that belonged to Casey's parents, so we're driving up to this place called Gosford, about an hour's drive away, to pick it up."

"Hmm, that sounds sinister."

"Well, let's hope it's not, for Casey's sake."

"Just let me know when your return flight is," Paxton said.

"Sure thing. How's Emily?"

"Great. Keeping us on our toes, but I wouldn't change it for anything, I'm pretty sure she misses her Uncle and Aunt though."

His comment made me smile. "Good, 'cause I'm the only one she has."

"Oh, and Nate, the papers came through for the house. Everything is finalized. She's all yours."

"That's great news. Okay, well, I'm going to get going and call the airlines, and I will speak with you soon. Give my love to Lynda and Emily."

"Aww, what, no love for your little brother? Now, that's not fair," Paxton said in an over the top baby voice.

"Fuck you."

"Yep, I love you too, bro," Paxton said before I disconnected our call. Stepping back into the kitchen, I was just about to check out available flights on my phone when I noticed a dim light coming from the living room. Walking over, I stopped when I saw Flynn leaning over the coffee table, which was covered in papers and folders, his eyes scanning over them intensely with both of his hands scrubbing through his hair in frustration. He lifted his head toward where I was standing in the doorway.

"Nate, what's up, mate?" he asked, slightly surprised by my presence.

"Just couldn't sleep, that jet lag really knocks you around," I said, sitting on the couch across from him. "What about you?" I asked, motioning at the mess of papers on the table.

He leaned back against the couch and let out a breath. "Just wanted to make sure everything is ready for Thursday."

"And is it?"

"I fucking hope so," he said with a shake of his head.

"So, what is it, Flynn?" I asked him, staring right into his eyes, making him look a little uncomfortable and perplexed at the question.

"I'm not sure what you mean," he said, his brows furrowed.

"Okay, let me put it this way. What is it that you know, but aren't telling Casey?"

With a pause, he looked down at the papers, back up to me, then shrugged. "Nothing," he finally said.

"And I think I'll call bullshit on that statement," I said, raising a skeptical eyebrow his way.

Flynn glanced around the room like he was searching for an answer that he thought would satisfy me, but then I saw the spark of defeat in his eyes as he realized that he couldn't hide anything from me.

"You know, I've tried almost everything to keep this fucker locked up for as long as possible, and the thing that has finally beaten me is time."

"Time?" I asked.

"Yep, time. As far as the government is concerned, he's done his time. He's been a model prisoner, accepted God into his life, and all the shit that goes with it, and I've racked my brain, trying to find some loophole to keep him there longer, but I have nothing, Nate. He's going to get parole, and there's not a fucking thing I can do to stop it," he said, his words filled with anger and defeat as he continued. "You know, I've protected Casey for so long, I'm not sure I can handle not being able to control this."

"Flynn, there's no point in beating yourself up, okay? Casey already has a feeling he's getting out, and I'm pretty sure she's dealing with it in her own way, but man, don't torture yourself. Nobody would have ever done for her what you have, and she knows it and respects it, so now we'll just deal with it and help her, okay?" Flynn took a moment before he gave me a nod.

"You know, I had to prepare myself to meet you," I said. "The way she talks about you and the bond you two share. I used to think that no man, unless he was deeply in love, would go to the lengths that you have for a woman, until I saw you two together, and I realized that you may not be blood-related, but you have a stronger bond with each other than I've seen in some families."

"Yeah, well what can I say? I love her. I would give my life for her," Flynn said with a strong determination. As he realized what he said, he quickly put up both hands. "Not like that, okay? Like a sister."

I grinned at him. "Yeah I know, and that is what we have in common."

"What's that?"

"I love her more than life itself. I would give my life for her, and I will never let anyone hurt her again, so I'd say she's pretty well protected with the both of us here, right?"

"Yeah, you're right. Thanks, Nate. I really needed this chat tonight," he said, grinning.

"Any time, Flynn, but I am curious about something."

"What's that?"

"When are you going to tell me what you really do?"

"Not sure what you mean, mate. I'm a lawyer," he said casually, shrugging off my question.

"Hey, it's okay, I understand. But I have a brother who is a lawyer, and he's damn good. Lots of connections that I don't even want to know how or where he makes them, but you..." I said, pointing a finger at him. "I'm pretty positive there's a lot more going on. I mean, you managed to wipe out Casey's whole history and give her a new identity that was almost impossible to dig up. So here's the deal. I'll tell you what I think because I just want to get it out there, and I don't expect any answers, okay?" Flynn slowly nodded, so I continued. "I'm not sure if you're undercover or you work for someone or something a lot bigger than your standard run-of-the-mill law firm, but what I am sure of is that you are very important to my girl. That makes you important to me unless you're involved in something that may ultimately hurt her. Then, that will be a whole different scenario, you get me?"

Flynn smiled, slowly shook his head, and said, "Yep, I get you loud and clear." With that, I had all the answers I needed, so I turned and walked upstairs, slipping back into bed next to Casey's warm body. As she turned and snuggled into me, I let out a huge, contented sigh.

Chapter Seven

C asey
Pulling out into the speeding traffic on the M1 freeway in Flynn's huge Jeep, I looked over at the horror on Nate's face as the lines on his forehead deepened from what I was sure was fear. "You okay?" I asked him with a chuckle.

"What? Yeah...sure," he said.

"You don't look okay, you look terrified."

"Who, me? Now, why should I be terrified? I mean, what could go wrong with a sweet, tiny woman driving this huge beast of a thing on the wrong side of the road?"

"Like I told you before, babe, it's you Americans that drive on the wrong side of the road, so just relax, enjoy the scenery, and I promise I will get you there in one piece." I gave him a huge, confident smile to try and put him at ease. Somehow, I didn't think it worked, because he seemed to have a death grip on the door handle for the whole trip to Gosford.

As soon as I drove down the familiar roads from my past, my earlier confidence started to drop a little and a coldness started to settle in the middle of my chest. Driving past my old school, I finally pulled up outside the house that I long tried to forget. Most kids have warm memories of their childhood homes, but this was never a home. It was a prison. Turning off the engine, I brushed my sweaty palms against my jeans and turned to look at the house. It was nothing fancy; just a regular looking brick home with a long veranda wrapping around the outside. The roof and fence had been repainted, and the garden was abundant with an assortment of trees, palms, and garden beds full of colorful flowers. The owners were obviously keen gardeners. My eyes roamed over the house, and I found the window of my old bedroom. An involuntary shiver ran through my body.

My thoughts were broken by the touch of a warm, strong hand that slipped around the back of my neck. Gentle fingers started to stroke the skin of my nape.

"Baby." The low growl of Nate's voice caused me to turn and look straight into his steel gray eyes. "You okay?" he asked.

"Yes...yes. It's just been a long time. I guess I wasn't expecting to feel anything about it," I said.

"And do you?" His brow quirked with concern.

"Well, I still hate it, so..." I smiled nervously at him.

"You don't have to...," he started, but I cut him off.

"Yes, I do, Nate. So let's go pull this Band-aid off quickly, okay?"

He looked at me hesitantly until I pulled the keys out of the ignition, opened the door, and slid out, my feet hitting the road with determination. Taking my hand in his, he led me up to the front door and pressed the doorbell. There was silence, followed by footsteps, and an older lady opened the door, her gray hair pulled up into a neat bun on the top of her head. She wiped her hands on a towel as she said, "Yes, can I help you?"

Clearing my throat, I smiled at her. "Hi, I'm Corrine and David Taylor's daughter, the previous owners. I was told that you found an old box that belonged to them?"

She instantly smiled when she recognized the names of my parents. "Oh, yes, please do come in. It's in my office." She motioned for us to follow her. Nate gave my hand a soft squeeze as he led me inside, following the woman down the hall into the kitchen area.

"Please, have a seat, and I'll get it for you, or feel free to look around. I'm guessing you will have some fond memories of growing up here?"

I just nodded and sat down in one of the chairs at the small wooden table. When she left the room, I said under my breath to myself, "If only you knew." But Nate heard me and started to ask, "Do you want to...?"

"No! I just want the box, and then we're out of here," I said quickly.

"Okay, baby," he said, resting his large hand on my shoulder, smoothing it in a small circular motion.

Looking down at where I nervously twisted my hands in my lap, I actually jumped at the sound of the box being placed on the table in front of me. It wasn't as big as I had expected. It was a little bit bigger than a shoe box and made of some type of wood. Lifting my hand, I ran my fingers over the carving on the lid following the letters that spelled out "Corrine."

"The box is locked. I'm sorry, we don't have a key for it, but I do hope it has something special in it for you," the woman said as I just stared at it.

I stood, picked it up, and looked at the kind woman's face. "Thank you," was all I could say to her as I walked toward the front door with just the low rumble of Nate's voice as he chatted briefly with the woman before he came out to see me tossing the box into the back seat of the Jeep and closing the door. He pulled me into his embrace.

"Hey, come here," he said as he stroked his hand tenderly up and down my back, making me melt into his hard, warm body.

"What did she say to you?" I asked into his chest.

"She just asked me if you were Catherine and always wondered if you were happy," he said, then continued, "I told her that you were very happy."

I looked up into his beautiful face to see his grin before I said, "You're right, I have you."

Leaning his head down, he brushed his lips against mine before saying, "Come on, let's get out of here."

The drive back was a silent one. Nate wanted to drive, but I told him I'd be fine. As I got lost in thoughts of what was in this box sitting behind me, I could feel his eyes watching me closely. Once home and inside, I looked in the kitchen drawers for something to pry the lock open, coming up with an old screwdriver. Nate immediately took it from me and started to pick the lock. I sat on the other side of the table and watched as he stabbed and pulled. Eventually, the box lid sprang open, and he turned it around to face me. Peering into it, the first things I saw were some old black and white photos. I picked them up and looked at them, but I didn't recognize anyone until I got to a color photo of my parents sitting on the side of a grassy hill. They looked so young in the picture. Placing the photos on the table, I sifted through the papers. There was what looked like my parents' marriage certificate, some more papers to do with the purchase of the house, but nothing of interest until I found something at the very bottom of the box: a small leather-bound book.

"What is it?" Nate asked as I just stared at it.

"Looks like a diary," I said, opening it up and flipping through the pages. The entries were handwritten with the date listed on the first page as June the 20th, 1985. Skimming through the pages, I took note of each date and realized that it went right through her pregnancy with me up until about a week before they were killed. Closing my eyes, I dropped the book onto the table, a shudder running through my body at the thought of having my mother's thoughts and feelings documented in this book before me. What the hell was I supposed to do with it?

"Baby?" I heard the low rumble of Nate's voice, causing me to let out the breath I had been holding and look up to see his concerned eyes. "What's in the book?" he asked.

"It's my mother's diary," I breathed out.

"What about the pictures?"

"I don't really know who they are of apart from the one of my parents. I'm guessing they must be friends or family of some kind," I said, picking up the old, weathered photos and absently shuffling through them before passing them to Nate.

"Maybe you have some family that you don't know about?" Nate said as he glanced down at the pictures.

"Not any that turned up at their funerals or offered me any support after the accident," I said, shaking my head. I stood up and pushed everything back into the box except the diary. I wanted to read it. Well, at least I thought I wanted to read it. Just not right now. Taking the box up to my room, I pushed it under the bed, turning to see Nate's curious look.

"You know, we could try and find out who those people are in the photos."

"Why?"

"Because you might actually have some family, and that's what you want right? A family to belong to? Casey, there are some things that you don't have to hide away under a bed, and if you have some family out there, Maybe it's worth it to try and find them," Nate said.

"The only thing that box will offer me is more pain, Nate. Besides, if I do have family and they are anything like my parents, I don't want to know them," I said, walking over and slipping my arms around his waist. "I have all the family I need right here." Feeling his strong arms wrapping around me and his warm breath against the top of my head was all the security I needed.

Chapter eight

N ate
Standing in her room, with her small arms around my waist and mine around her shoulders, I rubbed my chin against the top of her silken hair and inhaled. Vanilla mixed with her own unique intoxicating scent. After a few minutes of us standing in the same embrace, she moved her head to look up at me. "So, are you okay?" she asked, eyes tinged with worry.

"I'm fine, baby, why do you ask?"

"I don't know, it just seems that I'm dragging you into more of my drama."

"You're not dragging me into anything. If I remember correctly, I volunteered to come here, didn't I?" I said, pulling her head back to my chest.

"Yes, but...," she started, but I cut her words off.

"No 'buts.' I'm here because I want to be. I'm not too happy about you going into the parole hearing, but that's not my decision." Dropping her arms from around my waist and taking a step back, she rubbed at the small line that started to appear between her brows with her finger.

"I know you would rather me just write out a statement, but I think it might give me some kind of closure if I actually verbalize what I need to say."

"Verbalize to who, Casey? It's a parole hearing. He's not going to be there," I said, trying to keep my voice at a calm level.

"I know he won't be there in the room, but I feel like I need to tell them, the people that have the power to set him free, what he's taken from me." And when she looked at me in that moment, I could see the conflict in those beautiful eyes of hers, and I felt like we just took a huge step back to that vulnerable and pained woman of a few months ago. This was exactly what I was afraid of. She could play tough on the outside, but she was forgetting that I knew her much better than she thought, and I definitely knew how to read her eyes. Right now, the eyes I were looking into were telling me that she wanted to pull those shutters down on me, and I was not going to let that happen.

"You see, that look you have right now?" I said, pointing at her eyes. "That's a look I don't like."

Shaking her head and looking away from me, she turned, reached under the bed, and pulled out a dark blue suitcase, lifting it onto the bed and flipping it open.

"So what, you're just going to ignore me now?"

"No, I'm just not sure what to tell you," she said, pulling open the top drawer of the dresser and rummaging through what looked like panties. I walked over and took her hands in mine.

"Just tell me I'm wrong, Casey. Tell me you're strong enough to do this, because if you're not, we'll leave right now. Fuck the hearing," I said through gritted teeth.

Closing her eyes for just a moment then opening them again, she stared right into mine when she said, "I want to do this, and I know that I can, but I'm scared shitless, and I'd be a fool if I wasn't. But you being here is giving me the strength that I need, Nate. I'm sorry that you can read my eyes, I can't hide that, and I am trying my hardest to keep afloat. I just need you to warn me when I'm starting to sink, okay?"

Her words made my chest ache, but they were honest and for that, I was satisfied...for now.

Giving her a nod, I turned my attention to the open suitcase. "Do you need a hand with that?"

"No, I'm good. Why don't you go down, get a beer, and relax," she said, smiling.

"Sounds good, I'll leave you to it," I said before leaving the room and heading downstairs.

Keeping the promise I had made to Paxton before we left the US, I needed to give her some space and myself some much needed time to relax a little and get myself in check. I told Paxton that I would be on my best behavior and wouldn't smother Casey with my apparently dominant overprotectiveness, but I was finding that easier said than done at this point. I knew that she was dropping the walls she'd built around herself, but I could also see her building them back up again just as fast, and at the moment, I was caught between wanting to give her what she wanted and needed and taking what I wanted and needed, which was to get her the fuck back home and away from all this mess.

I grabbed a beer from the fridge, flipped the cap off, and took a long pull from the bottle. I headed toward the computer, figuring I might as well check through some emails and print off the tickets for the flight home on Saturday.

Three beers later, while catching up on the latest game scores on Fox Sport, I heard the front door open, and I turned to see Flynn walking through, carrying a briefcase in one hand and what looked like a plastic bag full of take-out containers.

"Hey, Nate," he said, as he dropped his case and bag down on the coffee table. He loosened his gray suit tie as he flipped the top button of his white dress shirt, then shucked out of his navy suit jacket, tossing it over a chair. I watched as he walked to the fridge, grabbed a beer, and almost drained the whole bottle in one hit. "So, how was the trip today?" Flynn asked.

"Interesting," I said, tilting my head to the side and lifting a brow at him.

"Really? How was Casey?" he asked as he flopped down in a chair across from me.

"Nervous, but she did it."

Flynn let out a heavy sigh. "Fuck."

"Yep, balls of steel, that woman," I said, trying to lighten the mood a little, which seemed to work because the lines on his face clearly relaxed.

"I thought about calling her this morning and insisting that I go out there," Flynn said.

"No, man, I think she needed to go. She seems to have an agenda of things she wants to conquer, and that one probably fit in perfectly."

"So, what about the box?" he asked taking another slug of his beer.

"Disturbing," I said, giving him a sideward glance that caused his eyes to widen.

"What do you mean?"

"It wasn't so much what was in it. It was what I kind of expected - some old photos and nondescript papers and a small journal that looks like it belonged to her mom. It was more her reaction to the things," I said, rubbing my fingers against my chin.

"Reaction?" Flynn asked, perplexed.

"Yes, she was very detached. As she flipped through the photos, there was nothing, no recognition, not even when she got to one of her parents. It was like her essence had left her body completely. It's just a little strange seeing her react to them like that."

"No, not for me," Flynn said. "They weren't traditional parents at all. They had no love for Casey, ever. To them, she was an inconvenience, an obstruction in their pathway to power. She was their mistake, and they reminded her of it every chance they got. No,

Nate, they were not parents. They were a pair of selfish animals who deserved what they got." Flynn's words were hard and tinged with a vicious anger, causing me to curse under my breath.

The room filled with a silent pause for a moment while the silent rage and fury of two men perforated the air around us until Flynn finally broke it and stood up.

"Well, better go up and get your girl. I brought us some Chinese take-out, and it's getting cold."

Chapter nine

C asey

Once Nate left the bedroom, I searched through my cupboards and drawers, picking out things that I wanted to take back to Portland with me and dropping the unwanted things into an empty box in the closet. Looking around the room now, I noticed how sparse it must have looked to Nate when he first came in here. I mean, it didn't actually look like a typical girly room, now that I looked at it. In fact, if it wasn't for it being my room, even I would think no one lived in it at all. But I guess that's how it was. I never wanted to keep anything from my childhood, not even any pictures, so the only thing I ever needed was clothes. I was never really a person that needed lots of belongings around me to make me feel at home because, in reality, I have never felt at home, anywhere...except in Portland with Nate.

Pushing everything I needed into the case and zipping it up, I sighed, grabbed my iPod, and pushed the buds into my ears. At the moment, I needed to put myself into a music coma with the help of Adele. Leaning my head back against my pillow, I closed my eyes with thoughts of sitting on the bottom stair of Paxton and Lynda's beach house, my feet sinking into the cool sand and the warm sun tickling across my face.

Still on the beach, I saw Nate's face come into view, his dark hair slick and wet with small beads of water from the ocean trickling down the side of his face and dripping off the scruff of his strong jaw. Reaching out with my hand, I traced a rivulet of water with one finger until I reached his bottom lip, sliding my finger over it with a light, lazy moan as he sucked it into the warmth of his mouth . It felt so real. I felt his tongue slide over the skin of my index finger, and damn, this feels too good and way too real to be a dream, and then my dream bubble popped as I was woken by a low, gravelly moan against my ear.

Opening my eyes slowly, I stared at his beautiful, eyes as he sucked my finger into his mouth again.

"Damn, that's hot," he groaned.

"Tell me about it. I guess dreams really can come true," I said as I smiled at him.

"Hmm, you were dreaming about me, huh?"

"I was until you woke me."

"Why dream when you can have the real thing any time you want?"

"Sounds good. I want. Now," I said, wrapping my arms around his neck.

"Me, too, but Flynn has dinner waiting for us downstairs, so as much as it pains me to say this," he said, emphasizing his point by grinding his hard length against my pelvis, "...later." Nate pulled me up from the bed, taking me with him to a standing position.

"Great timing, Flynn," I grumbled under my breath as we went down to eat.

The next few hours were filled with eating from a buffet of plastic containers filled with almost every Chinese dish you could imagine. Over a few beers and a bottle of white wine, Flynn went over the schedule for tomorrow and what to expect. Trying to reassure him that I would be fine and not to stress so much, he was starting to remind me of a mother duck making sure her babies were all together. Poor guy. I always knew he looked after me, but seeing the deep lines starting to appear on his face every time he looked at me made me realize just how much I wished he would take time for himself, to live the life he deserves.

That night, after Nate made sweet, gentle love to me, he pulled me into his strong arms, tucking me against the taut muscles of his chest. He kissed the top of my head, and the last words I heard him say before I fell asleep were, "It's almost over, baby."

I woke to the feeling of butterflies going crazy in my stomach, and I noticed that Nate wasn't next to me. Sitting up and scrubbing my hands over my face, I pulled myself up and got into the shower. After drying myself off, I dressed in a dark green wrap dress with long sleeves and a pair of black two-inch heels. I pulled my hair into a ponytail and applied a small amount of pink gloss across my lips. Running my palms over the front of my dress to make sure it was straight, I took one more look in the bathroom mirror, satisfied with the look that I was aiming for: professional and dignified.

Grabbing a matching black purse, I went downstairs and into the kitchen to where the two men in my life were sitting at the table having breakfast. Nate's head lifted to look at me as soon as I walked into the room, his eyes staying on mine as Flynn jumped up and motioned for me to sit while he got me some breakfast. "Just a cup of tea, please, Flynn. I don't think my stomach will cope with much this morning," I said.

Nate placed his hand on top of mine as he said to Flynn, "And a piece of toast, too." I narrowed my eyes at him, ready to disagree until I saw the slight lift of his brow and that warning light that flashed in his eyes..

Placing a hot, steaming mug of tea and a plate of toast in front of me, Flynn sat back down, taking a sip from his own mug. "You okay?" he asked me.

"A little nervous, but weirdly enough, I'm okay. I think I'm just ready for it to be over," I breathed out.

"And you've been over what you want to say?" Flynn asked, smiling when I gave him a nod.

"You'll do great, sweets."

"Thanks."

Nate sat in the back seat of Flynn's Jeep, gripping my hand. He was freshly shaved, wearing a white, button-down dress shirt and dark jeans. Looking at him made me think of how he always looked in his office, casual and relaxed, although I did miss the scruff that normally shadowed his strong jawline. For me, it didn't take long enough to get to the court in Parramatta, and with my hand still held tightly in Nate's, we walked up the stairs, where I glanced up briefly at the huge Australian Coat of Arms on the front of the building before we pushed through the glass doors and got into the lift.

When the doors opened, Flynn motioned for us to sit. "I'll go in and start, and when it's time, someone will come and get you, okay?" he said to me as he rubbed a soothing hand over my shoulder.

"Okay," I said, nodding before leaning back into the chair. As we waited, Nate was silent aside from the pulsating tick of the muscle on the side of his jaw that told me he was trying hard to relax and keep it together.

I jumped when the court door opened. An older woman wearing a conservative dark suit came out and motioned for me to come in. On somewhat shaky legs, I stood with Nate next to me, took a deep breath, and entered the courtroom. We were directed to sit in the front seats, directly behind where Flynn was sitting at a table covered in folders bursting with paper. As Flynn spoke, I zoned out, letting my eyes take in the surroundings. Sitting behind a long, heavy, carved wooden table were two men and a woman. The portly, balding, older gentleman that sat in the middle was introduced as a member of the judicial board. I could tell by his uniform that the other man was from the correctional facility, and the woman, a fairly young looking slim blonde, was a member of a community program that helped ex-offenders out on parole. At one end of the desk sat a slim monitor with a blank screen that flickered to life with an image that immediately caught my attention, making me suck in a gasp of air.

The face on the screen was that of an older man, face lined with years of severity and harshness, a spray of home-style tattoos decorating one side of his neck. His eyes were as black as night, dark bottomless holes of nothing, just the way I remembered them. I needed to look away...now. I turned to look at Nate. His eyes were my salvation and what I needed to concentrate on right now, and that's exactly what I did. I searched them for his strength, and although I saw a myriad of emotions swimming in them, I pushed past the anger and fury until I found it - understanding, validation, and love. I closed my eyes for a moment, just enough to balance myself, and when I opened them , I found his eyes searching mine. I gave him a slight nod, letting him know that I was okay.

We listened to statements from the prison facility in regards to Max Sullivan's long history of good behavior, steady work ethic while inside, his clean record in the last fifteen years, his clear mental state, and his newfound devotion to God. The young, blonde woman from the community support team had arranged for him to have somewhere to live, a part-time job, and his own private support team. I was starting to think that maybe I was the criminal because according to these people sitting in front of me, Max Sullivan was almost a perfect human being. If only they knew.

By the time Flynn turned and motioned for me to stand up at the podium in the front of the room to give my victim impact statement, I felt completely drained and disheartened. I realized quickly that it didn't matter what I said, they had already made their decision. I was only here as a formality, a tick in a procedural box, a duty from the State to the victim.

Standing up, I placed my hands on top of the podium in front of me,and slowly looked at the faces of the people in front of me for a moment, and inhaled deeply.

"Please, Miss Tyler, you may begin whenever you like. The court does not wish to take any more of your time than is absolutely necessary today." Looking up at the balding man sitting in the middle, I narrowed my eyes at him and swallowed hard, trying to push the instant anger his words had just caused down and away for later. Taking in a deep breath, I began.

"Time. That's a really important word to me because I have had a lot of it stolen from me; sixteen years, to be exact. I know what you see written in the papers in front of you. You see a man who has done his time in prison and apparently done it very well. You see a man who has paid his price to society and deserves a new start with somewhere to live, even a job and plenty of support, and it makes me wonder where my support has been for the last eighteen years. Because I wasn't as lucky as Max Sullivan. Nobody gave me back what he stole from me. A home, support...nothing." I took a moment to look at each and every one of them individually before I continued.

"Max Sullivan may have paid his debt to society, but he hasn't paid it to me. I can never get back what he took. I will never be the same, and where you see a man reformed, I see an evil animal. You only know him by what's written on the paper in front of you, but I know the real person, and that person is not human and will never be able to be helped or reformed. I see now, by being here today, that each one of you has already made a decision. Me being present here today is just a decent and morally courteous thing to do on behalf of the court. You are absolutely right. To continue this hearing is definitely a waste of my time, and quite frankly, I'm done wasting my time on Max Sullivan. Thank you."

I saw the somber looks on all three of their faces as I turned, grabbed my purse from the chair next to where Nate sat, and pushed my way out of the door to the outside hall. Nate caught up to me quickly, and I heard Flynn call out.

"Casey!" Stopping, I turned to him. "Please, sweets, wait. I just need to wrap this up."

I was just about to answer him when I heard the deep rumble of Nate's voice. "It's okay, you stay and do what you need to do, we'll get a taxi." Flynn nodded and looked at me with sadness in his eyes before Nate grabbed my hand and pulled me down the hall and outside the glass doors. Once outside, I stormed down to the footpath, pulling out my phone on the way to quickly order a taxi to pick us up from our current location. With arms folded and the feeling of Nate standing behind me, we waited in silence for the taxi and continued our silence all the way home.

Once inside, I threw my purse onto the kitchen table, went to the fridge, and pulled out a beer and a bottle of wine. I poured myself a solid, full glass and downed it before refilling it again.

"Casey." I heard the slight low warning tone of his voice before looking up at him, still standing with the unopened beer in his hand.

"Don't. I don't feel like getting a lecture on taking it easy with the wine, Nate. Right now, I just want to drink myself into a coma because that," I said, pointing at the front door with my full wine glass, "was a fucking load of crap."

"It wasn't good," he said in a low voice.

"And what the fuck? No one said anything about doing a video conference with that fucker, either. I was ready for it, you know, but *that* I was not ready for at all," I said taking another gulp of the wine. "You know, I wasn't kidding myself. I knew that logically, he would get parole, and I resigned myself to that fact. But sitting there, listening to those morons talk about him like he was some kind of saint and that what he did seemed so inconsequential and unimportant made me feel physically sick." Taking a seat at the dining table and dropping my face into my hands, I felt Nate pull a chair up next to me and start to gently rub a hand over my back.

"I'm sorry, baby," he said, making me shake my head.

"You have nothing to be sorry for, Nate. I need to apologize to you, for dragging you all the way here for nothing. Absolutely nothing."

"Not nothing. Never nothing, Casey. I'm here with you, and there is no place that I would rather be right now. I'm just sorry that you didn't get the closure that you needed."

Letting out the pent up breath that I had been holding, I turned and looked at him. He leaned his head down so our foreheads touched, and the anger drained from my body as he said, "I love you."

"I love you, too," I whispered back to him.

Nate grabbed my chair and turned it easily to face him. His large, strong, warm hands came up to hold my face in his palms, forcing me to look right at him. "Remember, this is not the end. It's a new beginning, so don't keep anything from me, okay? And I mean nothing. If you're stressed, worried, over thinking, pissed off, then do it with me, not at me, okay?" As soon as I nodded to agree, his warm lips were on mine, gently moving with a sweet caress, making me feel every bit of his love for me.

Chapter Ten

Nate

I ran Casey a bath as she got undressed, then helped her into the hot, bubbly water, handing her the rest of her wine. "You going to join me?" she asked.

"No, this is just for you this time, but make the most of it because this is a once only deal," I said, grinning as she leaned her head against the back of the tub and closed her eyes. "Just relax, okay? I need to call Paxton. He wanted to know how today went as soon we were done."

"Okay, just tell him it was fucked," she said as she smiled sardonically.

"I will," I said as I left her, pulling my phone out of my pocket as I went down the stairs. Paxton answered on the fifth ring with a sleepy voice.

"Hey, sorry I woke you," I said.

"No, no, it's cool. I was expecting it. Besides, Emily just went down not long ago," Paxton said.

"Is she okay?" I asked, concerned that she might be ill.

"Yeah, she's great, just hungry all the time. I have no idea where the hell she puts it all!" he said making me smile at the proud tone in his voice.

"If she's anything like us, she will have a mean appetite," I chuckled.

"Sooo, how did it go?" Paxton asked, making me pause for a moment to rub a hand over my face.

"Well, Casey told me to tell you it was fucked."

"And was it?"

"Pretty much. Besides having to listen to everything he had been charged with, the mother fucker was there."

"What, in the same room with Casey?" Paxton sounded both shocked and angry.

"No, by video conference, but Casey wasn't expecting it, and it momentarily rocked her concentration."

"Oh, fuck, is she okay?" he asked with genuine concern.

"She was pissed."

"I bet she was. And you? How are you doing?"

Sitting down on the couch and taking a minute to compose myself, I scrubbed my hand down my face and blew out a long-held breath, finally feeling my body relax from the tension I had been holding in all day.

"Nate?"

"Fuck, Paxton. I just...damn. Just hearing all the charges they had on him against her, I blanked it out halfway through. Put it this way, I now hate the word multiple."

"Jesus," was all Paxton could say.

"And watching that prick's face on the screen. Fuck, I just tried to concentrate on Casey and block out as much as I could, man. And you, you helped me a lot today."

"Me? How did I help?" he asked, sounding surprised at my statement.

"Because as I felt my blood pressure rising with every second that passed, I just kept hearing your fucking annoying voice in my head saying, 'Keep it calm, Nate, just get it done and get out.'"

"Hahaha, I'm glad you have my words of wisdom somewhere in that head of yours," he chuckled.

"Always, Paxton, you know that."

After a pause, Paxton continued, "So what now?"

"Now? I'm hoping it's over for my girl, and I can get her out of here."

"You leave Saturday, right?" he asked.

"Yeah."

"Do you need me to come pick you up?"

"Nah, I left the SUV at PDX. Besides, I'm pretty sure we will both be out of it with that damn time zone shit. I mean, we leave here Saturday morning at 7 a.m., travel for twenty plus hours, and land at PDX around 2 p.m. on the same day we left."

Paxton laughed as he spoke. "You should be used to that time zone shit with all the world traveling you've done in your time."

"Think I might be feeling my age," I chuckled.

"You? I doubt that, very much."

"I think I will be staying close to home from now on."

"Hey, I am keeping you to that promise. Just let me know if you need anything," he said.

"There is one thing. Can you contact Mrs. Winters and let her know that I'll need the pantry and fridge stocked for Saturday?"

"No problem," he said.

"Great. Okay, then, we will see you soon, little brother." I heard him cough at that before saying goodbye and ending the call.

Hearing light footsteps coming down the stairs, I looked up to see Casey dressed in a pair of black yoga pants and a loose fitting white t-shirt that slid off one shoulder. Her hair was still piled up on the top of her head, and a few stray, wet tendrils hung down, sticking to her neck and collarbone.

"You okay?" I asked her as she walked toward where I sat on the couch.

"I'm sure I'll live," she said with a forced, weak smile before I pulled her down onto my lap.

I wrapped my arms around her and pulled her into my chest, tucking her head under my chin. We stayed that way, just silence between us as though all we needed were the feelings transferring from her body to mine in that moment.

"Thank you for today," she said, almost in a whisper.

"For you? Any time," I said, trying to ease her obvious discomfort.

She absently rubbed her fingers over the buttons on the front of my shirt as she snuggled deeper into me, and in that moment, she felt so fucking good.

Later that night, we ordered pizza. The pizzas here were pretty small compared to the ones we had back home, but at least it was tasty. With two full stomachs, we stretched out on the couch and found a movie to watch. This was just how I liked it - nice, calm, relaxed, and getting closer to going home. Just as the credits for the movie started to roll up the screen, the front door opened and Flynn came in, looking pretty disheveled and exhausted. Dropping his briefcase at the front door, he pulled off his jacket before dropping himself down into one of the lounge chairs across from where we were laying on the couch. Casey took the remote from my hand, flipped off the TV, and sat up to face Flynn.

"You look like crap, Flynn," Casey said. Her voice was light as she spoke, but Flynn's face showed anything but being light. At this moment, he looked exasperated, like he had been put through the wringer a few times. He also had the distinct odor of scotch on him.

Scrubbing both hands down his face, then looking up at Casey, he said, "I'm so sorry, Casey." His voice was strained with regret.

"No, Flynn, it's okay. I know you busted your arse for me in there today, but it was obvious they had already made up their minds," Casey reassured him.

"That's a fucking understatement," Flynn spat out, causing Casey to flinch and me to sit up instantly.

"Please, Flynn, the last thing I want is for you to blame yourself. You did your best."

Flynn stood up and started to slowly pace the room before he stopped in front of where we were sitting.

"That's the point, though, I don't think I did do my best," Flynn said between gritted teeth.

"What are you talking about? Of course, you did," Casey said standing and watching as Flynn's eyes flashed with several different emotions until he came back to anger.

"It was a fucking whitewash, Casey. All of that, that stage show today, was just for you. It was all bullshit!" he yelled, causing me to stand up. I didn't like his tone of voice, and I wasn't sure if it was from the frustration of the day or the alcohol.

"What are you talking about, Flynn?" Casey said, obviously confused. "You're not making any sense. Look, I have no doubt that he will get parole, but I'm done, Flynn. I'm done with this whole thing. It's over, I will be long gone before he gets out, and I know he won't ever be able to follow me."

"That's the point though, sweets. He will be released on Friday." Flynn's words caused Casey's hand to fly to her mouth with a gasp.

"What?"

"The review board had already made their decision, and his release date had already been set," Flynn said.

"But how?"

"I have no fucking idea, it all had something to do with the public office wanting to show support for the victim, but in reality, their hands were tied. He's done his time and completed his re-socialization program. If they took the risk, had a legal parole hearing, and something went wrong, he could sue the government for millions. The whole thing today was fake. It was just for show, and I am so fucking stupid, I didn't even see any of it."

"Would they really go to all that trouble for him?" Casey asked, stunned at Flynn's words.

"To protect the government? To save money? To avoid any scandal in the press? Fuck yeah, for sure. But I've been thinking that I might be able to approach this from a different angle..." Flynn started, but was cut off by Casey.

"No, no angles, no nothing. It's done. Let it go, Flynn." Her words were hardened with a finality that made Flynn's head whip up to look at her.

"What? No, sweets. Listen, I can fix this..." he started, but she cut him off with a "NO!"

"But, Casey, we can't just let it..."

"Yes, we can, Flynn. It's done." Hearing the frailness in her tone, I had to intervene.

"Flynn," I said, my voice warning him to back off, but all it seemed to do was fire him up more. At least it was directed toward me now.

"Hey, mate, I respect you, but this is not the time for your opinion," he said, angrily pointing at me.

"Good, because it's not my opinion, it's a fact. Casey just told you to drop it, and I think you need to respect that," I said, taking a step closer to him. Flynn slowly shook his head before looking me straight in the eye and taking a step closer to me.

"Look, I know you're with her, but you don't own her. I looked out for Casey a long time before you came on the scene, so I'm pretty sure I know what she needs," Flynn said through gritted teeth.

Narrowing my stare at him, I could see that he was passionate about his words, but no other man would be telling me what my woman's needs were. I had a fleeting thought that I really needed to get a hold of the fury that was starting to burn through my veins, but that thought was interrupted by Casey wedging herself in between us.

"Hey, cool it, the pair of you! No one knows what my needs are except me, you got it?" Casey said, her voice strong and determined.

Her head turned to look at me and then back to Flynn. "I appreciate you, Flynn, and everything you've done, but I'm tired of fighting. I just want to get on with my life. It's been screwed up enough, and the last thing that I want is for the two most important men in my life to be locked into a testosterone-fueled pissing competition," she said, exasperated. My clenched fists loosened, and my body relaxed slightly. I looked at Flynn, and I could see his anger drain away with her words as he took a step back.

"I'm sorry, you're right," Flynn said, holding his hand out to me. After a moment's pause, I acquiesced and took it, giving him a firm shake that allowed Casey to let out a deep sigh.

"Okay, are we done now?" she asked, and Flynn and I both nodded at the same time. "Good, because it's been a long day, and I want to go to bed," she said as she grabbed my hand and led me upstairs to our room.

She slipped into bed before I could even get my shirt off. I turned off the light and slid into the bed behind her. She turned into my arms and snuggled into my chest before saying, "Your woman, hey?" making me chuckle as I pulled her in closer.

"Just stating the truth, baby."

"Okay, caveman." I could feel her smile against my chest.

"Where you're concerned, you bet your fucking ass I'm a caveman. Speaking of ass," I said, as I ran my hand down to grab a handful of a warm, soft, plump cheek, making her jump. "I've wanted to squeeze this all day."

"Really?" she said with a playful wiggle of her eyebrows. I reached over and grabbed her other ass cheek, pulling her up my body until her legs straddled my hips. The quick movement caused the top half of her body to fall forward. She giggled and lifted her face to mine, so close our noses were touching.

"Really," I growled and took a light bite of her bottom lip, sucking it into my mouth and causing her to moan into my mouth before her hands came up to cup my face. She kissed me back, slipping that warm tongue of hers into my mouth and over my own. My hand ran behind her head and gripped the back of her neck as I deepened the kiss even more, biting and nipping at her lips and her tongue with a fevered passion. I could never just have a taste of this woman, I had to have everything. I loosened my hold on the back of her neck slightly, giving her room to sit up and pull her t-shirt over her head, giving me an eyeful of her beautiful breasts, heaving with lust. With my hands on either side of her waist, I slid them up until I was cupping her breasts, one in each hand, and ran the pads of my thumbs over her delicious pink nipples, causing them to instantly harden under my touch. A low moan vibrated from deep in her throat as she started to make small circular movements, grinding her pelvis against my hard shaft. I could feel her wetness seeping through the thin material of her panties and soaking the front of my boxers, making my hard-on grow harder if that was even at all possible.

She leaned back down and started kissing me again. I ran my hands down to her panties, and I have no idea how, but I managed to tug them off before escaping the confines of my own underwear without breaking our kiss. What can I say? Where there's a will, there is definitely a way, and right now that way is up and in.

"I need to be inside you, now," I growled into her mouth. Casey sat up and lifted her hips up slightly, running a hand to the base of my shaft and rubbing the head between her wet folds. When I gripped her hips harder in protest of her teasing, she slowly eased herself down and took me inside. I was mesmerized as I watched her engulf every last inch until I was fully inside of her. She leaned back, placing her palms on my thighs and slowly started to ride me, a complete symphony of movement, changing in positions and rhythm. With shocks of electricity sparking up and down my spine and hitting my balls like a sledgehammer, I pulled her down harder as I thrust up into her tight, hot heat. She leaned forward with her palms on my chest, giving her more leverage. Her eyes focused on mine, and I watched the pleasure as it spiraled in her eyes as her sex tightened around my shaft and started to spasm. Her lips parted, and she moaned my name over and over, making me explode inside of her with my own orgasm finally released.

We stayed in that position for some time, with Casey still straddling me, her chest against mine, her head tucked under my chin, and my hands gently stroking her back as our quick, labored breaths settled and calmed. Eventually breaking our connection, I slipped her off and onto the bed next to me. I went to the bathroom to clean myself up, running a washcloth under the warm water before bringing it back to where she was laying and running it gently between her legs. Settling back into bed next to her, I pulled her back into my arms and kissed the top of her head.

Chapter eleven

Casey

Waking to the sun streaming through the window instantly reminded me that I'd forgotten to close the blinds last night. *Fat lot of good that does me now*, I thought. I grabbed my phone, turning to look at the clock that read 6:15 a.m. Seeing how early it was made me groan. Well, that, and the ache in my thigh muscles from last night. Slowly slipping from the death grip Nate had on me, I pulled down the blinds and put on a pair of sleep shorts and my t-shirt. I was just about to open the door when I heard Nate's sleepy voice.

"Where are you going?"

"Shh, go back to sleep. I'm just going down to get a drink," I said.

"Okay, just don't be long."

"Yes, sir," I said, giving him a mock salute that I knew he hated, but I watched as he rolled over and buried his face back into the pillow.

Trying to be as quiet as possible, I crept down the stairs and into the kitchen. I poured myself a glass of cold milk and sat down at the table.

Crossing my legs, with my elbow leaning on the table and my hand supporting my head, I absently stared out of the large glass sliding doors, out into the backyard, then up at the early morning sky. My mind drifted a little to the mornings that Nate and I had spent sitting on the beach at Paxton's. It seemed funny that no matter where you were in the world, whenever we gaze at the sky, the sun, or the moon, we are all looking at the same thing, just at different times in different places. The only thing different for me was that the feeling that I used to get from being in the safety of my own home, in my own country, just didn't seem to be as strong as it used to be, and for a moment, I wondered if that made me a traitor. I chuckled at the stupidity of my wandering thoughts.

I was also a little baffled at the absurdity of the whole parole hearing. What a waste of time, just for the sake of saving face. I wasn't sure if I just had a long time to think about the hearing or I had already resigned myself to the outcome, but I expected it to feel a lot harsher than it did, and with the reality of Flynn's words last night, there was no anger or defeat at all in me. If anything, I felt...relief. I felt like a huge weight had been lifted because I had made the decision to let it go. It was hard to explain, but I felt lighter, unimpeded by the past and the hold it used to have over me.

As I took a sip of milk from my glass, I heard footsteps on the stairs. Expecting to see Nate, I was surprised to see Flynn, his hair wet and slicked back from the shower, already dressed in black slacks, a crisp, white, tailored dress shirt with a dark red tie in place. I saw the slight falter in his step as he saw me sitting at the table.

"Hey, what are you doing up this early?" he asked as he poured himself a glass of orange juice from the fridge and brought it over to sit across from me.

"Just woke up early and came down for a drink."

"Are you okay?" he asked with concern.

"I know this sounds weird, but I feel bloody amazing," I said, smiling at him.

"Really?"

"Really. I was just sitting here thinking that I feel so relieved. Stupid, right?" I said, looking at him for some kind of confirmation or validation.

"I say if it feels good, own it," he said, smiling at me.

"I'm going to miss you," I said softly, causing him to stop mid-drink and place his glass on the table.

"I'm going to miss you, too, sweets, but I know that where you going, you're finally going to be happy and safe, and by watching you and Nate together, I can see that you have finally found what you've been looking for. That missing piece that you could never seem to find. Your freedom."

As I reached across the table and placed my hand on top of his, I could feel the burn of tears at the back of my eyes, but then he lightened the mood by saying, "Besides, it's a great excuse for me to come visit you and take in some of the beautiful ladies, I mean, sights over there."

"Trust you to think with your dick," I said, laughing.

"What can I say? I am but a mere man with a big libido."

"Sounds good. We can take turns! Well, once I'm settled and hopefully employed," I said with a grimace.

"You'll do it, look how far you've come."

"I guess, but it's taken a lot of help from the people around me."

"Aw, come on, don't sell yourself short. There aren't many people that would push through like you did. You certainly have balls of steel, woman," he said, chuckling.

"Nate and his family have been a huge help," I said.

"Yep, he's definitely a keeper, that one. And he is so in love with you."

I felt my cheeks redden with embarrassment at Flynn's words. "And that response," he said, motioning toward my face, "tells me that the feelings are mutual."

"Very much so," I said with a smile.

"So." Flynn clapped his hands together breaking the silence between us. "I need to get my things ready for work."

"Okay, you go do that, and I'll make some breakfast," I said standing. I headed for the kitchen and pulled a frying pan from the bottom cupboard.

"Sounds good to me," Flynn said, going into the living room, which was also his makeshift office.

I was standing in front of the stove, moving bacon around the pan while trying to dodge the spits of oil flying from it like fireworks when a strong pair of arms slipped around my waist, causing me to jump slightly.

Nate's face nuzzled against the side of my neck. "Mmm, now that's what I like to see. My beautiful girl dressed in a shorts, cooking my favorite food first thing in the morning." Turning my head, I kissed the underside of his jaw.

"Good morning, I thought you would sleep longer," I said.

"When I wake up with a raging hard-on, and you're not lying next to me, I need to find you," he growled into my neck, placing a warm, open-mouthed kiss against it.

"Go sit, this will be ready in a minute."

Nate grabbed a mug from the cupboard, filled it with black coffee, and took it to the table. Just as I was serving up the bacon, eggs, and toast, Flynn came in with his arms full of papers, along with his briefcase, and dropped them on the bench. As he sat down at the table, I placed a plate in front of him, then Nate, and one for myself.

"So, what have you got planned for today?" Flynn asked around a mouthful of scrambled eggs.

"A whole day in bed," Nate said just as I opened my mouth to answer. Ignoring his response, I looked at Flynn.

"Actually, I was thinking of taking Nate up to Bondi Beach and then spending the afternoon at Paddy's Market. I wanted to grab some presents to take back," I said, giving Nate a smile.

"Shopping?" Nate said, eyebrow raised in question.

"No, we'll go to Bondi for a while, then shopping," I said, grinning.

"Looks like your day is planned, mate," Flynn said to Nate.

"Seems so." Although Nate had an unhappy look on his face, I saw the corner of his lips quirk into a half grin.

"So listen, what time does your flight leave on Saturday?" Flynn asked Nate.

"7 a.m., so we'll be leaving very early."

"Okay, so tomorrow night, we'll go out, right?" Flynn said. "And I won't be taking no for an answer. It will be the last night we get to spend together for a while, so I was thinking dinner at the Tuscany winery and then onto the Pendulum for some drinks and dancing."

"Dinner sounds good, but the Pendulum? I was hoping to get an early night," I said.

"Come on, Casey, you can sleep on the plane! This will be our last night! Besides, I won't finish work till later tomorrow, and I want to spend the rest of the night with you guys," Flynn almost whined, making me feel bad and give in.

"Fine, but not an all-nighter, okay?"

"Okay," he relented. Flynn finished his breakfast and washed up his plate before grabbing his briefcase and leaving for work.

As promised, our day was a full one. After taking Nate to Bondi Beach, where we walked along the shoreline and took in the salty, fresh sea air, we found a small place to grab a bite to eat. We then headed up to the North Bondi Lookout, which is a cliff on the north side of Bondi that sits on a point, and it has the most spectacular views of the Pacific Ocean. I drove Nate crazy looking through the endless stalls at Paddy's Market, trying to decide on the perfect presents. I got Paxton another T-shirt with the Sydney Harbor Bridge on it together with a matching ball cap, and I purchased a beautiful, matching opal pendant and earring set for Lynda. When it came to buying for little Emily, there were so many pretty dresses, and tiny t-shirts with "Aussie Girl" across the front, and of course, I had to buy her a fluffy stuffed kangaroo. I just couldn't help myself. Thank goodness Nate stepped in and stopped me with the logic that we wouldn't be able to fit anything else in our luggage.

The day was topped off by dinner out on the patio with Flynn, and an evening relaxing. Nate and I had an early night followed by an early morning spent in bed, with Nate fulfilling his wish from the morning before. We pulled ourselves away from each other and into the shower, had something to eat, and spent the rest of the time repacking our bags to fit everything that I had purchased at the market. We just left out clothes to wear out that night and to travel in the next day, which was easy because it would all fit into our carry-on bag anyway.

Finding a nice, red, figure-hugging dress with a little bit of sparkle to it in my wardrobe and some black heels under my bed, I dressed, brushed out my long, blonde hair, and applied a little gloss to my lips before coming downstairs to a waiting Nate in a pair of jeans and a grey, silk button-down dress shirt. It didn't seem to matter what clothes he wore, he always looked as sexy as sin. *I might have to keep him close tonight*, I thought as his arms slipped around my waist, crushing me against his hard chest.

"You look delicious," he said, giving me a chaste kiss.

"You look pretty good yourself," I said, returning the compliment.

Hearing keys in the door, we both turned to see Flynn come in. "Hey, cool, you're ready. I'll just go change. I'll be quick, I saw the taxi waiting outside."

"What taxi?" I asked as I walked to the front door and opened it to take a look.

"There's a taxi waiting out there. I figured you called for it," he said, puzzled.

Looking out the door, I saw nothing. The street was empty. "There's nothing out there," I said to Flynn who now stood next to me.

"Huh, that's funny. It was there when I came in. It must have been for someone else in the street, and they got the wrong house. Awesome, now I have time to change," he said bounding up the stairs two at a time. Closing the door, I grabbed my purse and put my phone inside it. Within ten minutes, Flynn was back downstairs, dressed in a pair of black jeans and a dark green dress shirt, smelling fresh as a daisy. He pulled out his phone, dialed for a taxi, and we went outside to wait for it. No Jeep tonight, he told us he intended on showing us a good time.

The Tuscany winery restaurant was beautiful. We sat outside in the courtyard, and the trees there were covered in tiny white fairy lights that wound around the trunk and branches. The smell of the fresh night air mingled with the wonderful smells coming from the kitchen made my mouth water. We all ordered filet mignon, and the bottle of Merlot Cabernet Franc that Flynn ordered accompanied the meal beautifully. He wanted to order another, but when I rubbed my stomach and groaned that I wouldn't be able to have a drink at the Pendulum if we did, he conceded. I knew he would; any excuse to get there quicker.

The Pendulum Club at The Rocks was housed in an old stores building, and it was a pretty big place. The entry was through a huge archway that had two buildings on either side with a sandstone, outdoor courtyard area that joined them. It was kind of a mixture of old and new that came together effortlessly. On one side, there was a bar and seating with live entertainment, and on the other, a banging nightclub with high, small round tables and matching stools in the courtyard. We grabbed a table as soon as we saw one empty; the place was pretty full. Nate helped me up onto a stool, and Flynn took off to the bar, returning with a couple of beers and a glass of white wine for me. Even sitting in the courtyard, it was hard to hear each other talk, as there were so many bodies crowded around. The thumping music escaped from the nightclub and out into where we were sitting. Nate pulled his bar stool up close to me and had his protective arm around my waist.

When the courtyard starting filling up even more, and I was starting to feel a little buzzed from yet another glass of wine that Flynn had so graciously placed in my hand, I relented to his pouty begging to go into the nightclub to dance. I could see that Nate wasn't too impressed. His eyes were already darting around the swarming crowd around us. I also remembered how well he moved his body that night on the dance floor at the Bizarre, so with one of my hands in Flynn's and my other locked tightly in Nate's, I was dragged into the nightclub of spiraling flashing lights and loud thumping music coming from the DJ at the front. Somehow, in this huge mass of people, we moved with the crowd. I, with Nate's arms securely locked around me, almost crushing my body to his as Flynn latched onto a couple of women dancing together. It felt so good to let go and enjoy the music with my arms around Nate's neck and his eyes locked onto mine, our bodies moving rhythmically to the music.

After about an hour on the floor, our bodies were hot and sweaty, and our eardrums were humming. Nate and I moved to the outer floor and grabbed a beer from the bar. We watched Flynn enjoying the attention of the two gorgeous women on either side of him. After we finished our drinks, Nate looked over at Flynn, then motioned with his finger, pointing down at his watch. After a few words to his dance partners, he came off the floor and over to us.

"It's late, buddy, and we have an early flight, but you look like you're enjoying yourself. Why don't you stay?" Nate said.

"No, it's cool. I am totally wasted anyway. I need my bed," Flynn said as we started to make our way back out to the courtyard and out to the front where there was a huge line of people standing and waiting for a taxi.

Walking to the end of the line, I peered my head around the swaying line up of party goers before I said, "This is going to take a while, isn't it?"

"Yep, at least twenty minutes or so. Why, sweets?" Flynn asked.

"Do you think I will have enough time to run in and use the bathroom?" I asked with a slight grimace. I really hoped he would say yes because my bladder was about to explode.

"Sure, go for it. There's a bathroom just down the side there. Just be quick," Flynn said, pointing to a passageway at the side of the building. Turning, I hurried along the passageway, finding the door for a bathroom. After relieving my aching bladder, I washed my hands and wet a paper towel to dab some of the sweat from my face. Tossing it into the trash, I picked up my purse and quickly headed out the door. With my head down, concentrating on the uneven path and not wanting to get my heels stuck in any cracks, I was shocked when I slammed into someone. As I lifted my head to apologize, the words instantly stuck in my throat.

A face that I hadn't seen for a long time, now older, but I would never be able to erase it from my mind, stared back at me. A mixed ball of panic and fear rolled in my stomach causing bile to rise as I gagged at the sight in front of me. Max. Older, with a much thicker body, but those same evil eyes.

With my legs feeling like jelly, I leaned back against the wall, desperately seeking some kind of support. I tore my eyes away from his for a moment to look over his shoulder, hoping that someone, anyone, was coming this way, but there wasn't and with all the noise I didn't think anyone would hear me anyway. I opened my mouth to scream, but all that came out was silent, dry air. I could feel the icy terror coursing through every inch of my body, freezing me in place. It felt like everything was suddenly in slow motion as he lifted his hand and placed it flat on the wall behind me, bringing himself even closer. No longer able to look at him, I closed my eyes and wished that this was not happening, that it wasn't real, but when he spoke, I knew that wish was a really a nightmare.

"Look at me," he hissed into my face. Squeezing my eyes closed tighter and turning my head away from his hot breath and the stench of tobacco, I felt his roughened hand as it slowly slid from just below my breasts and up my neck until he had my jaw gripped in his palm. His thumb and forefinger pinched and squeezed as he turned my head to face him.

"Open your eyes, and look at me," he repeated, squeezing harder until the pain forced my eyes to open and look into his. I swallowed hard, trying to ease the dryness in my throat. His face was so close to mine our noses almost touched. His vile, crazed eyes stared so deeply into mine, I felt like I was looking into two windows of darkness. The skin of his mouth crinkled slightly at the corners as it turned into a psychotic smirk.

"I've been waiting for such a long time, and it looks like my little girl is all grown up," he said, the sound of his gravelly, low voice making me feel nauseous. When a tear slid from the corner of my eye and ran down the side of my cheek, he caught it with his thumb. "Aw, don't cry, little girl. I won't hurt you. You see, I've had a long time to think about what I did wrong, and I know now that I should have just been more patient with you." With my stomach churning and my heart almost beating out of my chest, I felt my breaths getting quicker and shorter as the fear started to take over. I needed to get it under control so I could clear my thoughts and do what I needed to survive.

Chapter twelve

Nate

The line of people in front of us was slowly getting shorter as the taxis pulled up and people fell into them. We were finally getting closer to the front. It had been a good night. The meal was spectacular, and it was good seeing Casey relaxed and enjoying her last night on the town with Flynn. But now, I found myself constantly staring over toward the passageway to the ladies bathroom, looking for Casey because we only had about six people in front of us. Why was she taking so long? Maybe there was a line for the bathroom, as well, I told myself. But when I looked at Flynn, we were both clearly having the same thought. Where the fuck was she?

When a taxi pulled up and four of the people in front of us jumped in, something didn't feel right, and my chest had an uncomfortable feeling in it.

"I'm going to go check on Casey," I told Flynn, making my way toward the passageway.

"Tell her to move her butt," I heard Flynn call out behind me. As I made my way down toward the ladies bathroom, I heard what sounded like low voices. Picking up my pace a little, I turned the final corner, and what I saw made my head explode in anger. Casey was being held against the wall by someone. My brain thumped with fury, and the blood coursing through my veins was so hot it felt like they were going to burst. All I could see was red. I took off running toward the scene that, in my head, looked like it was on a movie screen. I felt detached as I reached them and grabbed the asshole's shoulder, spinning him to face me. Out of the corner of my eye, I saw Casey slide down the wall into a sitting position, and the face I now stared at was the one person in this world that I wanted to kill. All I could get out was one word, "You," before my arm cocked back with a clenched fist and slammed into his face. I felt his nose crack on impact as blood sprayed from it, and once that first punch hit home, I lost it. Punch after punch followed as I gripped the front of his shirt. Every time my fist connected with his flesh, my adrenaline spiked even more. I wanted to hit him so hard that my fist would come out the other side of his skull. He dropped onto the floor. I stood over him and continued to pummel every inch of his now lifeless body. With the blood rushing through my ears like a freight train, I heard Casey's pleading voice as she said, "Stop him, Flynn! Please!" followed by strong arms wrapping around my chest, trying to cage my arms into my body.

"Nate! Stop, he's done," Flynn said, as I struggled to break his hold. With my chest heaving, I glanced to where Casey was sitting, her cheeks soaked with tears. When I saw the terror in her face, it kicked my brain back into gear. "Okay, let go of me," I growled at Flynn, which he instantly did. I crouched down to where Casey sat and scooped her up to a standing position, running my hand over her hair to the back of her neck. "What did he do?" I spat out.

"Nothing. I'm okay," she breathed out. Looking into her terrified eyes, I knew she was lying. I also knew I had to get her out of here. Flynn was bending over Max's limp, bloodied body. I watched as he placed two fingers against his neck, feeling for a pulse, then he looked up at us both. "Get her out of here."

"Flynn," Casey whimpered.

"Now! Grab a taxi and take her home, Nate. Leave it with me," he said with a low growl.

Looking at Flynn, something passed between us that made me instantly pull Casey against my chest, grab her purse off the ground, and walk her to the waiting taxi at the curb. Pushing in front of a guy just about to open the door, I grabbed hold of the handle first, helping Casey into the back seat.

"Sorry, pal, I think this one's mine," I grumbled as I got in next to her, giving the driver the address. Every muscle in my body was straining with tension, my hands still locked into fists, my breathing uneven, until I felt a hand slide across to mine with soft, trembling fingers gently brushing across my skin and pulling me from my darkness where bright blue eyes that shimmered with tears looked deep into mine. We had no words for each other at that moment, but all I needed right then was her touch.

As soon as we got inside the house, Casey went to the fridge, pulled out an ice pack, and pressed it against my throbbing knuckles. She motioned for me to sit as she pulled out two tumblers from the cupboard and a bottle of scotch, pouring the amber liquid into the glasses. She handed me one, then sat across from me with her own glass. Throwing back the scotch in one gulp, I felt it burn slightly as it went down, and Casey refilled it before going back to sipping hers.

"Are you okay?" I asked her gently, bringing her eyes up to mine.

"I think so. I'm not exactly sure what just happened though. Are you okay?" she responded, her eyes glancing down at my swollen and bloodied hands.

"Yeah, that's nothing," I said, shrugging off her concern.

"Nate, that was not nothing. What you did was..." Her voice trailed off as her eyes looked around for an answer.

"Was necessary, and believe me, he was lucky that Flynn turned up because when I saw his hands on you, all I could think of was ripping him to shreds," I said, shaking my head.

"But Nate, what if he is dead? What if someone saw...holy shit, Nate." I could hear the panic starting to rise in her voice as the shock was starting to wear off, leaving clear the whole situation. Dropping the ice pack on the table, I reached across, pulling her off her chair and sliding her shaking body onto my lap. I wrapped my arms tightly around her as her hands grasped at my shirt front. "What if...what if someone tells the police, and they come after you?"

"Shh," I hushed against the top of her head. "It's okay, baby. Flynn said he'd take care of it, and I trust him to do just that. Besides," I said, glancing down at my watch, "we'll be at the airport in a couple of hours on our way back to Portland, and if there's one person that I would never feel any guilt over putting six feet under, it's that fucker," I said with disdain.

"I couldn't take it if something happened to you knowing that I was the cause of it," she whispered. I pulled back so I could look into her eyes. I needed to make sure she heard and understood me.

"I told you I would kill for you, and I meant it. I promise you nothing will ever happen to me, okay?" I said. I pulled her back into my arms where we sat in silence. Sometime later, with Casey still on my lap and her eyes closed, I heard the front door open and saw a disheveled looking Flynn walk into the kitchen. He dropped his keys and phone on the table. He sat and grabbed the bottle of scotch, took a long swig from it, then leaned back into the chair and let out a long-held breath. Casey's eyes opened, and she pulled herself up to look at Flynn.

"Are you okay?" she asked him.

"Yeah, I'm fine. What about you two?" Flynn asked, his eyes darting between Casey and me.

"Nothing that an ice pack didn't fix," I said, looking at him. "And you?"

Flynn rolled his eyes and said, "It's been a long night."

"Is he..." Casey started to ask Flynn, but he cut her off.

"He's in a bad way. You gave him a good beating, mate; thanks for that."

His words made me grin. "You're welcome."

Casey stood up. "Seriously? I can't believe either of you are taking this so calmly. I mean, because of me, you've beaten someone half to death," she said, looking at me and then Flynn. "And you've helped cover up a crime, and you're both patting each other on the back?"

"I'm sorry, sweets, but Nate just did what I've wanted to do for so long. He deserves a pat on the back," Flynn chuckled, causing Casey's stance to stiffen as her hands fisted on her hips.

"It isn't funny, Flynn. What if someone saw, and he dies? Or he tells the police that Nate beat the hell out of him? Then they will come after the pair of you."

"Calm down, that's not going to happen," Flynn said calmly.

"How can you be so sure?" Casey asked him.

Flynn took another slug from the bottle of scotch in his hand.

"Because I was the one who called the cops and an ambulance for him, and I watched as the cops talked to people in the crowd. Everyone was so drunk and buzzed that no one saw anything," he said casually.

"You called the cops?" Casey asked.

"Yes, I just told them that I found him on my way to the bathroom."

"But what about when he talks to the cops?" she said, frustrated with Flynn's answers.

"It doesn't matter. He had so many drugs on him and in him that if he does regain consciousness, he'll go back inside for breaking his parole."

"What do you mean drugs? How do you know he had taken drugs?" Casey eyed Flynn with suspicion.

"I know because I put them on him and shoved a couple down his throat. The bastard had a bad gag reflex, too. Almost bit me."

"What the hell, Flynn?" Casey yelled, throwing her hands up in the air.

"Those two chicks that I was dancing with, they slipped me a little baggie. It had about 8 ecstasy pills in it, so before the cops got there, I shoved two down his throat and pushed the rest into his pocket, problem solved. Now, who's hungry? I am starving. How about I cook us up some bacon and eggs?" Flynn stood and went into the kitchen. He proceeded to pull out the bacon and a carton of eggs, placing them on the counter.

Casey stood, hands still firmly placed on her hips, with her mouth slightly ajar, staring at him until he finally looked at her.

"What?"

"I'm totally stunned, Flynn. I have no words."

"Humph, that would be a first," he chuckled as he pulled out a frying pan from under the counter and placed it on the stove top.

"I can't believe you did that. Who are you? Do I even know you?" she asked him, but before he could answer, I stood up and wrapped my arms around her waist.

"I'll tell you who he is, baby. He's your best friend, he loves you, and that's all you need to know, okay?" I felt her relax slightly at my words, and her stare softened as she looked back at Flynn.

She nodded, sighed, and then said, "You're right. I know everything I will ever need to know." She broke away from me and moved around the counter to Flynn, where he wrapped her in a ferocious bear hug, lifting her off her feet before placing her back down.

"Okay, now sit while I cook," he said, giving me a tip of his chin in gratitude for my support, but really, I owed him a lot more.

Chapter thirteen

Casey

After Flynn had loaded us all up with a plate full of crispy bacon and eggs, we had enough time to take a shower, get dressed, and leave for the airport. I sat in the back seat as Flynn drove us, and I could hear their low voices in the front. At another time, I would have struggled to listen, but at the moment, all I could think about was the previous night. I couldn't help but think how ludicrous it all was. I mean, how sick can a person be to spend the last fifteen years behind bars, only to be released and go straight back out into the public with the intent of continuing where he finished off? It was crazy. No, he was crazy. And Nate...I didn't think I had ever seen him that out of control before. The realization of how far he would go to protect me and what we have gave me an icy tingle down my spine. I had an underlying feeling of remorse and even guilt. Remorse for Nate losing it because of what Max had done, and guilt because as a doctor, my duty of care was to protect people from harm, but as Nate beat Max into a bloody mess, the only thing that I could think of was Nate's safety. Shit, now I was thinking too deeply about why the hell would I feel anything but hatred for Max fucking Sullivan. I think if anything, I was mad at myself for being a frozen statue in his grip and not kicking him in the balls myself.

As we pulled up at the Kingsford Smith Airport, my thoughts were pulled back into the present. Seeing the doors for international departure made me realize that we were going back home, getting out. Flynn pulled the luggage from the boot, then stood in front of us.

"Well, I guess this is where I leave you," Flynn said.

"You're not coming in?" I asked him.

"Nah, I hate goodbyes. Besides, I don't want to get a ticket for parking too long," he said, grinning. Wrapping my arms around his waist, he gave me a tight hug and whispered in my ear, "Love you, sweets."

"Love you, too. And it's not goodbye, it's see you later," I said.

After letting me go, he thrust out a hand to Nate, who took it. "Look after my girl," Flynn said as they shook hands.

"You know I will," Nate said. He clapped Flynn on the shoulder. "And thanks for everything. Remember, don't be a stranger. We'll have a room for you anytime you want, okay?" Flynn gave Nate a nod before rounding the Jeep, jumping in, and not looking back. I knew how hard this was for him, but I hoped he would be able to find his own peace and learn to live a little like I had. Besides, it wasn't as though I would never see him again.

Nate grabbed the suitcase, and we checked in our luggage. It was weird as I watched that one suitcase, which encompassed my entire life before I met Nate. It didn't seem like much to show for thirty years on this earth, but it was what it was, I guess. We waited in the Qantas lounge because, once again, Nate had managed to buy us business class tickets without my knowledge. This time, I wasn't going to argue with him; he deserved to have the extra leg room. It was going to be a long flight again, with a five-hour layover in Honolulu, but I was pretty sure we would definitely be getting some sleep considering we hadn't slept all night.

Before long, a female voice came over the loudspeaker. "Passengers flying Qantas flight 3711 traveling from Sydney to Honolulu then onto Portland, Oregon, please make your way to the departure desk. Your flight is now boarding."

Nate stood and took my hand in his as we walked to the boarding desk, handing over our boarding passes and passports, then making our way down to the waiting Airbus where we were shown to our luxurious seats. Once we took our seats, we were offered a glass of champagne. Nate gave me a wicked grin and said, "What, no complaints this time?"

"Nope, none at all," I said, smiling back at him.

As soon as we took off, Nate stretched out his long legs and was asleep before we reached cruising altitude. I leaned my seat back and lay on my side with my hands tucked under my cheek, watching him as he slept. His strong jawline was covered in a dark scruff, his full lips were parted ever so slightly, and his black hair was unruly, with a few stray locks almost covering his closed eyes. I actually felt relief for him. He was on his way home to his family, his penthouse, and his office - all places where he had some control. Coming with me to Australia must have been hard on him, but I so appreciated him being with me on this trip, even if it was a dramatic one. I wondered if there would ever be any words that I could give him to express exactly how much him being by my side through all of this meant to me. I guess I could only try.

I soon followed Nate in slumber, only waking briefly to decline an offer of lunch. I was so tired I couldn't even think of food. I briefly noticed Nate's empty seat. I guessed he had gone to the bathroom. I yawned, closed my eyes, and drifted back to sleep. The next time I woke, the cabin of the plane was in darkness. Nate was watching some action flick on the screen in front of him while wearing headphones. As I sat up and stretched my arms in the air, Nate looked at me, removing one of the headphones from his ear.

"Hey, sleepy girl," he said, smiling.

"Hi," I replied softly.

"I'll get the steward to get you something to eat," he said, pressing the button on the side of the chair.

"No, it's okay," I tried to say, but was stopped.

"You need to eat. You missed lunch and dinner. Don't argue," he said with a cheeky grin on his lips.

"Sure," I sighed. "I need to use the bathroom first," I said, standing and slipping into the aisle. Once I made it to the bathroom, I tried to finger comb my hair into a ponytail and splashed my face with cool water. I felt like I had slept for a week. My whole body felt really heavy. When I got back to my seat, there was a tray waiting for me with a selection of sandwiches, a chocolate muffin, and a bottle of water. I ate while Nate continued watching his movie.

I had to admit, the flight was better on the way back, even though we were late getting into Honolulu, so we didn't stay there as long as expected. Our final leg home went quickly, and we landed at PDX at 8:30 in the morning on the same day we left Sydney, which was always weird to think about. Once outside, we made our way to the long-term, secured parking where Nate picked up the keys to the SUV, and we were on our way back to the penthouse. I saw the instant relief in Nate's body language once he was back to driving on what he thought was the right side of the road, and I knew he must have felt good to be home.

As soon as we got into the penthouse, the bags were dropped outside the lift, and we both went upstairs and flopped into bed, both falling asleep almost instantly. The next time I woke was to the sound of the shower. Sitting up and pushing my legs out of bed, I groaned as I rubbed my temples. My head felt like I had been hit with a sledgehammer, and they were still pounding on it. Taking a few minutes to ride out the dizziness that went along with the pounding, I slowly walked into the bathroom where, through the steamy glass of the shower, I watched as Nate stood with his back to me, both palms resting against the tiles with his head bent under a stream of water. I was mesmerized by his solid body. I watched as the taut muscles in his back twitched as he moved his head back and forth. I loved that the ink of his colorful tattoos were more vibrant with the water running over them.

The thudding in my head brought me back, and I moved toward the glass cabinet above the sink in search of some pain relief. As I opened it, Nate's head lifted to look at me through the glass. "Hey," he greeted, but all I could do was groan.

"You alright?"

"My head is killing me," I said, continuing my search through the collection of aftershave bottles, new tubes of toothpaste, and various other bathroom essentials.

"There's some Tylenol in the drawer next to the stove in the kitchen," Nate said, turning off the shower and stepping out. I passed him a towel that he quickly rubbed through his hair and wrapped around his waist. "Why don't you hop in the shower, and I'll grab you some," he said, dropping a quick kiss on my lips before heading out of the bathroom.

Stripping myself of the clothes that I had been wearing for the past 24 hours and had just slept in, I got into the shower and turned it on. Before the water had even wet my body, Nate was back with two pills and a glass of water. "Thanks," I said, taking the glass, downing the pills, and handing the glass back to him.

"Are you okay? You look pretty pale," he said, his eyes showing concern.

"Just all the travel and a messed up body clock. I'll be okay. What about you?"

"It's just good to be home," he said, smiling. Then he added, "If you're okay, I'm going to get dressed and go down to the office."

"Yeah, you go see your brother. I'll be fine."

"Okay, be back soon," he said and left the bathroom to get dressed. I stayed in the shower until my fingertips started to shrivel, and then I dragged myself out, dried off, and slipped into a pair of shorts and tank top. I headed downstairs to the kitchen and poured a large glass of orange juice that I took over to the wall of glass to gaze out at the city beneath us. As I sipped the juice, the pain in my head finally started to ease. Grabbing my phone, I sat on the couch and flipped Flynn a text message letting him know that we had arrived home safely and that I would call later when he was awake.

Draining the glass, I dragged the suitcase and our bags into the bedroom and started to unpack. I was transferring things from the case to the closet when my fingers hit something firm. Pulling it out from under the clothing, I realized it was my mother's journal, which I had thrown into the suitcase. I just stared at the worn cover. I did want to read it, but I still wasn't ready. Walking around to the side of the bed, I slipped it into the drawer of the bedside table and went back to putting things away. I shoved the huge pile of laundry I had collected into the washing machine before heading back to the kitchen to make myself something to eat.

Chapter fourteen

N^{ate}

As soon as the elevator doors opened into the lobby of my office, I finally felt at home. Ignoring my office doors, I walked past them and down to Paxton's office, knocking once before entering. Paxton sat behind his heavy, glass desk reading something on the computer screen that sat in front of him.

"What?" he said, sounding slightly angry without taking his eyes away from the screen.

"Fuck you, too," I said.

Paxton's head whipped up, his face breaking into a huge smile. He immediately got up and came around his desk to greet me with a brotherly bear hug. "What are you doing here? I thought you would be sleeping off the jet lag," Paxton said, pulling back and looking me over.

"Yeah, we did sleep some of it off. We got back pretty early this morning."

"I am so glad you are back. I feel like I can breathe again now," he said, grinning.

"Smartass," I said, sitting in one of the two black leather chairs that sat in front of his desk as he dropped into the other.

"Really, Nate, I'm glad you're back," Paxton said.

"Me, too. I mean, don't get me wrong, what little I saw of Australia was spectacular, and I can't wait to go back, but hopefully under different circumstances. I'm glad I went with Casey, but damn, it's good to be back on home ground again. Speaking of home, why are you here at work on a Sunday when you have a wife and daughter at home?"

Paxton's brow raised as he looked at me. "I think that jet lag has rattled your brain more than you think because today is Saturday."

"Shit, you're right. The time difference is a bit of a mind fuck," I said, scrubbing a hand over my face.

"Anyway, I needed to catch up on some work, and it was a good excuse to be here when you got back. Speaking of paperwork...," Paxton said. He got up, rounded his desk, and opened the top drawer, pulling out a large white envelope. He dropped it into my lap before taking a seat again. "That's the deed to your new home."

Lifting the envelope, I tore open the top, pulling out the papers, followed by several keys on a small silver ring. "That was fast work," I said, giving him an appreciative smile.

"You're welcome."

Pushing the papers back inside the envelope and pocketing the keys, I said, "No, this is really great, it's just what Casey needs."

"And before I forget, Lynda is expecting you both at the beach house tonight for dinner. She's missed you both."

Pulling out my phone, I tapped out a quick message to Casey, letting her know to pack an overnight bag for the beach house.

"Don't tell me you have to ask the little woman first," Paxton said, grinning.

"Fuck off," I playfully sneered back at him.

"So, fill me in on your trip."

"You're up to speed on most of it, the whole whitewash with the parole hearing and shit."

"Yeah, that was bullshit. How the fuck did they get away with that one?"

"I have no idea. Flynn filed a grievance with the courts, but Casey wanted it dropped."

"I can understand why. How is she?" Paxton asked, concerned.

"She's amazingly good. All she wanted to do was get back here. You should have seen her, Paxton. She didn't even look like she belonged in her own home. It was weird."

"Yeah, well, I guess it doesn't hold any good memories for her," he said.

"The only one she has there is Flynn, and he's got a lot more going on than he's letting on."

"What do you mean?"

"I can't be sure, but I think he is much more than just a lawyer. I'm pretty sure he has some kind of double life thing going on."

"What, you mean like undercover type thing or illegal type thing?" Paxton asked, looking interested.

"No, I don't think it's anything illegal, but there's more to him than meets the eye."

Paxton nodded and then studied me for a moment. "So, what are you not telling me?"

Taken aback by his question, I smiled as I realized that I could never hide anything from him.

"Are you sure you want to go there?" I asked him with a slight grimace.

"What did you do?" he asked, his annoyance obvious in the tone of his voice.

"Nothing that you wouldn't have done," I said, placating him.

"Nate," Paxton growled.

Rubbing my hand on the back of my neck, I tried to think of just how to put it all into words.

"On the last night, Flynn took us out for a meal and then onto this weird kind of cross between an old style bar, lounge, and nightclub place. It was a good night."

"And..." Paxton said.

"And that fucker, Max Sullivan, turned up. He grabbed Casey while Flynn and I were waiting for a taxi."

"What the fuck?"

"She had gone to use the bathroom, and when I got to her, he had her by the throat, pressed up against the wall," I said, my anger resurfacing at the memory.

Paxton stood shaking his head. "Please, don't say what I think you're going to say," he said, pushing his hands into his pockets.

"Depends what you think I'm going to say," I said sheepishly.

He huffed out a breath before saying, "Well, if some sicko had Lynda pushed against a wall, I would rip him to pieces with my bare hands."

"When I saw that bastard with his hands on her, Paxton, I saw blood," I said through gritted teeth, looking straight at him. "I didn't think at all; I just reacted."

"Fuck, Nate. At least tell me you didn't kill him?" When I shrugged my shoulders, Paxton started to pace. "Did anyone see you? What about cops?" He started a barrage of questions that I halted by standing right in front of him and placing a hand on his shoulder.

"Look, the last thing that I know is that he was in the hospital, unconscious. There were no witnesses, and Flynn took care of everything. He's going to keep me updated, okay?"

Paxton reluctantly gave me a nod before saying, "So, Casey...she's alright?"

"Yeah, she's good. What about Peterson, anything new?"

"Nah, I've been keeping an eye on the little fucker. Nothing since you and Jax paid him a visit."

"That's just the way I like it."

Making my way back up to the penthouse with a promise to Paxton that we would meet him down in the garage in an hour and with the large white envelope clutched in my hand, I was hit by loud music playing as soon as the elevator doors opened. Walking in, my heart hitched a little at the sight of Casey dancing around in the kitchen, cleaning down the counters. I leaned against the wall for a moment and watched her wiggle and sway to the loud, thumping music as she busied herself with the task at hand. She looked so comfortable and relaxed, and it was a welcome sight to see this beautiful woman clearly very comfortable in my home. When she turned and saw me staring at her, she smiled, picking up the remote and silencing the music.

"Sorry, I didn't see you there," she said, her cheeks turning a little pink with embarrassment.

"Please, don't stop. I was enjoying the show."

"Funny guy," she said leaning a hip against the kitchen island.

"You know I have a housekeeper who does all the cleaning, right?" I asked her.

"Yes, the elusive and stealthy Mrs. Winters. I've heard her name and woken up in the morning to a clean place and a well-stocked fridge, but I haven't been quick enough to see her yet." She smiled.

"Well, I'm pretty sure you'll be seeing a lot more of her over the next couple of weeks."

"Really? Why is that?" she asked, brows raised in curiosity. Walking closer to her, I reached into my pocket and pulled out the bunch of keys.

"Because over the next few weeks, I have a feeling that I am going to be pretty busy with the Bank contract, and I don't want you to be on your own for long periods of time." She opened her mouth to protest, but I held a finger against her lips and continued. "Besides, even though I know how incredible you are at multitasking, I still think you'll need a hand looking after two places, and I'd like to know you have some help decorating this." Holding up the keys, I gently swayed them in front of her eyes. She looked at the keys then back to me, and I noticed as a small crease formed in between her brows.

I watched as she studied the keys for a moment. Then she broke into a huge smile and said, "The beach house?" I took her hand and nodded, placing the keys into her palm, closing her fingers over them.

"It's all yours."

Looking down at her hand then back up to me, she whispered, "Ours."

Wrapping my arms around her and pulling her against me, I kissed her forehead. "I didn't expect it to happen so fast," she said.

"You can thank Paxton for that. I have no idea how he gets things accomplished so fast, but he's a slick little shit, and this is the one time I am not going to question him."

"I'll thank him later, then."

"Speaking of which, we had better go down to the garage before he comes looking for us," I said, giving her ass a squeeze.

Chapter Fifteen

Casey

We had just put our overnight bags and a bag full of presents into the boot of the Audi when the lift doors opened and Paxton strode out, arms open to engulf me in a warm hug.

"Hey, Casey, how are you doing?" he asked as he pulled me back, looking at me with concern.

"I'm great, Paxton, and really glad to be back."

"Well, we sure did miss you both. Speaking of which, we better hit the road before Lynda starts calling me to see where we are."

"Don't have to tell me twice; I can't wait to see them both."

We followed behind Paxton for most of the journey. It didn't matter how many times we made this road trip, I still loved taking in the view from the window. I was conscious of the change in the air. The smell of the salty breeze coming from the ocean and the sound of the waves got louder the closer we got to the beach house. As soon as we pulled up outside the house, Lynda was at the door with Emily in her arms, her face alight with an excitement that matched my own. Jumping out, we embraced each other, being careful not to crush Emily who was sandwiched between two sets of boobs. Breaking apart, I took Emily from Lynda and hugged her close, breathing in her beautiful baby scent and dropping a light kiss on her forehead. "Look at you, little girl! You have grown so much," I said, looking into her sweet little face before turning to look at Lynda. "And you look wonderful! I see motherhood agrees with you."

"It does, but not so much at three in the morning!" Lynda said, smiling. She continued, "Come on in, I am dying to hear about your trip."

Leaving Paxton and Nate to bring in our bags, I followed Lynda into the house where we sat opposite each other on the couch. With Emily still in my arms, we both broke into a flurry of excited chatter at the same time. Lynda bombarded me with questions about our trip that I tried to answer quickly before asking her questions about Emily. We didn't even notice the men come in. It was only when they both joined us in the living room, each holding opened bottles of beer, that we broke from our talking. Nate placed his beer on the coffee table. He came to sit next to me, and I handed him his niece. He was just as lost as I had been in the little bundle, cooing at her and gently running his fingers over her wispy hair and chubby cheeks. I watched as his eyes softened and then grew wide with love as she blew little raspberries as he spoke to her.

"She is so beautiful," he said, looking up at Paxton.

"What do you expect, with two of the most beautiful people in the world as her parents?" Paxton said, grinning.

"Well, at least one," Nate said to Paxton.

The afternoon was spent catching up, watching as Paxton and Lynda enjoyed the gifts that we brought back with us, and of course, play time with little Emily. We thoroughly enjoyed the wonderful dinner and time out on the back deck with a glass of wine, surrounded by the smells and sounds of the ocean.

"So, I hear you have a new house to furnish," Lynda said, patting my leg.

"I guess we do," I said, looking over to where Nate sat stretched out in an armchair, making him grin before he said, "Oh, no, that's all yours, baby."

"I don't think so, you'll be living there, as well."

"Yeah, but shopping is not my thing," he said, rubbing his fingers along his chin.

"And it's not mine either, remember?"

"Really?" Lynda said, a slightly shocked look on her face as she looked at Nate and me. "You're just as bad as each other."

"Yeah, what woman doesn't like to shop?" Paxton said.

In unison, both Nate and I pointed in my direction with me saying, "Me," and Nate saying, "Her," making us break out into laughter.

"Then you might have a bit of a problem. I mean, you do need something to have that wild monkey sex on, otherwise you guys are going to end up with splinters," Paxton said, smiling. We were all silent for a moment, contemplating an easy solution to our decorating dilemma when Lynda jumped with excitement.

"I know, you can purchase furniture online! All we need is a computer, some more wine, Nate's credit card, and we can fill that house with everything you'll need."

"Sounds good to me," Nate said, looking straight at me. "What do you think?"

"I think it sounds great, but you still need to be involved," I said, giving Nate a pointed look.

"Really?" he almost whined like a 10-year-old being told he had to clean his room.

"Of course. I don't want to be responsible for buying some ugly couch that you decide is uncomfortable down the road. I'll never hear the end of it!"

"Fine," he breathed out. "Go grab the laptop, and let's do this before I change my mind."

"You wouldn't dare," I said, causing his brow to arch as he said, "Try me."

Over the next couple of hours, another bottle of wine, and a few beers, we managed to furnish our new home from top to bottom with the basics to move in. The purchases included an obscenely sized, flat screen TV with a complete surround sound system to go with it, of course, at Nate's request. When I saw the total of the invoice, I opened my mouth to protest, but quickly decided to zip it when Nate gave me a shake of his head and a wicked death stare as he pulled out his credit card and tapped in the number and delivery address. I was amazed at just how much you could purchase online without even stepping foot into a showroom. Satisfied with our furniture quest for the night, we headed off to bed where I quickly fell asleep, my cheek pressed against Nate's hard chest with the excitement of exploring our new home in the morning.

Driving up the gravel driveway the next morning, I saw the white house come into view. Nerves rumbled in the pit of my belly with anticipation. We'd only been here once before, but it felt so familiar, so comfortable, so homely. Nate pulled the Audi up at the front stairs, and as we climbed them together up onto the front porch, the smell of the sea in the breeze seemed to envelop me in its essence. Nate took my hand and pressed the keys into my palm. I looked into the depths of his eyes for just a moment before unlocking the door, turning the handle, and pushing it open. I was hit with the smell of fresh paint combined with a woodsy aroma. Walking inside, I made my way down the long hallway, which opened up to the kitchen with its large expanse of tri-fold windows. I stood there, silently taking in the beauty of the wide, wraparound deck overlooking the picture perfect view of the blue ocean. Standing beside me, Nate unlocked the wall of glass and slid it open to where the smell and sound of the crashing waves seemed to go right through me and infiltrate every part of the house.

Nate pulled me into his arms as we just stood and looked out at nature's wonderful painting in front of us.

"What are you thinking?" he asked, stroking a hand down my back.

"I'm wondering if this is all real," I said. Nate's hand moved under my chin, tilting it up to him.

"I ask myself that same question every time I look at you," he said, his voice low. Swallowing hard, I felt my eyes start to well with tears from his words and the overwhelming feeling of belonging somewhere and to someone. I felt a tear slowly slide down my cheek. Nate's thumb caught it gently before his lips touched mine softly.

"I want to give you everything," he breathed against my mouth.

"You already have," I said, closing my eyes and pressing my cheek against his chest.

We spent the morning exploring the rest of the house. It wasn't huge, but it certainly wasn't small either, I had no idea what we were going to do with all the empty rooms. The largest bedroom had its own bathroom and more large glass windows that opened up to its own spectacular view of the ocean. Most of the walls were painted white, but Nate assured me that we could repaint them any color we desired, and my mind started envisioning splashes of color everywhere.

Locking up the house, we went back to Paxton's for a late lunch before we headed back to the penthouse. Nate had a huge workload to catch up on now that we were back, and I had some organizing to do. We talked about the move on the way back. Nate didn't want to take much with him from the penthouse as we would be traveling back and forth between the beach and the city. Turning slightly in my seat to look at Nate, I said, "What do you think about giving the beach house a name?" He glanced at me, one brow arched with amused puzzlement.

"A name?"

"Yes, you know, like 'The Manor' or 'Beach Villa.' Something other than 'The Beach House.'"

"It's entirely up to you, baby," he said, smiling. "Do you have something in mind?"

"Kind of."

"And...?" he urged.

"Well, back home, we have these really beautiful trees called jacarandas. They're strong, with a sturdy trunk, and have the most beautiful, lilac-colored flowers..."

Before I could finish, Nate jumped in. "Sounds perfect. That description reminds me of you."

Looking down, feeling my cheeks warm slightly, I said "So, you think 'Jacaranda House' sounds okay?"

"Absolutely," he said, smiling.

"You are just too good to me, Nathanial King."

"I love it when you say my full name in that sexy accent," he said with a wicked grin.

"You are just too easy to please," I laughed.

"When it involves you naked and me inside of you, I'd have to agree."

"Dirty boy," I said, smacking his thigh playfully.

"Oh, believe me, baby, I intend to be very dirty when we get back."

"You do have work tomorrow, remember?"

"And your point is?" he said with a raised brow.

"I just thought you would turn in early tonight."

"I am, with you," he said with an almost serious look on his face.

"Do you have a lot to catch up on?"

"Yeah, I need to finalize the security plan for the bank contract, and I need to go over to the club. Apparently, they've been having some issues with the alarms."

"What, at the Bizarre?" I asked him.

"Yes, it seems the Bizarre is going to be a huge pain in my ass," he said, shaking his head.

"I'm sure you'll work it out," I said, smoothing my hand over his forearm.

Once we got back to the penthouse, Nate retreated to his office to make some calls, and I made us a simple chicken salad for dinner. Dinner was followed by a shared shower where Nate kept his promise of being a dirty boy. We started in the shower and continued into the bedroom. Sated and sweaty, I cuddled into his strong embrace, where the last thing I felt before falling asleep was his kiss on the top of my head.

Nate's kiss was also the first thing I felt when I woke, my eyes opening to the feeling of his lips sofly pressed to mine. Warmed by waking in such a wonderful way, I stretched my arms above my head, then rubbed the sleep out of my eyes to find him dressed in a white button-down shirt and a pair of jeans, smelling delicious as usual and leaning over me.

"Morning," I said sleepily.

"Morning, beautiful." The deep rumble of his voice combined with his freshly showered and clean linen smell made my thighs clench. Rolling over onto my stomach, I groaned in frustration. I felt his hand grab my ass cheek and squeeze before he said, "You need to get up, babe. You have a guest downstairs."

"What? Who?"

"I have to run, text me if you need me, okay?" he said quickly, exiting the bedroom and ignoring my question. Guest? What the hell did he mean? Feeling a little confused but curious, I jumped out of bed and headed for the bathroom to wash, brush my teeth, and pull my hair into a ponytail before pulling on a pair of shorts and a t-shirt. I slowly headed downstairs to see just who this guest was.

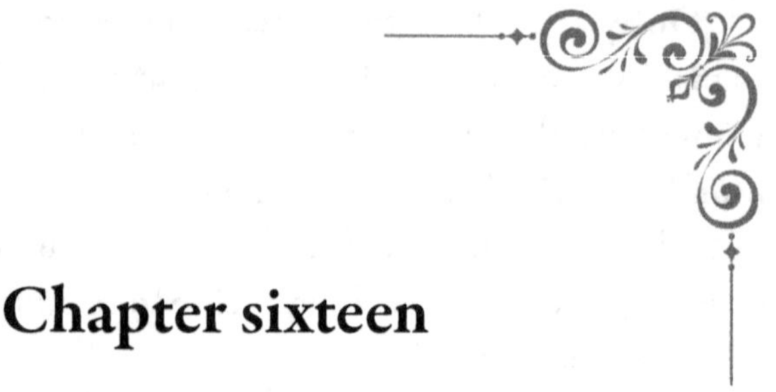

Chapter sixteen

N^{ate}

Leaning back in the chair behind my desk, I never thought I would ever feel excited to be back in my office, but I was. Damn, what has this woman done to me? "Fucking made you domesticated, that's what," I answered myself out loud just as a knock came at the door. Paxton walked in carrying an arm full of folders, dumping them in front of me.

"Okay, where do you want to start?" he sighed.

"I'm all yours to direct," I told him.

And that's what we did over the next few hours, taking a quick break for lunch before continuing. This bank contract was a huge deal for the company, and it was extremely important to get it right. I didn't want any mistakes like it appeared we were having with the night club. Paxton had been filling me in on the different issues the club had been having since its opening night, but the more he talked, the more suspicious I became. It was clearly way more than just a faulty alarm system. I let Paxton know I would get on to it once we had the bank deal wrapped up, and it seemed to ease his anxiety over the whole situation.

The next time I glanced down at my watch, I realized we had been deep into the bank contract most of the day. Paxton and I agreed everything was in place to launch the takeover, so I went to the bar. Grabbing a couple of tumblers, I poured each of us two fingers of scotch and handed one to Paxton.

"So, now that we're done with that, we need to discuss Casey," Paxton said, grabbing my full attention.

"What about Casey?" I asked carefully.

"Chill out, nothing bad. Just concerning her work visa."

Instantly relieved by the subject, I nodded for him to continue. "Well, I have started the ball rolling, but first, they will want to verify her medical degrees and relevant paperwork. She will need to sit for the US medical licensing exam to start with before moving into a residency program. I've also got someone looking into getting Casey some volunteer work at one of the free medical clinics in town. It will probably help with her visa application, as well."

"Fuck me, Paxton, that's a lot," I said, sitting forward in my chair.

"I know, but I'm afraid that's what it's going to take. The US has very strict rules where foreign doctors are concerned."

"I knew it wasn't going to be easy, but you really need to be talking to Casey about all this, not me. Hell, I don't care what it takes to get her a green card as long as she gets one." Taking a moment, I ran my tongue along my bottom lip with a thought, then asked, "What if we get married?"

Paxton's head whipped up so fast I'm sure I heard a crack. "What?"

"You know, marriage. Wouldn't that help?" I said, ignoring his shocked look.

"You, married?" Paxton said, tapping both his hands against his ears. "Sorry, could you repeat that? I think my hearing just went out on me."

"Fuck you, asshat, why is that so shocking to hear?"

"Because Nathanial King and marriage are just three words I thought I would never hear in the same sentence...ever."

"Yeah, well things change, life changes. I mean, I didn't expect to meet someone like Casey," I said, glancing out the large windows, lost in thought about her and what she had brought into my life. It was true, marriage was something that had never been on my agenda. I never wanted to have the extra responsibility of having someone in my life, someone else to have to think about when making any decisions. That all changed when I met Casey. She changed everything, and I would do anything for her. If that meant getting married earlier than I had planned to make sure that nothing could take her away from me, then I would do it in a heartbeat.

Turning my gaze from the outside view back to a now shocked-looking Paxton, I said, "I don't care what it takes, Paxton, just make it happen."

"You know I will, but you are right. This conversation needs to be with Casey."

"Yeah, I'll just have to tread carefully with that one. If she thinks I only want to get married to keep her in the country, she will dig her heels in, and most likely kick me in the balls." I chuckled at the thought.

"I think we should try my way first, and I'm pretty sure you like your balls too much at this stage to lose them," Paxton laughed. "Besides, I think she would much prefer it if you proposed marriage for the right reasons, don't you?"

"Absolutely."

Once we finished our drinks and Paxton went back to his office, I picked up my phone, scrolling through the contacts until I found Alonzo Reed, the Bizarre Club owner's number, and pressed it. It rang three times, and a deeply accented voice answered. "Hello?"

"Alonzo, its Nathanial King."

"Ahh, Nate. Glad you called. We need to meet, my friend."

"Yes, I agree. I've heard you're having some problems with security?"

"Yes, too many," he sighed into the phone.

"Okay, when are you free to meet?" I asked.

"As soon as possible, if we could?"

"Well, where are you? I have some time now. I was just going to head home."

"That sounds perfect. I am at the club, come on around."

"Okay, give me about twenty," I said, ending the call. I shut down my computers for the night and headed down to the garage.

Pulling up outside the club, it looked completely different in the daylight. Quiet and empty, almost like an abandoned building. No glittering lights, half-naked bodies, or circus acts swarming around the front entrance. I walked up to the huge double glass door and knocked loudly, hoping someone was close enough to hear. Waiting a few minutes before knocking again, I saw Alonzo striding toward the door. He flipped the lock to open it.

"Nate, please come in," he said, standing to the side for me to enter before locking the doors again. "This way," he gestured before walking ahead of me, beckoning me to follow. We arrived at a back office that I knew was his, and he gestured for me to sit in one of the chairs as he sat opposite me behind his sleek, black desk. "I'm glad you could come. Can I get you something to drink?"

"No, thank you. I'm driving," I told him.

"Paxton told me you have been on an overseas trip. A holiday?" he asked with a slight grin.

"Unfortunately, no."

"No?"

"My girlfriend is from Australia, and we needed to go back and deal with some...family issues." I didn't want to go into detail with Alonzo. I liked the guy, and he checked out, but I was always of the conviction that in my line of work, one can never be too careful.

"So sorry to hear that. I hope everything is alright now?"

"Yes, everything is fine, thank you," I said, giving him a reassuring smile before quickly changing the subject. "So, tell me what's been going on around here. Paxton tells me you've been having some problems with the alarm systems that we put in place?"

Alonzo leaned back into his chair and rubbed a finger back and forth over his bottom lip in thought. "Yes, the alarms have been going off unnecessarily and at inappropriate times," he said, but it was what he wasn't saying that got my attention.

"Alonzo?" I said, drawing his attention back to me as he seemed to drift a little looking down at the top of his desk. "What is it?" I asked him, but he waved away my question.

"Nothing. I think maybe we just need a new alarm system."

"There's more to it though, isn't there? Because the words that just came out of your mouth sounded more like you were trying to convince yourself more than you were me." I gave him a questioning look. I needed to know what was going on, or what he thought was going on before I could fix anything. Sighing, he turned his computer screen around to face me and started moving the mouse around, clicking on different files before pulling up a video screen that was broken into four separate squares. This was of what looked like footage from the security cameras around the club. I looked at it, then at him.

"I think the alarms are being set off as a distraction," Alonzo said suspiciously.

"For what?"

"Watch," he said, motioning to the screen and clicking the cursor on one of the squares, making the picture bigger. He zoomed into one of the smaller bars at the back of the club. Moving closer to the screen, I watched as the barman served some drinks to a couple of young women sitting at the bar. A guy walked to the end of the bar, right in the corner, and sat on a stool. He looked around, then up toward the camera, then quickly back down again as the barman walked over to him, placing an open bottle of beer on the counter in front of him. The guy pushed what looked like a large wad of cash to the barman, who took it, pushing it into his pocket before walking away to serve someone else. Alonzo clicked pause.

"So, tell me what you saw," he said.

Taking a moment to go over the video, it didn't take a brain surgeon to work out what had just transpired. "Well, it looks like you have a crooked barman, who is either pocketing your money or running drugs," I said matter-of-factly.

"Drugs?" Alonzo looked pretty shocked at my analysis of the situation. "Pilfering money, yes. But drugs?"

"Yes, did you notice the large pile of cash he handed over for the beer? I know your club is pretty top end, Alonzo, but I don't think your beer charges are that exuberant, do you? I am pretty sure that guy," I said, pointing to the nervous looking customer, "has only a few bills in his hand, but it's what's wrapped up in the bills that's more suspicious. I think he is passing drugs to the bartender, who is most likely selling them to your patrons and making some extra cash on the side."

Alonzo leaned back into his chair and pinched the bridge of his nose between his thumb and finger, closing his eyes and shaking his head in what I was hoping was shocked disgust. He took a moment to think before he slammed his fist down on his desk. That's when I knew it had definitely hit home. "That little bastard! I'll have his balls," he seethed.

"Yes, I agree, but I think maybe we should play this one a little smarter. First, catch the bartender with the goods, then take out the supplier. Otherwise, you might get rid of him, but not the actual problem. You want to make sure none of your other staff are involved, as well, otherwise it will be an ongoing issue that you'll never get rid of."

"You're right," Alonzo said, nodding in agreement. "I don't want this garbage in my club. Once it gets in, it's like getting rid of the stench of a dead rat in the walls, and I don't want that smell in my club or on me."

"Okay, well, I know this will be hard to sit on for a couple of days, but give me time to work out a plan, and we will clean out the stench, okay?" Alonzo smiled a little and seemed to relax at my words. As I stood, he extended his hand and shook mine.

"Thank you. Please let me know when, okay?"

"I'll give you a call very soon," I reassured him.

Chapter Seventeen

Casey

Walking down the stairs, I could hear movement coming from the kitchen, and the soft, low humming of a female voice, followed by the sound of water running in the kitchen sink. Tentatively, I made my way down to the bottom stair and looked over at the kitchen...which was empty. Confused, I walked closer to the marble bench, when a head popped up from the other side, making me jump with a little squeak and a hand to my chest. We just stood for a moment, looking at each other. The elusive Mrs. Winters wasn't very tall. She had a slight frame with short, wavy, dark hair streaked with a few strands of grey. She looked to be in her late 50s with beautiful, pale skin and warm, brown eyes.

"Oh, darlin', I didn't mean to give you a fright," she exclaimed in a soft, southern drawl.

"No, it's okay. I heard noises down here, and when I came down, I didn't see you. For a minute there, I thought we might have a ghost!" I chuckled.

"Well, I've been compared to many things, but never a ghost," she said, walking around the bench and wiping her hands on a towel until she was standing in front of me. She held out her hand, which I took. "Well, I'm guessing you must be Miss. Tyler?"

"Please, call me Casey. And you must be Mrs. Winters?"

"Oh, honey, you make me feel like my mother calling me that. You just call me Carmel."

"Okay, Carmel," I said, smiling. "Its really nice to meet you. I have no idea how I've been here all this time, but never seen you!"

"Oh, I always like to sneak in at the crack of dawn, get it done quickly, and get out. I don't believe in intruding on peoples' lives."

"Oh, and the meals you leave in the freezer are amazing," I told her. I watched as she grabbed two glasses from the cupboard, took a pitcher of juice out of the refrigerator, filled the glasses, and slid one across the counter toward me.

"That's sweet of you to say, honey. I do like to cook, but Mr. King is the only one I actually do it for. He's kind of special," she said with a slight twinkle in her eye.

Taking a sip of juice from my glass, I looked at her over the rim with a raised eyebrow and a grin. "I don't have something to worry about here, do I?" I teased.

Carmel looked up at me with a shocked expression. "Oh, Lord! No, girl, I'm old enough to be his mama!" When she saw the impish look I was giving her, she laughed at my insinuation and said conspiratorily, "No harm in looking, though."

"Yeah, well, I don't blame you there. He's definitely easy on the eyes!"

"He and Jackson sure are a pretty pair of bookends," she sighed.

"You know Jackson?" I asked her.

"Sure do. He's my cousin, Lilly's, boy. He and Mr. King have been close friends from the minute they joined the Marines."

"Jax is a great guy."

"He always was a good boy. Looks after his family well. That's why when Mr. King was looking for a housekeeper, Jackson sent me to look after him, but I think he looks after me better." She smiled. "But enough talk about me, I want to know about that accent of yours! Where is it from?"

"Australia."

"What? My Lord, that's on the other side of the world, girl! What are you doing here?"

Chewing my bottom lip, thinking of where to begin my story, I looked up into her kind face, and for some reason, felt an instant sense of calm with this woman.

"I guess you could say it was a string of unfortunate circumstances," I said, grimacing.

"Well, in that case, I think I will cook us up something, and you can tell me all about it over some food. What do you think?"

"Sounds great, I'm starving."

"Good, I like a girl with an appetite. You're too skinny anyways. You sit, and I'll whip us something up," she said. Carmel pulled out bowls and pans from the cupboard, and I watched as she skillfully made us up a batch of pancakes and listened as I told her about my contract with IMA and how I came to meet Nate. I told her about the kidnapping threat and why he had brought me here, but I didn't go into everything. There were just some parts of my life that I still wasn't ready to share, especially with a woman I had just met, even if she did make me feel instantly comfortable. Helping Carmel load the dishwasher with our dirty dishes, I was caught off guard when she said, "I think we are going to have a great time at the house."

"You mean the beach house?" I asked, giving her a slightly puzzled look that she immediately noticed. Turning to me with her hands on her hips, she said, "Please tell me that boy told you."

"Told me?"

"That he wants me to spend a couple of days a week down there, as well as here."

"What? I don't understand," I said, baffled as to why Nate would think that we would need a housekeeper when there would only be the two of us living there. Seeing the look on my face, she continued.

"Oh, honey. I'm sorry, I know how it can feel having another woman in your castle, and its fine, but maybe you need to talk to Mr. King about it."

Instantly, my hand reached out to touch her arm, regretting my reaction. I didn't want her to feel rejected or awkward in any way.

"No, no it's fine. I'm just trying to work out why, that's all. It seems a little over the top to have a housekeeper there. I mean it's just a house, not like this place," I said, spreading a hand out to the penthouse.

"That's okay, sweetie, I'm in no way offended at all. I'm guessing he might have wanted you to have some help setting up a home for you both. Anyway, you talk to that man first, okay?" she said, patting my arm.

"Yes, I'll do that. Thanks."

After Carmel left, I headed up to the gym and spent some time in there, still baffled by why Nate would want a housekeeper. I mean, I knew that to him, it was probably a normal thing to have, but not to me. Even though I was pretty sure I would love Carmel's company, I was still looking forward to having alone time, something that I was very used to. Another thing that was laying heavily on my mind was Max Sullivan. I'd spoken to Flynn, who was being pretty closed-lipped and not giving any further information other than that Sullivan was still in the hospital, he would keep me updated, and that I should forget about him entirely. How the hell did he expect me to do that? Not only had he been a huge part of my life, but I was now in danger of him affecting Nate's life, as well. I knew that Flynn had said there were no witnesses that night, but what if someone came forward somewhere down the track? Would Nate be safe now that we were back in Portland? Flynn assured me there was nothing to worry about, but in my experience, your past always comes back to haunt you, and the last thing that I wanted was for MY past to come back and haunt Nate.

I was standing at the stove, pushing stir-fry around in the sizzling pan when I heard the ding of the lift and the doors sliding open. Looking up, I watched as Nate came in, dropped his phone and keys on the coffee table, and then came around to where I was standing. Inhaling the aroma, he said, "Smells good, I am starving," before dropping a kiss on the back of my neck. "I'll just take a quick shower."

I was momentarily distracted from serving dinner by Nate's bare chest and low slung sleep pants when he appeared downstairs soon after. It didn't matter how many times I saw his perfect body covered in that amazingly intricate ink or that sexy V that disappeared below the top of his pants, it still sent a shiver of desire up my spine, and the way he was looking at me, he knew it.

"You look a bit flustered there," he said with a knowing smile.

Bringing myself to finish the task at hand without spilling vegetables and meat all over the kitchen island, then dumping the pan in the sink, I chose to ignore his comment. After all, I had just been caught eye fucking him. Over dinner, Nate filled me in on his day, including his conversation with Paxton over my visa and residency in the US.

"But I told him it was something he needed to discuss with you," Nate said.

"Sounds good. I'll go through my paperwork and get together what he needs so we can get things moving."

"You know there's no hurry, right?"

"Nate," I warned, knowing where this conversation was heading.

"I'm just saying, don't feel pressured into anything. I just want you to take your time in deciding what you want to do."

Looking at him curiously, I asked, "What do you mean, deciding what I want to do? I already have a career, Nate."

I watched as he put another forkful of food into his mouth, contemplating my words. "You're right I apologize," he said. "I just didn't want you to feel obligated to moving faster than you wanted. That's all."

"Speaking of which," I said, brow raised, "I met Mrs. Winters this morning."

"Good! I'm glad you two finally got to meet. She's great, isn't she?"

"Yes, she's lovely. She also told me that you want her to work at the beach house?" I asked.

"Yeah, well, I thought she would be able to help you out and keep you company," he said, placing his fork down on his now empty plate. Sighing, I picked up my half-eaten dinner plate along with his. I walked into the kitchen, placing them in the sink with enough of a crash to get his attention.

"What?" he asked, coming to stand in front of me when I turned to face him.

"A babysitter, Nate. You want Mrs. Winters to babysit me," I said, feeling my anger starting to bubble and grow with the way he almost scoffed at the idea.

"She's not a babysitter."

"Yes, Nate, she is. The house isn't big enough to need a housekeeper," I said, looking deep into his eyes, wanting him to feel the burn of my irritation.

"Baby," he said, his voice low and placating as he placed his hands on my hips and pulled me closer to him. "I'd feel better knowing you had someone there with you when I'm here working." He nuzzled into my neck.

"I don't need protecting 24 hours a day, Nate. You need to get that into your head."

Letting out a deep, hot breath against my skin, he said, "I will never stop protecting you. Ever. But you're right."

Pulling back from him slightly so that he was looking at me, I softened when I saw the pained look on his face. "There's a difference between being protective and being obsessively overbearing and suffocating. I understand that's your job. Our shaky start to this relationship probably gave you cause to feel like this, but there needs to be some boundaries, Nate."

"I know. All I can do is try, okay?"

Leaning into me with his hands on either side of the marble bench top, he imprisoned me between his body and the sink. He bowed his head slightly until his eyes were level with mine, and what I saw swimming in them was not resistance to my words. Those gray eyes swirled with a darkness of lust and heat, flickering between my eyes, then darting to my mouth. With just that look of hunger, I felt my anger slowly ebbing away as my breathing grew heavier with the warmth of his closeness. I watched his beautiful mouth as he spoke in a low gravelly tone. "There are a lot of things that I love about you, but right now, it's your need to psychoanalyze me and that hot temper of yours."

"Nate?" I whispered huskily.

"Hmm?" he breathed into my neck.

"Stop," I said without an ounce of conviction in my voice.

"No," he said as he started to kiss along my collarbone and slowly up the side of my neck, where he gently bit then licked the spot before moving his mouth over my lips. With our breathing starting to accelerate with the rising heat between us, I felt his warm breath tickle over my mouth as his eyes bored into mine. Pools of liquid gray, full of a hunger that I could only compare to my own, I felt his hand slide down to the waistband of my shorts, yank open the button, then slide down the zipper. His hand slid down into my panties, where his fingers started to gently caress my wet folds. A low moan somewhere deep in my throat escaped my parted lips.

"Looks like I'm not the only one who gets turned on by a disagreement," he said against my mouth.

His hand cupped my mound, and he slipped a finger deep inside of my wetness, making me gasp in pleasure at the invasion. Taking my gasp into his mouth when his lips crashed down onto mine, he tasted of spices from our meal as his tongue swept inside and over my own. As he pushed his body into mine, I could feel how hard he was through his sleep pants. With the kiss becoming frantic and in a bid to get closer to each other, I was stunned when he suddenly pulled back and knelt down in front of me, pulling my shorts and panties down and off in one swoop. He was at eye level with the swollen apex in between my thighs. Just watching his greedy look made me squeeze my thighs together tighter in an effort to relieve the pressure.

Running his palms up the back of my legs, he lifted one of them, placing it over his shoulder. He then ran his hand up my stomach, under my shirt to the middle of my breasts where he gently pressed to encourage me to lean back against the bench. The next thing I felt was his mouth on my sex, sucking and licking with a ravenous hunger. With my head thrown back in pleasure, I dug my hands into his luscious, thick, black hair in an effort to hold him exactly where I needed him to be while I rode through the intensity of my orgasm which hit me with wave after wave of intimate pleasure.

Without giving me time to recover, Nate removed my leg from his shoulder and stood, wiping the evidence of my orgasm off his lips with the back of his hand. Then he lifted me onto the bench, pushing his pants down where they pooled on the floor at his feet. I looked down to find him fisting his huge erection before pushing my legs apart and rubbing the head over my still wet lips. With one thrust, he buried himself deep inside of me, and I instinctively wrapped my legs around his waist as his hands came around my lower back where he had control of the depth and our movement. The kitchen filled with noises of passion and heat as he fucked me so hard I thought something might break. He rained open-mouthed kisses against my throat and mouth with whispered curses and moans that ended in a spiral of out of control movements and thrashing that left me gasping out his name when I came once again, this time with the feeling of his liquid heat filling me with his own ferocious climax.

Panting, I let my legs slide down as I leaned my head on his shoulder, trying to catch my breath. I could feel his body still shuddering with the aftershocks for several moments after as we gently kissed. He slipped from my body, helping me down off the kitchen bench. Still breathing hard, he said, "Fuck, woman, you are going to be the death of me," making me giggle.

"Me? I think you might have created a monster."

"I didn't have to create anything, baby. It's all you."

Chapter eighteen

Nate

The next few days were beyond busy. More like hectic as hell, with the furniture getting delivered out to the beach house, the contract for West Bank getting closer to being launched, and researching Alonzo's employees. I facilitated a compromise with Casey regarding Mrs. Winters spending some time helping her to get the house organized. That turned out to be harder than negotiating a million dollar contract. Damn, that woman could be so stubborn and combative at times. Casey eventually agreed to have Mrs. Winters at the house a couple of days a week at first, then once a week. She argued that looking after the penthouse was a big enough job on its own for Mrs. Winters without considering the new house, as well.

The thing I really loved though, was the look on Casey's face every time we drove up the driveway of that house. Her smile was so big, it seemed to spread from ear to ear. I realized that buying the house was one of the best decisions I had ever made. Well, besides taking on a feisty, stubborn, strong Aussie woman as my live-in girlfriend. Now, that was the absolutely best decision I had ever made in my entire life. Now I just wanted to see her happy in a home that was her own, where she felt comfortable and like she belonged.

Looking down at my watch, I noticed that it was just after 11 a.m. when there was a knock on my office door. "Come in," I answered. Leaning back into my chair, I watched as the door slowly opened, and in walked the beautiful woman I had just been thinking about. She was wearing a light blue sundress that came to just above her knees, showing off those long, tanned legs. Her almost white, blonde hair was twisted into a braid that hung down over one tanned shoulder. Pure perfection.

"Hi, what do I owe the pleasure?" I asked, smiling at her.

Giving me a knowing look, she said, "Keep your mind out of the gutter, Mr. King. I just came down to see Paxton. I brought all the paperwork he needs from me."

"When you visit me in my office, baby, nothing but filth runs through my mind."

"Really? What kind?" she asked, sitting in one of the leather chairs opposite my desk. I watched as she slowly crossed her legs. Leaning forward and placing my elbows on the desk in front of me, I sighed.

"Hmm, let's see...you sitting right here," I said, patting the top of my desk. "Spread out in front of me, naked under that dress, a feast fit for a King." I grinned as her cheeks flushed slightly. "Or you on your knees around this side of the desk," I continued, liking the fact that my words seemed to make her squirm a little in her chair.

"I'll keep that in mind for future reference," she said, grinning at me.

"You do that," I said, leaning back in my chair again.

"I see you have a new secretary," she said, motioning toward the door.

"Yes, Laura. She started yesterday."

"How is she?"

"She's nice enough. Too early to tell at this point," I said, shrugging.

"She's very pretty," she said, and I noticed a slight hitch in her voice. Getting up, I walked around to the front of my desk, leaning against it and crossing my arms.

"Casey, although my ego is slightly pleased with your small show of jealousy, I can assure you there is no other woman that compares to you." She looked up at me, slightly embarrassed.

"Stupid, huh?"

"No, baby. At least you're calm about it. If the situation was reversed and that was a male out there, I'm pretty sure I would be grabbing him by the throat and escorting him off the premises by now." I chuckled, but was relieved when she let out a relaxed laugh.

"So, did you get everything sorted out with Paxton? Give the little paper muncher all the documentation he needed?"

"Yeah, he's happy. Now he can get started on keeping me in the country legally," she said, smiling.

"That's great, the quicker the better."

"Although he did bring up something that we probably need to talk about," she said hesitantly, which sparked my attention.

"Go on," I encouraged.

"Well, he suggested doing some volunteer work at a free community clinic. Paxton thinks it will help in two ways: both with my green card and to stop me from getting bored."

"I agree," I said, rubbing my fingers over the stubble on my chin. I didn't want her to get any kind of reaction from me. If she knew what was really going through my mind right now, like I was going to choke the living shit out of my brother when I saw him, it would most likely cause an argument.

"You agree?" she asked, slight shock in her voice.

"Play it safe here, tread carefully. Remember to reign in the overprotective Nate and search for that smooth, calm one instead," I thought to myself.

"Honestly?" I asked with a raised eyebrow.

"Yes, Nate, honestly."

Blowing out a long-held breath, I said "I don't like the thought of you working in one of those community clinics. They attract trouble, and I'm not comfortable with it at all." Seeing that she was going to protest, I raised my hands to stop her before she could and continued. "That being said, I trust you to make the right decision for you, and if it's something that you want to do, then I want you to do it. Just please, give me the satisfaction of knowing that Nick will drop you off and be there to pick you up, okay?"

Casey stood up from the chair, walked to stand in front of me, and wound her hands around the back of my neck. Stretching up, she placed a light kiss on my jaw. "Thank you. I thought that was going to be a lot harder than it was."

Reaching my hands around to grab her ass, I said "Oh, believe me, in my head, it was."

Placing a quick kiss on her lips, I smacked her on the ass. "So, if you're finished with Paxton, do you want to head out to the beach house and arrange some furniture?"

"I would love to. That is, if you're finished here? If not, I can wait in the penthouse until you're done."

"No, I'm good. Let's get out of here," I said, switching off my computer and grabbing my phone and keys. Taking her hand, I almost pulled her out and into the elevator.

"Nate, it gets prettier every time we come here," she said with awe as the house slowly came into view. Switching the engine off, I turned my gaze to her and watched as she looked out at the front door as though she was mesmerized by it, just like I was mesmerized by her.

"Yes, it does," I said.

Breaking the moment, she turned to see me looking intently at her and not the house. Her look softened with realization. She reached her hand over to brush along the side of my face and whispered, "Have I ever told you how much I love you?"

"You have, but you can tell me again anytime," I said. She just gave me a huge smile, jumped out of the SUV, and ran up to the front door with the keys. The door swung open, and she dashed inside while I opened the trunk and grabbed the bags of groceries we purchased on the way before I followed her.

As I dumped the bags on the wooden counter in the kitchen, I could hear as she moved from room to room, mumbling under her breath. I noticed the furniture, wrapped in thick plastic, had been distributed into the rooms by the delivery guys as we instructed. Casey ran past me into the kitchen, pulling open a drawer and coming back with what looked like an old, rusty carving knife. "What the fuck?" I exclaimed as she passed me again, heading for the living room.

"I saw it there the other day," she said over her shoulder as she started cutting into the plastic on one of the couches.

"Damn, woman, be careful with that thing."

"Trust me, I'm a surgeon," she laughed before going back to mercilessly ripping off the plastic until she uncovered the black leather couch. As she flopped onto it, the joy that was written all over her face was intoxicating. Walking over to the tri-fold windows, I unlocked them, slid them open, and I was instantly hit by the force of the ocean breeze that filled the house. Over the next few hours, we got lost in the layers of plastic wrap that seemed to cover everything. Once everything was in place, Casey started filling the kitchen cupboards, opening boxes and pulling out an assortment of glasses, plates, you name it. It seemed to be all in that box. Who would have ever thought that it would be so easy to set up a home with just a few clicks of a mouse on a computer? A perfect solution for someone who hates shopping. I busied myself with setting up the "man" portion of the house; the important things like the sound system, TV, and surround sound. I was concentrating deeply on it until Casey dragged me away to assemble the king-sized bed in the bedroom.

Later that night, exhausted but content, we sat out on the back deck stairs with a beer and listened to the roll of the ocean. We finally climbed into that damn bed that took me hours to put together and fell asleep quickly and easily into its inviting comfort.

Chapter Nineteen

Casey

After having one of the best night's sleep I think I had ever had, it was topped off by waking up to the sounds and smell of the ocean and a warm, hard body wrapped around me. After some encouragement, and Nate finally realizing that Paxton would be coming to pick him up in the next few minutes, he was up, showered, dressed, and kissing me goodbye at the front door as he left for work. It was so surreal, I felt like I was in some kind of happily-ever-after movie. I had the whole house to myself. I couldn't remember feeling this much excitement for such a long time. I mean, who the hell gets excited about making the bed and tidying the kitchen from breakfast? Me, that's who, finally feeling part of a normal life.

I spent most of the day exploring. Not just the house in detail, but the surrounding beach. The back of the house hid a small cove that wound around us, giving us almost total privacy, and the view was just breathtaking. After taking a walk along the beach, I stood at the top of the stairs on the back deck, breathing in the therapeutic air that seemed to settle on every inch of my skin, causing a relaxing warmth and calmness to flood through my body. I realized that, at last, I felt like I was home.

By mid-afternoon, I started to prepare dinner. Nate had sent me a text earlier letting me know he would be home around six. He had gotten a lift that morning with Paxton, leaving the SUV, and was driving the Audi home tonight. He believed that it was good to have a car parked in the driveway as much as possible, letting people know that someone was living in the house. I was just putting some chicken in the fridge to marinate when my phone started to ring with Flynn's familiar ringtone. I picked it up and pressed the green "Accept" button with an excited, "Flynn?!"

"Hey, sweets, how are you?" he asked, sounding very awake.

"Is everything okay? It's pretty late there," I asked, a little worried.

"Everything's great. I had a late night, and I thought I would give you a buzz before heading to bed."

"Oh, okay. You had me worried there for a minute," I said, relieved.

"So, have you moved in yet?"

"Yes, and Flynn, it is so friggin' awesome!" I gushed excitedly.

"Good, I'm glad! Listen, I wanted to give you a heads up on our little problem," he said seriously.

"Okay..." I dragged out the word cautiously.

"Don't worry, everything is fine."

"And...?"

"Well, unfortunately, the bastard is recovering slowly. Nate did quite a job on him, and fortunately, he can't remember a thing. Now, I'm not sure if he can and he's just not talking or maybe it's an aftereffect from all the drugs I shoved down his throat." He laughed. "Sorry, that was just wishful thinking. Anyway, it doesn't matter. He broke his parole, so as soon as he's cleared by the hospital, he is heading straight back to his cozy jail cell with a lot of extra time."

"How much?"

"Not sure yet, but I'm sure I can tweak things just a little in that department," he said mischievously.

"You need to be careful, Flynn," I warned him.

"Always, sweets. You know me."

"Yeah, sometimes too well," I said, laughing.

"So, the house is good?" he asked, drastically changing the subject.

"Yes, it is. Beyond good. More than I could ever dream of."

"And you have a spare room for me, right?"

"Of course! That was my top priority."

"Good, that's the way it should be," he chuckled.

We talked for about another ten minutes, and when I finished the call I felt better with the knowledge that Max was alive and didn't remember anything. Even though I had always wished him dead, just knowing that Nate's actions would not lead to consequences coming back and biting us on the arse in the future was a relief. Even if the bastard was still alive, I felt safer knowing that he was a long way from me now.

Just after six, I saw the lights of the Audi coming up the driveway. I quickly wiped my hand on a towel, dropped it on the kitchen bench, and made my way to the front door. With anticipation, I listened as the roar of the engine came to a stop, the door opened and closed, his heavy footsteps crunching along the gravel path, then up the front stairs, the sound of his key as he slipped it into the lock and turned the handle. He was looking down at some papers in his hand as he walked in, not noticing me standing there. I took in his large frame dressed in his normal office attire of jeans and a white button-down shirt that clung to every hard muscle in his chest, the sleeves rolled up to his elbows showing the colorful art along his arms. He was so magnificent to look at. Dropping his phone and keys in the small glass bowl on the table at the entry, he finally looked up to see me standing and watching him like a pervert.

I slowly walked toward him and wrapped my arms around his neck, feeling the soft hair at his collar. He ran his hands down to my ass and pulled me up, so I could wrap my legs around his waist, before kissing him so deeply I lost my own breath in the process.

With me still wrapped around him, he carried me with ease into the living room, sitting down on the couch with me now straddling him.

"Hi," he said, voice husky from our kiss.

"Well, hello," I whispered against his throat, snuggling into his warmth.

"Are you alright?" he asked slowly.

"Hmm, more than alright," I breathed against his skin. "How was your day?"

"Productive, and yours?"

"Mine was...perfect," I said, giving him another kiss.

"I take it you like it here," he chuckled.

"I love it. Almost as much as I love you," I teased.

"Well if you keep rubbing your ass against me like that, I will be taking you to bed to show you just how much I love you."

"Dinner is almost ready, so you might have to save that thought for later," I said, giving him a wink and climbing off his lap.

"Tease."

"Yep, so go take a shower, and I'll get dinner on the table."

Seeing the slight look of disappointment on his face, I hurried into the kitchen before I changed my own mind and left dinner until later. He walked out of the bathroom several minutes later, dressed in his sleep pants, his hair still wet, and sat at the table where dinner was waiting for him.

"This looks good. Don't tell me my tough Aussie is getting domesticated," he teased.

"Is that bad?" I cringed.

"Nope. If I had my way, I would have you barefoot and pregnant and chained to my bed at night..." His words tapered off as he realized what he had said, reaching his hand across the table and placing it on top of mine. "Shit. Sorry, babe, I didn't mean..."

"It's fine," I said, waving away his concern, hating the look of regret in his eyes. I looked down at the food on my plate and picked up my fork.

"Eat, it will get cold," I said, giving him a quick smile, motioning to his food. We ate in silence for the first few minutes until I decided to change the subject. "I got a call from Flynn today."

Looking at me with a raised brow, he said, "And?"

"He just wanted to let me know that the asshole was slowly recovering, and once he's medically cleared, he'll be heading back to prison."

"Pity," Nate said under his breath.

"Hey, no one wants him gone for good more than I do, but I'm just glad nothing is going to come back onto you."

Nate looked back down at his plate before continuing to eat. I could tell he wanted to say more by the twitch thumping furiously at his jawline. I knew this whole thing made him crazy, so I changed the subject. "Is Paxton picking you up again in the morning?"

"No, I'll take the Audi, it's faster," he said with a slight lift to the corner of his mouth. "What about you? Mrs. Winters is coming over in the morning, right?"

"Yep, I think she said something about taking me to some local markets, which will be interesting." After rinsing the dishes and placing them into the dishwasher, Nate grabbed us both a beer from the refrigerator, flipping the cap before handing me one, then opening his own while we got comfortable on the couch. Nate flipped through the channels, looking for something to watch. I placed my beer on the coffee table and stretched out, laying my head in his lap. Once he had settled on the local news channel, he stroked his hand gently through my hair.

"I might be a little late tomorrow, but I will text you and let you know," he said.

"Something big?" I queried.

"Just going over to the Bizarre. Alonzo needs some help with his security, so I'll need to head over there when it opens at 7."

"Sounds like it will be a late night, then?"

"Yeah, maybe you should come with me and wait at the penthouse until I'm done."

"I'm sure I'll be perfectly fine here. That is, unless you think you'll be too tired to drive back and you want to stay at the penthouse?"

"No, it shouldn't take long."

"Is it the alarm system again?" I asked, looking up at him.

"Yeah," he said, draining the last of his beer from the bottle. When we finally went to bed, Nate kept his earlier promise of loving me. He did so thoroughly, in fact, that I dropped into a deep sleep before he had even gotten back from the bathroom with a warm cloth for me. The next thing I remembered was waking to him giving me a soft kiss before saying goodbye and leaving while I stretched out in the huge bed and languished in the musky scent he left behind on the sheets for a while. Eventually, I pulled myself up and into the shower before Carmel arrived.

I had just poured myself a hot cup of tea when there was a knock at the door. As soon as I opened it, I was greeted with her warm smile.

"Morning, sugar," she said in her wonderful southern drawl as she walked in and set her bag down on the entrance table.

"Good morning to you. Come into the kitchen. Would you like some tea?" I asked, holding up my mug.

"I'm afraid I'm a black coffee girl," she said.

"Not a problem, it's over there. Nate put it on this morning," I said, grabbing the glass jug from the machine, filling a mug with the black brew, and handing it to her. Cradling the mug in her fingers, she inhaled the steam before taking a sip.

"Mm, just how I like it, nice and strong." We both moved over to the small kitchen table and sat. Carmel looked around and out of the windows beside her. "What a beautiful view," she said, her eyes wide in awe as she looked out at the ocean.

"Yes, it is. Come on, I'll give you a tour," I said, setting my mug down on the table. I stood and reached for her hand. Carmel took it and hung on whilst I almost dragged her around, showing her every room with an abundance of enthusiastic babble. I explained what was going into each specific space. By the time I had finished, I felt breathless with excitement.

"Well, I can see you're in love with this place already," Carmel said as she smiled at me.

"I am. I can't explain it, but from the first time I stepped in here, I felt like I belonged. Like this house needed me as much as I needed it." Looking at her face, I scoffed at my words. "Sounds silly, doesn't it?"

Carmel reached out her hand, resting it on my arm soothingly. "No child, I believe that a house is just as alive as any person, and just like we all have a soul mate out there waiting for us, a house has its owner in just the same way. Some things are just meant to be."

"And what about you? Did you find your soul mate? Your home?" I asked curiously. I didn't know much about this woman, yet I felt like I had known her for a long time. Letting her hand slip from my arm, she walked over to the window and stared out. I saw the emotions swimming in her eyes as she became locked in a memory.

"I did. Charlie and I were high school sweethearts. Did the whole thing: dating, marriage, a beautiful home. We had forty unforgettable years together before cancer took him from me," she said, looking down for a moment.

"I'm so sorry," I whispered, feeling bad that I had brought up a subject that obviously caused her pain. But then she turned to look at me.

"No need to be sorry. I wouldn't have swapped those years for anything. The only thing that I regret is not being able to give my Charlie any babies. Not from lack of trying, of course, but it just didn't happen."

"Carmel..." She turned fully to face me, stopping my words.

"Like I said, best years of my life. Now, let's put these memories away. I have plans for the day," she said, her face filling with excitement.

"You do?"

"Well, I figured you probably wouldn't have much for me to do around here, so we are taking a trip to Manzanita."

"Where?"

"It's a little place about ten miles up the oceanfront, but they have a little street market there today, and I thought we might find some little treasures to fill this place with."

Even though I hated shopping, I actually found myself shivering a little in anticipation, not just for finding some treasure, but also to spend more time with this wonderful woman.

"Okay, let's do it," I said, picking up my purse and dropping my phone into it.

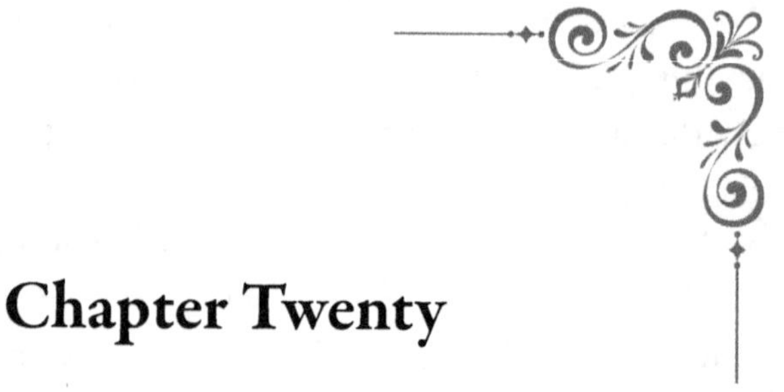

Chapter Twenty

N^{ate}

"I'm not sure about this, Nate. You know there's more to that club than meets the eye, right?" Paxton said, giving me that certain look he has when he wants to say more but is deciding not to. "I think you should leave it up to the police," he said as he worriedly paced my office.

"You worry too much, Paxton. It's not a big deal, and the cops will be involved. Alonzo just wants some help grabbing not just the barman, but his supplier, as well, and he wants to do it without any disruption to the club," I told him with as much reassurance as I could. I knew what Paxton was like whenever I got personally involved with any kind of security operation. If there was one thing that I always appreciated about my little brother, it was his dedication to having my back at all times, even though sometimes I had to do a little sugar coating.

Paxton was always the one who loved to sit behind the protection of a desk in a building and wreak havoc through legal channels, and I've always been the complete opposite. I liked being hands on. I liked the dirty work. I always liked the excitement, the thrill of a challenge. That's what made us a great team and why we always got things done.

"It'll be fine, I promise. Just sit, will you? You're going to walk a permanent path in my floor." I grinned at him, causing him to let out a sigh and drop into a chair opposite my desk.

"Fine, but I just don't understand why you can never do things the easy way."

"Because life would be boring then, and I'm an asshole." Paxton visibly relaxed, laughed, and nodded in agreement.

"You got that right."

I arrived at The Bizarre just before 7 that evening. The large, bald security guard standing at the front door gave me a nod and opened the door, letting me into the club where I made my way through to Alonzo's office at the back. A last minute decision to stop off at Stella's restaurant to grab a quick bite before coming here was a good one. I knocked on Alonzo's heavy, wood door and entered when I heard him say, "Come in."

As soon as I walked in, he rose from the chair behind his desk, coming around to grasp my hand in his.

"Hey, great to see you again. Please, take a seat," Alonzo said, gesturing toward a chair in front of his desk. I watched as he strolled toward the small bar in the corner, pulled out two crystal tumblers, and poured us both a drink. He handed me one of the glasses as he took his own and sat in the chair next to me. Bringing the tumbler to my mouth, I inhaled the woodsy smell of the aged whiskey before taking a drink and letting the amber liquid warm my stomach and relax me from the inside out.

"It won't take long for the club to fill tonight. There's already a long line outside," Alonzo said, pointing to one of the screens attached to the wall in his office. I looked up to see the large crowd of people starting to gather at the front door, waiting to gain access via the same security guard who let me in just moments before.

"Yes, I saw a line out there as I came in. Looks like business is doing well?"

"Yes, very well. We are full every night, and on Friday and Saturday, we always have to turn people away."

"That's good. We all want our businesses to be successful," I said, raising my glass to him.

"Yes, but we also want our business to have a good, clean reputation. That is very important for me," Alonzo said.

"I agree, and that's why we are going to do some cleaning tonight," I said, grinning.

We both sat and watched the several screens that were attached to the wall, showing all the major areas in the club. We kept the middle screen focused on the bar where we had previously identified the suspicious deal, and flipped the others between other areas of the club. The plan was to catch a deal taking place on camera between the barman in question and his accomplice. I would then take one of the bouncers down to the bar, have him cover the door, and grab the supplier as he tried to leave. In theory, we would catch them both in action, then take them into Alonzo's office for some questioning before calling in the cops.

As the night progressed, I was starting to get annoyed that nothing had happened, I had hoped this was going to be quick so I could get home. I hated leaving Casey out at the beach house on her own for such a long time. I was starting to think it might have been a better idea to have brought her to stay at the penthouse for the night, but it was too late now. I would just have to ride this thing out and hope this didn't turn out to be a big waste of time. I was just starting to lose patience when I noticed the same guy from the other night slowly move up to the bar and pull himself up onto a stool. Standing, I pointed to the screen.

"Okay, that's him right there," I said, heading for the door, leaving Alonzo to make sure they get the video evidence we needed. I lifted my chin to the bouncer waiting outside Alonzo's office door, signaling for him to follow. Once at the bar, the bouncer made his way to the closest and only exit while I made my way to the end and sat on a stool. I was a few seats down from the dealer; not too far away, but not close enough to make him suspicious either. I watched as the barman served drinks to other patrons standing at the bar before serving his buddy a beer. I closely watched the interaction between the two men through their eye contact. It was like they were having a conversation without words, which confirmed my suspicion that these two had been working as a team for a long time. The supplier was on his third beer when he signaled to the barman to settle up. I watched as his hand, covering a large wad of cash, moved toward the barman, who, in turn, took it, stuffed it into his pocket, and then passed something back. Looking over at the bouncer standing at the exit, I gave him a nod and then slid off the stool, making my way behind the bar. My eyes darted between the three men in motion, and I saw the supplier look at me nervously before moving away from the bar. The barman looked up at me.

"Hey man, only staff are allowed back here," was all he managed to get out before I stood directly in front of him and said, "I guess it's good that I'm staff then, isn't it?" before grabbing his arm. With a quick twist and bend, I pulled his arm behind his back in a stronghold.

"Fuck, man, what are you doing?" the barman yelled out over the thumping music.

"Putting an end to your drug career," I growled as I pushed him from behind the bar and down the hall to Alonzo's office. The door was already open, and I pushed him inside and then, with my other hand on his shoulder, I pushed him down. This forced him to sit in the chair directly across from where Alonzo sat, elbows leaning on his desk with his fingers laced together in front of him, his eyes now focused on his barman in front of him, who now nervously looked around the room while rubbing his shoulder.

"What the hell is going on?" he asked, his voice sounding jittery.

Alonzo just stared at him for a few minutes, making him squirm uncomfortably in his chair. Then he looked down at a piece of paper in front of him before looking back up. "Travis, isn't it?" he asked.

"Yes."

"And how long have you worked for me, Travis?"

"Since you opened," Travis answered with slight hesitancy.

"And how long have you been dealing drugs in my club?" Alonzo roared out, smashing both his palms on his desk and standing. Travis slunk back into his chair, trying to get as far away as possible.

"I don't know what you're talking about," Travis answered in a low voice.

"Don't lie to me. I have been watching you for some time now, and it's all on camera," Alonso said, pointing up at the screens on the wall.

Travis looked up and saw the paused picture on the middle screen that showed a close up of his hand passing the buyer a small white package, then breathed out a defeated sounding breath.

"It's not a big deal, and it's good for your club. The customers get high, they enjoy the night, and drink more, so it's a win-win situation," Travis said nonchalantly.

"A win-win situation?" Alonzo seethed out between gritted teeth. "I thought your little friend was your supplier, but now I see it is you that is the supplier. In my club, do you know what would happen if we were caught with drugs on the premises? My business, my reputation, everything would be gone in the blink of an eye, and you sit there telling me that you are providing my club with a good service?"

Travis just shrugged in response, which only ignited Alonzo's fury more. "People like you make me sick. You get paid well, you get great tips and bonuses, but it's still not enough, and your only response is to shrug." Alonzo shook his head in disgust then looked straight at me, his eyes almost burning red. "Please, get him out of my face before I do something that I will regret. The police are outside waiting for him."

"Sure thing," I said. Slapping a hand to the collar of his shirt and pulling Travis up to a standing position, I pushed him toward the door.

"By the way, Travis, you're fired!" Alonzo spat out.

Once outside the office, I noticed the bouncer walking toward me, alone. "I'm sorry, Mr. King. The little prick was fast. I lost him."

Letting out a curse and shaking my head in frustration, I just looked at him, completely baffled at how a guy this big, standing at the only exit from the bar, could let someone get past him so easily. "Then you had better go tell your boss that yourself, but I'm warning you, he's not in the best of moods right now."

Letting out a sigh, with shoulders slumped, the burly bouncer knocked on Alonzo's door and entered.

Pushing Travis in the back to make him move in the direction of the front door to the awaiting police car, he stumbled, but straightened himself before walking. "I just don't understand what the big deal is, man," Travis said, looking over his shoulder to talk to me as we continued to walk.

"That's your problem. Save it for the cops," I growled.

"Come on, give me a break," he almost whined.

"Shut the fuck up and move," I said, giving him another shove toward the door, his bargaining technique of whining starting to grate on my nerves. Moving through the crowd of people, I stuck close to the little prick. I had no intention of letting him slip into the crowd. Almost at the glass front door, I could see two police officers, and I gave Travis one last push to the middle of his back into the bouncer, who wrapped a huge looking hand around Travis's neck before opening the door to escort him out. It was then I noticed the look on the bouncer's face. His eyes were locked on something behind me, wide and glaring. I saw his hand come up in a stop motion, and then I felt a hard whack at the back of my skull, followed by the sound of splintering glass. A sharp pain speared through the back of my head causing me to see tiny stars floating in front of my eyes, and then...blackness.

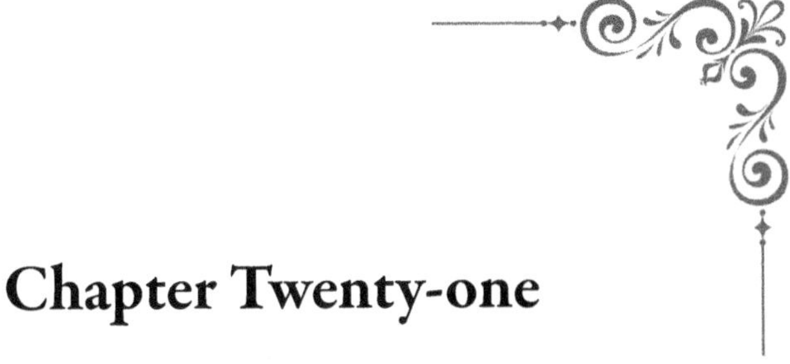

Chapter Twenty-one

Casey

I never thought I would use the words "shopping" and "great day" in the same sentence, but that's exactly what today was. After spending time at the street markets with Carmel, there was no other way to explain it. We went from trawling through colorful pillows and throw rugs, to picking through boxes of fruit, squeezing, smelling, and purchasing enough fruit to live on for a month. Carmel showed me her secret to picking the freshest fruit available and how to get a great bargain on anything. I don't think I have ever laughed so much, listening to her barter a good price on what I considered already cheap fruit. She joked and chatted with the vendors, and after seeing her in action, I was pretty sure she could charm the pants of a car salesman.

We found a small café on the beachfront where we stopped, ordered some lunch, and continued to chat and laugh about all the bargains we had accumulated. After lunch, we drove back to Jacaranda House, where she helped me carry all of my purchases from the boot of her car to stack them in the middle of the living room. "Thank you so much, Carmel. I had such a great day," I said as we walked back out to her car.

"No, thank you, sweetie. I had a ball, although I didn't really earn my wages today," she said, stepping in and giving me a hug.

"Oh, believe me, you certainly did," I said, smiling at her.

"Well, I will make sure I plan something fun for next week then, as well," she said as she slid into her car and closed the door. With a wave, I watched as she drove down the driveway and out of sight. I went inside to have a good look through my shopping bags with excitement.

After distributing pillows, throw rugs and various little pieces of colorful pottery that I had picked up at the market, it was starting to get dark outside. I locked all the doors, as instructed by Nate, then made myself a quick sandwich and a hot cup of tea, and settled down on the couch with the remote, intent on doing some channel surfing until Nate got back.

Waking with a startled jump at the sound of a huge explosion, I quickly sat up and squinted my eyes at the large TV screen. It was full of bright orange flames and exploding cars from the action movie that must have followed the romance movie I was watching when I fell asleep. Grabbing the remote, I flicked off the TV and was instantly thrown in to the silence of nothing but the crash of the waves outside. Rubbing my eyes, trying to wake myself up, I jumped again when I heard my phone ringing in the kitchen. Hopping up, I headed over to it and just caught it as it almost vibrated off the kitchen island. Looking down, I saw Paxton's name flashing across the screen.

"Paxton?" I answered sleepily.

"Casey." The urgency in his voice instantly snapped me to attention.

"Paxton, what's wrong?"

"It's Nate, we're at the hospital," was all I heard before the phone line crackled and cut off. Frantically, I dialed his number and got nothing. I cursed and dialed Nate's phone, which went straight to voicemail. Pacing back and forth in the kitchen, I kept dialing between Paxton and Nate's phone, and still nothing. Frustrated, I threw my phone toward the couch, where it bounced off onto the floor.

What the fuck was happening? My mind was chaotic with potential scenarios, and all that was going through my head was Paxton's words, "It's Nate, we're at the hospital." Nate was hurt, and they were at the hospital. "Shit, shit, shit," I said out loud. I ran into the bedroom, pulled on a pair of jeans, grabbed a jacket from the closet, and slipped on a pair of sneakers. I ran back out to the living room, picking up my purse and retrieving my phone from the floor.

At the front door, I searched the keys in the glass bowl, pulling out the ones for the SUV. I ran out, slamming the door behind me. Pressing the fob for the lock, with the blink of the lights, I yanked open the door and slid into the driver's seat. My anxiety started to heighten as I pushed the key into the ignition and fastened my seat belt. With both hands gripping the steering wheel, I let out a deep breath whilst dropping my forehead down to lean against my now white knuckles.

"You can do this, get a grip. Nate is hurt," I said to myself. I was trying to muster up enough courage to drive this fucking monster truck on the opposite side of the bloody road. Just the thought made my stomach start to churn and the beginnings of nausea started to form with the anxiety. My mind kept replaying Paxton's words. *It's Nate, we're at the hospital.* That was enough to make me force the rising bile back down, take a deep breath, then slowly let it out. I turned the key, bringing the motor to life and shifted into gear before punching "Portland hospital" into the GPS and driving down the driveway.

After a couple of miles out on the open road, I felt myself starting to relax. As long as I didn't hug the curb too tightly whilst trying to stay as far to the right-hand side of the road as possible, I would be okay. I told myself, logically, that I had been driving for years and that I could do this to take my mind off going through all the different scenarios as to why Nate was at the hospital. What the hell happened? Was he hurt? Just the thought of him being hurt in any way caused the nausea to start forming again in my stomach. Pulling myself back into reality, I concentrated on the road in front of me, the white lines, the lights, and the cheery voice of the woman giving me directions from the GPS - anything but Nate right now.

By the time I saw the sign for the hospital, I felt beads of sweat gathering along my forehead. I pulled into the first parking spot I saw, flinging the door open, grabbing my purse, and dropping down from the SUV. Clicking the lock button on the fob over my shoulder, I almost ran across to the front entry, coming to a stop at the receptionist sitting at a desk behind a wall of glass with just a small opening for her to hear.

"Can I help you, ma'am?" the petite, dark-haired woman asked, peering over her gold-rimmed glasses.

"Nathanial King, I got a phone call," I panted.

"Okay, calm yourself now while I take a look," she said as she tapped at the keys on her keyboard and looked at the screen in front of her. After a few moments, she looked back up at me. "Are you family?"

"I'm his wife," I quickly lied, chewing on my bottom lip as she eyed me coyly for a minute then pointed at the screen.

"Here we are, Nathanial King. He's still being seen by the ER doctors, but if you take a seat, I will give them a call and see what I can do to get you in to see your husband."

"Thank you," I said, giving her a weak smile and sitting down on one of the hard plastic chairs that made up several identical rows. Other anxious strangers waited nervously in the waiting room around me. As a doctor, it felt strange being on this side of the large metal doors. I pulled my phone from my purse, dialed Paxton's number again, and listened as it went straight to voicemail. With a combination of frustration of not knowing and the stress of driving to the hospital, I felt myself starting to get that cold, familiar feeling in the middle of my chest. It's hard to explain, but it started as an empty, cold void, which seemed to grow as it pulled all irrational thoughts from me into it, making it gain strength. It was followed by a tight feeling in my lungs that seemed to suck all the oxygen out of my body. Feeling the coldness starting, I pulled my earphones from my purse and pushed the buds into my ears. Connecting them to my phone, I flipped through my playlist, finding Enigma and pressing play. I closed my eyes and started to tame my breathing, matching it to the slow, pulsating beat of the music that started to permeate my brain, until it slowed, and I felt the coldness start to disappear. I visualized the music as patterns to distract me from the visions of Nate laying on a gurney somewhere beyond those doors.

Feeling a tap on my shoulder, I opened my eyes to find the receptionist standing in front of me. "Follow me, Mrs. King. I'll take you through to your husband." I stood, stuffed my phone back into my purse, and followed her to some glass doors, which slid open as she waved her ID over a small sensor on the wall. Walking behind her past the numerous doorways to rooms with patients lying in beds, I scanned my surroundings, taking in the hospital and the busy atmosphere of its halls. They were filled with trolleys, gurneys, staff, and patients, some sitting on the same hard, bright, red plastic chairs that were out in the waiting room. It felt like years since I had been a part of a hospital crew, working the floors assisting multiple patients. I hadn't actually thought about work since I had been with Nate. Being back in this environment, with its familiar sterile scent and bustle of movement made me remember just for a second how much I loved my profession. My thoughts were interrupted by the sight of Paxton sitting outside a room, his elbows leaning on his knees. I raced up to where he sat, giving the kind receptionist a quick, "Thanks," as I did.

"Paxton," I said, causing his head to dart up and his eyes to lock on mine with surprise.

"Casey, how the fuck did you get here?" he said, standing to place his hands on my shoulders.

"I drove, what happened?"

"You drove?" he asked incredulously.

"Paxton, that doesn't matter. Where is he, and what happened?" I asked again, raising my voice in frustration as I gripped his forearms. Seeing my anxiety, he pulled me into his arms.

"He's okay. The doctor is with him now. He took a hit in the back of the head with a bottle, and it knocked him out cold. He lost consciousness for a while. That's why they bought him to the hospital. Well, that, and because he needed stitches." I felt myself relax just a little knowing that Nate wasn't seriously hurt. At least he was alive. Paxton pulled back from me, and we sat down.

"Fuck, Casey, I didn't mean to scare you like that. I just wanted to let you know where we were and why Nate would be late getting back, but my phone cut off, and I couldn't get any reception once they brought me back here to wait."

"It's okay, Paxton. I'm glad you called me."

"Well, I'm not. Nate's going to beat my ass when he finds out I caused you to panic enough to drive all the way here," he said, shaking his head. I patted his arm with reassurance.

"Don't worry about that. I'm just glad he's alright, but I think you have a story to tell me while we wait, don't you think?" I asked with a lifted brow.

Paxton cursed under his breath before laying out the whole story of what went down at the club that night. He mentioned that he had tried to reason with Nate to let the police handle the situation. I stopped him when he tried to explain why Nate tends to do things his own way because I knew exactly how he liked to have control of all situations. The door next to us opened, and a nurse came out and said, "You can come in and see him now."

Standing, Paxton grabbed hold of my hand and led me in behind him. The first thing I saw was a paper bag sitting on a chair with Nate's white shirt half hanging out of it, now soaked in blood. Looking over to the bed, my eyes locked onto his pale face, head propped up, his hair damp, and I could see the red stains from the blood still on the back of his neck and partly covering the top of one shoulder. His powerful chest was bare down to his waist, where a sheet covered his legs. My heart sank at the sight of him in this position, eyes closed, and looking so still. Walking to the side of the bed, I stroked my hand across his, feeling for its reassuring warmth. It caused his eyes to flutter open, and the corner of his mouth twitched into a grin.

"Casey?" his words sounded low and gruff.

"I'm here. How are you feeling?"

"Like I've been hit in the head with a bottle," he said, chuckling, then wincing at the effort.

"Very funny," I said before turning my attention to the doctor, who was writing something on a hospital chart. I cleared my throat. "So, how is he?"

Placing the chart into its holder at the end of the bed, he turned to look at me.

"Remarkably good considering the power of the hit he took to the back of his skull. Hello, I'm Dr. Thomas, Head of Neurology," he said, holding his hand out for me to shake.

"Casey," I replied as I took his hand. "So, what's the damage?"

"Nothing major, luckily. He has a 5 cm gash to the back of his head and a mild concussion. I've sutured the wound, but we want to keep him here overnight under observation due to the fact that he lost consciousness for a short period of time. He's had an MRI that looks fine with no indication of anything abnormal. His films were actually pretty clear."

"That's good," I sighed out with relief.

"Good, that means I can get out of here," Nate said as he sat up on the bed, letting out a low hiss of pain and quickly bringing his hand to rub across his forehead.

"Oh, no, Mr. King. I'm afraid you'll be spending the night here so we can keep a close eye on you. That was a serious blow to the head you took tonight. Everything looks good at the moment, but with a head injury, that can change over a 24-hour period," Dr. Thomas said sternly.

Nate sat up on the bed, pulling the sheet from around his legs and dropping his feet to the floor. Thankfully, he still had his jeans on. "It's alright, Doc, she's a doctor," he said, pointing at me. Dr. Thomas turned to me, and I gave him a nod.

"Yes, I'm an ER surgeon, but the doctor is right. You need to spend the night," I said, looking at Nate who had already pulled on his boots and was pulling his blood-soaked shirt from the paper bag it was in.

"I'm fine, and there's nothing more they can do here that you can't do at home."

"Nate, please don't be stubborn about this. I'll stay, as well, and I'll sleep in the chair."

Nate turned his sights on Paxton, who was leaning against the wall. "Paxton," he said in a cross between a pleading and a commanding tone.

"Come on, Nate, don't give them a hard time. Just stay for the night," Paxton said, walking toward his brother.

Nate continued to pull on his shirt and do up the buttons. "Look, Doc, I appreciate that you're worried about my health, but I can assure you, I have managed to survive much more serious wounds than this," he said, motioning to the back of his head. "And I promise that if I feel worse overnight, I will come straight back to the hospital, but right now, I want to get into my own bed, in my own home, and sleep. So just give me the discharge papers, and I will sign myself out and take full responsibility."

Nate's eyes flittered between Paxton, Dr. Thomas, and me, and seeing the look of determination in his eyes, combined with pain and just plain exhaustion, I backed down and acquiesced to his wish. "It's okay, Dr. Thomas. Just let me take him home. I will be with him all night, and I'll check his neuro obs hourly. I can assure you that if there is the slightest change, he will be coming back to the hospital, even if I have to drag him here kicking and screaming," I said through tight lips to Nate, and the cheeky asshole winked at me.

"Okay, I don't agree, but at least he's with a professional. I'll just get your discharge form and get you something for the pain." Dr. Thomas sighed in defeat as he left the room.

"What the fuck, Nate?" Paxton bit out, causing Nate to wince.

"Please, don't yell, and don't lecture me, Paxton. I just want to go home, okay?"

It took about another twenty minutes of sitting in the waiting room until we had the discharge papers and some strong pain medication before we could finally leave. Walking out of the front doors, Paxton said, "I'm parked in the secure parking under the hospital, so I'll drive us back and pick up my car tomorrow. Where did you park, Casey?"

I pointed over at the SUV. "I'm parked over here," I said, pulling the keys from my purse and unlocking it. Nate just stopped and gazed at me.

"You drove here?" he asked between gritted teeth.

"Uh huh."

Then he turned to look at Paxton. "And you let her?" he growled.

"No one *let* me do anything. I drove here to get to you, so stop with all this alpha shit, and get in the back seat," I seethed through pursed lips at Nate and tossed the keys to Paxton to drive, getting in the back seat with Nate.

"Here, put your head on my lap, and try and sleep on the way back," I told Nate.

"Babe," he started to protest, but I stopped him.

"Can you please, just for once, not question anything," I said, and with a sigh, he stretched out as much as he could on the back seat, placing his head on my lap. He brought his arm up over my knees so his hand was holding my waist. It was as though he wanted to bury his face into my stomach. Stroking my hand softly over his forehead, I pushed the hair away from his eyes, leaned down, and placed a kiss against his temple. "Just relax and sleep," I whispered against his cheek, and within minutes, I felt his body relax as his breathing became deeper.

The drive home was silent, and when we pulled up at the house, Paxton helped me get a sleepy Nate out of the SUV and into bed. He took the SUV home and arranged to get his own car back in the morning. He figured Nate wouldn't be needing it tomorrow, as he wouldn't be fit to come into work anyway. With a hug and a goodbye, I was left to look after the bear with a sore head, literally. I always thought he would be a nightmare of a patient to look after, and so far, I was right. Going into the bathroom, I filled up a bowl with warm water and grabbed a cloth, taking it around to where he lay on the bed and placing it on the bedside table. I also took two of the pills the doctor had prescribed and a glass of water to him.

"Nate, open your mouth and swallow these, they will help with the pain." He groaned, opened his eyes then his mouth for me to place the pills on his tongue, followed by a sip of water. I pulled at the bloodied shirt he was wearing and eventually got it free. After squeezing out the warm, wet cloth, I wiped some of the dried blood off his shoulder and around his neck. It wasn't a great job, but it was better than nothing.

Standing, I undid the belt on his jeans and pulled them down and off, dropping them onto the floor and covering him with the sheet. Sitting down next to him, I took the small torch that I kept in the bedside table and lifted first his right eyelid, then his left, and checked his pupils, making him groan again. *It's going to be a long night,* I thought, pulling up the armchair next to the bed. I wrapped myself in a blanket and curled up next to him with my phone. My alarm was set for precisely one hour. At this stage, I was completely drained, and I knew that as soon as I relaxed into the chair, I would be asleep, but as long as I had the alarm to keep waking me every hour to check his neuro obs, I would be happy.

Throughout the night, I checked Nate hourly. The medication they gave him at the hospital seemed to keep him pain free and fast asleep, which was exactly what he needed. I slept in between the alarms until morning, when I watched the sun come up over the ocean with a hot, strong mug of tea in my hand out on the back porch, I came back in when I heard Nate's gravelly sounding voice calling out.

"Casey?"

"I'm here," I called out as I went into the bedroom and sat on the bed next to him. "Hey, how's your head feeling this morning?" I said, running my fingers softly over his brows.

"Like shit. What time is it?" he asked groggily.

"Just after 6 a.m."

He leaned up on his elbows before wincing and laying his head back onto the pillow. "Now, now, big guy, take it easy. I'll get you some more pain meds and some coffee, okay? You just stay where you are. Don't even think about getting out of bed today," I warned him.

When I returned with some hot, buttered toast and a hot mug of black coffee, he was sitting up in bed, leaning against the headboard. I placed the plate with the toast on the bedside table and handed him the coffee. He drank a mouthful and moaned, "That tastes so good."

"I bet it does. I think they kept you nil by mouth at the hospital last night."

"How the fuck did you manage to drive to the hospital?" he asked.

"Don't you think you had better tell me how the fuck you ended up in the hospital with a hole in your head first?" I retorted.

"It's a long story."

"I have time because you are not going anywhere today," I said, prodding my index finger into the middle of his chest.

While Nate explained the events that unfolded at the club last night, I helped him eat his toast. Well, more like I hand fed him his toast because he never ate breakfast unless I made him.

"So, they at least arrested one of them right? The barman?" I said.

"Yeah, but I don't think it will take them long to coax a name out of him," he said.

"I hope so. The coward hit you from behind," I said angrily.

"I've had worse," Nate shrugged.

"I've no doubt you have, you just didn't have me to frantically worry about you."

Nate placed his empty mug on the bedside table. "Come here," he said, pulling me into his arms and running a hand through my hair. "I'm sorry, babe. I really didn't expect there to be a problem. I didn't mean for you to worry, and I certainly didn't mean for you to drive. Jesus, if anything had happened to you..."

"Well, it didn't. I did alright, actually. I mean, I almost had a heart attack and peed myself when I first got onto the road. I'm pretty sure anyone behind me went around because I was hugging the curb, but it wasn't too bad. In fact, I think it's something I will enjoy." I grinned at him, and he kissed the top of my head.

"You'll get used to it. I just planned on being in the SUV with you the first time you went out on the road."

I stayed there, wrapped in his arms with my cheek pressed against his naked warm chest for a while, just enjoying his touch and the feeling of relief that he was alright. Although he hated being treated like an invalid, I pulled away from him to checks his neuro obs again. Once I was satisfied that everything was okay and the wound on the back of his head was not bleeding, I assisted him with taking a shower. He didn't seem to mind that part of being an invalid at all, especially when I helped to wash all the remnants of blood from the back of his neck whilst keeping the wound and stitches dry. It always amazed me how men, no matter how sick or injured they were, could always manage to get an erection in any situation. I convinced him, with great difficulty, that having any kind of sexual activity at the moment was not good for his concussion, and that he didn't need to be doing anything that might raise his blood pressure. I did allow him to trade our bed for the couch in the living room, though, so he could relax in front of the TV. Honestly, I was pretty sure he enjoyed being pampered for the day, even though he would never admit it.

Chapter Twenty-two

Nate

Waking up this morning was painful. My head throbbed like a son of a bitch, and the pain in the back of my head stung. Opening my eyes, even slowly, caused discomfort, but I wanted to make sure that I was in my own bed. I remembered insisting on leaving the hospital and getting into the SUV. Then I remembered the distinct smell and feel of Casey and laying down alongside the comfort of her presence, allowing me to drift back to sleep. I struggled to recall much more until I turned to see Casey curled up in a chair next to the bed. This was my heaven, watching her while she slept. I craved these moments when I woke before her and watched her in that blissful state. I think it's because when she's asleep, she looks like she doesn't have a care in the world, like she's not worried about anything, completely relaxed.

Her feet were curled up under her and her hands were clasped together against her cheek as she leaned against them. Her lips were slightly parted, and I could see her pulse beating steadily under the soft, creamy skin of her throat. Damn, why was she sleeping in a chair and not in bed? A pang of guilt hit me when I remembered the doctor at the hospital saying something about checking me every hour. Shit! That's what she had done. She'd stayed up all night just to take care of me, and now she was cramped up in a chair. I tried to lever myself into a sitting position, but my head was hit with an explosion of pain that instantly made me retreat and drop my head back onto the pillow. I closed my eyes for a moment to try and ease the throbbing behind my eyelids. The next thing that I remembered was opening my eyes and looking at a now empty chair. Calling out her name, I was instantly rewarded with the sight of her sitting in front of me, her beautiful, blue eyes wide and tinged with worry as she asked, "Hey, how's your head feeling this morning?"

Although I was peeved at being treated like a patient, I was pleased with moving to the couch and being able to watch my girl as she lay on the other one with her head buried in a huge book. She was wearing a very short pair of denim shorts, and her tanned legs were stretched out along the length of the couch. Moving my eyes up her legs, I caught sight of a small strip of bare skin of her stomach from where her tank top had ridden up, and once again I felt like a starving animal, watching and waiting to pounce on its prey with the slightest movement. Ever since she washed me in the shower this morning, I had a hard-on that wouldn't back down, and sweet Jesus, I tried to control it. I respected her opinion as a doctor that raising my blood pressure was not good for my head injury, but honestly, I didn't give a damn. All I could think about was crawling up her body and sinking into her, and that thought made me groan out loud as I tried to adjust myself.

Without even looking at me or moving the book she was reading, her voice came from behind it. "Keep it in your pants, because it's not going to happen today," she almost sang.

"Come on, you are torturing me. First, you run your soapy hands all over my body, and now, all I can see are your beautiful naked legs," I moaned.

Still ignoring me, Casey lifted a hand to the blanket draped over the back of the couch and pulled it down to cover her legs.

"Smartass," I said, tossing a pillow at her, making her finally drop the book she was reading onto her lap. "What the hell are you reading anyway? Looks like a telephone book."

"It's a medical, surgical book. I have to read up on American protocols to pass the exams."

"Crap, I forgot about those. When are they scheduled?" I asked, absently rubbing my forehead, noticing that the pain was starting to move into a dull ache.

Casey stood up, went to the kitchen, and came back with a glass of water and two white pills in her palm, holding them out to me. "Take these, they'll help." I swallowed the pills with half of the water. She sat next to me and gently stroked her fingers across my brow. "Just close your eyes for a while. I told you getting horny would hurt." Ignoring her smart remark, I closed my eyes and relaxed into the soft touch of her fingertips as they moved slowly back and forth across my forehead. It felt so good that the pain started to subside a little, beckoning me back to sleep.

The next time I woke was to a spicy aroma in the air. I slowly sat up and planted my bare feet on the polished wooden floor and realized I actually felt good. The relentless pain in my head was now a low, dull ache at the back of my skull.

"Hey, how's your head?" Casey said, coming to stand in front of me.

"A lot better, thanks to you," I said, sliding my hands up her outer thighs to grip her hips and drag her down onto my lap.

"Hey!" she exclaimed in a little squeak.

"It's okay. I think I learned my lesson earlier. No dirty stuff. Well, at least for the night. I just want to hold you," I said, pulling her tighter into my arms and inhaling her wonderful vanilla scent.

"But dinner is ready."

"Fuck dinner," I said, making her chuckle against my neck. God, she felt so good, and that was where we stayed for the next few minutes, just sitting and absorbing each other's warmth until she stood and mouthed the word, "Dinner," to me. We ate out on the deck. The combination of the setting sun over the ocean and the cool salty breeze was almost as picturesque as looking at Casey. I couldn't believe that everything I had done in my life had brought me here, right now, with her. My mom always said life had its own plan for each of us, and I think it just hit me how right she was, because this was something I had never envisioned for myself...ever. Yet, here I was, content and consumed by this woman and all she had to offer me.

I woke early the next morning, this time with Casey wrapped around me in a tangle of limbs. I was relieved that I managed to talk her out of sleeping in the damn chair again. She argued that it was easier for her to keep an eye on me, but I pulled the old wounded dog look. You know, droopy, forlorn eyes. I explained that I slept much better knowing that she was lying next to me in the bed; therefore, causing me less pain and distress through the night. I gave myself a silent victory high five when she slipped under the covers next to me. Pushing down my morning wood and the temptation to ravish her naked body took immense strength, but I promised her I would try and behave for a few days.

But now, as I gently tried to untangle myself from her naked body, I wondered if it would be worth annoying her for a quickie before I headed into work. Mulling it over for a few minutes, I realized that I had an even bigger problem: telling her I was going to work. So at this stage, I decided to forego the quickie with pained reluctance and quietly extricated myself from the bed. I stealthily moved into the bathroom for a quick shower, quietly grabbing some clean clothes on the way. But on exiting the bathroom, now dressed, I was confronted by an annoyed Casey standing with her legs apart and her hands locked onto her hips.

"What are you doing?" she asked.

"Going into work."

"Ah, I don't think so."

"Ah, I do."

"Nate," she growled at me, and it sounded so adorable and sexy.

"I'm good, babe. Honestly, I feel great. I think it helped to have my own doctor looking after me," I said, walking over to her and casually giving her a kiss on her firm, angry lips.

"Well, this doctor thinks you need more time," she huffed out as she followed behind me into the kitchen. Her arms were now folded across her chest with one hip leaning against the counter, and she watched as I poured myself a cup of coffee and took a sip.

"I promise, I feel as good as new," I tried to reassure her. "I need to help Paxton with the bank project. I keep dumping stuff on him, and he never complains, but I know he would like to spend less time behind a desk right now." With the sudden softened look on her face, I knew she got what I was talking about. So much had been happening that Paxton hadn't had much time to spend with Lynda and Emily, especially with our trip back to Australia. Walking to me and placing her palm on my chest, she just nodded and gave me a knowing smile.

When I got outside, Paxton was parked, waiting for me in my SUV. He had kept it until we could get back to the hospital to pick up his car.

Getting into the passenger seat, I was assaulted by a strong, pungent smell of musk. "Holy shit, my car stinks! Whatever you're wearing, I think you overdid it this morning, bro."

"Good morning to you, too, and it was a gift from Lynda," Paxton said, smiling as he took off down the driveway. "So, how are you doing?"

"I'm good. Just a slight headache, but that'll pass." I waved off his look of concern.

"You sure? I can handle everything if you need more time."

"Thanks, but I need to get back to work so I can give you some time off."

"I'm fine," Paxton insisted.

"Yeah, but I don't think your wife shares the same sentiment as you," I said, grinning at him.

"What, why? Has Lynda said something to Casey?"

"No, not that I know of," I said, shaking my head. "I'm just taking a guess. You've spent so much time covering my ass that you haven't had nearly enough time for your family."

"It's cool, Nate. Don't worry."

"It's not cool, and it needs to change, so I'll take the reins next week. You spend some time with Lynda and Emily, okay?"

"What? No, impossible. We're in the middle of the West Bank project!" he said.

"I know, so do what you can by the weekend, and I'll get into it next week. No buts, Paxton, you need a break."

Blowing out a sigh, he said, "Okay, if you're sure."

"Very sure, and Paxton?"

"Yeah."

"I appreciate everything you do for me."

"You're welcome. Anytime."

Stopping in at the hospital on the way in, we picked up Paxton's car, and he followed me back to the office. The rest of the day was as hectic as I thought it would be. By lunchtime, I felt my head starting to throb again, so I asked Laura to hold my calls for an hour. I took a couple of pain killers and closed my eyes for a while until it started to clear, then it was back to work. Giving Alonzo a quick call later in the afternoon, he told me that the barman had given up his buddy in crime, and they had both been charged with intent to sell and supply drugs and assault with a deadly weapon causing bodily harm. Alonzo thanked me several times and gave me an open invitation to bring Casey to the club any time with drinks on him. The only problem was that I had no intention of taking Casey to the club. It seemed like every time I went to the place, I had a bad experience. Nope, hopefully I wouldn't have to step foot in that place again any time soon.

Chapter Twenty-three

Casey

I was just putting the plate of sandwiches I'd made into the refrigerator when I heard a knock at the door. Lynda was bringing Emily over for lunch today. She'd had a tour of the house when it was empty, but now it was full of furniture, and as I looked around with pride at our home, I was excited to see what she thought. I threw open the front door to Lynda's bright smile. She had a bottle of white wine in one hand, a baby bag on her shoulder, and Emily in her car seat. "Here, let me help," I said, rushing to take Emily from her.

"Thanks," she said, following me inside and down to the kitchen where I sat Emily's car seat on the kitchen bench top. Lynda dropped her bag and slid the wine into the refrigerator, then gave me a hug. "It's so good to see you!"

"You, too!"

"Wow, this place looks magnificent," she said, walking into the living room and looking around.

"Thanks! Come on, I'll give you a tour, then we'll have some lunch," I said as she unstrapped Emily and placed her on her hip.

"Lead the way!"

After the tour, we sat outside and enjoyed some lunch with a nicely chilled glass of wine while Emily kicked up her legs on a blanket on the floor between us. "So, are you enjoying it here?" Lynda asked.

"Yes, it's wonderful! What about you? Have you managed to do any painting?"

"Not yet," she said with a frown.

"Why not?"

"I don't know. I get Emily down for a nap, but then there's always something else that needs attention, like bottles or laundry. By the time I'm free, she's awake again. Not that I'm blaming her or anything. I think I need a little more time to get into a good routine," she said, taking another sip of her wine.

"Well, I can always come over and watch her for a while and help out while you paint, or you can bring her here for a few hours, if that will help."

"Sounds tempting, but I don't want to intrude on your time and force you to be a babysitter."

"Nonsense, it'll be fun."

"Really?" she asked, and I knew exactly what she was thinking with the slight look of sadness she gave me.

"Yes, really. I would love to. That is, if you trust me, of course?"

"Are you kidding me? Did you really just ask me that question?" She almost glared at me, and I just shrugged. "Of course I trust you, you idiot! I just didn't want to put you in an uncomfortable situation."

"It's all good. I love spending time with her, and it will be good for both of us."

"Sounds great to me! You just let me know when it's a good time for you. I know you have your exams coming up."

"I know," I groaned. "The first one is next week."

"I see you're not looking forward to it then." She giggled at my lack of enthusiasm.

"Not really, but it's a means to an end. As soon as I take the exams with the medical board, Paxton has arranged for me to do some volunteer work at a free clinic in Portland."

"Yeah, he told me that. Is that a good thing?" she asked tentatively, trying to read my reaction.

"Well, it is for me. I mean, although I love being a lady of leisure out here in my own private paradise, I need to get back into it or I'll start losing my clinical skills. Besides, my mind is starting to get lazy."

"And Nate?" She raised a brow at me.

"Nate is Nate. He's not happy about the area where the clinic is located, but he's okay with it as long as Nick drops me off and picks me up," I said, rolling my eyes.

"That's not a bad thing, Casey. Sometimes those free clinics can attract some bad people."

"I know, but even bad people need medical attention. I think it will be a good experience."

"Well, as long as it's what you want to do, that's great."

After Lynda left late that afternoon, I took one of the frozen lasagnas Carmel had brought over out of the freezer and sat it on the bench to thaw along with some garlic bread. Then I went into the bathroom and ran a hot bath, filling it with a silky, sweet-smelling bath oil that I had brought from the penthouse. I stripped down and sank into the luxuriously steamy water. That, combined with the sound of the waves outside crashing against the shoreline, and the mingling scent of salt and bath oil was so relaxing and decadent. I was perfectly accurate with what I had said to Lynda over lunch. This was definitely my little slice of paradise.

I must have fallen asleep in the tub because when I opened my eyes, it was dark outside. Pulling the plug and getting out, I wrapped a fluffy towel around my body, still covered with soap suds, and ran into the bedroom to get dry. I selected and put on a pair of black panties and grabbed a long loose t-shirt to throw on, but as I turned, I noticed myself in the full-length mirror in our bedroom. Standing up straight, I dropped my hands to my sides and gazed at my reflection. I couldn't remember the last time I actually had a long look at myself in a mirror, and I was momentarily shocked at what I saw. Bringing my hand up to my stomach, I ran my fingers over my scars, feeling the bumpy, flawed skin along the zigzag scar tissue that ran in a line just under my belly button. I looked at the raised dots and further up to the red, perfect slice marks around the areola of my nipples. A flash of a thin, silver-tipped blade invaded my mind, then the hot, glowing red tip of a cigarette. I inhaled sharply with a hiss, remembering the burn and the slight smell of charred flesh. Closing my eyes tightly, I tried to squeeze the tears back as I concentrated on my breathing, willing myself to escape the memory. I felt a single tear run down my cheek, and I heard a soft, low voice behind me.

"Baby?" The intrusion made me jump. I opened my eyes to see Nate standing behind me, his eyes filled with concern. I quickly pulled the t-shirt I was still holding tightly in my hand up to cover the front of me when I felt his arms snake around my waist. Nate pulled me back against his chest. He said nothing, just breathed into my neck, holding me so tight that I knew he was trying to absorb the pain that I was feeling.

"Please, don't cry," he whispered.

"I'm sorry," I said as I wiped away the tear with the back of my hand.

"You know you have nothing to be sorry for, sweetheart. Just talk to me," he pleaded.

"I don't know. I just saw myself in the mirror...and remembered how flawed I am."

"No, no, no. You're not flawed at all, baby. You may have some battle scars like me, but you're perfect. Let me show you," he said, reaching around to take the t-shirt from my hands and dropping it on the floor. Kneeling down behind me and placing his palms against the outside of my calves, he slowly ran them up my legs and settled on my hips. "Beautiful, long, tanned, and soft legs," he said. His hands then moved around to my bottom, where he gently squeezed. "A luscious, biteable ass, beautiful hips, and beautiful, soft skin." His hands moved over my belly and up to cup my breasts. "Plump, soft breasts with the tastiest nipples." Then, his hands slid up my throat, and he turned me to face him. "You are flawless," he said, cupping my face and rubbing his thumbs over my cheeks. "The most beautiful woman I have ever known. There is no one like you, baby, and you are mine."

I closed my eyes when his lips softly brushed across mine and I just felt him.

"I love everything about you. Don't you ever doubt that."

I wrapped my arms around his waist. "I just got lost in a memory, that's all."

"And I'll always be here to find you and bring you back to me, okay?" Giving him a nod, I rested my cheek against his chest.

"How is your head?" I asked him.

"It's fine. Don't worry. Right now, I'm more interested in you."

"I'm okay," I reassured him.

"I have an idea, but I need you to trust me," he said, making me look up at him questioningly.

"I think together we've experienced a lot of pleasure, but maybe you need to get to know your own body again, explore the changes in it, trust it, and take back some control." Nodding, he led me over to the bed and slid my panties off, motioning for me to lay on the bed. "I'll be right back," he said. He left the bedroom and came back several minutes later with my iPod, a pair of earphones, a sleeping mask, and an unlabeled bottle. I watched as he unbuttoned his shirt and let it drop to the floor, followed by his boots and jeans, leaving just his black boxers on. Lifting my legs, he sat on the bed, draping them over his thighs so he was cross-legged in between my legs. He took my iPod and flipped through the playlists, plugging the earphones into it.

"Now, if you feel uncomfortable or uncertain at any time, just tell me, okay?"

I nodded, and he placed the sleep mask over my head. "I'm going to cover your eyes and put the earphones on you, and I just want you to get lost in your music with no sight distractions. I just want you to feel, okay?" I nodded hesitantly. He placed the mask over my eyes and the earphones over my ears. Then, with a faint click, I heard the sound of Enigma filtering through. He chose a beautiful, relaxing song, and even though the darkness of the sleep mask was a little daunting at first, I knew that the only two people in the room were Nate and myself.

As the slow, rhythmic notes penetrated my mind, I felt something warm and silky trickle onto my belly. His large hands were rubbing what felt like oil around and up to my breasts, cupping them before running a soft oily fingertip over my nipples, making them tingle and harden under his touch. I felt myself relax as his hands explored my body, covering every inch of skin with the oil, over the full length of my legs and up my inner thighs, then finally coating my sex. I felt his hands take mine, guide them to my breasts, opening my fingers in his slippery hands and moving my own palms over my taut nipples, causing me to let out a small gasp of excitement. With his hands still on mine, he moved them down my stomach and brushed my fingers over the slippery naked lips of my sex, singling out my index finger and placing the tip right on my swollen nub, moving it in small, slow circular motions. Giving myself pleasure was something so new to me, I thought I would be embarrassed at the thought of Nate watching me, but it just heightened the warm pleasure seeping through every vein in my body. As my fingers stroked in between my legs, I felt so uninhibited, so intimate with my body. As I felt myself starting to climb toward release, I felt Nate's hand join mine as he slowly slid a finger inside of me, making me groan louder with the surge in pleasure running through my body.

His finger moved in and out, making my own fingers move faster. I needed release. Opening my legs wider, I felt him slide another finger inside of me. Nate's touch started to push me over the edge, and I screamed out his name as my inner walls tightened around his fingers. I crushed my thighs together tighter, savoring the feeling until I dropped my hands to my sides and shivered from the aftershocks.

I felt the earphones being taken away, and then the sleep mask was removed. I squinted against the intrusion of light into my eyes. When they focused again, they were drawn into a pair of wide gray eyes, now swimming with a hungry lust of their own. "Fuck." Nate's curse came out in a long growl. "That was the sexiest thing I have ever seen."

"That was the sexiest thing I have ever done," I panted, and reached down to the huge bulge pushing through his boxers.

"No, baby, this was all for you."

"But I want you," I breathed.

"Casey," he groaned.

"I need you, Nate," was all I said before sitting up and helping him to get naked and in between my legs. He pushed inside of me, where my inner walls were still tingling and raw with pleasure, making me instantly want more of him. Wrapping my legs around his waist and pushing my heels into his ass made him groan even louder. With his chest pressed against mine, the oil between us made my nipples slide against the hard muscles of his chest, making them hypersensitive and responsive to the friction between us as he ground his pelvis into me. His mouth crashed down onto mine in a kiss that told me just how hungry he was. His tongue slid into my mouth and over mine, making the pleasure soar through my body once again. With my eyes closed, my body arched into his, absorbing every inch of him. We were so close I felt as though we are fusing together and becoming one. One entity, one soul. The ultimate euphoria felt so deep I never wanted it to end.

"Look at me," I heard him breathe out in a low growl that made me open my eyes. I saw the same feelings reflected in his hungry eyes, and I couldn't hold back the building pressure in my body any longer. I chanted his name over and over, his thrusts coming harder and deeper until he reached his own pinnacle, pulling me over the edge of pure ecstasy with his release. Nate leaned his forehead against mine, his heavy breathing warming my lips as we both trembled and slowly calmed our bodies before he slid to my side, pulling me onto his chest, his strong arms locking around my naked, spent body.

Needless to say, dinner was very late. We dozed off for a while, then got up and jumped in the shower to wash the oil off of both of us. Nothing needed to be said. Our eyes said it all. He thanked me for trusting him, and I thanked him for giving me such a wonderful and enlightening experience.

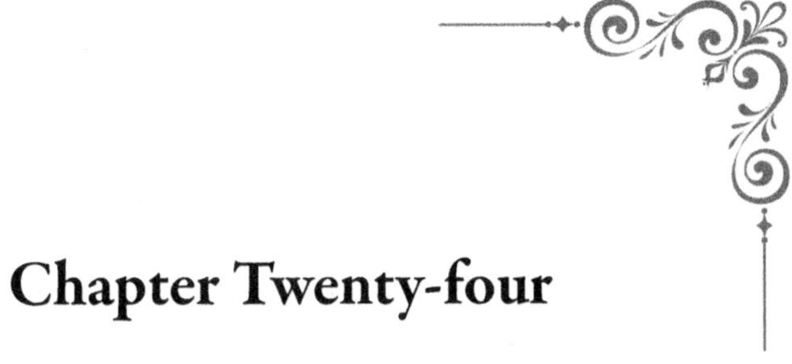

Chapter Twenty-four

Nate

On the drive into Portland the next morning, the only thoughts I had running through my mind were of Casey and the trust she showed in me last night. We had been talking one night a couple of weeks ago, and she suggested that she was ready for me to push some boundaries with her in bed. It seemed the more pleasure she experienced, the more confident she became. I loved seeing her take control of her sexuality after all the years of being forced to bury it. I thought if I could take her into one of her relaxing music comas where she felt safe while not allowing her to feel self-conscious about herself and her perceived imperfections, I could help her to explore her own body and realize just how beautiful and desired she was. I just needed to take very small steps and wait for the right moment. I would never want her to do anything that made her uncomfortable, and I certainly would never want her to do anything that I knew she was doing just to please me. Now, that would really piss me off. And I really needed her to understand that all I loved and cared about was her. As long as she was next to me, that was all that mattered. Last night, when I walked in and saw her looking at her reflection in the mirror with pain in her eyes and that single tear silently falling down her cheek, it fucking broke me into a million pieces.

She would never be broken to me, ever, but I also wanted her to know that she controlled her own body's wants, needs, and pleasure. Last night, she certainly did just that. She blew my own fucking world in the process, and damned if I wasn't walking bow-legged this morning myself.

Pulling the Audi into the reserved space in the garage, I got out and pressed the elevator button. It was going to be a long day, I could just feel it. As soon as the elevator opened on my office floor, my new secretary, Laura, had a pile of messages that I needed to follow up on, and so it began. Some files had also arrived to go through, courtesy of Paxton, who had them delivered by courier this morning. That asshole was supposed to be taking some time off, not working on shit at home and sending it in here.

Dropping everything onto my desk, I pulled my cell phone from the back pocket of my jeans, bringing the screen to life and pressing the contact for Paxton. I stood, looking out through the huge wall of glass in front of me where I could see the hustle and bustle of life going on below. Paxton answered on the second ring with a, "Hey, Nate, did you get my package?"

"Yes, I did, thank you, but why didn't you just call me this morning and get me to pick them up? Oh, and why the hell are you working when you're supposed to be chilling with the family?"

"I am having a great time being at home, I promise. These were just the final copies of the contracts for the West Bank deal that I wanted you to have one more look at before faxing through to their head office. Fuck knows why I didn't get you to pick them up on your way in this morning. I guess I'm having a hard time remembering that you live basically down the road now," he chuckled into the phone.

"Okay, I'll take a look at them now, but I'm sure they are perfectly fine, Paxton. I mean, how many times have you gone over them and tweaked them?"

"I'm sorry, what can I say? You know how anal I am about these things."

"That's an understatement. You need to relax, Paxton. Everything is going smoothly, and you worry too much."

"Yeah, well, I have to do it for both of us."

"Funny guy, go back to your wife and daughter, and leave me alone," I said jokingly.

"Okay. Well, I'll see you Saturday then."

"What's on Saturday?" I asked, puzzled.

"Casey invited us over for dinner. A kind of housewarming, I think."

"Sounds good, I'll see you then," I said, ending the call and taking one last look out the windows before flopping into my chair and pulling it up to the desk with determination.

Pressing the button on the intercom for Laura to come in, I handed her the finalized papers with instructions to have them couriered to The West Bank and to make arrangements for a trip to their head office in Washington, D.C. for the next week. I had already talked to the head of operations over there, and Laura was liaising with them to arrange a conference time and date with instructions for a fly in, fly out itinerary. The quicker we set this deal in motion, the quicker I could move on and concentrate on other things.

Near the end of the day, I decided to check my emails when I noticed an advertisement flash up alongside the page for a local animal shelter. The huge flashing banner caught my attention across the top with the words "Adopt me" on it, with a before and after photo of a dog. The before photo showed a skinny, dirty, flea-ridden looking, poor excuse for a dog lying on a dirty blanket. The after photo showed the same dog, only now in much better condition with some meat on his bones. Clean, golden fur covered his body, and he sat with a blue ball in his mouth like he was waiting for someone to play with. The text under the photos read:

*HI, MY NAME IS CHANCE. I was in a bad state before I came
to the Portland Dog Shelter. Now, all I need is a loving home.
I am happy and friendly, I love to play fetch and to run.
Please, take a Chance on me and adopt me. I promise I will be
your faithful companion.*

I had never, ever thought about getting a pet, but there was something about this dog's face that I swore said, "You need me." Well, that together with the thought of how much better I would feel knowing that Casey had a guard dog with her when I wasn't there made me make the impulsive and rash decision to call the shelter.

After a brief stop at a pet store on the way home to pick up some doggy essentials for the new addition, I pulled up in front of the house two hours later with a furry friend in the passenger seat. His tongue was hanging out as his head whipped from side to side, checking out his new surroundings with interest. I pulled into the driveway and opened the car door. My new friend leapt across my lap, down onto the ground, and headed fast for the nearest tree to relieve himself. Walking up to the front door, I patted the side of my leg to get Chance next to me then commanded him to "Sit" and "Stay." I knocked on the door, and I heard Casey approaching while mumbling something about me forgetting my keys. She opened the door, and before she could say anything, I said, "I brought a house guest," as I pointed down to Chance. Casey's eyes dropped down to Chance with an instant softness before she crouched before him. It was clearly love at first sight. Chance jumped all over her, his tail wagging furiously and his wet tongue licking her face.

"Hey, buddy, who might you be?" she said, gently fending off his overly enthusiastic greeting.

"This is Chance. He's around one year old, and I thought he might be a good guard dog for the place," I said matter-of-factly, still trying to convince myself that I had made a good decision.

"Really? You brought us a pet?" she asked wide-eyed.

"No, I brought us a guard dog," I said, trying to keep my voice as stern as possible.

"You mean, like a stay outside working dog?"

"Exactly."

"Yeah, right, like that's going to happen," she said, raising her eyebrows questioningly at me. "Come on, Chance, let's show you your new home," she said, patting her leg for him to follow her down the hall and into the kitchen. Going back out to the car, I unloaded the dog food and bed and realized right then and there that if I thought this dog was going to live outside of this house, I was fucking kidding myself. I was going to be lucky if there would be enough room for me in our bed tonight if Casey got her way. I had to admit, she could wrap me around her little finger at times, but there was no way that dog was sleeping with us tonight. Not now, not ever.

Lying in bed that night with her cuddled up against my side, stroking my hand down the warm, soft skin of her naked back, she said, "Chance is a good, symbolic name, don't you think?"

"I think that's what caught my attention. His name did seem somehow appropriate for us."

"Thank you. I'm in love with him already," she said, and I felt her smile against my chest.

"So, I was thinking, next week is your first exam. Maybe we should spend the night before at the penthouse. I know you need to be there early, so it might make sense to be closer?"

"Sounds good, but what about Chance? We can't leave him here by himself," she said, concerned.

"We'll take him with us."

"To the penthouse? Is that allowed?"

"Baby, I own the building. I'm pretty sure it's okay with the landlord."

"Good point," she laughed.

As she snuggled in closer to me, I felt the bottom of the bed press down and the slow slide of a furry body, cautiously inching his way up the bed between us. Sitting up and looking at those big brown, puppy dog eyes, I pointed to the dog bed in the corner of the room.

"Down," I commanded.

"Nate, he's lonely," Casey pleaded.

"Look, I let you talk me into letting him sleep in our room, but he's not sleeping in our bed." Pointing again to the dog bed in the corner, I told Chance, "Bed, now." Looking at me once more, he slowly stood, jumped off the bed, and ambled toward his bed. I swore he fucking sighed in disgust. "Stay," I told him, before laying back down and pulling Casey back into my arms again.

"Nate," she whispered.

"Nope, not happening. Now, get some sleep."

"Goodnight," she sighed with defeat and wrapped her arm around my waist, pulling the sheet up with it.

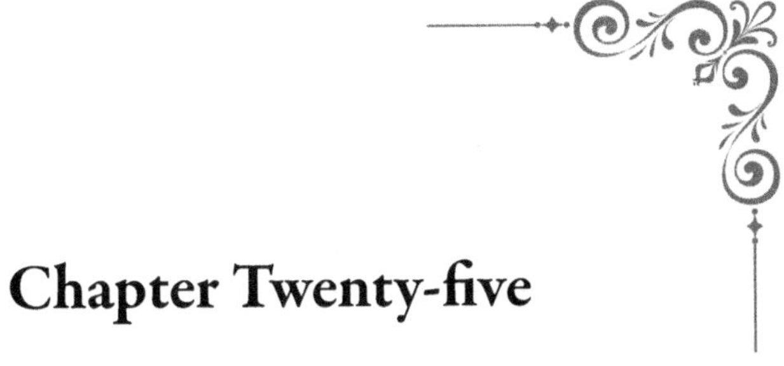

Chapter Twenty-five

Casey

After Nate left for work the next morning, I took Chance for a walk along the beach, throwing one of the many balls that Nate purchased for him yesterday. I actually couldn't believe we had a dog. A friggin' dog! Ever since I could remember, I had wanted a dog. I longed for my own pet as a child, but I was always told that animals required great responsibility, and I was already too much to look after, never mind a pet. I even remembered a friend from school had a dog that had puppies one summer, and I took one home, hopeful my parents would somehow soften and let me keep it. After spending the afternoon begging, pleading, and negotiating with them that it would make a good guard dog, and that I would get a paper round to feed it, I was told absolutely not.

Tears streamed down my face as I carried the fluffy little puppy back to its mother. I never thought I would feel that kind of pain in my chest again. I ended up getting grounded for a month, as well, not that it made too much of a difference. I never went anywhere other than next door to play with Flynn, and my parents always returned after dark, so they never suspected a thing anyway.

I scooped up the ball and threw it for Chance. I watched him run, wagging his tail. *He is mine,* I thought happily. His exuberance and playful nature made me laugh so loud that he looked at me like I was crazy as he dropped the ball at my feet. Chance sat and tilted his head, first to one side, then the other. Reaching out, I gave him a scratch behind his ears. "Come on, boy, let's go get you some water."

The next few days went by so fast and I was sure it was partly due to having Chance with me at Jacaranda House. He was so good and made himself right at home, even down to chewing holes in a pair of Nate's boxers that I found in the corner of the kitchen one morning. He must have stolen them from the washing basket. After showing him the now chewed material and letting him know that he was a bad boy, I quickly shoved them into the bottom of the trash and hoped that they weren't a favorite pair that Nate would miss.

Paxton and Lynda brought Emily over on Saturday, and we spent the day swimming, eating, and polishing off a few bottles of wine. Now that Lynda wasn't breastfeeding Emily, she really wanted to make up for some lost time. It was a really good family day that ended with us all watching a movie with a huge bowl of popcorn before Paxton drove his pleasantly buzzed wife and sleeping daughter home. On Monday, we packed Chance into the SUV and headed back to Portland, where I spent most of the day laying on the couch reading my medical books with Chance at my feet. My first exam was in the morning, and I needed to be prepared. This was an important step in my new life, and I wanted to make sure I had every topic covered.

When Nate got back to the penthouse just after 6 p.m., he suggested that we take Chance for a walk and have dinner at Stella's, which didn't take much convincing. I remembered the first meal I had there, and every time Nate mentioned the place, I started to salivate. We sat at an outside table, tying Chance's lead to one of the legs, where he flopped down. That is, until Stella came out with one of her special pizzas, a bowl of her homemade garlic pasta, and some fresh crusty bread. Then he was up in begging mode.

"So, how are you feeling about tomorrow? Nervous?" Nate asked as he took a huge bite of his slice of cheesy pizza. I watched, amused, as he tried to contain the gooey, stringy, cheese trail it left from the pizza to his mouth.

"A little," I confessed.

"You'll be fine, you know your stuff."

"I know, but knowing it when you're using it is sometimes different from when you're asked to explain it," I said, grinning at him.

"Just relax and breathe."

"I will, I promise," I told him and found him looking at me in an odd way. Grabbing my napkin, I wiped my mouth.

"What's wrong, have I got sauce on my face?" I asked, smiling, and he slowly shook his head.

"No, just looking at you and thinking how beautiful you are."

"Nate," I whispered, feeling my cheeks blush with his compliment. Nate reached across the table and took my hand in his.

"You are, and I am so lucky that you're mine."

"Not sure about lucky. More like crazy," I said as I smiled at him.

"Well, that, too, but I mean it, babe. You are the best thing that has ever happened in my life." Looking into his eyes and seeing his sincerity caused a shiver to run down my spine.

"Thank you, but you know it's the other way around, right?"

"Okay, no competition. We are even on this one," he said, grinning and slipping the last piece of his pizza into his mouth.

We took Chance for a walk in the park before heading back to the penthouse for an early night. Nate had arranged for Nick to pick me up in front of the building at 8 a.m., and I wanted to get up a couple of hours early to go over some notes before we left. Nate wanted to take me in, but I knew how busy he and Paxton were at the moment with the bank deal, and I eventually convinced him that it would be pretty boring waiting for me to finish. If there was one thing that I knew, it was that Nate hated waiting around, so I made sure I put a lot of emphasis on how long it would take. When the alarm went off at 6 the next morning, I dressed in some sweats and sneakers, took Chance out to do his business, and came back up to get stuck into the books again. I studied until Nate got up about an hour later, and we had some breakfast together before I went downstairs to meet Nick.

I was pretty sure I went to the bathroom to pee more times than necessary before I entered the exam room. There were several others in there taking the exam, as well, and we were told that it would be split into seven, sixty-minute blocks and spread over an eight-hour period.

My stomach started to do flip-flop motions as I sat down, but as soon as I turned over the papers and picked up my pen on the first exam paper, I seemed to breeze through it. Everything that was on the paper felt like second nature, and the more questions I answered, the easier it became, giving me even more confidence in the fact that I hadn't forgotten anything. The day was long and arduous, but I felt good about the results.

When I finished, they told us that we should get our results in the mail over the next few days along with a time and date for the second exam. I was feeling so good, I almost skipped out and into the waiting car outside. I got off the elevator at the King Security floor and walked over to the secretary's desk, where she had her head down and her fingers gliding over the computer keyboard so fast, I swore I could almost see smoke rising. It took a few moments before she looked up and saw me standing there, but then I noticed why as she pulled out a pair of black earbuds from her ears and pressed a button on a small black box that was connected to the computer.

"So sorry, I didn't see you there," she said, her apology sincere.

"That's okay, you look pretty busy."

"Mr. King wants this, like, yesterday," she said, pointing to the computer screen, making me chuckle.

"It's alright, I didn't want to disturb you. Is he busy?" I asked her.

"I'll just check," she said, picking up the phone and pressing a button on it. "Mr. King, Miss Tyler is here to see you." Placing the phone back, she said, "Go right in."

"Thank you, Laura," I said as I slowly pushed open the door and walked into his office. Nate was in front of me almost instantaneously, snaking one arm around my waist as he pushed his palm against the door, closing it. His hand came up to the back of my head, holding it firmly as his mouth met mine in a knee-trembling, scorching hot kiss. When his head drew away, I said, "Wow, now that's what I call a welcome."

"How did it go?"

"It was good. Easier than I thought it was going to be, but way too long," I said, reaching up and running a finger across his one black curl that always seemed to drop into his eyes.

"I thought about you all day," he growled into my neck.

"Well, I'm afraid you might have to do some more thinking about me because I need to get up to the penthouse and take Chance out for a walk before he leaves us a present up there," I said, tilting my head back to give him easier access to my neck and running my fingers through the hair at the back of his neck.

"Fuck," he cursed into my skin disappointedly.

"Sorry, babe, but I'm pretty sure you don't want to put your foot in something wet and squishy later."

Sighing, he pulled his head back with a frustrated and horny look on his face. He gave me one last kiss, then smoothed down the front of his shirt, collecting himself. "Think I'm starting to have regrets," he said, one brow raised.

"About Chance? Don't even think about it," I said, scowling at him.

"I think I'm getting jealous already. You're going to go upstairs and let a dog do what I want to do."

"What, poop on the floor?" I laughed.

"Funny. I mean more like lick you all over, then he gets you stroking him for the rest of the afternoon."

"Aww, my poor baby. Don't worry, I will let you lick me all over tonight, then I will stroke you anywhere you want me to," I said as I pushed myself onto my tippy toes and kissed the tip of his nose, making him growl in frustration once again.

After Nate finished work that night, we drove back out to the beach house, although I had to keep reminding him to keep his eyes on the road instead of me with those lustful gray eyes of his. I think when I made him the promise about licking and stroking this afternoon, I might just have bitten off more than I could chew. This became more apparent when he almost skidded to a stop in front of the house, grabbed Chance's leash to take him for a quick walk, and growled out to me to get in the bedroom and get naked. This time, Chance was left outside of our bedroom.

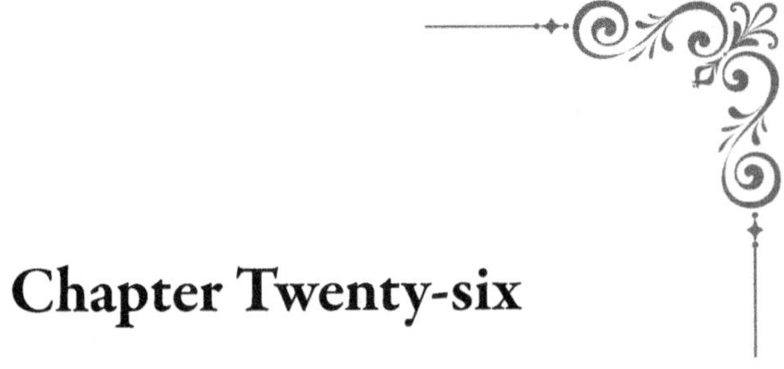

Chapter Twenty-six

Nate

I had no idea how I got through the day. My thoughts were totally consumed by Casey taking her exams, which morphed into Casey walking into my office naked and perching on my desk in front of me. And all that fantasy did was give me a painful hard-on for the rest of the day. When Laura buzzed, letting me know Casey was outside my office door, I thought my luck had changed. It might have if it wasn't for her reminding me that Chance was likely crapping on the floor upstairs in the penthouse, and she needed to take him out.

That last revelation was more than enough to put a downer on my carnal thoughts involving her, although when we got home that night, I made good on my promise of licking and stroking her all over, which I had to say was worth my day of some painful blue balls. When I woke in the morning, her side of the bed was empty. Running my hand across the sheet and feeling that it was cold, I pulled myself up to sit on the side of the bed. Running my hands down my face, scratching at the scruff on my chin, I took a quick glance at the time on my phone, seeing that it was just after 7 a.m. I headed to the bathroom for a shower and a shave.

Once dressed in my usual office attire - jeans, boots and a navy blue, silk dress shirt - I opened the bedroom door to the smell of fresh coffee and something fried. Filling a mug with the hot liquid, I looked around for my girl, and I saw movement out on the sand.

Walking out onto the back deck, I saw her dressed in only a pair of shorts and an almost see-through white shirt that had slid down, exposing her shoulders. Leaning a hip against the deck rail, I sipped my coffee and watched as she tossed the ball for the dog and laughed when he brought it back and dropped it at her feet. The morning sun was warm, but the ocean breeze was cool. Still, she ran with the dog, her long, blonde hair flying around carelessly in the breeze, her cheeks slightly pink with delight. I loved seeing her like this. She looked so happy, elated, and so free.

"Morning," I shouted out, making her turn and then run up the beach and up the stairs to me.

"Morning," she said, placing a hand on my chest and leaning in for a kiss, which I obliged by stooping down to catch her lips with mine.

"Mmm, you smell good," she moaned, running a hand over my freshly shaven cheek.

"You always smell good, baby."

"You want some breakfast? I cooked you some bacon and eggs and put them in the oven to keep them warm," she said, going into the kitchen. Grabbing a glove and pulling out the plate from the oven, I placed it on the table before grabbing some utensils from the drawer. Sitting down, I inhaled the wonderful smell of bacon before starting to eat.

"You know you don't have to cook for me all the time, right?" I said around a mouthful of fluffy scrambled eggs.

"I like to cook for you, but I can stop if you want me to."

"No, no not at all. I just don't want you to think it's something you're expected to do, you know?"

"Relax, Nate, I'm messing with you. I have always loved to cook, but now I really love to cook for you," she said, giving me that beautiful smile of hers.

"So, how would you feel about a house guest this weekend?"

"A house guest? Who?" she asked, her eyes wide with curiosity.

"Remember how I told you that Paxton and I have to fly to Washington, D.C. for the day on Monday?" I asked, and she gave me a nod. "Well, I want Jax there as well, so I thought I might see if he wants to come over on the weekend so you two can catch up before we leave. What do you think?"

"What do I think? Are you kidding me?" she said, jumping up and kissing me on the cheek. "I say get that cowboy here, so I can turn him into a beach bum," she said excitedly. It should have pissed me off at how happy she was at the idea of seeing Jax, but it didn't because I knew they had formed a close brother/sister bond. It took me a while to realize that Jax would protect her with his life and that Casey loved me and only me.

As soon as I got into my office, I pulled up the contact list on my phone and pressed Jax's name. It took several rings before he answered. "Hey, buddy, how the hell are you?"

"I'm good, what about you? You enjoying some well-earned time off?" I asked him, relaxing in my chair, turning it toward the windows.

"Hell yeah! I'm enjoying it while it lasts, but considering you're calling me right now, it seems my enjoyment might be coming to an end," he chuckled into the phone.

"Yeah, sorry, man, but Paxton and I need you with us in Washington, D.C. on Monday for the West Bank contract," I said apologetically.

"Not a problem. Where and what time?"

"Well, I was thinking you could fly in here on Friday and stay for the weekend before we head out on Monday. That is, if you're not busy?"

"Sounds good. So, I get to see your new place, huh?"

"Of course."

"And that sweet little woman of yours, too? Maybe in a swimsuit?" I could almost see the evil bastard grinning on the other end of the phone.

"You're pushing your luck now, Jax, but yes, Casey is very excited to see you."

"Ah, what can I say? I am an expert at getting women excited," he said, laughing.

"Yeah, yeah. And on that note, I will say goodbye. Call me when you land, and I'll pick you up on the way home." Jax was still laughing when I ended the call.

The West Bank deal was one of the biggest contracts King Security had ever taken on. It covered every branch of their banks throughout the United States with an upgrade to their security protocols and included installing all new, state-of-the-art cameras and equipment. After this trip to D.C. to finalize the contract with the board, King Security was going to become the biggest security company in the country. Not bad, considering it started with a retired cop, a rundown building, and a dream. My father's dream was becoming a reality.

I pulled up outside arrivals at PDX on Friday afternoon. Jax ambled out and over to the SUV dressed in jeans, a black t-shirt, and his favorite black Stetson. Pulling open the door, he threw his duffle bag into the back seat and slid into the passenger side. "Jesus, Jax, when are you going to buy yourself a new duffle? That thing stinks of horse shit," I said, watching as he pulled his seatbelt on.

"It's my lucky duffle," he said, smiling. "And hello to you, too."

Pulling the SUV out into traffic, we spent the drive catching up, and I filled him in on our trip to Australia. I also brought him up to speed on the bank contract.

"So, how is she?" he asked, his voice tinged with concern.

"She's good. Really good, surprisingly," I told him.

"Sounds like she's been through hell," Jax said, looking out of the window.

"I know, but she's back. You'll see," I said, pulling into the long driveway that led up to the white house at the top and coming to a stop. Before our feet hit the gravel, the front door opened, and Casey ran down the stairs toward us with Chance barking behind. Jax caught hold of Casey in his arms, lifting her up and spinning her around.

"Hey, little lady! Well, look at you," he said, putting her down and taking a step back to look her over. Walking over, I put an arm around her waist, pulling her into my side.

"Not for too long," I said to Jax.

"Come on in," Casey said, motioning to the front door. Jax bent down to pat Chance.

"I can't believe you bought a dog," he said, looking at Casey with a chuckle.

"I didn't, Nate bought him," she said, making Jax turn to me with a raised brow.

"What? I wanted a guard dog," I said, shrugging.

"Okay, what did you do with my buddy, Nate? Because this guy here is just too domesticated and homely. I mean, a house with a white picket fence and a dog?" Jax said with his hands spread out at his sides.

"Fuck you, I'm not domesticated," I said, walking into the house.

"Almost," Casey said, giving me a cheeky grin.

"I'll deal with you later," I said to her over my shoulder in a warning tone.

Jax walked through to the living area and stood in front of the open glass doors that led out onto the back deck. He pulled off his hat and dropped it on a chair outside while he was taking in the view. "Holy shit, this is amazing," he said, his words filled with awe at the sight. Casey came from the kitchen with a couple of beers, handing one to Jax then the other to me. We enjoyed some time catching up while taking in the magnificent ocean view.

The weekend was full of cookouts on the beach and lots of swimming, and I had to admit, I did insist that Casey wear the ugliest one-piece swimsuit she could find in the closet. Which, in all honesty, made no difference whatsoever because she was beautiful regardless of what she wore, but I was much more interested in limiting the amount of her skin Jax got to see. Paxton came over on Sunday with Lynda and the baby, and Casey called Mrs. Winters and invited her over to join us. We all enjoyed the evening talking over a wonderful meal cooked by the ladies. It was pure delight to watch my girl laugh, smile, and look more comfortable than I had ever seen her before.

Chapter Twenty-seven

Casey

What a weekend! It was so good having everyone over on Sunday, and I absolutely loved having Jax here for the weekend. I loved hearing stories from their time in the Marines and their travels. These were things Nate never really talked about much. I had tried to get him to talk about it before, but he just shrugged it off and said it held more bad memories than good, so I didn't want to push him on the subject. But while Jax was here, he seemed a lot more relaxed and open, as though it helped to think about those memories with the support of someone else who was there with him, to help buffer the painful ones.

On Monday morning, after a kiss and hug from Jax with a promise that we had to do this more often and a long, lingering, hot kiss from Nate, they left to pick up Paxton to head to the airport for the flight to D.C. I settled in for a long day of study and revision for my next medical board exam. Later that afternoon, I was down on the beach playing with Chance when I heard my phone ringing. Running up the stairs, I picked it up, looking at the screen that read "Unknown caller," and answering it with a "Hello?" I waited for a voice, but there was nothing, just silence. "Hello?" I said again, but the line was blank. "Damn telemarketers can find you anywhere," I said to myself, cutting off the call and going inside.

After making a sandwich, I took it into the living room along with a glass of milk and got comfy on the couch with a plan of finding a movie to get engrossed in until Nate got back. He texted me when he arrived in D.C., and he also sent me a text letting me know their flight had been delayed and that he should be home around 11 that night. After polishing off the sandwich and milk, I found an old horror movie to watch and curled up on the couch with a blanket and Chance's warm body covering my feet. I must have dozed off because I was woken by him sitting up and growling.

"What's up, boy?" I said, patting the top of his head. His body was stiff, and I noticed a small line of hair along his back sticking up. His eyes were pinned to the front door, and a low growl persisted to roll through his body. Thinking it might be Nate coming up the driveway, I went to the front door to make sure the lights were turned on and looked through the small window next to it, but there was nothing. Walking around the house, I went to every window, looking through them and checking if they were locked with Chance at my side, still not happy. Once I was sure everything was locked up, I sat back on the couch, picked up the remote, and changed the channel, giving Chance another pat. "No more spooky movies for us tonight, hey, boy?" I said to him, convinced he must have heard an animal outside that spooked him.

I climbed into bed just after 11 p.m. that night, unable to stay awake any longer, and fell asleep with the comfortable knowledge that Chance was laying right next to me. The next morning, he was curled up on his bed in the corner of the bedroom, and I had a large, warm body wrapped around my own. I could feel Nate's heavy breathing behind me, telling me he was still asleep. I reached up behind me and stroked my hand through his hair, causing a low moan to rumble in his chest. "What time did you get in?" I asked him.

"Around 1 a.m. Not sure what you got up to yesterday, but you were so out of it, you didn't even stir when I got into bed. Not even when your guard dog over there started growling at me."

"You should have woken me," I said sleepily.

"You forget, sweetheart, watching you sleep is my favorite pastime."

"So, how did it all go?" I asked, trying to ignore his growing erection that was now pressing against my lower back.

"Great. It all went to plan. Now the heavy work begins."

"I'm so proud of you and Paxton. This was a huge deal to organize, and you both did it even with all my problems interfering with the process," I said.

"You will never be a problem. You are a pleasure, and I have a very efficient and smart brother," he said with pride.

"It couldn't have been done without you, either. Don't sell yourself short, Nate. Paxton might be efficient and smart, but your vision, drive, and security knowledge played a huge part, as well."

"I missed you," he breathed into the back of my neck, his warm mouth placing small kisses against my skin.

"I missed you, too," I told him as I rolled over to face him and his huge erection head on.

"Hmm, we both missed you," he said as he pulled me closer, rolling his hips to press his hard shaft against the skin of my stomach.

"I guess we'd better do something to fix that then, huh?"

"You read my mind completely," he breathed, just before his lips hit mine.

The following weeks flew by in a whirlwind of normality. Well, here at home, at least. Not so much for Nate and Paxton at King Security. There, it had become a little hectic since they took on the West Bank contract, which was understandable with the size of the job. They had also taken on another contract from a huge supermarket chain, three more nightclubs, and a couple of private contracts, as well. Needless to say, when Nate came home at night, he was pretty exhausted from the day.

My days, on the other hand, were quite the opposite. Carmel always came early every Monday morning with a plan of helping me around the house, but really, there was nothing for her to do. And she always turned up with a frozen lasagna or casseroles that went straight into the freezer. I had stopped arguing the point that she didn't need to cook for us when I realized that she liked to do it, and she seemed to get so much pleasure from sharing her own family recipes with us. So Mondays became exploration days for us both. We would check websites to find out what was happening around the community and troll street markets looking for bargains. I loved spending time with her. She had become a great friend, and we always seemed to find something to talk about, sometimes for hours out on the back deck as we watched the ocean and sipped on her famous iced sweet tea.

Usually on Tuesdays, Lynda would bring Emily over for a few hours, and we would have lunch and chat. Then she would leave Emily with me for the rest of the afternoon, going home to work on her latest painting. I was so glad that she had started again. Her skill with a paintbrush was just amazing, and I loved spending time with the little tyke while Lynda enjoyed some time to herself. Emily and I spent some quality time together, which included me getting puked and dribbled on several times, not to mention the stench that oozed from her diapers. Now, that was so bad, I'm pretty sure it could melt the wax in your ears. This little bundle of joy was definitely an overall smelly, eating, pooping world champion.

I also got to enjoy the good parts, from the wonderful, fresh, clean baby smell of her soft skin to her little giggles as I blew raspberries against her soft, warm tummy to watching her small, bow-like pink lips as she slept. She was just so beautiful and so thought provoking. Every time I looked at her, I swore my ovaries pulsed with the need to have a baby of my own. Since I had been spending so much time with this little bundle of perfection, I had been thinking more and more about Nate wanting a family some day, and then a pang of guilt hit me hard at the thought of not being able to provide him with his own biological children. We had talked about it, and he was aware of the slim to none chance of me ever being able to get pregnant or even carry a baby to full term after the mess my reproductive system was left in. It was also something I had never really looked into thoroughly, either. I mean, I remembered what the doctors had told me years ago in regards to my possible future infertility due to all the scar tissue inside of my body, but it wasn't something I had ever thought about. At the time, it seemed inconsequential, until now.

Nate would always get home a little earlier on the afternoons that Emily was here. He absolutely loved to spend time playing with his niece. After giving me a quick kiss on the top of my head, he pulled off his boots and got onto the floor to join us in our play. I adored watching him play with Emily, giving her little kisses and watching as his huge, strong hands gently stroked her hair and tickled her tiny feet. Watching him in this way caused a pain to ripple across my heart with the thought of never being able to carry his baby in my belly.

I drew my thoughts back into myself. I didn't want Nate to think that spending time with Emily might be painful for me. I knew how protective he was of me emotionally, and if he ever suspected that by looking after her that I was torturing myself, I knew he would try to shield me from it in any way possible. Thankfully, at the moment, he was too engrossed in playing peek-a-boo with her to notice me immersed in my own deep thoughts.

The next day, he surprised me with an early delivery from a garden center in Florida. He had found me some Jacaranda trees online and had purchased six small spruces to plant around the garden. I was so excited, I almost knocked him down when he walked through the door that night, and let's just say he also got very lucky that night.

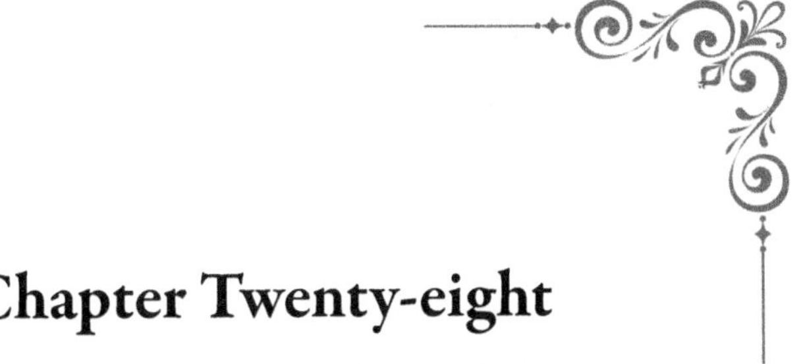

Chapter Twenty-eight

Nate

As soon as I got into my office Monday morning, I received a text from Paxton asking me to come down to his office. Making my way down the hallway toward his door, his secretary, Gloria, an older woman who had worked in that position for at least the last five years, looked up from where she was typing.

"Good morning, Mr. King. Please, go right in."

"Thanks, Gloria," I said as I knocked and then pushed open his door. Paxton's office was the complete opposite of my own. While I liked the huge wall of glass, he liked the windows covered with stiff, gray blinds. My office was tidy and minimal, but his was wall-to-wall bookcases and filing cabinets, all crammed full. His desk held two computer screens and a pile of files and papers so tall I could hardly see him sitting behind them. He stood up from behind his desk looking slightly disheveled, with his suit jacket off, the top button of his crisp, white dress shirt undone, and his tie loosened. He looked stressed, which was an unusual look for my little brother first thing in the morning. Shoving his hands into his dress pant pockets, he leaned against the front of his desk.

"What is it, Paxton?" I asked with concern.

"We have a bit of a problem with one of the private contracts we took on," he breathed out with exasperated annoyance.

"Which one?"

"Barrett Adams."

"The state senator?" I questioned, and he nodded. "What kind of a problem?"

"Well, the contract is for the senator's private protection, right?"

"Yes, for a conference he's attending."

"Well, the senator asked for you to take on the role personally."

"I know, and that's not a problem," I reassured him.

"Yes, well, I didn't think it would be either until I just received his itinerary." Paxton blew out a breath and then reached behind him, grabbing a sheet of paper and handing it to me. Looking down at it, all I saw were three words: "FOUR DAYS" and "LONDON." I looked back up to Paxton with fury.

"Four days in London? For fuck's sake, Paxton, I thought this was a one day gig in the next state or something, not on the other side of the pond!"

"I know. I'm sorry, Nate, I should have asked more questions before I agreed for you to do it," Paxton said, sounding deflated.

"Four days in the U.K.?" I repeated.

"Yes, he's attending the Sedex Conference, and he'll be staying at the Rosewood Hotel near the Covent Gardens in London. That's where you'll be staying, as well."

"Fuck," I seethed. I pushed a hand through my hair, then started to pace his office, trying to contain my anger to keep it from igniting and exploding onto Paxton. I knew it wasn't his fault, but I fucking promised myself that I would never be away from Casey or the office for more than a day. Maybe I could take her with me? No, that wasn't a good idea. Not when I'm on a job doing private protection. I might inadvertently put her in danger if anything happened to the senator while we were there.

"Nate," Paxton said, breaking into my train of thought. Looking up at him, I could see the lines of worry etched on his face.

"Relax, Paxton. I'm not going to rip your head off. I know it's not your fault; it's just business. It's just...I don't like to be away from Casey. Especially for four fucking days in another country."

"I understand. I did try and talk him into having someone else, but he insisted on you. Or we could just cancel the contract. I mean, it might cause a few problems, but I'm sure I could work it out."

"No, Paxton, it's fine. You know once we take on a contract, we see it through to the end," I said, looking at him as he nodded.

"Casey can come stay with us while you're gone. Lynda would love it," he said.

"If only it was that simple. I know her too well. She will insist on staying at home, giving me a big lecture on how she's not a baby, she doesn't need a sitter, and she doesn't want to put you both out." I sighed in frustration at her stubbornness.

Paxton's eyes roamed around his office as we both tried to think of another solution. "What about Mrs. Winters ?" Paxton said suddenly.

"Mrs. Winters?" I asked, perplexed.

"Yes, what if she stays with Casey?"

"Now, that might work," I said, pointing a finger at him.

"It's worth a try, Nate. And I am sorry about all this. I am even pissed at myself. I'm always nagging at you to let others take the risks, and here I am, throwing you into the deep end."

"Like I said, don't worry. It doesn't seem like a risky job. It's more the being away, you know?" I asked, rubbing a finger along my bottom lip in thought.

"Yeah, I do. I wouldn't want to leave my two girls to go over the other side of the pond either," he said with a grimace, and I could see he was pretty disappointed in himself with the whole situation, and it bugged me to see him this way. Moving over to him, I gave him a brotherly slap on the back.

"Don't worry, it'll be fine," I told him, but the look he gave me told me that he would continue to beat himself up over it for the next few days no matter what I said to him.

I pulled into the driveway later that afternoon, and as I got closer to the house, I saw Casey with a shovel in her hand, digging at one side of the house. Pulling up in front of the house, I watched her for just a few moments. She was wearing a thin, white sundress and a pair of sneakers with her beautiful golden hair pulled into a braid down her back. She looked so intense, but humorous at the same time as she rammed the shovel into the ground, scooping dirt from a hole at her feet. As much as I loved to just watch whatever she was doing, I really wanted to take over for her. Climbing out of the car, I walked across the grass to where she was working. I lifted her face to look at me. Her cheeks were flushed, and small beads of sweat trickled down the side of her face. Her smile was wide and beaming. "Hi," she said as she brushed the sweat off her brow with the back of her hand.

"You know I would have helped you with this on Saturday, right?"

"I know, I just thought I would get a head start."

Reaching out for the shovel, I said, "Here, let me. You look hot." Handing me the shovel, she sighed, and I was sure she was happy with my offer as she took a step back and watched as I made quick work of getting the hole to the depth required for the Jacaranda spruce she already had in her hand, ready for planting. An hour later, all six trees were planted in the allocated spots that she randomly picked out around the house. We headed inside and took a shower where I spent some time giving her a more proper and longer greeting with my mouth.

Clean and sweat-free, we sat out on the back deck with a bottle of water each, and I figured it was the perfect moment for me to let her know about my trip. But before I could speak she said, "So, what's on your mind?"

Turning toward her with a raised brow, I took a drink from the water bottle and said, "What makes you think I have something on my mind?"

"Because the muscle in the side of your jaw is twitching, and it only seems to do that if you're pissed at me or you want to talk about something that you think will upset me or piss me off," she said, grinning.

"Hmm, I think I might have to be more aware of that twitching in the future, then."

"Okay, spill it, Mr. King. What's on your mind?" she asked, leaning her head against my shoulder.

"One of the private contracts Paxton took on is private security for a senator attending a conference, who requested me personally," I started.

"Okay, go on," she said slowly.

"It's for four days, and it's in London," I finished. She sat silently for a few minutes.

"Is it dangerous?" she asked quietly.

"No. No, baby, it's not that," I said, realizing that her first thought was worry about my safety. I cupped her face in my hands. I needed her to see my eyes and see that I was far from worried about that.

"Then what is it, Nate?"

"You, baby. I don't want to leave you." I felt the tension ease from her through my hands. She placed her hands over mine.

"Look, I know this is part of your job, Nate, and as long as you're safe, then I'll be fine." Closing my eyes, I leaned my forehead against hers and just breathed her in.

"I love you so fucking much," I said.

"I love you, too. Just be safe," she whispered against my lips, her breath warm with a slight hint of mint.

"Okay, then we need to get inside," I growled.

"Why is that?" she asked with a grin.

"Because I only have the next few days to fuck you on every surface and in every position before I leave, and I want to get my fill of you before I go, so we need to get started right now," I said as I stood, grabbed her hand, and pulled her inside behind me, captivated by her excited giggle as I almost dragged her into the bedroom.

Chapter Twenty-nine

Casey

It was morning, and I stood outside, wrapped tightly in Nate's arms, my hands gripping onto the back of his black, silk dress shirt, and my cheek pressed against his chest. I just needed to absorb him - his touch, his smell, everything. Over the past few days, we had done nothing but be with each other, and I reasoned with myself by reminding myself that I spent many years by myself, and this would be easy. But in those lonely years of mine, I didn't have him, and now that it was time for him to leave, it was more painful than I could have imagined. I closed my eyes and just felt him before he put a finger under my chin, tilting it up to him and placing a soft kiss on my lips.

"You okay?" he asked, his eyes searching mine for confirmation, and I nodded. "Remember to have Mrs. Winters stay over, and if you need anything, just call Paxton, okay?"

"I will."

"I'll call you when I get to the hotel."

"You do that," I said to him, and with one last kiss, I watched as he slid into the Audi, started the engine, and drove off down the driveway and out of my line of sight. Wrapping my arms around my waist, I lost myself for a few moments in the emptiness I was left with until I was brought back to reality by the feeling of a ball being dropped at my feet. When I looked down into Chance's large, brown eyes with his wagging tail and excited tongue hanging out, salivating at the expected play time, it made me smile and scratch the top of his head before picking up the ball and tossing it down the gravel driveway. I laughed as I watched him run after it, and his playfulness made me realize that I was going to be fine, and I wasn't alone.

As expected, Carmel turned up on the doorstep later that morning carrying several bags full of groceries. "You didn't have to bring all that," I said, pointing to the bulging bags as she hefted them onto the kitchen island.

"I know, but I have plans for us," she said with a wicked grin.

"Oh yes, what kind of plans?"

"I thought we might do some old-fashioned baking. You know, cook us up a batch of double chocolate fudge brownies and some chocolate chips cookies."

"Oh my, that does sound good," I said, my mouth watering at the thought.

"Yeah, well there ain't nothing better when you're feeling blue than watching a good movie and eating yourself into a chocolate coma. It always eases the pain," she said, giving me a wink.

"You are such a gem," I said, giving her a hug of appreciation that she knew exactly how I felt without me having to say anything.

And that was how we spent our day - covered in flour, sugar, and chocolate with the sweet, warm smells penetrating the walls of every room in the house. It was heavenly. We didn't even bother to cook anything for dinner because we were so full just from licking our fingers and tasting everything. By the time we sunk into the couch and looked for a movie to watch, we were both starting to feel too sick in the stomach to even think about eating anything for the rest of the week. After the movie, which Carmel chose (big mistake because I should have known she would want to watch an old cowboy movie that seemed to never end), I locked up the house, showed Carmel to the guest room that I had made up earlier, and said goodnight before getting into bed, which, at the moment, seemed way too big and empty without Nate's large frame in it. Pulling his pillow close to my body and inhaling his musky, clean scent, I hugged it tight and fell asleep.

Startled by my phone ringing, I reached out toward the bedside table and saw Nate's name flash across the screen. I answered it with a sleepy, "Hi."

"Sorry I woke you, baby. I know it's late," he said, and the sound of his voice put a smile on my lips instantly. Sitting up, I rubbed my eyes.

"No, I'm glad you did. I wanted you to," I reassured him. "How was your flight?"

"Long and boring."

"What, even in business class?" I asked, smiling to myself.

"Yes, because I didn't have you as my blanket."

"Are you at the hotel?"

"Yeah, I'm going to take a shower and get some sleep. I need to be up early in the morning. I just wanted to call and hear your voice. I miss you."

"I miss you, too. So much," I said, cradling the phone tenderly like I was actually touching him.

"I know, it feels wrong being without you."

"It'll go fast," I said.

"It better because I will not be doing it again. Is Mrs. Winters there with you?"

"Yes, she turned up with bags full of food, and we did some baking," I said, smiling as I remembered how much fun I'd had.

"Yeah, well, she's a great cook."

"That she is. At this rate, I'll be twice as big by the time you get back," I laughed.

"Good, more of you for me to play with," he said playfully, and I could feel his grin radiating through the phone. With a hesitant goodbye, I hung up the phone and lay down to cuddle back up to his pillow.

I awoke to the wonderful, mouth-watering smell of bacon frying. The odor streaming through the air and under the bedroom door made my stomach growl in response. Getting up and pulling on a pair of shorts and t-shirt, I made my way out to the kitchen, following the smell in a trance.

Carmel was standing at the stove when I entered the kitchen. She looked up from the frying pan that she was concentrating on as she moved crispy bacon and fried eggs around in it. "Morning, sugar, did you sleep well?" she asked, her southern drawl stronger this morning.

"Yes, thank you. Nate called around 1 a.m. He got to the hotel in London," I told her.

"Oh, that's good to hear. You hungry?" she asked as she pulled a couple of plates from the overhead cupboard.

"Starving."

"Then you go sit down, and I'll fix you a plate. This is ready for eating," she said and started to serve what looked like a huge helping of bacon, eggs, and fried potatoes. "There you go, honey, tuck in," she said, placing the plate in front of me.

Holy crap, there was enough food on my plate to feed at least four people. I was still staring at my plate when she brought two glasses of orange juice to the table followed by her own plate. She picked up her fork and noticed I was still staring at my plate of food.

"Come on, eat up," she said, pointing to my plate with her fork.

"All of it?" I asked, wide-eyed.

"Yep, every last bite," she said, giving me a cheeky, playful grin.

"I'll do my best," I said, diving into the mountain of bacon and filling my mouth with it. There was no way on earth I was able to finish it all, but I did manage to convince her that I would keep the rest for lunch later. Carmel left around 10 a.m. to run some errands, and there were some things to take care of at the penthouse. I knew that Nate would rather have had her stay here with me the whole time, but she was very proud and particular about her job, and she liked to keep on top of the cleaning at the penthouse. She told me that it only took one day of not dusting, and the place would look like a crop duster had flown through. It did take a little convincing on my part in reassuring her that I would be fine, and that she shouldn't change her routine because of Nate's overprotective nature. Eventually, she relented, even agreeing to me cooking a meal for her tonight. Yes! I was starting to win with this woman.

After tidying up the kitchen, I went back into the bedroom to make the bed that I had hastily exited this morning. Tucking the sheets into my side of the bed, I spotted a hair tie on the floor. Picking it up, I opened the drawer on the bedside table to put it back into a small heart-shaped container that I kept in there. While I was putting my hair tie in the container, my fingers brushed against my mother's diary. I pulled it out and sat on the side of the bed. I ran my fingers over the thin, leather lace that was wrapped around it and tied in a bow at the front. The whole book was bound in leather with my mother's initials carved into the front cover. In the corner were small, carved flower heads surrounded by tiny leaves. Someone had spent a lot of time crafting it, and I wondered for a moment if maybe my father had made it for her. Thinking back to my childhood, I couldn't actually remember much about him at all. I never saw him do anything physical around the house, like mowing the lawn or gardening. I never even saw him tinkering under the hood of the car. He mostly stayed in his study when he was at home, and I was pretty sure if he had made something as elegant as this diary, my mother would have surely bragged to her friends when they came over for her elaborate dinner parties that took place at least once a month.

I winced as I remembered those dinner parties. I knew when one was coming up, due to the ugly, frilly dresses that would appear on the end of my bed, along with a frilly pair of white socks and a pair of shiny, polished black shoes. It reminded me of an outfit for an old style baby doll, with layers of taffeta and bows. I was always instructed to take a bath, wash my hair, and get dressed. Then, she would come up to my room and do her inspection, making sure everything was in place just how she liked it. I would also receive a lecture on how she expected me to behave in front of her friends that evening, which usually consisted of me standing up straight with my hands behind my back, smile, be polite, and answer only if spoken to. Once the façade was over, I was sent up to my room to change, which was the best part because the dresses were always uncomfortable and itchy. After dinner, I was expected to be in bed, my dress neatly hung in the closet when mother came up with a sandwich and a glass of milk and a small after dinner mint as a treat for behaving myself. Getting the dress off and savoring the dark chocolate with its minty center was the best part of those dinner parties.

Looking down at the book in my hand, I contemplated opening it. Did I really want to know what was written on the pages? It was a diary...maybe if I read it, I might have a better understanding of my mother's feelings, her thoughts. Torn between wanting to read it and wanting to burn it, I realized that if I didn't want to read it, then I would never have saved it from the box it was in and brought it with me. Pulling the leather lace bow, I unwrapped the book from its bindings and opened the stiff cover. On the top right-hand corner were the words, "My darling Corrine, love always, David." The diary started on the 1st of January 1985, so I guessed it must have been a Christmas present from my father, and she had dutifully started writing in it at the start of a new year.

As I started scanning through the pages at her neat, flowing handwriting, I noticed that her words were so shallow and pompous. She discussed various cases she was working on. Not in detail, and without any names, of course, but she would also write down her thoughts of people that she worked with, which were just nasty and derogatory, and she did name those people. Names that were very familiar. As I kept reading, it struck me like a lightning bolt that all of these people that she talked about with such malice and hatred were the people that attended her monthly dinner parties. Flipping through the pages, I read as she talked about their cheap clothes and endless trips into hospital for plastic surgery, affairs, and gossip. This woman was just a pure bitch. Slamming the book closed, I placed it back into the drawer, wiping my hands down my thighs as though it would wipe the stain of her hateful words away. My thoughts were broken by the vibrating sound of my phone as it silently rang and moved across the bedside table. Picking it up, I pressed the green accept button and put it to my ear.

"Hi," I breathed out shakily.

"Casey?" Nate said, his voice sounding concerned. "Are you okay?"

"Yes, I'm fine. Did you get some sleep?" I asked, trying to brighten my tone.

"Don't change the subject," he growled. "What's wrong?"

"Nothing. I was just in the bedroom looking for something, and I was getting frustrated at not finding it," I said more confidently.

Silence.

"Nate?"

"I'm here."

"Are you okay?" I asked, now concerned that he wasn't.

"I'm fine. It's you I'm concerned about. When you answered, you sounded...agitated. Upset."

"Well, I'm fine. Honestly, you just caught me when I was starting to get pissed off at all the crap in the closet, that's all. Now, tell me about you," I said, trying to steer the conversation off of me and on to him. Just when I thought I was starting to lose this battle, he sighed over the line.

"I'm fine, just missing you."

"I know that feeling well. I am missing you like crazy, too. So, what are your plans for today, Mr. King?"

"I'm escorting the senator to his conference, then he has a dinner to attend after. Then, back to the hotel."

"Sounds exciting."

"Yeah, about as exciting as getting my fingernails pulled out with a rusty pair of pliers."

"Come on, it can't be that bad. What about seeing some of London while you're there?"

"No time for that. Anyway, I've seen it plenty of times before, I just..." he trailed off, and I could hear the frustration in them.

"I know, I feel the same. Just try and relax. The more you think about it, the longer time will drag, okay?"

"Yeah, I know. You're right."

"I know I am," I said, grinning.

"Oh, crap, did I just say that out loud?" he asked with a playful tone in his voice. "Damn."

"You sure did, and you can't take it back," I laughed. I was so glad he sounded less tense than when I first answered the phone. We chatted for a while longer as he told me about his room, the food, and the weather before he let out a relaxed sigh.

"I love hearing your voice," he said.

"Yes, well, I think we may have become addicted to each other because I love hearing yours, too. Is that a bad thing?" I asked him.

"Nope, and if it is, then I am really, really bad."

After hanging up with Nate, I glanced at the drawer in the bedside table again, thinking about the diary inside of it. I felt the need to read more now that I had started it, and yet I also felt like I should leave it. After a few moments, I decided to leave it where it was for now. By the time Carmel came back later that afternoon, I had cooked us a chicken curry with vegetables and rice, heaped some into two bowls, and we sat and ate in front of the TV. This was starting to feel like a girls' weekend, sitting around watching old movies and chatting. She was curious about Australia. My home country was a subject that I could ramble on about for hours, and I did. By the time we had eaten, done the dishes, and tidied up the kitchen, she let out a big yawn, making me realize that this poor woman had been gone all day working, so I fixed us both a mug of hot chocolate and ushered her off to bed.

I took my own mug into my bedroom and climbed into bed. Chance jumped on the bottom and stretched himself out. "You better enjoy it while you can because in a couple of days, you will be back in your own bed," I said, giving him a smile and a scratch behind his ears. Opening the drawer and pulling out the diary, I laid it on my lap and stared at it as I sipped my hot chocolate.

Chapter Thirty

Casey

Still staring at it half an hour later, I placed my empty mug on the bedside table and let temptation get the better of me. I opened up the diary to the last page I had read. By looking at the dates at the top of each page, she didn't seem to write in it every day, but at least one or two times a week. A lot of what she wrote, I considered egotistical shit. And that was being nice. She was just so shallow and self-centered, so unemotional that the only thing she seemed to talk about with any form of enthusiasm was herself and occasionally my father. Flipping through the pages and skimming over her words, I glanced back up to the date again at the top of the page and looked at the year: 1985. My stomach did a tiny somersault as I went through the math in my brain, trying to count back from when I was born. I flipped the pages past April and May until I got to June, 1st, 2nd, 3rd, nothing. 4th, 5th, nothing. And then on the 6th, there it was, right in front of my eyes, so clear and shocking for me to see that I dropped the diary back onto the bed as I put both hands to my mouth with a gasp.

Staring down at the open book on the bed in front of me was all I could do. I never thought when I started reading it that it would bring me to my mother's feelings while she was pregnant with me, yet just a glance at her words on the paper caused me to feel torn once again, not sure of whether I should continue to read or stop. Getting up from the bed, I walked into the kitchen, and made myself a hot cup of tea to take back into the bedroom. Sitting back on the bed, I leaned back against the headboard and sipped my tea, my eyes glued to the still open diary like if I blinked, it was going to close itself and disappear or something. Or maybe that's what I really wanted it to do? Fuck, this was crazy. Finishing off my tea, I picked up the diary and started to read.

JUNE 6TH, 1985

Today, I feel as though my life is over. I went to see Dr. Woods about some worrying symptoms that I thought may be due to early menopause last week. I had some blood tests done while I was there, and I have just received a phone call from her with the results. It seems that I am expecting a baby. I'm not sure it has fully sunk in yet, even after talking to David about it. He was just as shocked as I was, as our whole married life we have been so very careful. What is even more devastating is that David will not even consider having an abortion, as it's against God's will. This is something I am unprepared for. I cannot find the words to describe how I am feeling at the moment, and with no abortion or even giving the child up for adoption after it's born. David said if it's God's will that we must have a child, then we will abide by it. I think it has nothing to do with God, as this child is a curse and I am beside myself.

I wasn't sure how one should feel as they were reading their mother's experience and emotional state on the day she found out she was pregnant, but after reading her words, I was pretty sure it wasn't hatred. For most women, it would be a joyful day, but not for this emotionally inept one. Turning the page, it had skipped to the following week.

June 13th, 1985

I am still in a state of turmoil with this thing growing inside of me. It makes me feel so tired, and the constant feeling of illness makes it very hard to get through the day at the office. I have no plan of telling anyone until I really have to, as it will be hard to hide the shame and pretend to be happy about the whole thing. Dr. Woods has advised me to limit my wine to one glass a day, but I have no intentions of doing that. In fact, I may increase it, and when this constant sickness wears off, I am going to take up running in the afternoons. Maybe with the increased alcohol consumption and vigorous exercise, this thing may just fall out of its own accord.

Slamming the book closed in fury at the thought of this woman trying on purpose to harm an innocent baby made bile start to rise in my belly. What made it even worse was that the innocent baby was me.

Shoving the diary into the bedside drawer, I switched off the lamp and snuggled down under the covers, reaching for Nate's pillow to cuddle into, taking comfort in the knowledge that he would be home soon. I woke early the next morning after a terrible night. I guess that's what you get for reading a horror story just before you go to sleep. After I showered and dressed, I went out into the kitchen and started making some breakfast for Carmel before she headed off for work.

Throughout the day, as much as I tried, I just couldn't get my mother's words out of my head. I mean, I knew she was a bitch, but I think when I decided to read her diary I thought I might find some kind of reason for why she hated me so much. I guess I was looking for some kind of silver lining amongst the shitty clouds of my childhood. I had, and so far, I was getting exactly what my parents had given me my whole life...nothing. My phone started to ring just after lunch. Picking it up, I saw Paxton's name on the screen. "Hey, Paxton," I answered.

"How you doing, Casey?" he asked.

"I'm great. Missing Nate, but I'm good."

"Yep, I miss the asshole, as well, but he'll be back tomorrow."

"What time does his flight get in?" I asked.

"Around five in the afternoon. I offered to pick him up, but he took the Audi and left it in long-term parking. He said he wanted to get home fast, and something along the lines of me driving like an old lady," he chuckled.

"Well, Paxton, I like old lady driving just fine."

"Listen, I just wanted to let you know that I organized your volunteer work at the free clinic. All your paperwork came through from the medical board, so I thought you might be eager for something to do until you get an internship at the hospital."

"That's great, Paxton, I'm really looking forward to it."

"Good. I just wanted to double check and to see when you might want to start?"

"As soon as they need me," I answered eagerly.

"They're a free clinic, Casey. They wanted you, like, yesterday," he said with amusement.

"Well, any day next week will be fine."

"Okay. I'll get on it today, and I'll give you a call and let you know when."

"Thanks, Paxton, for everything."

"For you, Casey, anything."

After hanging up the phone, I took Chance out for a walk on the beach, and he decided to take a swim. I had to admit, he looked like he was having a great time trying to bite at the frothy waves along the shoreline. Just watching him with his mouth wide open, tongue hanging out aimlessly, snapping at thin air made me laugh so much I almost peed myself a little. Taking him back up the back deck stairs, I gave him a spray with the hose to get the sand out of his fur, then started to rub him down with a beach towel. When I heard my phone ring in the kitchen, I was torn between answering it and letting him inside still wet. I let it ring out and finished drying him off. When I got back inside, I picked the phone up off the kitchen island. Looking down at the screen, it showed a missed call from Carmel, so I pressed her number.

"Casey?" she answered, sounding a little annoyed.

"Carmel, are you okay?" I asked, concerned at the tone of her voice.

"Yes, honey, I'm fine. I just wanted to call and let you know I might be late. My damn car got a flat, and I had to call triple A. I'm waiting on them now."

"That's a pain in the arse. Are you alright, though?"

"Yes, sugar, I'm fine. Just not sure when I'll get there."

"Well, are you close to your apartment?" I asked her.

"About ten minutes, why?"

"Once your flat is fixed, why don't you just go home? You will be exhausted."

"That's okay, honey, I don't mind."

"Well, I do. I would be much happier if you went straight home."

"What about you?"

"I'm fine. Nate will be home tomorrow," I said, giving her as much reassurance as I could because I knew how stubborn this woman was.

"I don't know, Casey...I promised Mr. King," she started to say, but I quickly cut her off.

"Please, Carmel, I'm fine. I promise. In fact, I think I'll be having an early night tonight." After a short pause in the conversation, I heard her let out a sigh.

"Well, if you're sure about this?"

"I'm sure, Carmel. I would rather you go home and get a good night's sleep after such a long day than drive all the way down here to babysit me," I chuckled.

"Well, okay. Just as long as you call me if you need me, okay?"

"I promise. Just send me a text when you get home safe."

"I will, sugar. You make sure you lock up the house," she said, her voice taking on a stern, motherly tone.

"I will."

After locking up the house so securely that a fly couldn't even sneak in, I made myself a bowl of chicken soup from a can in the cupboard and sat on the couch in the living room, flicking the TV on to watch the local news and weather. Later, after cleaning up and taking a shower, I was just coming out of the bathroom, wrapped in a towel, when I heard my phone ringing again. I rushed to get to it without slipping on the floor with my wet feet. I grabbed it, pressed the green button, and put it to my ear.

"Hello?" Nothing, just silence. Looking down at the screen, there wasn't even a name or number on the screen. Lifting it back up to my ear, I tried again. "Hello?" Still hearing nothing, I hung up and dropped the phone back onto the kitchen table. Maybe it was just a wrong number, unless Nate was trying to call me from the phone in his hotel room? Thinking that the caller was most likely him, I made sure I took my phone with me into the bedroom, placing it on the bedside table. I changed for bed, and with Chance already staking his claim on the bottom half of the bed, I clicked the lock on the bedroom door and slid in between the sheets. Then, I reached into the drawer and pulled out the diary. I'm not sure why I seemed to be so compelled to read it, but I was. I felt like it was some kind of history that I needed to know even if it was a hard one to read. But as I opened it up to the last page I read, I just wished that I wasn't so hungry for information from this woman I once called mother.

July 1st, 1985

I haven't been well enough to write anything in this journal, which is a real shame because I do find it very cathartic after a long day in court, which is what I had today. I spoke to David about the child, but he is not interested, which is alright for him because he's not having to put up with all the relentless exhaustion and sickness. I did tell a few of my closest friends, who were very happy and excited for some reason, so I just gave them my best smile when they congratulated me. Why someone would be so excited about the indignity of going through childbirth and then being stuck with another responsibility for so many years, I have no idea. I need to put it out of my mind because just the thought makes me feel even sicker.

Chance shifted on the bed and moved up closer to me. For a moment, I wondered if he sensed the tension radiating through my body. Leaning my head against the headboard, I placed my hand on the top of his head and softly stroked his thick fur, the action bringing me some well-needed comfort before I picked up the book again. The new entry jumped almost two months ahead.

September 10th, 1985

Well, I am starting to grow out of my clothes. This disgusting bulge has made it impossible to wear any of my pants, and I really don't want to go out and waste money on maternity clothes. After all, they will never be used again. I spent the afternoon looking through my wardrobe, and I have managed to find some loose-fitting dresses and some skirts with a little more room in them, so tomorrow, I will go into town and purchase a good, strong fitting corset. That should keep this bulge under some control. I really hate my body at the moment. David said that we will need to employ a nanny to look after the child when it is born, but that will not be happening. Mrs. Dawson, the housekeeper, has agreed to look after it through the week, so I will just look for a babysitter for the weekends. I have promised myself that I will not allow this child to cause any undue disruptions to our lives, and I plan to keep that promise.

Closing the book, I slipped it back into the drawer and then pinched the bridge of my nose, searching for some kind of understanding and tolerance for this woman somewhere deep inside, but I came up empty. I had nothing, so I pulled the bed covers up around me, closed my eyes, and fell asleep.

The next time I opened my eyes, it was still dark outside, and I wondered what the time was, but before I could pick up my phone to check, Chance jumped up into a sitting position. His ears pricked up, and a low growl emanated from deep in his belly, causing me to sit up as well. Stroking a hand down his back to calm him, I said, "Hey, boy, what's the matter?" But he didn't move from his rigid stance, his eyes still locked on the bedroom door. Cautiously, I got up from the bed and turned on the main light before moving to the window. Chance jumped down onto the floor and sat in front of the door. Moving the blinds away from the window, I looked out onto the back deck. I couldn't see anything, but something was bothering him. opening the closet I pull out Nate's baseball bat and slowly click back the bolt the lock on the bedroom door. Opening it and quietly making my way down the hall turning lights on as I go.

Chance bolted out and ran ahead of me as soon as the door opened, and he started running from window to window, jumping up at each, pushing his head under the blinds, growling. His persistent agitation was starting to make my stomach roll with anxiety as I moved over to the back door and peered through the glass pane. I turned on the outside security light, illuminating the back deck only to see a dark figure jump over the side of the deck railing and take off down the side of the house. The shock of actually seeing someone out there made me jump back from the door with a yelp.

"Chance, come," I commanded as I almost ran back up the hall and into the bedroom, slamming the door and locking it behind me. Grabbing my phone, I saw that it was just after 5 a.m. "Shit, shit, shit," I cursed as I pulled up my contacts list and scrolled through until I found Paxton's number. I tapped it, and it started to ring. "Come on, come on," I chanted as it kept ringing.

"Casey?" Paxton answered groggily.

"Paxton, someone is at the house." I spoke fast and urgently enough for him to realize something was wrong.

"What?" he asked, now sounding wide awake.

"Something woke me up, and Chance was growling. I turned on all the lights, and when I looked out onto the back deck, I saw someone jump over the rails."

"Okay, where are you now?"

"Locked in the bedroom."

"Stay right where you are, I'm on my way," he said, and I heard Lynda's sleepy voice asking what was wrong and Paxton telling her that everything was okay. "Stay on the phone with me, okay?" he said, and I heard the muffled sounds of him moving around and then the jingle of the keys. He talked to me as he got into his car, then put me on speaker phone once I heard him start to drive. Within ten minutes, he said, "Okay, I'm pulling into the driveway now. Just stay in the bedroom until I look around."

"Please, Paxton, be careful," I said as I sat in the middle of the bed, holding onto Chance's collar as he growled at what was now Paxton outside.

"I can't see anyone, Casey. Everything looks okay out here. You can come open the door and let me in."

"Okay." I hung up and unlocked the bedroom door. I made my way to the front door, turning the lock and opening it to a frazzled-looking Paxton. His hair was messy, and his shorts and t-shirt looked like they were on inside out, making me feel instantly guilty as he walked inside.

"I'm so sorry, Paxton," I said, looking down at my hands twisting nervously together.

"Shit, Casey. No, don't be sorry. I'm glad you called me. Come here." He pulled me into his arms and hugged me hard, rubbing his hands up and down my back. "Are you okay?"

"Yeah, it was just unexpected, I guess. Maybe it was a stray dog or something," I said, second guessing what I saw outside, wondering now if I had made a mistake.

"Not sure, but there's nothing out there now."

"Let me at least make you a cup of coffee before you leave. I feel like such an idiot." I led him into the kitchen where I fixed us both a cup of coffee. As we sat down at the kitchen table, the sun just started to rise outside.

"I thought Mrs. Winters was staying with you?" he asked.

"She has been, but she had a flat tire on her way back, and she was waiting for Triple A. She was closer to home, and I didn't want her to drive out here after that," I said, shrugging.

"You should have called me earlier. I would have come out and got you to stay with us for the night," he said with a scowl.

"I was fine, Paxton, and I have Chance with me."

"I guess. So, has anything else been happening? You know, anything out of the ordinary?"

"Not that I can think of. Oh, wait! Not sure if this is anything, but I have had a couple of phone calls where no one talks. They just hang up."

"What the fuck, Casey! When?" he demanded.

"Last week. Then one last night."

"Why didn't you say anything?"

"I don't know. Last week, I thought it was probably one of those telemarketers. I thought the one last night might have been Nate trying to call me from the hotel phone in his room."

"Jesus, fuck...," he spat out as he pulled out his phone.

"What are you doing?"

"Calling Nate."

"No, Paxton. He'll be back today. If you call him now, he'll be pissed off the whole trip back. Please, just let me tell him when he gets home." I was pleading with him, and I watched as his face changed with understanding.

"Fine, but if you don't tell him as soon as he gets back, I will," he said as he rubbed a hand through his hair in agitation. "Fuck. If he finds out that I didn't tell him, he'll kick my ass."

"I promise I'll tell him," I said with the sweetest smile I could manage as I took a sip from my cup.

After some persuasive talking on my part that it was now daylight, and I would be perfectly fine, I managed to convince Paxton to go home to his family. Giving him a thankful hug and promising once again to talk to Nate as soon as he was back, he finally left, and I let Chance outside to take care of his business before I jumped into the shower and relaxed under the hot water.

Chapter Thirty-one

Nate

London is a beautiful place to visit, but the next time I travel here, it will be with Casey. This whole being apart from each other, even if it was only for four days, was unsettling. A very unusual feeling for me after all the traveling I've done over the years. I had never experienced such a feeling of emptiness like I had over these past four days. The job itself was a piece of cake. No drama or being asked to supply anything illegal for the senator's pleasure. In fact, Barrett Adams was one of the good guys. He was married with a couple of kids, and I could see that he was just as anxious to get home to his family as I was.

The KLM flight left dead on time from Heathrow Airport at 6:30 a.m., and as the plane took off, we left a pretty dark and rainy London behind as we climbed into the clouds. This trip had only one stop in Amsterdam for almost an hour, then connected to Delta Airlines for the remaining twelve-hour flight, getting me back into PDX just after midday. I was not even going to think about the time difference. All I knew was that I intended to slip on some earphones, lay back and watch a movie, and hopefully fall asleep until we landed. That hope went right out the damn window because as soon as I closed my eyes, all I could see was Casey sitting on the beach, tossing the ball for that mutt while we talked on the phone yesterday afternoon. We had managed to fit in a few short phone calls through the day, but damn, it was hard to hear her voice and not be able to touch her warm, soft skin as we talked. It might have only been for four days, but it was four days too many. I guess I had to admit that I was just addicted to the woman, and that was an addiction I could live with. Three glasses of scotch later, I finally fell asleep with the thought of my girl in my mind.

After landing at PDX, it didn't take long to grab my bag and head over to the secured parking lot to pick up the Audi. As I pulled out onto the road home, I pressed Paxton's number on my phone and put it on speaker. He picked up on the second ring.

"Nate?"

"Hey, Paxton, I just landed, and I'm heading home unless you need me to call into the office on the way?"

"No, everything's good here. Glad you're back. How was it?"

"Fine. Everything ran smoothly. Glad to leave the miserable weather behind though."

"I bet you are. You just head on home. We'll catch up later. I'm sure you'll be ready for some sleep."

"I'm ready for something, but I can tell you right now that it's not sleeping." I grinned to myself.

"Alright, keep your dirty bed play to yourself. I'll call you later," he laughed.

"Okay, talk later." Hanging up, I concentrated on the road and not the painful ache in my crotch that was growing exponentially with every mile.

I pulled into the driveway, my anticipation almost killing me as I dialed Casey's number. When she answered, I just said, "Baby, I'm almost at the front door, so you had better lock that mutt in the spare room."

"What?" was all she could sputter out.

"You heard me, do it now," I said and hung up just as I pulled to a sliding stop on the gravel outside. I jumped out of the car and ran up the front steps. I reached the front door as she opened it, and

I was dazzled by her beautiful smile. Before she could say a word, I wrapped my hand around the back of her neck, pulling her close to me. My mouth crashed down on hers, and I took it with the ferocity of a starving man because that's exactly what I felt like - starved for her. Snaking my arm around her waist, I pulled her hard against my body as I took all that I needed from her mouth.

With our mouths still connected, I ran both my hands down to her plump ass and lifted her up before moving back and sitting her on the entry table. "I'm so glad you're wearing a dress today," I growled into her ear before gently biting the lobe.

"Why is that?" she asked breathlessly.

I answered her by lifting up the short sundress, slipping a hand into her panties, pulling them down her legs, and dropping them onto the floor. "Because I need to be inside of you right now," I said, taking her mouth again with mine and drinking her in. I felt her own urgency in her hands as she reached down, undoing my belt and the button of my jeans. She slid the zipper down and fisted my hard erection in her soft, warm hand, sliding it up and down twice before I needed to take over. Nudging her legs further apart, I slid my shaft over her sex, coating it in her hot, wet juices. As she wrapped her legs around my waist, I plunged into her with one swift move, fully sheathing myself in her warmth from root to tip, causing her to let out a small squeal. "I'm sorry, baby, are you okay?" I asked, panting out the words.

"Yes," she breathed, and I started to pump into her with long, hard, deep strokes. Our mouths and tongues danced against each other, mingled with the sounds of pleasurable moans and heated breaths, losing ourselves in each other. Breaking the kiss, she threw back her head and screamed out my name, her thighs tightening around my waist as her sex throbbed and pulsated, causing me to lose myself in her. Thrusting into her one last time, I reached my own frenzied climax and came deep inside her body. Leaning my forehead against hers, both of us panting, she said, "I guess you missed me then?"

"That is a fucking understatement," I said, placing a kiss on the tip of her nose. "That will never be happening again."

"What, the spontaneous sex at the front door before I even get a hello?" She grinned wickedly at me.

"Now, that will definitely be happening again, but being away from you for more than a day? Never again unless you come with me," I said. Her hands smoothed through my hair as we stayed exactly where we were until our breathing slowed. With her legs still wrapped tightly around my waist and me still inside of her, I took a careful and slow walk to the bedroom, gently laying her on the bed before pulling out of her, rolling to the side, and pulling her close into my body. We lay there for several minutes with her cheek pressed against my chest. I was lost in the beauty and feel of her soft hair as I aimlessly combed my fingers through it. Damn, it was so good to be home.

"So, how was your trip?" Casey asked, breaking the silence.

"Hell without you," I told her, and she playfully slapped my chest, lifting her head to look at me.

"You already told me that. I mean, overall, how was it?"

"Well, compared to any other job I've done in private protection, it was pretty tame. The Senator is a nice, quiet family man. No fancy requests at 3 in the morning, no drunken bar fights, no picking up women on the side of the road for him..." I started to say, but Casey cut my words off with a death stare from hell.

"Wait, what? Drunken bar fights? Women?"

"Yeah. Well, normally these senators like to play hard once they get away from their wives, but Adams was different."

"And by different, you mean he chose to respect his marriage vows and his wife while he was at this conference?" she asked, her voice strained with venom.

"Hey, calm down. Nothing happened."

"I'm glad to hear that because if I thought that you were out supplying a Senator with some tits and arse for the night, I'd have your balls in a vice grip by now," she said, sliding her hand down and stopping on said balls. Her action and rising temper made me laugh as I pulled her to lay on top of me. She struggled a little, but I tightened my arms around her, keeping her in place.

"You know, I can think of a lot of better things for you to do with my balls rather than rip them off."

My words brought her eyes to mine. "This isn't funny, Nate. It's disgusting."

I tried to rein in my laughter at her spiking temper that I could see in the thin line of her lips and the pinkness rising in her cheeks. I said, "I know, baby. You're right, and like I said, nothing happened. I was just messing with you."

"You're just saying that now to save your balls," she said, eyeing me with suspicion. I couldn't help the laugh that escaped my mouth.

"Well, I am rather attached to them."

"Why would you say that, you shithead?" She smiled and softened in my arms, laying her head down on my chest. I kissed the top of her head.

"Yeah, I know, I just couldn't help it. I just love it when you get fired up." With that, I rolled her over until she lay under me, and I proceeded to make up for the last four days of not being able to have her.

Chapter Thirty-Two

Casey

Waking up with Nate stretched out next to me felt so good. I missed his warm body in bed, and now here he was. He looked exhausted from the flight. Sliding from the bed and scooping my dress from the floor, I was about to leave the bedroom when a thought hit me as I got to the door. Turning back to my bedside table, I slowly slid open the drawer and pulled out the diary, then quietly left the bedroom and headed down to the kitchen, slipping my sundress on as I walked. I let Chance out of the spare room and out onto the back porch while I searched through the freezer for one of Carmel's frozen casseroles before taking it out and sliding into the oven, turning the heat on low to give Nate a good few hours to sleep.

Grabbing a bottle of water from the refrigerator, I went outside and sat in one of the chairs on the back deck, closing my eyes, and breathing in the fresh, salty sea air for a few minutes before opening the diary, readying myself for more of my mother's wonderfully brutal words.

November 2nd, 1985

Damn this child. Not even born yet, but is making my life a misery. Besides my growing belly, it moves around at the most inconvenient times, like when I am trying to sleep, or even worse, when I am with a client. Everyone around me always wants to touch my belly and feel the baby move, a feeling that disgusts me. I lay awake the other night thinking, "Why? Why me? What did I do to deserve this punishment?"

I will be glad when it is over and done with, and I can go back to living my life.

December 24th, 1985

Well, it's Christmas Eve, and I am sitting in my office, enjoying a large glass of brandy and feeling miserable with the thought that this will be the last year that David and I will be alone. I have tried to talk to him about my feelings, but he just doesn't want to listen. He just makes comments about how other women do it all the time, or that I am overreacting, and I need to pull myself together. Easy for him to say. I am finding that even my feelings for David at the moment are questionable. This baby has done exactly what I knew it would do: ruined my life and my marriage.

February 20th, 1986

Today, I went to my doctor's appointment. All seems to be on track for the birth, although my doctor has suggested that I have a cesarean section due to having a small pelvis. I must admit, the thought of being put to sleep instead of enduring the hours of labor pain sounds perfectly fine to me. The best news today was that I have a date for the birth, so I can plan my calendar to fit around it, which means less disruption to my schedule than I expected. It seems there might just be a silver lining for me after all.

March 10th, 1986

Free at last! I have my body back. The child was born on the 1st of March as planned, and because of the surgery, I didn't have to see her straight away. Yes, a daughter apparently weighing 7lbs. 5oz. The nurses keep telling me how beautiful she is and sympathize that I have been too ill to see her, but they just don't know how wonderful it feels to have my body back and finally be free of the burden. David has been to visit me. He told me that he has called the child Catherine, after his mother. Seems a fitting name as I couldn't stand the old witch.

The last sentence actually made my stomach roll with nausea, I just couldn't understand where all her hatred came from. I thought that by reading her diary, I might get a small glimpse into what drove her to be so evil, but so far I saw nothing. No drugs or poverty, no constant beatings from a husband. She seemed to have a pretty great life, so why the hell did she hate me so much? I mean, I didn't ask to be born. I didn't ask for any of it, and the more I read her words, the more I realized she was just a selfish, self-indulgent, spiteful poor excuse for a human being. I just couldn't seem to fathom how anyone could have those types of thoughts and feelings about an innocent baby.

I was still lost in my thoughts when I heard the ding of the oven timer letting me know that dinner was ready. As I pulled the dish out of the oven, Nate walked out of the bedroom in his low slung sleep pants. Looking up at his messy black hair, unshaven face, and those perfect V lines that disappeared down the front of his pants, the dish almost slipped from my oven gloved hands. Standing up and quickly sliding it onto the stove top, I managed to pull myself back into reality.

"Hi, did you get good sleep?" I asked Nate, watching him slowly amble toward me and pull me into his arms.

"I did. Sorry, I didn't mean to sleep the day away."

"Don't be silly, you needed it. Are you hungry?"

"Hmm, but not for food," he moaned into my neck.

"Well, that's tough luck for you because dinner is ready," I said, pulling away to get some plates out and take them to the table before grabbing the beef casserole and placing it in the middle along with some crusty bread rolls and motioning for Nate to sit. As soon as he placed the first forkful of delicious tender meat into his mouth, his eyes closed with a moan. "Mrs. Winters?"

"Yep, she is a fantastic cook, plus the fact that I can't seem to stop her from supplying us with endless frozen meals."

"Good, don't even think of stopping her," Nate said, scooping more of the casserole into his mouth.

"Hey my cooking's not that bad." I pouted at his overenthusiasm at eating Carmel's cooking.

"Your cooking is perfect, baby, but damn, Mrs. Winters has a way of cooking that homestyle way my mom used to."

"That's nice. I'm glad she gives you some good memories," I said sincerely. Nate picked up a bread roll, tore it in half, then stopped to look at me.

"I wish my mom could have met you, baby. She would have fallen in love with you and been thankful that you were willing to take me on."

"Me, take you on? You mean the opposite, don't you?" I said, grinning.

"What can I say, I was always the one to take on a good challenge," he said, grinning back at me. "So, speaking of Mrs. Winters, what did you two get up to while I was gone?"

"Let's just say the woman likes to shop and shop for bargains. I think we went to every market in Oregon."

"And you went with her?" he said, stopping mid-chew to look at me.

"Yep."

"And you enjoyed it?"

"Yep, it was good. I think it's because the market stalls were outside. They don't feel as suffocating and crowded as a shopping mall. Plus, we would have lunch and talk. She's a very interesting woman," I said.

"I'm glad. I knew you two would get along. You're both very similar."

"We are?" I asked, slightly shocked by his observation.

"Yep. You're both strong, independent woman who've had a tough road in life."

Remembering what Carmel had told me about her life, I thought that maybe he was right. Maybe that was why we got along so well. "I guess," I said absently.

After dinner, we took Chance out onto the beach for a walk before curling into each other on the couch.

"This is what I missed the most," Nate said as he stroked my hair back, tucking a strand behind my ear before placing a gentle kiss against my neck.

"Did you?" I asked him, my question causing him to stop placing tiny kisses on my neck.

"What, miss being with you? Are you really asking me that?"

"No, I just wondered if maybe you missed your life before. You know, being able to take off overseas on a moment's notice, without any worries?"

"If you're asking me if I liked the idea of not being attached, then the answer is a definite no. A few years ago, I would have enjoyed every minute of it, but being away from you made me feel like I had an empty hole in the middle of my chest, and all I wanted to do was come home to you."

"That's so sweet," I breathed out, touched at his words and knowing exactly how he felt.

"Yeah, well, never again, baby."

Reaching up with my hand, I ran my fingers over his jaw, trying to soothe the seriousness of his words. "I love you, Nathaniel King."

"I love you, too, Casey Tyler. Too much," he said as he brought his mouth down to mine.

By the time Nate came out of the bedroom in the morning, ready for work with his phone pressed against his ear, I had already made him some breakfast. "Yeah, sure, Paxton. I don't think it will be a problem," Nate said into the phone, followed by, "Okay, see you then." He hung up, sitting down at the kitchen table.

"Everything alright?" I asked, motioning toward the phone.

"Yeah, but it looks like you'll be coming in with me today," he said, taking a drink of his coffee.

"Why is that?"

"Paxton has some papers for you to look over and sign. Apparently the clinic would like you to start straight away." I was slightly shocked, and I noticed the two small lines of annoyance furrow on his forehead.

"Wow, your brother works fast."

"Too fast," I heard Nate say under his breath.

Totally ignoring his tone, I said, "Okay, I'll just take a quick shower and get dressed then." Walking away from him toward the bathroom, I could feel the burn of his glare as it penetrated my back.

I was deep in thought about giving Chance the run of the house while we were gone, crossing my fingers that he would behave himself and not eat any of the furniture. I wasn't sure if I would be required to go into the clinic today, and leaving Chance locked up in the penthouse with all its finery did not sound like a good idea. I turned to look at Nate. He looked deep in thought, and that stern, concentrated look on his face told me he wasn't too happy.

"Okay, big guy, spill it," I said, breaking the silence and causing him to look at me just for a moment before turning his eyes back to the road.

"Spill what?"

"What's causing those little crease lines in your forehead to get deeper every time I look at you," I said nonchalantly. He briefly looked at me again before speaking.

"You know what's pissing me off, so why are you asking me?" he said testily.

"Because I want to know why," I said, turning slightly in my chair so I could look at him better.

"I don't know, would you like me to make a list up for you?" he said, raising his eyebrow when he glanced at me.

"It's only for one, maybe two, days a week."

"Yeah, in the scummiest part of Portland that has a higher crime rate than any other suburb. Fucking awesome, Casey," he said, and I noticed not just his hands tighten on the steering wheel, but also the tiny muscle in his jaw, which had started to twitch. Placing my hand on his thigh, I tried to put him at ease.

"Hey, I'll be alright. I've done some research on the place, and it has nothing on some of the shit that I had to deal with at the hospital in Sydney. You forget, I'm used to working in this kind of environment. Plus, you need to have a little faith in me, Nate."

"It's not you I don't have faith in, it's all the other scumbags that you'll be dealing with," he said through a clenched jaw.

"Look, how about a compromise? I'll give it a month's trial. I won't ever leave the building unless it's with Nick, and then we'll revisit this conversation, okay?" I said, lightly slapping his thigh, hoping my suggestion would soothe his bubbling anger with the whole situation.

"No, it's not okay, but it's something, I guess. I just don't understand why you can't just wait until you start your residency. You know, in a nice, safe hospital"

"Believe me, no hospital is safe, and I'm not sure how long it will take for me to get one Nate. It could take months." As I waited for him to throw another counter argument my way again, I noticed as the tenseness in his body visibly started to subside, and he slowly shook his head.

"You're right. Doesn't mean I have to like it though. Stubborn woman," he mumbled.

"I heard that."

"Good, because if you don't stick with Nick going and returning from that shit box clinic, I promise you will be hearing a lot more than that," he said, a slight grin creasing the corner of his mouth, making me sit back into my seat and relax with a quiet victory smile on my lips.

Chapter Thirty-three

N ate

I pulled the Audi into my parking space under the King Security building. We got out and into the elevator, stopping at my office floor first. Before we even got to my door, I saw Paxton coming down the hallway.

"Hey, bro, nice to have you back," he said, giving me a slap on my shoulder. "Hi, Casey," he said, smiling at her.

"Hey, Paxton," she replied.

"I have all the papers for you to go over," he said, looking at her and holding up a slim white folder, but before she could say anything, I took the folder from his fingers.

"Thanks, I would like to take a look myself," I said, turning and entering my office with both of them behind me. I knew I was being an overprotective ass about this, but I'd be damned if I wasn't going to check out this place thoroughly before Casey even stepped foot in it. Rounding my desk and sitting down behind it, I looked up into two shocked faces.

"What? I want to know what she's getting herself into," I said, looking at Paxton and noticing as Casey folded her arms over her chest. She turned to look at Paxton.

"Just ignore him, Paxton. He's just practicing being an asshole at the moment," she bit out, and Paxton's face morphed from shock to a grin before he slowly started to back out of my office.

"Okaaaay." He drew the word out slowly. "I think I'll leave you two alone for a while. Just drop the papers off in my office, Casey," he said before closing the door, leaving Casey still standing almost at attention in front of my desk.

"What? You think I'm being unreasonable?" I asked with a raised brow. Letting out a sigh, she flopped into a chair.

"Honestly, I think you're acting like an idiot, but I understand that you have this compulsion to act like a caveman sometimes, so I am guessing this is just one of those times."

"I just want to know if you're going to be safe, that's all."

"And I understand completely. I mean you do own your own security company, so I wouldn't expect anything less. But as far as the paperwork, I'm pretty sure that really intelligent brother of yours has been through it with a fine-toothed comb to make sure there is nothing hidden in between the lines. I'm also pretty sure that I can handle it myself, but thanks for the offer," she stated as she leapt up from the chair and snatched the file off the desk in front of me before heading for the door. "I'll be in the penthouse, reading," she called out as she waved the file above her head, slamming the door behind her. I should have been pissed, but all I could do was smile at her sassy mouth and the sweet sight of her ass as it swayed out of my office.

Turning on my computer, I waded my way through the emails waiting for me before digging into the huge pile of contracts stacked on the side of my desk. Since we took over the security of The West Bank, business had grown exponentially, with a major shopping mall chain, private contracts, and now a chain of fitness centers to add to the pile of the already extensive list of clients we already had. King Security was becoming bigger than we ever expected. Pulling up the free clinic on the computer, I sent a quick email with the address over to Paxton with a request for the building specs, including the surrounding buildings. Then, I perused as much information on the place as I could. It was a pretty small place, housed in what used to be one of the original council offices in Portland, with minimal funding from government agencies and various charities around the area, which was pretty normal for a free clinic. Within an hour, Paxton walked through my door with the building specs and a spreadsheet of everything: average patient count, average criminal activity in the area, and an all over list of everything that had happened at the clinic since it opened its doors just over three years ago.

"That was fast work," I told him as he took a seat.

"Already had everything. What can I say? I know you too well," he said with a wide grin.

"Didn't realize I was that easy to read," I mumbled to myself as I flipped through the pages.

"I heard that, and yes you are. To me, anyway."

"Nothing wrong with checking out the place. I mean, that is what we do right? Security?" I said a little too harshly.

"Hey, back down there. I would do exactly the same thing if it was Lynda," he said, holding up his hands in surrender.

"Yeah, well, this bit of information here," I said, motioning to the file in front of me, "is just between you and me. okay?"

"Sure, not a problem," he said, making the motion of zipping his lips closed, before continuing. "So, where's Casey?" he asked.

"Gone up to the penthouse to look over the paperwork. She thinks I'm interfering."

"She's right, you are."

"I don't care. I just want to make sure she's safe," I told him.

"So, I take it she's not happy with you interfering?" he said, making little air quotes on the last word.

"Nope, but she wasn't too happy with the little chat we had on the way here anyway."

"Oh, okay, so you and she talked this morning?" Paxton asked.

"Yes," I dragged the word out slowly, looking at my brother with curiosity at his question. "Why?"

"Nothing, as long as you guys talked and everything is cool," he said with a little nervous tremor coming from his voice. Placing the file down on the desk and leaning forward, I looked at Paxton.

"Am I missing something here?"

"Nope, not at all," he said, glancing down at his watch. "Damn, is that the time? I have to get back. I have a conference call coming in soon. Just tell Casey to drop the papers off at my office when she's done," he said, standing and heading toward the door. I stood and followed closely behind him.

"Paxton," I growled, making him turn.

"Yeah," he said, turning and pushing his hands into his pockets, looking at me way too innocently.

"You know you're really bad at hiding things, right?" Looking at Paxton, I could tell there was something he needed to get out. He just had that guilty look plastered all over his face.

"I'm not hiding anything."

"Liar."

"Really?"

"Still lying."

"Nate." He spoke with a plea that said, *please, let it go*, but there was no way that was happening, and I knew he's saw the determination in my face when he said, "I just don't want to cause any friction between you and Casey. She told me she was going to talk to you about the situation, and I don't want to overstep any boundaries here."

"What the fuck are you talking about? Boundaries? Friction? And what situation?" I said my voice slightly rising in irritation.

Taking in a huge breath before releasing it, he said, "Casey called me early this morning. She thought she saw someone out on the back deck at Jacaranda House." He quickly added, "But there was no one there, Nate. I got there about ten minutes after she called me and looked the whole place over. She thinks it might have been a stray dog or something."

Saying nothing, I walked back to my desk before turning to look at him. "A dog?"

"That's what she said, and I thought maybe she might be right until she told me that she'd also received two phone calls with no one on the other end."

"What the fuck, Paxton?" I exploded.

"I know, and I had the exact same reaction as you."

"So why didn't you call me?"

"I was going to, but Casey said that she was going to talk to you this morning about it."

"Damn that stubborn woman!" I spat out.

"Nate, I..." Paxton started to say, but I put up my hand to stop him.

"It's okay. I know what a force she is to reckon with, Paxton, but you still should have told me." My words sounded harsher than I wanted them to, so I softened my tone. "Just don't listen to her the next time, alright?" I said, and Paxton just nodded.

After Paxton left my office, I sat and turned my chair toward the glass wall of windows, staring at the blue sky beyond it and contemplating what Paxton had told me before he left. Was it Peterson again? Was he trying to push my buttons? Because if he was, it was a huge mistake on his part, and if I needed to pay him another visit, this time there wouldn't be any kid glove treatment for him. Getting up and slowly starting to pace my office floor, I tried to think of anyone else. Sullivan wasn't a threat anymore, but if it wasn't Peterson, then who? I needed to talk to Casey and find out exactly what happened with the visitor and the phone calls or I would end up going around in circles and tying myself in what could only be unnecessary knots.

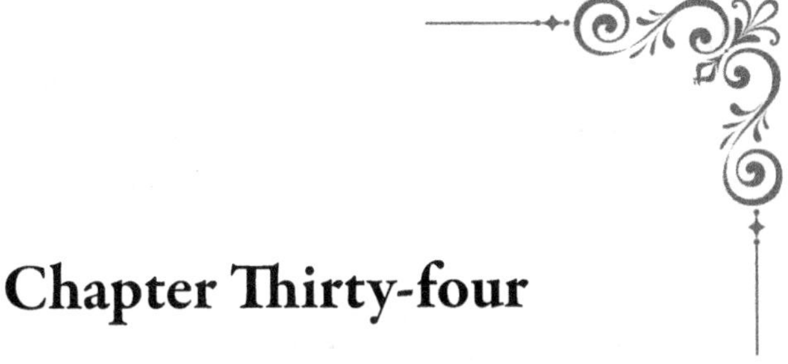

Chapter Thirty-four

Casey

I left Nate's office with the papers clutched firmly in my hand. I took the lift up to the penthouse. I hadn't been here for what felt like weeks, but as I stepped out into the tiled foyer, I inhaled the sweet smell of fresh flowers. Sure enough, sitting on the kitchen island was an arrangement of white and red roses in a crystal cut vase. A card was propped in front of it. I picked up the small, silver envelope and slid out the card. I recognized Nate's heavy, yet elegant, handwriting with the words, "I love you," written on it. I leaned into the small buds and breathed in their beautiful scent while holding the small card to my chest as I smiled at his thoughtfulness. Now I felt like crap for giving him a hard time. Pulling myself up onto the stool, I sat for a while, just staring at the flowers and silently kicking myself for being angry with him this morning. I started to read through the paperwork that Paxton had given me. It was all standard protocol, no surgical practice unless under supervision, no prescription writing, insurance cover while I worked at the clinic, blah, blah, blah. I knew it was going to be hard to work under someone's supervision considering my surgical background, but I also knew it would be part of the parcel, and I was actually really just glad to be getting back into what I knew. I had to admit I was pretty excited about it.

I had just signed my name at the bottom of the page accepting all of their conditions when I heard the ding of the elevator and the doors slide open. Slipping off the stool, I watched Nate as he walked into the kitchen and pulled a glass from one cupboard and a bottle of Jack from another before pouring himself a drink and swallowing a huge mouthful before putting the glass down on the bench. When his eyes focused on mine, I knew something was wrong. The bubbling fury behind his stare was difficult to miss.

"Something wrong?" I asked tentatively.

"That depends," he almost growled.

"On?"

"On what you have no need to tell me."

When I saw that twitchy muscle in his jaw start to pulsate, I knew I was in some deep shit, but for what? I had no idea. I casually looked around the penthouse, up at the ceiling, chewing at my bottom lip and generally trying to look like I was deep in thought when he said through gritted teeth, "Are you kidding me, Casey?"

"Sorry, I'm just trying to figure out why you're so pissed at me."

"So while I was away, nothing happened?" he growled.

"Nothing out of the ordinary," I said, shaking my head.

"Are you sure about that?" he asked, and now I was starting to get annoyed.

"Can we just stop playing twenty questions and just please explain to me what has got your boxer shorts in a twist?" I said, placing my hands on my hips and facing him as he walked around the kitchen island and stood in front of me.

"So, seeing someone out on the back deck at the beach house in the early hours of the morning isn't out of the ordinary? Or is that something that frequently happens? And the strange phone calls, also not out of the ordinary?" his words dripped with so much sarcasm and bite that I actually cringed.

"Oh," was the only word that came out because now I knew why he was so combustible.

"Yeah, 'oh.'" He emphasized my own word, causing me to break his intense eye contact and look down at my shoeless feet.

"So as I said, is there something you need to tell me?" he reiterated.

"Not much point now, you seem to know it all," I said, lifting my head to look straight back into his eyes. I watched as they moved around, searching mine for an answer to his question.

"I want to hear it from you," he finally said, and when I walked over to sit on one of the couches, he sat on the coffee table in front of me. Great, he was going to do his usual trick of fencing me in so I would have no escape from this conversation.

"I'm sorry. I was going to tell you, but you came back and fucked the sense out of me, and I forgot. I didn't think it was a big deal anyway. I told Paxton I was probably overreacting."

His eyebrow quirked, and he said, "Everything that happens to you or in your life is a big deal to me."

"Look, I just got spooked because I was on my own and Chance started growling at something outside. When I went to look out of the window, I just saw a shadow, that's all. It was probably a stray dog or something," I shrugged.

"If it was nothing, why did it scare you so much that you called Paxton? I know you too well, Casey, and it would take a lot more than a shadow of a stray animal to scare you into to calling for help."

Looking at the smug look on his face was very frustrating because he was right, but I wasn't going to let him know that. "I don't know, I guess I panicked."

"And the phone calls?"

"I don't know. Telemarketers? Wrong number?" I looked at him and watched as he rubbed a hand through his hair and down his face.

"Seems a little coincidental, don't you think?" he said, cocking his head to one side.

"I don't know, you're the security expert," I said shrugging.

"I wish you would have told me," he said with a sigh, shaking his head.

"Look, I think we both have become stuck in a world of watching our backs and living a very fragile and suspicious life since we met. And just maybe, we might be looking for something that's not there and can be explained by something simple, but out of the ordinary, and just coincidental," I said, placing my hands on top of his thighs. "I just don't want you to spend so much time worrying about me or my safety, Nate."

"Well, I can't promise you that, baby," he said, his body slightly losing the tension in it.

"I know, and I don't expect you to, and I love that you want to protect me, but at some point, we need to live, Nate, and not in a protective bubble." This time, when his eyes met mine, the anger had disappeared and was replaced with a softness and an understanding of what I was trying to tell him.

"All I can do is try, but you need to promise me that if anything like this happens again, you'll tell me, okay?" he said, taking both of my cheeks in his hands.

"I promise," I said, nodding, and his lips gently brushed against mine.

On the way back to Jacaranda House, we talked about the paperwork for the free clinic, and just as I thought, he had already read over them and didn't see any problems, although he did stipulate, again, that I would be driven to and from the clinic by Nick. With an eye roll, I let him have his way with that. If it would make him feel better, then so be it.

Once we got home, I was relieved to see that the house was still in one piece and Chance hadn't decided to eat any of the furniture. Nate took him out for a walk on the beach, while I got stuck preparing dinner. I placed some fresh prawns that we had picked up on the way home into a container with a marinade and placed it into the fridge. By the time a heavily breathing Nate walked in the back door, closely followed by a panting dog, I had everything in the pan cooking. As I loaded up two plates, Nate opened up a bottle of Riesling, pouring us each a glass. We sat out on the deck, enjoying our meal while watching the moon dance on the rolling waves coming into shore. A wonderful, soft breeze encircled us as we ate and chatted while sipping the wine. It was a perfect end to the day.

The next morning, after Nate left, my fingers were itching to pick up the diary, but I paced myself by doing the laundry, then taking Chance out for a walk before grabbing it and flopping on the couch. I pulled my legs up and tucked them under me before finding the last page I had read. After my birth, there seemed to be huge blanks between dates until my 1st birthday, where apparently I had been given a small party to celebrate. Although upon reading the entry, it seemed more like one of her dinner parties, as no children attended, just some friends of my parents.

Flipping through the pages, the breaks between her entries seemed to get even bigger, and anything she did write was always about work or the most important person in her life...her. And even though I didn't remember ever taking a vacation with my parents, there were entries made about ones they had taken that I had no recollection of. The next mention of me was on my 10th birthday.

1st March 1996

What a dreadful day it was today, David had insisted that we have a small dinner for friends to celebrate the child's birthday, and I had brought her a beautiful, quite expensive white silk dress to wear. The ungrateful child stained it by dropping food down the front, absolutely ruining it. I was so embarrassed that I sent her straight up to her room for the rest of the night without finishing her meal. I'm sure my guests were appalled at her table manners and the ghastly animal we had brought into this world.

I jumped and slammed the book closed when there was a knock at the door. Placing the diary on the table, I tried to fight my way past Chance as he weaved in and around my legs, finally reaching the door and opening it to Carmel's smiling face.

"Hey, honey, how are you doing?"

"I'm good, is something wrong?" I asked her, a little perplexed at her coming by.

"No, why, sugar?" she asked, walking past me and into the kitchen, stopping to pat an excited Chance on her way.

"No reason. I just didn't expect you today, that's all."

"Oh, shit, I should have called before I turned up on your doorstep shouldn't I have?" she asked, looking a little crestfallen.

"No, no it's fine. Just unexpected," I said, smiling at her.

"Is it a bad time?"

"No, it's fine, honestly"

"Good, because I brought us some homemade apple pie that's still warm, so you need to brew us up some coffee, girl," she said as she pulled out a covered pie plate from the basket she was carrying and slid it onto the table, right next to the diary. I saw her eyes glance at it then back to me. "Did I disturb you from reading a good book, honey?"

"I wouldn't say it was a good book," I said, grimacing. "It's my mother's diary."

"Oh, wow, how exciting," she said, her eyes wide.

"I wouldn't say that either."

"That bad, huh?"

"I'll fix us some coffee," I said, walking into the kitchen. I pulled two mugs out of the cupboard and handed her two small plates for the pie. As we sat down at the kitchen table across from each other, the smell of the pie made my mouth water. The pastry was thick and buttery with slices of apple coated in brown sugar and cinnamon spilling from it.

"Oh, my God, this is delicious," I said with a moan as soon as I placed a spoonful into my mouth.

"It's my grandma's recipe. She always did make a tasty pie. Just you mind you save some of it for Mr. King now," she said, pointing an accusatory spoon in my direction, causing me to smile and give her a nod.

"So, you want to talk about it?" Carmel asked, a more serious but cautious tone to her voice. I wasn't sure what she was referring to until I saw her eyes drop to the diary. Placing my spoon down onto my plate, I felt my shoulders sag in response.

"It's complicated," I sighed.

Placing her mug of coffee down on the table, she reached across and placed her hand on top of mine. "Honey, I know you have a lot of things in your past that you keep private, and I respect that, but in all the time we've spent together, I can see that whatever it was, it hurt you bad, and I have seen it in your eyes many times. I've also seen you wash that pain away just as quickly as it comes. There's nothing wrong with showing you're in pain, but sometimes you need to realize that you have a whole bunch of people around you to help you carry it now, and I'd like to think I am one of those people."

"You are, very much so," I said with so much honesty I felt it stinging the back of my eyes.

"Now, like I said, I'm always here if you want to talk about it."

Seeing the sincerity in her wide brown eyes, I was momentarily torn as the emotional swirl of uncertainty started to roll through my head, and it must have shown because Carmel patted my hand, stood, and picked up our dirty plates, taking them into the kitchen.

"I thought I might find something more about my mother's thoughts and feelings if I read it." I started nervously. Carmel placed the plates into the sink and came back over to sit opposite me at the table, the expression in her eyes and on her face showing me that she was there to do one thing, listen.

"I thought that if I read it, I would find a reason for her hate toward me. You know like maybe she was unsure of how to be a mother, or she was an alcoholic or suffered from postnatal depression or something. I don't, I knew it was just something to blame her actions on," I said as I concentrated on twisting my fingers together in my lap.

"And did you?" Carmel asked.

"No, I guess before I started reading, it I had some deep-seated hope that she had an excuse for who she was, but the more I read, that hope just disappears"

"I'm so sorry, honey," she said tenderly.

"So am I," I whispered.

"Some people are just not worthy of treasuring the gift of a child. I never understood why that happened in life, but I do know it does." I heard the sadness in her voice as she remembered her own struggles to have a child of her own, and I reached out to placed my hand on top of hers in comfort.

"I'm sorry, I didn't mean to bring up any painful memories for you." She shook her head slightly, and we just sat there for a few moments, comforting each other for our own losses in life.

"Well the way I look at it, I think the world somehow might have done us both a favor amongst all this heartache."

"What do you mean?"

"Your momma's loss ended up being my gain." Standing up, I leaned down and wrapped my arms around her shoulders. This woman, who had come into my life only a short time ago, had just given me more than my own mother had given me in a lifetime.

That afternoon, after Carmel had left, I placed the diary back into the drawer of the bedside table. I needed to take a break from it for a few days. I also needed to concentrate on my first shift, which started at 10 a.m. Monday morning.

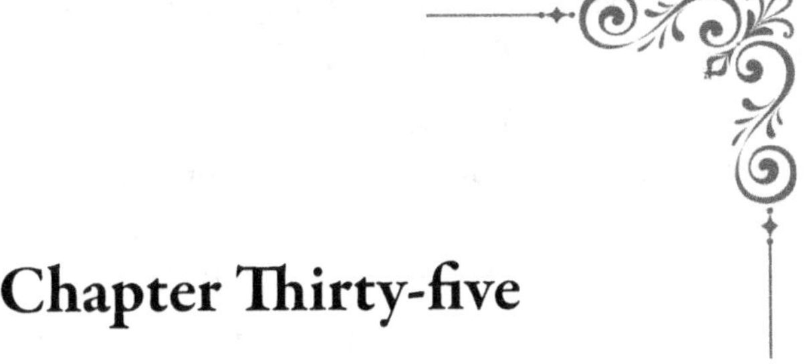

Chapter Thirty-five

N^{ate}

Seeing the excited look on Casey's face as she almost dove into the town car that was waiting for her outside King Security this morning almost made me feel guilty about any of the apprehensions I had about her volunteering at the clinic. But being protective of her was something that I didn't think I would ever be able to turn off. I just needed to learn to hide it better. At least she'd agreed to Nick driving her there and picking her up at the end of her day. This was something we had discussed in great detail; a lot over the weekend. I couldn't believe that she actually intended on walking there. Stubborn woman.

She wasn't so stubborn this morning, though. When I went back into the bedroom after taking a shower, I found her laying on her stomach, clutching onto my pillow with her leg bent and thrown over the cover. Her white tank top had slid up far enough to reveal a red pair of panties covering that fantastic peach of an ass. I couldn't help myself. I just had to touch her warm, soft skin, running my hand from her ankle slowly up to the back of her knee, then gliding my fingertips up to her ass and sliding my fingers under the lace of her panties, making her stir enough for me to replace my fingers with my mouth. Moving the lacy material to one side, I placed open mouthed kisses on the soft cheeks of her warm flesh, then took a gentle bite, causing her to moan and sleepily say, "You must be really hungry this morning." Looking up at her blonde, tangled hair, I could still see those sparkling, blue eyes with their thick, long lashes peeking through a fringe of golden silk. Fuck, talk about bedroom eyes. She had bedroom everything.

Kissing a path along the top of her ass and over her hip bone, she turned to lay on her back, and I continued the path of tiny kisses across her pelvis and right to the front of those naughty, red panties of hers, inhaling the beautiful, erotic scent of her that always drove me insane. "I am going to have an early breakfast," I breathed against the front of the lace, making her squirm her ass around in anticipation. I loved how free she had become with her sexuality, never afraid to try or enjoy anything in the bedroom. Slipping my fingers into the side of her panties, I slowly slid them down her legs, letting my fingers caress her soft skin until they reached her ankles and fell onto the floor. Running both palms up the inside of her legs, I slowly pushed them open wider and crawled further up the bed in between them. I was right where I wanted to be to enjoy my breakfast, and I did so thoroughly.

On the drive into Portland, she fidgeted in her seat with excitement almost the whole way there. She had dressed casually in a pair of black skinny jeans, a cream colored blouse, and a pair of tan leather boots that came up to her knees. She also had a black sweater folded neatly on her knees, with her beautiful, long blonde hair pulled back into a ponytail that sat high on the back of her head. Even without a scrap of makeup on, she looked absolutely beautiful. After I parked the car, I escorted her up in the elevator and out to a waiting Nick at the front of the building and then turned to her. "You have Nick's number in your phone, so just give him a call when you're ready, and he'll bring you back here, okay?"

"Yes, boss," she said with a mock salute. Then, standing on her tiptoes, her mouth touched mine with a soft kiss. "Wish me luck," she said as she got into the town car and closed the door. Shoving my hands into my pockets, I stood and watched as Nick drove away and out of sight before heading up to my office.

Sitting down in the leather chair behind my desk and turning on the computer, I buzzed for Laura to come in with her notepad. Within a minute, there was a soft knock on the door and Laura was standing in front of my desk. I'm not sure where Paxton found her, but so far she was proving to be one very intelligent, organized, and really efficient secretary who was very easy to work with.

"Take a seat. I need some files brought up from Paxton's office, and it's a pretty big list. Also, I was wondering if you could book a table for two for dinner tonight at Giorgio's around 7 p.m."

"Of course, Mr. King," she said, then started to jot down the file names and numbers that I gave her. Twenty minutes later, Laura pushed a small trolley with a basket full of folders in it back through the door with Paxton following closely behind her.

"Thanks, Laura," I said as she left the office, closing the door behind her. Paxton dropped down into one of the chairs opposite me.

"Looks like you have a full day ahead of you," Paxton said with a grin and a nod toward the trolley.

"Yep," I said as I grabbed a stack of the folders and dumped them onto my desk, sitting down and taking the top one, before looking at him.

"Is there something you need?" I asked him.

"Just wondered where all the files were heading to, but I think I got my answer," he said with a grin.

"And what's that supposed to mean?"

"You, needing something to occupy your brain for the day instead of thinking about Casey," he said, standing to leave.

"That has nothing to do with it, I just want to get a head start on some of the contracts," I said nonchalantly.

"Okay, whatever you say. I'll be in my office if you need me," he said as he left.

Smug bastard that he was being right now, I had to hand it to him. He'd hit the nail on the head. I really did need something to sink my teeth into today or I was going to sit here wondering how Casey was doing. I had to get a grip. She was right. Our relationship had been forged on me protecting her, and I needed to trust her judgment with this and roll with it, "Pftt, easier said than done, babe," I said to myself, running a hand through my hair, sitting back in my chair, and opening the first folder.

The first file was for a small gym franchise aptly named "Ship Shape." They had a total of twelve gyms scattered around the country. Reading through their requirements for the business, it looked like all they really needed was a well-monitored security system and hourly checks by a security guard. The gyms were open 24 hours a day, 7 days a week and could only be entered by a swipe card. Jotting down a quick plan on the pad on my desk, I closed up the file and took another one off the pile in front of me.

A small supermarket chain with only three stores operating in the area needed the same, a good security system, but more surveillance and some permanently placed security guards. The areas the businesses were situated in weren't high risk areas for crime, but not low either. I made some more notes, then grabbed another file. Another nightclub that was just over the river in Vancouver with plans to open up two more later in the year. Going through each folder, I placed them in order of priority, as well as in order of difficulty and planning. By 1 p.m., and with my stomach starting to growl like an angry bear, I sent a text to Paxton to see if he wanted to grab some lunch with me. I felt satisfied that I managed to steer my thoughts away from Casey. It seemed my plan had worked - so far, anyway.

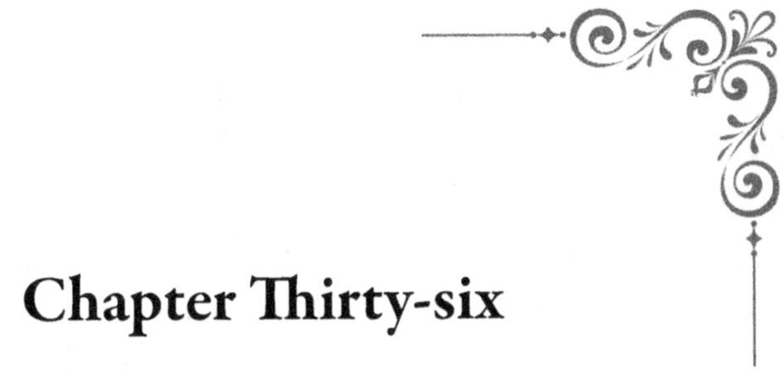

Chapter Thirty-six

Casey

Nick pulled up outside an old red brick building with a sign above the single glass door that read "Healthy Life." I opened the back door before he even had time to shut the engine off. "Thanks, Nick," I said as I climbed out, turning back briefly to see the look of annoyance on his face. "I'll call you when I'm done."

He replied, "Yes, ma'am," and I closed the door and walked up the four steps to enter the building. Walking inside, I was surprised to see that someone had done some serious refurbishing. From the outside, the building looked a little old and run down, but inside, it looked freshly painted with an array of colorful artwork placed in a single line along the walls. The decor was clean and simple with black leather bench seats running down either side of the long room, separated by small tables covered in magazines. Walking down toward the reception area, I noticed that the bottom half was a solid wall and the top half was glass. Peeking through to the empty desk and chair on the other side, I noticed a door to the right of the reception desk with a small swipe card screen and a "Press for service" button next to it, so that was what I did.

I waited and then started to wonder why everything was so quiet and empty. Was this place open today? Had I come on the wrong day? I thought that maybe I should give Paxton a call just to make sure I was at the right place. Fishing around in my purse for my phone, I found the ID card that Paxton had given me when I signed the paperwork. It had my name on it, followed by volunteer Doctor, and it had the same name on the card that was written on the sign hung above the door outside, so yep, I seemed to be at the right place, and I was sure Nick knew where he was going. Just as I was about to grab my phone to call Paxton, there was a noise from the door that was beyond the wall of glass in front of me. As it opened, a young, raven-haired woman walked through. She looked to be in her mid-twenties, dressed casually in a pair of black leggings and a bright blue sweater. She smiled when she saw me and made her way over to the desk.

"Hi, welcome to Healthy Life, how can I help you this morning?" she said in a what sounded like a well-rehearsed chirpy tone. Taking the ID card I had in my hand, I slipped it through the small gap in the glass onto the desktop.

"Hi, I'm Casey Tyler, the new volunteer doctor," I said with a smile. She looked down at my ID, then back up at me, smiling.

"Well, hello, Dr. Tyler. So sorry to keep you waiting," she said apologetically.

"That's okay. I was just a little worried that I'd come to the wrong place," I said, looking behind me to the empty room.

"Don't worry about that, it will start filling up soon enough," she said, looking down at the watch on her wrist. "If you go to that door over there, I'll buzz you in and give you the tour before it gets crazy," she said, pointing to the door to the right of me. With a buzz and click, the door unlocked. I walked inside and turned the corner, putting me behind the reception counter where the young woman handed back my ID card and then offered me her hand.

"I'm Tessa. I work the office, appointments, and referee any fights that break out," she said as I shook her hand.

"Fights?" I asked.

"Yes, normally due to a patient not understanding the concept of waiting patiently for your turn," she laughed. "Come on, I'll take you out the back and introduce you to the team," she said. she turned and headed for the door that she had entered from, and I followed behind. Walking through it, we stepped into another corridor, but this one had numbered doors on either side. "These are the examination rooms where the patients are seen," Tessa said as we continued to walk past them. It looked like there were around ten rooms altogether. "And in here is the heart of the place," she said, swiping a card against an ID reader and pushing it open.

We walked inside, and I saw that the much larger room housed a few work stations with desks and computers, a small triage area, and an open area with a large table and chairs and a small kitchen in the corner. There was a huge whiteboard attached the wall with the room numbers and what looked like names written next to them. To the left of me was another couple of doors and beyond that, what looked like an office with the door open.

"You will be assigned your own treatment room for the day, and then your name will be written on the whiteboard next to the number for that room," Tessa said, pointing at the whiteboard. "That is the medication room, and that one is the supply room," she said, pointing at the doors to the left. "In here is our floor coordinator. Come on in," she said, walking to the open office door before giving the door a quick tap. "Hey, Diane, our new volunteer, Dr. Tyler, is here," she said. As I walked through the door, an older woman with a mass of frizzy red curls and black-rimmed glasses stood from the other side of the desk, quickly making her way around to the front of it and greeting me with a handshake.

"Welcome, Dr. Tyler. I'm Diane Banks," she said as she shook my hand with enthusiasm.

"Please, call me Casey," I told her.

"Diane," she nodded back to me. "Please, take a seat," she said, motioning to one of the chairs in front of her desk, and then turning to Tessa. "Thank you, Tessa."

"You're welcome, I'll catch up with you sometime later," she said, looking at me with a smile.

"I'd like that, thanks," I said and noticed that she closed the office door on her way out.

Diane leaned forward with her elbows on the desk and her fingers linked together in front of her. "I'm so happy to meet you. I've read your file; very impressive." Her compliment made me feel warmth flood my face.

"Thank you, I'm just happy you let me volunteer my services."

"Oh, no, we are very honored to have someone with your experience," Diane beamed at me, making my cheeks flush a little more with embarrassment at her words.

"Well, thank you. I'm not sure if have any more experience than anyone else around here, though."

"Now, you're being modest. I've read through your qualification transcripts, and your experience is just astonishing. I'm just sorry that you have to go through so much red tape to work here in the US," she said with a frown.

"That's okay, I understand. Besides, sometimes it's good to go back to the beginning and refresh the brain," I said, giving my temple a tap with my finger.

"Well, we have a great team of volunteers here, and I'm sure you will be a perfect fit, so how about I give you the big tour and you can meet some of the other staff members?"

"Sounds great," I said, standing to join her as we left the office.

It was a well set up little clinic, with several doctors and nurses and a list of specialists who volunteered their time from the local Hospital. It was pretty impressive for a free clinic that survived on funds that were mostly donated by charity organizations and some help from local government funding. After the grand tour of the place and meeting some of the other staff members that were working that day, Diane led me into the staff room area I had seen earlier, where she made us both a cup of coffee, and we sat down at the table.

"So, what do you think?" Diane asked as she took a sip from her cup.

"I think that I am going to like it here," I said, giving her a smile.

"That's fantastic. We are certainly going to like having you here," she said enthusiastically. "Have you thought about how many days you might be able to come in?" she asked.

"I was thinking maybe two days a week? If that's okay?" I said.

"That would be great, just what we need," she said, smiling in a warm, friendly way that made me like her. She made me feel at ease in this new environment, and she spoke about the clinic with a lot of pride and joy in her voice. As we sat and drank our coffee, we slipped into an easy conversation about our lives and families. Diane asked me what had brought me to the US, and I briefly told her that I had met someone while working for International Medical Assist on a US military base in Ashgabat. She was interested to get more of my story, but I kept it pretty nondescript and managed to change the direction of conversation onto her story. Diane proceeded to tell me that she was born and raised in Portland, she was married to her high school sweetheart, who also became a doctor, and they had two grown-up children. Apparently, when the children moved out of the home, she decided to put her secretarial skills combined with her knowledge of the medical system to work and applied it to running the clinic. She had just started to tell me about her children in more detail when a tall, slim woman walked in. Looking at her, I wasn't sure if she was a staff member or a patient that had somehow wandered into the back of the clinic. She wore a pair of torn jeans and a black t-shirt with a band logo across the front in bold letters. Her black hair was short and spiky, and both arms had some serious and colorful ink on them. She looked like she had just stepped down from the stage at a rock concert after playing bass guitar for the last hour.

"Oh, Maddie, great timing. This is Dr. Casey Tyler. She will be joining our team. Casey, this is Maddie Price. She is our counselor. She works for the juvenile services for troubled youth and volunteers here in her spare time," Diane said, introducing us. Maddie sat down at the table and offered her hand, which I took.

"Nice to meet you, Maddie," I said, giving her a smile.

"Great to have you on board. And where the hell is that accent from?"

"Australia," I said, laughing at her question.

"How the hell did you get stuck in Portland?"

Still laughing, I said, "It's a long story. Remind me to tell you about it over a coffee sometime."

"Definitely," she said with a grin and a shake of her head.

I guess she wasn't the most typical-looking counselor I had ever come into contact with. She looked more like a rough biker chick, but I liked her. She was laid back and relaxed. After the tour and more paperwork to fill out, Diane told me to come in for my first shift on Monday. As I left the building with as much enthusiasm and bounce as I had walked in there with that morning, I scooped my phone from my purse and dutifully sent Nick a text.

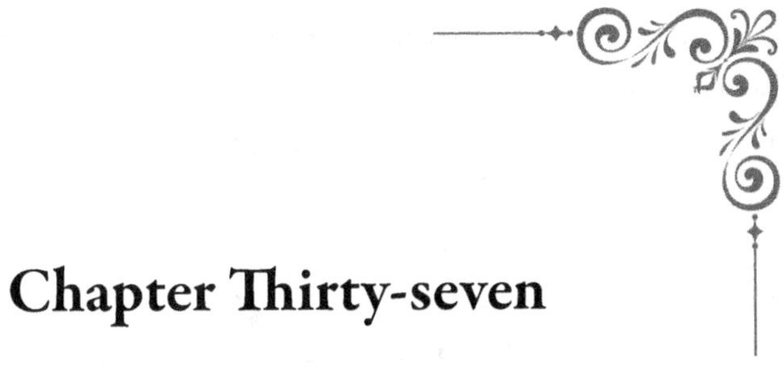

Chapter Thirty-seven

Nate

Deep in conversation with Paxton as we plowed through the pile of contracts that were sitting on my desk, I realized that I hadn't actually glanced down at my watch so obsessively as I did earlier this morning. Well, until now, anyway.

"Quit it," Paxton said.

"Quit what?"

"Looking at the time. She'll get here when she gets here. Damn," he said with an exasperated sigh.

"You say that like I have been watching the clock all day."

"You have."

"Funny, I was just thinking the opposite," I said, running a hand through my hair, a little confused.

"Believe me, you might not think you were doing it, but you have been," he said, looking at me with a grin.

"And I think you're just yanking my chain, little brother," I said, looking at him through narrowed eyes. I watched as he was opening his mouth to protest when there was a knock at the door. "Come in," I answered. When the door opened, I felt my body instantly relax from a tension that I didn't even realize was in it until now. Casey walked in with an obvious gentle bounce to her step and a beautiful, penetrating smile spread across her wonderful lips.

"Thank fuck," Paxton breathed out under his breath as he sat back down into his chair, and I guessed he was relieved that the object of my obsession was back in the building.

"Hey." I greeted her by coming around my desk and scooping her into my arms, planting a kiss on her beautiful mouth. "You look happy. I take it everything went well?"

"Everything was perfect. The place is definitely not what I expected," she said, looking over at Paxton.

"I told you it was good," he said matter-of-factly and with a slight air of satisfaction.

Turning my attention back to Casey, I smoothed my thumb over the soft skin of her cheek. "That's great, baby, I'm really happy for you," I told her with genuine pleasure as I looked into her eyes that were bursting with a combination of happiness and excitement. Giving her another chaste kiss on her lips, I dropped my arms from her and went over to the bar, pulling out a bottle of wine and holding it up. "Well, we don't have any champagne to celebrate, but I do have this bottle of Cabernet Sauvignon from Napa Valley."

"Sounds good," Casey said as I took three wine glasses off the shelf and poured us all a glass. I handed the first one to Casey, then the other to Paxton. As we stood facing each other, I lifted my glass. "To new beginnings," I said, smiling at Casey as we clinked glasses and took a sip.

"Damn, that's good," Paxton said in appreciation of the wine. "Never realized my brother had such good taste for good wine," he smirked at Casey.

"Very funny. Just drink your wine before I kick your ass out of my office," I said, making him chuckle.

All three of us spent the next hour polishing off the bottle of wine and listening to Casey's excited recall of the tour of the facility and the different staff members she had met that day. I watched in fascination as she bubbled over with enthusiasm about returning back to the work I knew she loved. Seeing that made me realize that I needed to back off and let this woman spread her wings and shine.

Later in the afternoon, Casey went up to the penthouse to take a shower and see if she had left anything in the closet for her to wear that would be dressy enough for dinner. I made the mistake of naming the restaurant that I had booked for us to eat at before we returned home, and she googled it. Then she got annoyed because I should have told her to bring something nice to wear with her this morning. It made no difference when I told her that it didn't matter what she wore, we were going there to eat, not to be in a fashion parade.

I realized that this relationship stuff was all new to me, but I didn't think I would ever fully understand the way a woman's mind works, and to be honest, I don't think I really want to.

After Paxton left my office to head home, I tried to put the pile of files that were sitting on my desk into some kind of an assemblance, but in the end, I totally gave up the fight and left it for the morning because I intended on taking my girl out on a date.

As I opened the door of the Audi for Casey to get in, I was still amazed at how stunning this woman was. In the small amount of time she had had to get ready, she had managed to shower and find a short-sleeved little black dress that fit to every sensual curve of her body, a pair of red heels, and she had brushed her beautiful golden blonde hair out until it shimmered down her back in a river of silk. She looked absolutely stunning, and I couldn't keep my eyes off of her the whole drive to Giorgio's. I definitely had to adjust myself a few times before we were even seated at a table. I watched as Casey looked around, taking in the elegant dining room until she brought her eyes to mine.

"See, I'm glad I googled this place. It's way too ritzy for a pair of jeans and a sweater," she said in a low voice so only I could hear her.

"If you think this place is ritzy, wait until you taste the food," I said.

"That good, huh?"

"Baby, it will blow your mind," I said, giving her a wink.

After watching her eat said meal, I realized I needed to rethink my words. As I watched her eyes close as she moaned out her enjoyment with every mouthful of pasta she put in it, all I could think of was getting her home so she could blow my mind. As she placed the last bite of chocolate tiramisu into her mouth, I almost lost my load.

"Are you alright?" she asked as she placed her dessert fork on her plate and lifted up her glass of water to take a sip.

"Yep, fine," I said.

"Are you sure? Because with the look on your face at the moment, you look...pretty uncomfortable," she said with a wicked grin. Picking up my glass of scotch and rolling the amber liquid around in it before taking a mouthful, I leaned in closer to her.

"I just watched you orgasm your way through an entree, a main meal, and now dessert so yeah, I guess you could say I'm pretty uncomfortable right now," I said, taking another slug of scotch from my glass and leaning back in my chair.

"Maybe we need to go home then," she said, lifting an eyebrow and wearing a wicked grin across her lips. Suddenly, I felt something brush against the front of my pants under the table. Putting down my glass, I lifted the white tablecloth slightly to see her naked foot with her dark red, glossy nail polished toes perched on my chair in between my legs. Dropping the tablecloth back into place, my eyes shot up to meet hers.

"You have got to be kidding me right?" I said, and was met with the sparkle of lust in her perfect blue eyes. Signaling for the waiter to bring the check for our meal, I handed him my credit card. As soon as I signed the check, I took Casey's hand and almost dragged her out of the restaurant and back to the car with the sounds of her giggles mocking my fast pace and our hasty exit. Opening the car door, I rushed her in, slamming the door, and got into the driver's seat, turning the ignition before slamming it into gear, all to the sound of her soft, low laughter.

"I think you might need to watch your speed, Nate," she said as we sped down the highway toward home.

"Don't worry, baby, I'm doing the speed limit," I gritted out between clenched teeth, which only made her laugh again. "I'm glad you think this is so amusing," I said, taking a sideways glance at her. She looked totally relaxed in the seat next to me, with just a wide smile on her beautiful mouth. Fuck, I really needed to look at the road and not at her. *Don't look at her, don't look at her,* I silently chanted to myself, which was working until I heard a click, which made me turn my head slightly to look at her. She had undone her seat belt and turned slightly toward me.

"What the fuck are you doing? Fasten your seatbelt before we get booked!"

"Are there any cops around?" she asked, looking out of the side window, then turning in her seat to look out the back window.

"No, but it's dangerous," I said, teetering between frustration and a little bit of anger at her unsafe behavior.

"Okay, chill out," she said, sitting back into her seat and clipping the belt back into place before placing both of her naked feet up onto the dashboard in front of her, causing her already short dress to ride further up, revealing more of her smooth legs and thighs. Then, trying my hardest to keep my eyes on the road in front of me but flicking between the road and those long sexy legs of hers, I watched as her hands slowly moved down to her knees and brushed up the hem of her dress. As she slid the material higher, I caught a glimpse of her black, lace-topped thigh highs and silky black panties.

"Fuck," I hissed as I moved in my seat with discomfort. I was so hard the zipper on my jeans was groaning with the strain.

"Are you okay?" she asked innocently.

"No, and you aren't going to be either in about five more minutes," I growled.

"Is this bothering you?" she asked, motioning to her legs. "Do you want me to put them down?"

"Don't you dare, I'm enjoying the view."

Leaving one hand on the steering wheel, I moved my other hand down toward the front of her panties and gently ran a finger over the front of the lace, causing a little moan to escape from her mouth.

"You're soaking wet," I managed to breathe out before pulling my hand away and turning up the driveway with my foot planted hard on the accelerator, pulling the car to a sliding stop on the gravel in front of the house. Getting out into a cloud of dust, I yanked open the passenger side door and pulled her out and into my arms, pressing my mouth against hers in a hot, ravenous kiss. "You make me so fucking hungry," I managed to growl out in between our lips tasting each others.

"Do I?" she teased. "Then maybe you better take me to bed."

"I can't wait that long," I said, breaking the kiss and turning her around so she was facing the hood of the Audi. I slipped my hands around to the front of her dress and cupped her breasts in my hands. I start to knead them, instantly feeling her nipples harden under my palms. She moaned and pushed her ass back against my groin while her head dropped back against my chest, giving me perfect access to the creamy, white skin of her neck. Bending my knees slightly, I pushed my raging hard-on into the cleft of her ass, rubbing against her as I ran my tongue along the soft skin at the side of her neck, gently nipping and biting at the tender flesh before biting the lobe of her ear.

"I'm going to take you right here, right now," I breathed into her ear. "It's going to be hard and fast," I continued as her body moved against mine, her breathing pattern changing with a want and need of her own. "Are you okay with that?" I asked her in a low, urgent tone because it didn't matter how bad I wanted to fuck her on the hood of my car or how hard my dick was or how I could feel the blood pumping through my veins so hard that it felt like I might have a stroke if I didn't get inside of her. I would never fuck her until she gave me permission to do so. I hear a soft sigh as she gave me a slight nod.

"Words, Casey. I need to hear the words," I growled out.

"Yes, I'm okay," she managed to breathe out before I gently pushed her to bend over the car, her chest pressed against the hood. Grabbing the hem of her dress, I pulled it up until it bunched around her waist. Grabbing the back of those tantalizing black panties, I quickly pulled them down her legs until they were around her ankles. With one hand splayed against her back to hold her in place, I worked the buckle of my belt open with the other and undid my jeans, my erection springing out before I had the zipper fully down. I stepped closer in between her legs, nudging them open further with my knees. Taking my shaft in my hand, I rubbed the head over her slick entrance once before plunging into her with one quick, deep thrust, so hard her body jerked and slid further onto the hood of the car as she let out a moan of pleasure. Her tight, warm channel clamped around me, sending shockwaves into my balls. I started to move inside of her with fast, deep strokes, and the deeper I thrusted, the deeper I wanted to go. I couldn't seem to get enough to satiate my hunger for her. The only sounds were of the ocean on the other side of the house that were mingled with Casey's panting moans and my own hard breaths and grunts of pure pleasure. When I felt her moving back against me even harder, meeting my thrusts, I knew she was chasing her own climax, and that made me thrust faster into her warmth. I felt her low moan that seemed to start at the base of her spine and travel upwards. Then I felt the tightening of her body as she screamed out my name into the dark night, and I instantly felt the ripples of her orgasm roll through her body, followed by the liquid heat that now surrounded my shaft, causing me to thrust once more, coming hard and deep into her body. Leaning forward, my chest against her back, I placed soft, open mouthed kisses against the side of her neck as she turned her head to the side, giving me her mouth. I kissed her lips between our heated, panting breaths until we came down from the sexual heaven we just traveled to.

Eventually, feeling the tremble in my leg muscles starting to ease, I stood up and tucked myself back into my pants, then reached down and slowly pulled her panties back up over her beautiful ass before pulling her dress back into place. Reaching down, I pulled her up into a standing position to face me, gently moving her hair away from her face and out of her eyes because I needed to see those eyes as I asked, "Okay?" As I looked into them, searching for anything that told me that she wasn't, but all I saw was pure contentment.

Chapter Thirty-eight

C asey

Looking up into Nate's eyes, still filled with the fire from his own orgasm, all I could say to him was, "Oh, I'm more than okay." I smiled, making him relax and grin before bending down, lifting me up and throwing me over his shoulder, fireman style.

"Nate, what are you doing!" I squealed in shock.

"Taking you to bed like you asked me to do," he said before smacking my ass and running up the front stairs, taking two at a time as we both laughed. As he pushed the front door open, we were greeted by a very excited dog. Chance jumped up, placing his paws against Nate's side and giving me a wet doggie kiss against the side of my upside down face before running out the front door and making a beeline for the grass. Nate carried me inside, dropping me onto the couch, then pointed a finger at me. "Don't even think about moving. I'll take care of Chance, then I'm taking you for a shower."

"Yes, boss." I said, smiling as I watched his fine ass walk toward the door and outside.

The following week was so different from what life had been like since we came back from Sydney and moved into the house at the beach. I had to say that my life had been a pretty lazy one. But this week was the total opposite. I had baby Emily for two days this week so Lynda could not only have some time for herself to paint, but also run some errands, and to be honest, I loved every minute of it. Emily seemed to be growing so fast and doing something different every time I saw her. At the moment, she appeared to have found another use for her mouth in the form of blowing raspberries. Taking great pleasure in her own little party trick, she also started rolling onto her tummy and looking around, and she loved it when Chance flopped down next to her and proceeded to lick the top of her head.

My first shift at the clinic was pretty eventful. Very different from when I had the grand tour of the place. On that day, it was quite empty, but not today. Today, when I walked through the front door, the waiting room was packed to the rafters, mostly woman with small children and a few elderly people. Making my way through the crowd of bored, tired, and crying babies, I finally reached the entry door into the back where I swiped my ID card. I pushed it open, and the first person who greeted me was Maddie.

"Hi, Doc, glad you could make it," she said, smiling at me.

"It's pretty crowded out there," I said, gesturing behind me with my thumb.

"Oh, yeah. I hope you wore some comfortable footwear today because I have a feeling today is going to be a bitch," she said, and hung a black stethoscope around my neck before tucking an arm through mine. "Come on, I'll lead you into the lion's den," she laughed as we walked toward triage.

By the time I had messaged Nick to come pick me up, I was totally exhausted. I had no idea how many patients I saw today because I totally lost count after about fifteen. They just kept bringing them, and I kept treating them before passing them on to the doctor that was in charge for that day so he could prescribe any medications that they needed. I could treat them for almost any ailments they had, but not prescribe any meds, not yet anyway. The day's work had certainly reminded me of what a long, hard day at work was like. Nick dropped me off in front of King Security, and I made my way inside, getting into the elevator and pressing the button for the penthouse for a much needed shower before going down to Nate's office.

Feeling clean and more human, I headed down to the office floor with my fingers crossed that Nate was close to finishing for the day. I hated leaving Chance at Jacaranda House all day by himself. Although he'd been great and hadn't done anything yet, there was always a first time, plus it didn't seem fair to him. He loved being around people. I did console my guilt by at least knowing that I would only be away for one or two days a week, though.

When the elevator doors opened, there seemed to be a flurry of people everywhere. "What the fuck?" I said to myself as I headed to Nate's office. Laura sat at her desk. "Is he in there?" I asked her, pointing to the large wooden doors.

"Yes, Miss Tyler. I'll tell him you're here," she said, looking flustered as she picked up the phone, pressed a button, and announced my arrival. Hanging up, she said, "Go on in."

"Thanks," I said as I pushed open the doors to a room full of chaos. There were several computers set up all over his office, and Paxton sat behind Nate's desk, almost invisible behind the stack of files in front of him. Nate paced back and forth in front of the huge window, his phone pressed against his ear, his body rigid and tense as he took big strides across the room, then turned back to pace the same path. What the hell was going on? It had to be something bad because I had never seen Paxton ever look as worried as he looked right now. Walking over to Nate, he looked up and held up a finger, letting me know he would be off the phone in a minute.

"I don't give a fuck, Tony, I need it done now!" he yelled into the phone before ending the call and tossing his phone on the desk.

"What's going on?" I asked with concern.

Nate rubbed a hand down his face and closed his eyes. "The servers went down this morning, and we had a breach in the network."

"What? How?" I asked in shock.

"No fucking idea. Some shithead hacker got in through a back door, I'm guessing," he spat out.

"Did they get anything of importance?"

"We don't think so. Paxton was able to shut everything down as soon as it was breached."

"Jeez," was the only thing I could say.

I think Nate noticed my zero knowledge of computers when he saw the clueless look I had on my face as I looked over at Paxton. Walking over to me, he slid a finger under my chin, tilting it up to face him. "We could be here for another couple of hours," he said with a tinge of regret in his voice.

"That's okay. I'll go up to the penthouse and take a nap," I said. "Unless you need my help with anything?"

"Are you okay?" he asked with concern as his eyes searched mine.

"Yeah, I'm fine. Just a bit tired. It was a pretty rough first day," I said, smiling at him.

"I guess that answers my next question of how was your day, then."

"Later. You get back to what you're doing. You know where to find me," I said as he leaned his head down, pressing his lips against mine. I walked out of the office and back up to the penthouse where I pulled out my iPod, slipped in the earbuds, stretched out on one of the black leather couches, and fell asleep listening to the soulful tones of Adele.

When Nate woke me from my slumber with soft kisses on my forehead, it was pretty late, and he looked so tired. I suggested that we should spend the night here and took a gamble that Chance wouldn't eat anything other than the full bowl of food that I'd left him this morning, but Nate said he was fine, and he wanted to go home. It was actually nice to hear him say that because the penthouse had been his home for so long.

On the drive back, Nate went over what had happened with the breach in the network and how Paxton and their tech guy, Tony, had locked down the system until they could repair any damage to the firewalls and get it back up and running before investigating who was responsible. Looking over at him, I could see his whole body was wrecked with fatigue. The creases in his forehead seemed much deeper than normal, and I wondered if there might be more to this than he was telling me. But when I pressed him a little, he was unsure of what the culprits were looking for. Still, it didn't change the fact that he needed to find out. Then he changed the subject and asked me about my day. Not wanting to bore him to sleep in his depleted state, I kept it brief and light until we pulled up outside the front door to a barking dog and the sound of him furiously scratching at the door.

Once the door was open, and he rushed past us, I instructed Nate to go take a shower and get into bed. With a slight reluctance, he did because by the time I got into the bedroom, he was laying on his back with one arm slung across his eyes. A soft, exhausted snore slipped from between his lips. Sliding in next to him, I snuggled into his side, draping an arm over his waist and for a while, I just lay there, listening to the gentle rhythm of his breathing and feeling the rise and fall of his chest.

When I woke the next morning, the space next to me was empty. Rolling over, I ran my hand over the space that still felt a little warm, so I got up and walked down into the kitchen. The large, glass tri-fold doors were pushed back, letting in a subtle ocean breeze. As I walked to the opening, I could see the blue sky with not a cloud in sight. Stepping out onto the deck, I spotted Chance running at the edge of the water, playing his usual game, which included biting aimlessly at the frothy waves as they rolled in and retreated back into the ocean. Nate was sitting on the top step, still dressed in his sleep pants and nothing else. I watched as his winged man tattoo that was spread over his entire back flexed and moved as he lifted a mug of coffee to his mouth and took a sip while he watched Chance and his antics with a faint smile. His strong profile was shadowed with not only a dark few days beard growth, but something more. He looked relaxed, but in a tense way, if that could even be possible. His black, tousled hair was picked up by the breeze, and I couldn't help but stand behind him and stroke it.

"Hey," I said, running my fingers through his hair.

"Good morning," he said, reaching a hand up to take mine and guide me to sit next to him on the step.

"Did you sleep alright?" I asked, placing my palm against the side of his face.

"I slept like a log," he said, grinning at me.

"You looked beat."

"Yeah, well, it was a hard day," he said, taking another sip of his coffee.

"And what about today?" I asked.

"Today is a new day."

"So you fixed the problem?"

"Yeah, we did, thankfully," he said with a sigh.

"Then what's bothering you?"

"I don't know, exactly," he mused.

"Did they get anything important or anything detrimental to the business?"

"No, they didn't have enough time to get into our system," he said.

"Then what is it? Because something's on your mind," I said, and he turned to face me.

"I'm not sure. It's just a gut feeling that something's not right," and I could see in his eyes that his mind had been working overtime while he slept.

"Have you talked to Paxton?"

"Yep, and he's going to do his sniffer dog routine today. I gotta hand it to him, he is definitely the brains in the family."

"Don't sell yourself short, you're a smart cookie," I said, smiling at him.

"Nah, I'm just the muscle," he chuckled.

"That's a load of crap, and you know it. You are both very talented and intelligent men who make a great team."

"And you're biased," he said, smiling.

"Give yourself some credit, and trust your gut instinct. You always have before," I said before kissing his lips and standing. "Come on, let's get some breakfast."

Just over an hour later, Nate was showered, dressed, and fed, and had left for the office, looking happier than he had earlier. I hated seeing his stress this morning but I guess when you run a large security company and someone hacks into your system, it must destabilize your own sense of security and force you into a deeper awareness. Knowing Nate's need of control, I'd say this would have knocked him off kilter a little and unsettled him. I also knew that by the time he got back tonight, he would have that control firmly back in his hands.

Chapter Thirty-nine

Nate

On the drive into Portland, I was still wracking my brain, to make sense of the events that had happened yesterday, trying to think if I had missed anything. By the time I pulled into my parking space at King Security, I had nothing. Zero, zilch. So it seemed I had given myself a headache for nothing. As soon as I entered my office, I grabbed the box of Tylenol from the top drawer of my desk and popped out a couple of pills, throwing them back with a mouthful of water. Pushing my hands into the front of my jeans, I walked over to my view of the world below me, taking in the bustle of traffic and people as I inhaled deeply, trying to let my stress out with an exhale as I remembered what Casey had said before I left this morning. *"Talk to Paxton."* My thoughts of those beautiful sapphire eyes of hers were interrupted by a knock on the door. "Yes," I called out, and Paxton strolled in.

"I thought I told you to come in later today," I said.

"I know, but I thought I might as well be here rather than stressing at home," he said, sounding tired.

"I know the feeling, but there's not much we can do about it now. Just make sure nothing was stolen and move forward."

"Aren't you the optimistic soldier this morning?" he said, grinning.

"Yeah, well, what can I say. It's Casey's influence," I said, shrugging.

"Well, the good news is that nothing has been stolen, and the even better news is that Tony was up most of the night tracing the hack until he pinpointed the shithead."

"Really?" I said, looking at him.

"Yeah, turns out it was just some wannabe hackers. Teenagers in Rochester. Apparently, they tried to get into a few different places."

"Jesus, Paxton." I breathed out a sigh of relief.

"I know, but it's all good. Tony has been in contact with the local police there, and they're investigating it. They'll contact us when they press charges."

"Yeah, thanks to you and Tony," I said, sounding a little defeated.

"And by that you mean?" Paxton asked with a raised brow.

"It means you were awesome yesterday," I said.

"So were you."

"Not sure I was much help on the tech side of things, but I did do a lot of yelling," I said, grinning at him.

"Hey, we work as a team," Paxton said, walking closer to me.

"I know," I said, turning to gaze out of the window again.

"Okay, what gives? What's on your mind?" Paxton asked, now joining me to look out of the window.

"A few things," I said wistfully.

"Like?"

"Like I'm lucky to have such a smart brother."

"What, and you've only just realized that now?" Paxton gasped slapping a hand against his chest. "I'm hurt," he said, mock pouting like a school girl, and it made me smile.

"You know what I mean. I'm not sure I would have handled it as well as you did yesterday."

"Bullshit."

"No, really. I mean it, take credit where it's due."

"Look, the only reason that we work," he said, waving his hand between me and him, "is because I'm calm when it's needed, and you're tough when it's needed. You might be lucky to have me, brother, but I am equally lucky to have you, okay?"

"I don't know, Paxton," I said, shrugging. "Maybe it's been a little harder for me to transition back into to the office from the field than I thought it would be."

"I'd say you're transitioning just fine. Just give it time. We work well together, Nate, and that's all that matters. Now, what else is one your mind?"

After a slight pause, I turned to look at Paxton. "I realized yesterday when we had to shut everything down that the first thought that came into my mind was not the security of our clients' information like it probably should have been. I was thinking about the security of our families."

"I agree, I had the exact same thought," he said, nodding.

"You did?"

"Yep. Then I tried to rationalize with myself that a money hungry business owner maybe wouldn't think that way, but that's not what we are, thankfully," he said, smiling.

"So whatever happens in the future, we agree that Lynda, Emily, and Casey's security comes before business, right?"

"Absolutely, one hundred percent," Paxton said, nodding.

"Good," I said, knowing all too well that Paxton and I would always be on the same page where family was concerned.

"Okay, what else? Because I can see that brain of yours still ticking away."

"I'm not sure. I just have this gut feeling that there's more to this. Maybe I'm just overthinking things. I don't know," I said, shaking my head.

"Well, not wanting to burn your ego here, and normally I trust your gut, as well, but I can assure you everything is fine. It's probably because for the last few years you've been on high alert to any inconsistencies or anything out of the ordinary. Plus, you've had a lot on your plate with Casey, so it's understandable."

"Yeah, you're probably right," I told him.

"I am, but you can't help your suspicious brain," he said, grinning.

"Yeah, that's me," I agreed, relaxing more than I was on the drive in here, and glad I listened to Casey. It was humbling to realize that my little brother didn't need me to protect him anymore, although if anyone touched him, I would still break every fucking bone in their body.

Chapter Forty

C asey

After Nate left, I tidied up and loaded the dishwasher. My phone rang just before lunch, and I answered it to a frazzled-sounding Lynda. "Hey, what's up?" I asked.

"Casey, are you at home today?"

"Yes, why? Is everything okay?" I asked, slightly concerned with the urgency in her voice.

"Everything's fine, I just need a huge favor."

"Sure, what do you need?" I said, relaxing.

"Well, remember I told you about the little art gallery that opened up in Portland? The one on Irving Street?"

"Is that the one you sent some photos of your work to the other week?"

"Yes, that's it. Well, they just called, and they would like to display a few of my pieces. They want me to drop them off today," she said excitedly.

"That's fantastic, Lynda! I am so proud of you."

"Thanks! I'm pretty nervous, though."

"Don't be. Your work is incredible, so what can I do to help?"

"Well, Emily was up most of the night teething, and I just got her settled down."

"Say no more, do you want me to come over?"

"No, I'll drop her off there. The only thing that got her to sleep was putting her in her car seat, so I think it will be easier."

"Okay, no problem."

"Thanks, Casey, you are an angel. I should be there in about fifteen minutes," she said before hanging up. Right on time, at fifteen minutes, she was knocking at the door with a sleeping Emily in her car seat and a bag full of baby goodies in the other, dressed impeccably in a black knee-length pencil skirt and a cream silk blouse. Opening the door. I took them from her, and she kissed my cheek.

"Thank you so much. Everything she needs is in the bag. I shouldn't be too long."

"She'll be fine, take all the time you need. You look great," I said as she turned away to head back to her car. "Hey, you did remember to put the paintings in the car, right?" I giggled.

"Sure did," she said, laughing. She waved as she took off down the driveway, and I took Emily into the living room and gently set the car seat down next to the couch. She looked totally worn out. Her eyes looked a little red and puffy, matching her flushed, chubby cheeks from an obviously tearful night.

"You poor baby," I whispered to her before I put Chance out on the deck. I really didn't want his enthusiasm for licking Emily's face off like he normally did to disturb her while she was sleeping. Leaving the bedroom door wide open, so I had a clear view of her, I pulled some nice, crisp, clean sheets onto the bed and finished making it. Just as I placed the last of the pillows on the bed, my eyes drifted to the bedside table for a few moments before I sat down on the side of the bed. I continued to stare at it, picturing the diary that sat inside. My mind started waging war against itself again. If I left it in there, was I going to have this turmoil every time I looked at the bedside table? Yes, I was. Should I pull it out and throw it in the garbage? Yes, I should. Should I read the rest of it? No, absolutely not. It was only going to bring up things that didn't deserve my time.

Was I not only talking to myself right now, but also answering myself back? Yep, I certainly was because having that thing in that drawer was essentially driving me insane. Therefore, I needed to get rid of it. Nodding at my final decision, I opened the drawer and pulled out the diary. With it clutched firmly in my hand, I walked to the kitchen and pressed the pedal on the trash can, opening the lid, intent on dropping it where it belonged. Then I paused long enough for my mind to say, *Are you going to regret not finishing it?* Taking in a long, deep breath and closing my eyes, I moved my foot, letting the trash can lid close and exhale with an accompanying, "Fuck," from me. I opened the refrigerator and pulled out a cold bottle of beer. I took it and the diary to the couch, where I dropped onto it, tucking my legs underneath me and flipping the cap of the beer. Emily was still fast asleep. As I brought the bottle to my lips and took a mouthfull of the cold liquid, I opened the diary.

Flipping through the pages, I was at least glad that she wrote the dates at the top of them because I knew exactly what I was looking for; what I had always wanted to know. I knew it when I picked this diary out of that box and put it in my suitcase. I needed to know about that date. And there it was, staring right at me: March 3, 2000. The day I was taken.

3rd March 2000

I'm not sure if this is something that I should be writing in this journal, but I think for my own sanity, it's something that I need to do. The other day, I arrived home to an empty house. I languished in the peace of it. That is, until David asked me where our daughter was at the dinner table. Catherine has been old enough for quite some years now to take care of not only herself, but the upkeep of the house, as well. After all, she needs to learn how to earn her keep, and the earlier she realizes that nothing is free in this world, the better. But today, she did not come home for dinner, and David was furious with the child. At last, he sees how ungrateful she really is, but I left him with his fury and retired to bed. I have a busy day tomorrow, and I will not be losing any sleep over a 14-year-old who has decided to stay out all night with her friends.

5th March 2000

I stayed at the office longer than normal today just to enjoy some peace and quiet for just a little longer. I just cannot face going home and any more of David's incessant ranting and insistence that somehow it is my fault that the child is still not home and that I need to do something.

6th March 2000

When I arrived home this evening, I was ready for another night of arguments. Instead, I found David accompanied by two police officers, and I watched the color slowly drain from my husband's face as they told us that Catherine was seen getting into a car and they were treating it as suspicious. Apparently, David had felt guilty and called them. The stupid man. He is going to look rather silly when she turns up in a few days time having done God knows what with God knows who. I really hope no one saw the police here. That's all we need; a scandal, fodder for the community gossip.

7th March 2000

This will be my last entry into this diary, and then I intend on tossing into the fireplace, but before I do, I need to get something off my chest because I will not be taking this to church and into confessional like I should do. I know that God sees all, and I know he will see my words and grant my forgiveness. Today, I received a phone call from a man who claimed to have taken our daughter. He demanded a ludicrous amount of money for her return. He could have been anyone, and I asked for some kind of validation that he had her, which he supplied a few minutes later with one whispered word down the phone line. "Mother." I did discuss what was said in the phone call with both David and the police. The police agreed with my decision not to pay anything, but David was unsure, and when the caller called me again the next day, I told him that we would not be paying any ransom money. He became very angry and abusive, and let me know that if I didn't pay him what he wanted, we would never see our daughter again. I told him I didn't care what he did with her, although I kept this small part of the call to myself. The police have advised us to stay away from the press and let them do their job. They have told us that in ninety percent of these types of abductions, if there is no money, they won't keep the abductee. What puzzles me the most is that my husband is clearly not happy with the situation, but in time, I'm sure he will come to realize that this is truly a blessing, and I am sure that the child will be dumped off somewhere and hopefully find her own way in life and not come back here. Now I feel that my conscience has been cleared, and at last, after much sacrifice, I can have my life back.

I flipped over the last few pages, but they were all blank. Closing the diary, I just stared at it, amazed that this woman ever existed. She actually thought that by writing it down that she would be forgiven? Didn't she realize that on that date, she sealed my fate? Forever? My stomach rolled as bile started to rise into my throat, making me swallow hard to get it back down as my mind whirred into overdrive. This woman obviously had some kind of mental disorder, because no normal person would think like her about a child, would they? Closing my eyes and leaning my head against the back of the couch, I tried to reel in the downpour of emotions and thoughts that were running through my mind, and thankfully, I was saved by the tiny, soft whimper of a beautiful little angel who was sitting in her car seat, now wide awake, with her huge blue eyes focused on me. Getting up, I lifted her into my arms, feeling her warmth against my chest, stroking the back of her head, as I look into her eyes. "Hey, beautiful girl. You woke up just at the right time," I said, sniffing back the threatening tears as I softly placed a kiss on the top of her head.

Chapter Forty-one

N^ate
Pressing the button on my phone, I let Laura know that she could come in and collect the papers I had just spent over an hour signing. A few minutes later, she entered, briskly walking to the front of my desk. Handing her the file with a, "Thank you," she exited, and I turned off my computer. Leaning back in my chair, I rubbed a hand over my face, feeling a sense of relief and calm that Paxton and I had talked this morning. For me, it cleared the path to have another talk with him about me spending less time in the office and more time out in the field. Spending all day cooped up behind a desk was starting to feel a little confining, and I had no intention of leaving Casey for any amount of time, so there would be no private contracts or overseas trips. I just wanted to have some time out among our clients, being more hands-on with advice and setting up security.

I just wanted to find some way to split my time between the office and being out and involved in the business for my own sanity's sake. Standing up, I pushed my chair under my desk and pocketed my phone. Grabbing the keys for the Audi, I left the office and headed down to the garage. As I opened the car door, my phone started to vibrate in my pocket. When I pulled it out, I saw Lynda's name flashing on the screen.

"Hey, what's a pretty momma like you doing calling me? Isn't Paxton home yet?" I asked her.

"Yeah, he's taking a shower," she said, but there was something strange in her tone.

"What's up?"

"It's probably nothing, but Casey had Emily over at your place today while I ran an errand."

"Okay." I dragged out the word slowly, wondering where this conversation was going.

"When I picked Emily up, Casey seemed to be acting a little...strange."

"What do you mean?"

"I don't know exactly. It might just be nothing, but she was different this afternoon than she was when I dropped the baby off."

"Did she say anything to you?"

"No, but that's what's bugging me, Nate. On the outside, she appeared happy and smiling, but it seemed...forced, if that makes sense?"

"I see," I said, being careful to hide the concern in my voice.

"Look, it's probably nothing, I just wanted you to know, okay?" Lynda's voice flooded the line with light heartedness, but I could still hear her worry.

"That's okay. I'm just about to get into the car and head home anyway."

"Great, that's good. Just send me a text and let me know that everything's alright, will you? Or I will be up all night with it on my mind."

"Sure thing. Thanks, Lynda," I said, ending the call.

I drove just a little bit over the speed limit on the way home. I did shoot Casey a quick text before pulling out of King Security to let her know that I was on my way. She texted me back with her usual red love heart emoji, so I thought that maybe Lynda was worried over nothing, but just to be sure, I wanted to get back as quickly as possible, preferably without a ticket.

Pulling into the driveway half an hour faster than normal, I noticed that the house was dark as I drove toward it. Not a single light was on inside at all. Coming to a stop out the front and getting out, I pressed the key fob for the car to lock over my shoulder as I took the front stairs two at a time and pushed my key into the front door. Entering, I dropped my phone and keys into the glass bowl at the entry and made my way down the hall, checking the rooms as I went until I reached the living area and the kitchen. All the lights were out, and the house was eerily quiet, apart from the sound of the ocean coming in from outside.

Turning on the lamp in the living room and walking to the tri-fold glass doors that were fully opened, I walked out onto the deck and leaned against the rail. There, in the middle of the beach, was a roaring fire. It wasn't a huge fire, but the flames were pretty high. Chance was laying curled up on one side, and Casey sat on the other side of the fire pit, her arms wrapped around her bent knees. Relief flooded through my body with a relieving sigh that nothing seemed to be wrong. She looked alright from here. Stepping down the stairs and onto the beach, I pushed my hands into the pockets of my jeans and started to walk toward her with a smile. I was just about to admonish her for starting a fire on a private beach when my words caught in my throat as I saw her face. I'd seen that look of pain and foreboding before, that empty, lost look. Her eyes were glassy and red and staring straight into the flames in front of her. I could tell she'd been crying, and that was not something that this woman did easily. When I got to the fire pit, she didn't even look up at me.

"Baby?" I cautiously said, but still nothing. Chance got up and came to me, wagging his tail with excitement. I scratched behind his ears while keeping my eyes directly on Casey.

"Casey?" I said a little louder, causing her to look up at me. Her eyes were so wide I could see the reflection of the flames dancing in them.

"What are you doing, baby?" I asked, and she just stared at me for a moment before she spoke.

"I'm having a funeral, and this," she said as she motioned to the fire pit, "is my crematorium." She held out a brown, leather bound book that looked oddly familiar. I quickly scanned my memory for where I had seen it before, and then it hit me like a lightning strike. It was the book that was in the box that we collected from her childhood home back in Sydney.

Chapter Forty-two

C asey
Earlier that afternoon

After feeding and changing Emily, I took her out onto the back deck. The sun had disappeared, and the sky was full of slightly gray-looking clouds. Sitting down in one of the deck chairs, I cuddled and chatted away to her. My mouth was engaged on our conversation and her gurgles, but my brain was starting to drift a little, and I needed to pull myself together until Lynda came back, which thankfully was sooner rather than later. We were still sitting out on the back deck when she stepped out onto it.

"Hi! Sorry, I'm a little late," she said.

"No, its fine. We've had a great time, haven't we, beautiful girl?" I cooed at Emily before placing a kiss on her forehead. "How did it go?" I asked her.

"Great, they were really impressed and enthusiastic." She smiled with pride.

"And they should be. You're a great artist. They should be honored."

"Well, thank you for the support, but we'll see what happens. At least it's a start, right?" she said holding her hands out to Emily, who immediately went to her mom. "I hope you were a good girl for Aunty Casey," Lynda cooed sweetly to Emily.

"She was perfect, as usual. I'll get her things together for you," I said, getting up and walking into the living room to pick up her blanket and toys, which were still spread out over the floor where we had been playing earlier. Placing everything into the baby bag and zipping it up, I looked up to find Lynda staring at me.

"Are you alright?" she asked.

"Me?"

"Yeah, you look completely drained. I hope Emily didn't wear you out."

"Not at all, just feeling really tired today for some reason," I said, rubbing a hand over my face in an effort to look more awake than I was feeling.

"I hope you're not coming down with something. I've heard there's a stomach flu going around," Lynda said.

"I'm sure it's more from not getting enough sleep. I stayed up late last night, talking to Flynn for ages," I said, waving off her concerns.

"Oh, okay. How is he?"

"He's good. Busy as always, but he's hoping to come over for a visit soon."

"Sounds good, I can't wait to meet him."

"You and Paxton will love him," I said, smiling.

"Okay, well, I had better get this little lady home for a bath, and you should crash on the couch for a snooze. You look wasted," she said, grinning.

"Yeah, I will," I assured her, then walked with her out the front door and to her car, where she clipped in the baby seat and turned to give me a hug.

"Hey, do you want to do dinner Saturday? My house?" she said.

"Yeah, sure. Sounds good."

"Okay, see you around seven then. And thanks for today, Casey."

"No problem. Anytime," I said as I waved at Emily in the back seat, then watched as they drove away.

Walking back inside, I dropped onto the couch and curled up, pulling the rug that hung over the back of it down to cover me. My eyes closed with an exhausted heaviness, and I sank into sleep.

I woke startled, sitting up with a gasp, pushing my hair away from my face. I quickly looked around the living room, a little disorientated for a few minutes, until I realized where I was. Looking at the time on my phone, I saw that I'd been asleep for just over two hours, and the whole time, my sleep was marred by a disturbing dream of a jumbled mixture of images from my childhood up until today. But the one picture that kept flashing into my dream was that of my mother's diary. Not her face, because truthfully, I have never been able to picture her face in detail. I think it's because I hardly ever saw her and what few times I did, she was always scowling or angry. She pretty much scared the hell out of me for as long as I could remember. Getting up, I started to pace around the room, trying to get rid of the turmoilof thoughts in my head. Chance followed behind me, tilting his head and looking at me curiously every time I stopped. Looking up, I spotted the bottle of scotch in the corner on the bench in the kitchen. Grabbing it, I filled a glass almost to the rim with the pungent liquid before taking a large gulp. The burn of it sliding down my throat was repulsive, but the warmth when it hit my belly and spread had a slight comforting effect, so I took another slug, draining the glass, and poured another one. By the time I'd finished that one, my body felt loose and relaxed, and my head fuzzy and numb. Just what I was aiming for.

Pacing between the kitchen and the living area, I stopped and gazed at the book sitting on the coffee table for a moment before continuing my pacing. The sun had just gone down, and the house was dark. I stood out on the back deck just looking out as the moon cast it's light on the ocean, and then it hit me. I needed to get rid of this book permanently. I never wanted to see it again. Grabbing the book, I searched through the kitchen drawers until I found a box of matches that Nate kept in there, he'd all but given up smoking, but I knew he still liked to have the occasional one now and then.

"Bingo," I said as my hand found what I was looking for. Making my way down the back stairs onto the sand, I scoured around the house for some kindling, and was lucky enough to find a pile of it stacked under the house. I took what I needed down to the middle of the beach, where I made myself a fire.

It took some coaxing to get the flames going. Between the effects of the alcohol and blowing on the small flames to get the fire started, I made myself dizzy enough that it dropped me on my ass on the sand. By the time I had gotten my head to stop swimming, the flames of the fire were burning strong and steady.

Gazing into the fire, Chance lay next to me. I wasn't sure how long I sat there for, but I did know that somewhere deep in my mind, I heard a familiar voice saying my name. I snapped out of my reverie, looking up into Nate's wide eyes.

"What are you doing, baby?" he asked, his tone low and cautious.

"I'm having a funeral, and this is my crematorium", I announced, holding up the diary and pointing to the fire with a slur in my voice.

I watched as Nate's eyes flickered back and forth between mine and the book that I held out, and I saw the minute he recognized it.

"Baby," he said, sadness flashing across his face.

"Nope, this is not a time for sadness. It's a time to celebrate," I said, holding up a hand to stop him from coming any closer to me.

"You've been drinking?"

"I sure have, and do you want to know why? Because I needed a few drinks to read the shit that was in this diary," I said, holding the book up higher.

"Fuck," he cursed under his breath.

"Yep, that's a fitting word for this disgusting account of a deranged woman's thoughts."

"Your mom?" he asked.

"Pfft, she wasn't a mother, she was a monster. Do you know, she never wanted me from the minute she found out she was pregnant? She tried to get an abortion, but it was against my father's religion. So she tried other ways to try to get rid of me. She drank, she exercised like crazy, she even wore a tight-fitting corset. I'm amazed she didn't throw herself down the stairs. No, wait, she wouldn't have done that because it might have left a mark on her precious face."

"I'm so sorry, baby."

"You know what the hardest part to read was?" I asked, looking at him as he slowly shook his head. "She was the one who decided not to pay the ransom, and she was so happy that she didn't have to think about me again, she fucked up my life and gave me to that fucking rapist to torture for almost three years, Nate. And do you know how much it would have cost her for me to have had a normal life, instead of one that included me being tortured, starved, raped and beaten half to death? $10,000. That's all she had to pay. Ten lousy fucking thousand dollars, Nate. Why would someone do that to a child?"

"Because she was evil, Casey, and that's why both she and your father got their justice in the end."

"Yeah, well I hope she fucking died in pain," I said, standing up and dropping the diary onto the flames. I watched in silence as the leather smoldered and curled under the intense heat until the pages inside caught aflame. "Now, you can burn in hell, you fucking bitch," I spat, wrapping my arms tightly around my middle.

"You're free of her, baby. You have been for a long time. You're strong, and you have a new family now, one that loves you more than words will ever be able to express."

"But am I, Nate? Am I free of her? Because it feels like no matter what I do, I will always be tied by my wrists to her and what happened. I thought I had found freedom, but once again, she's made everything twisted again," I said. Looking up at him, the tears that I had managed to keep contained by my anger burst free, and I could feel their wetness running down my cheeks, but before I could say anything else, he had me enclosed in his strong arms.

"That's it, baby. Let it all go," Nate whispered at my temple.

And with his words, I did. I cried hard with shuddering sobs like I'd never cried before because in reality, I never had. I cried for the unwanted child, I cried for the abused child, and I cried for the forgotten child. My heart broke for all of those lost years that I could never get back, and when I thought I had finished, the pain resurfaced again and again, reigniting the torrent of emotion that I had kept locked inside for all of those years. Always blaming myself for being worthless, broken, and unworthy of anything, always searching for something that was missing. After reading her diary, I finally realized that it wasn't me that was worthless and broken. It was them. My parents. They were the ones unworthy of ever having a child.

My hands fisted tightly at the front of Nate's shirt and my cheek pressed against his chest. My endless tears had soaked the front of his shirt, and the whole time I had been falling apart, he was there to hold me together.

I could feel the strength in his arms and in his low words of comfort as he spoke them against my temple. This man had once again given me the freedom to cut the bindings of my past and free myself at last. Exhausted and emotionally drained, I felt myself starting to crumble, but before I could slide away from his body, he hooked an arm around the back of my knees and scooped me up into his arms, walking back up the beach and into the house.

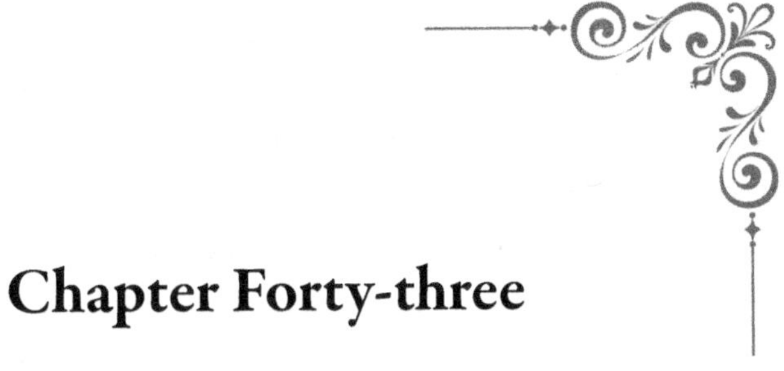

Chapter Forty-three

Nate

Watching my girl fall apart sent a spear of pain right through my heart. As hard as it was to feel the pain shuddering through her body as she sobbed in my arms, I think that it had been a long time coming, and it might have been just what she needed. I held her tight as she cried. I needed her to feel me. I wanted her to know that I was right here with her, so I gently stroked her soft hair and planted soft kisses at her temple and over her wet cheeks, attempting to soothe her pain as much as I could. But how could I soothe away a pain that had been ingrained in her for her whole life? I felt so fucking hopeless. I wished her parents were still alive just so I could kill the motherfuckers myself. I was lost as to how I could take away this pain from her, so I did the only thing I could. I picked her up into my arms and carried her up the beach and into the house. She was still clinging to my shirt with ferocity when I gently placed her feet back on the ground in the bathroom and turned on the water to fill the bathtub. Sliding my fingers over hers, I brushed away the tension in them and gently undressed her. With her head bowed and silent, I lifted her into the bath and bathed her, washing away not only the sand from her body and the smoke from her hair, but hopefully, some of her pain.

Once she was wrapped in a towel, I pulled one of my t-shirts over her head and guided her in between the sheets, laying down next to her before taking her back into my arms. No words were needed at that moment. Everything was said with just touch. I stroked her hair tenderly until I felt her body relax and her breathing took on a deep, slow rhythm, telling me that she had fallen into a deep sleep. I slowly extricated my arms from around her and left her to sleep, quietly closing the bedroom door behind me. Heading into the kitchen, I grabbed a cold bottle of beer from the refrigerator, flipped the cap, and took a long pull from the bottle. The chill of the amber fluid cooled my anger toward what Casey had been through. Taking my beer with me, I picked up my phone, went outside, sat on the back deck, and dialed Lynda's phone number.

She picked up on the third ring with an anxious, "Nate?"

"Yeah, are you busy?"

"I am never too busy for you. Is everything alright? How's Casey?"

"Yeah, she's fast asleep at the moment. I'm pretty sure she's going to feel like crap in the morning."

"That bad, huh?"

"Let's just say it hasn't been a great night," I said, sighing into the phone.

"Why, what happened?" Lynda asked.

"It seems she has been reading a diary that belonged to her mother, and she got the answers to most of her questions."

"A diary?"

"Yeah. When we were in Sydney, it turned up in a box that was left at her childhood home, along with some old photos. She threw everything else away, but obviously, she kept the diary."

"Ah, Jesus, Nate. Was it bad?"

"I'm guessing it was with the small pieces of information that came out tonight. I mean I guessed that her parents were pieces of shit, but it appears her mother was pretty much a monster." I heard Lynda draw in a sharp gasp.

"And it looks like she gave Casey a raw narrative on how much she didn't want a baby in her life, right up until she decided to basically give her 14-year-old daughter to her rapist."

"What?" Lynda gasped.

"Yeah, I know. It sounds pretty fucked up, but that's what it boils down to. Her mother was abusive and neglectful, and when her daughter was kidnapped, she made the decision not to pay the ransom," I said through gritted teeth.

"God, that's terrible, Nate. How can a mother do that to a child? Poor Casey. She's been through so much. It doesn't seem fair that one person should have to endure so much pain in their life."

"I know."

"So, how are you doing?" Lynda asked with concern.

"Yeah, well, that's why I called you."

"Ah, I see. So you needed a sounding board, huh?" she said.

"Something like that. I just want to take it all for her, you know?"

"I know, but you can't. And maybe, although it was a painful experience, it might have actually been what she needed, Nate. Maybe it's come full circle for her now, and she just needs to do some healing."

"I really hope so."

"You just keep doing what you're good at."

"What's that?"

"Loving her. That's all you have to do right now. Just let her know how much she's loved and needed by you and by us, and just be patient."

"See, I knew there was a reason I wanted to talk to you," I said, smiling into the phone.

"What can I say, I am just an awesome sister-in-law," Lynda chuckled.

"You certainly are that. Thanks, Lynda."

"Anytime," she said before we said goodnight, and I polished off the rest of my beer.

The sound that woke me the next morning was far from a pleasant one. I opened my eyes to an empty space next to me and the sound of heaving and groaning coming from the bathroom. I got up and went in to the sight of Casey hugging the toilet bowl as her body heaved out empty the contents of her stomach. Moving to her, I gathered her hair in my hand and moved it away from the target zone until she had nothing else left to come out. She sat back onto the bathroom floor, leaning her head against the wall. Wetting a cloth, I wiped her face down.

"Feel better?" I asked her.

"Oh, my God. Remind me never to drink scotch again," she groaned before taking the wet cloth from me and scrubbing at her face.

Helping her to her feet, she tentatively moved to the sink where she rinsed out her mouth, brushed her teeth, and pulled her long, loose hair into a messy looking bun on the top of her head. When she turned around to look at me, she looked completely washed out from the night before.

"Thank you," she said, placing her palm against my cheek.

"For what?"

"For being here and putting up with my shit," she said and rolled her eyes. Pulling her into my arms, I kissed the top of her head.

"Don't sweat it, baby. Come on, let's go get some breakfast," I said, leading her out and down to the kitchen. I sat her at the table and placed a glass of water and two Tylenol in front of her. "Take those, and I'll cook you up an omelet," I said, heading back into the kitchen.

"I'm not sure I can handle eggs at the moment," she said as she downed the Tylenol.

"Tough, that's what you're getting. You need to put something back into that empty stomach," I said, pointing a finger at her.

"Aren't you going to be late for work?" she asked.

"Nice try, sweetheart, but I'm taking the day off."

"Please don't, Nate. I'll be fine," she half groaned.

"I know you'll be fine because I'll be here to take care of you," I said as I flipped the omelet onto a plate with some toast and put it down in front of her.

Chapter Forty-four

Casey

Looking up at Nate, I tried to give him my best doe-eyed look of mercy, but all he said was, "Eat," and pointed down at the fluffy, yellow omelet on the plate. I expected to gag on the first mouthful, but I was surprised when it went down with a tasty swallow, and before I knew it, my plate was empty. Nate sat back into his chair and took a sip from his coffee cup.

"Feel better?" he asked over the top of the cup.

"Surprisingly, yes," I said, smiling.

"So, I was thinking that we would relax and take it easy today. Maybe go for a walk down the shoreline, then come back and talk," he said, with one eyebrow raised.

"Talk? Do we have to?" I said.

"Yep."

"Okay," I said, dragging the word out slowly and looking at him through narrowed eyes.

"Well, I was thinking that this is something that we really need to talk about, get it all out and...fuck. I don't know, try and make some sense of it all. Remember, no secrets, and we promised to talk about things." Nate said, rubbing a hand through his hair.

"I'm pretty sure you know all of my secrets. Not much more to tell. Well, I hope there isn't anyway."

Standing up, Nate picked up both plates and placed them in the sink, then came back to the table. "Come on, let's take that walk."

Sighing in defeat, I stood and went into the bedroom to change into a pair of shorts and a t-shirt, then joined Nate and Chance, who were standing on the beach at the bottom of the stairs, waiting for me. As soon as my feet hit the sand, Nate took my hand and threaded our fingers together as we walked past the remnants of last night's fire, down to the water's edge, and along the shore. Nothing was said while we walked. We just enjoyed the warm sun, the clear, blue sky, and the fresh smell of the clean ocean air as the breeze whipped around us. It was nice and calming, and that, along with breakfast, made me feel so much better.

When our walk was over, Nate stayed true to his word, and we sat on the couch. I turned to face him with my legs crossed under me.

"So, what do you want to know?" I asked him.

"Well, you could start with the diary."

"I brought it with me, intent on reading it, although I did go back and forth with that decision for a while. I suppose in the end, it was just too tempting. Look, I know it sounds stupid, but I thought by reading it, I might get a different picture of my parents. I mean, they always treated me like I was invisible, and I don't know, I thought maybe I would find a reason or something. Not that there is ever a good reason to treat another human being, let alone a child, like they did."

"No, there isn't," Nate said stiffly.

"I guess I thought that maybe she had some kind of mental issue going on, or that her relationship with my father was abusive or something. I don't know, just something," I said, exasperated.

"So what did you find?"

Taking a deep breath, I gave Nate the short version of what was in the diary, I didn't want to go too much into detail because just with the words I had spoken, his body language went through several different stages of tension. Not to mention his facial expressions. Tight lips, furrowed brows, and his eyes were like windows filled with raging anger that I knew he was keeping a tight rein on until I finished telling him what made me go down onto the beach last night and build a fire.

Shrugging, I said. "I found out that my mother was exactly what I always thought she was. A selfish, self-absorbed, evil bitch. I also realized that I didn't do anything. It wasn't my fault, it was theirs," I said, looking up into Nate's eyes, which were now filled with sympathy and understanding.

"You see, I've always thought that it was my fault. That I had done something to cause them not to want me, but I hadn't." Nate reached out and stroked my cheek with the back of his fingers.

"Baby, how could you have done anything wrong? The only thing you did was be born to a couple of abusive parents, who had no right to do what they did." As he spoke, I felt the tension in his body start to appear, and I placed my hand on top of his as he stroked my face.

"Nate, please don't be angry about something that you had no control over."

"I'm trying hard not to, babe," he said as he continued to stroke my cheek tenderly.

"I'm sorry about last night. I needed a bit of liquid courage to finish reading it, and then all I could think about was getting rid of it for good. I suppose I thought it was only fitting that the spawn of the devil needed to burn in hell," I said, looking down at my hands that were now rubbing against each other.

"Hey, look at me," Nate demanded, placing a finger under my chin and tilting my face up to his.

"You have nothing to be sorry for." Reaching out both arms, he pulled me onto his lap and close into his body. We sat like that for a few moments in silence, until I whispered into his chest, "I told you I was broken." His body stiffened at my words.

"No, baby, you're far from being broken. You are the strongest person I have ever met in my life. I mean, how many people can go through what you went through and survive? Think about it. You have fought your whole life, starting from the womb, for fuck's sake. And still, after everything you endured, you picked yourself up and put yourself through medical school. Hell, you even took a contract to work overseas under conditions that some soldiers wouldn't work in. All your parents ever did for you was donate some biological material, but everything you are and everything you have become is down to you. You did it, no one else. So listen to me when I tell you you're not broken. You are perfect, and better still, I'm the lucky bastard that gets to keep you." Slowly, I traced a finger over the lines of muscle under his t-shirt.

"So, does that mean you don't want to trade me in then?" I said, looking up at him sheepishly.

"Not yet," he chuckled. "Although, I might think about it if you keep hiding things from me. If there's something on your mind, you need to talk to me, okay? You need to learn to share the load."

"I will, I promise. I just want it all to go away. I'm tired of it hanging around my neck like an anchor, and honestly, I really didn't think reading the diary was going to devastate me as much as it did."

"Yeah, well, I think that was a long time coming. I have a feeling you needed to cry it all out for once instead of putting on the tough act and keeping it all inside," he said, touching my nose with the tip of his finger.

"It's not an act, you asshole," I laughed, giving him a light slap against his chest.

"Whatever," he sighed before continuing. "Just remember, we are your family now, and this is the time for you to have control and steer your happiness in the direction that I tell you to." I stared at him, wide-eyed, with my mouth gaping open until he couldn't keep the laughter in any longer. "Just kidding, babe," he said as he pulled me further up his body and planted his mouth on mine with a searing kiss. "I love you, babe," he said against my lips.

"And I love you," I said, kissing him back.

Over the next couple of weeks, life settled down more and more every day. Nate was right. Since that night on the beach when I sobbed out my pain, I felt so much lighter in my body, mind, and soul. I felt as though I had purged myself of a lifetime of tears that I had never shed before. Nate and I spent almost that whole day relaxing and talking about anything and everything until he was satisfied that my diary burning decision was the best thing I could have done. For me, it was a symbolic end to my past and a new beginning with Nate.

I started working at the free clinic two days a week, and I was enjoying it immensely. I loved being part of a team again, and on the days that it wasn't so busy, we had a lot of fun, joking around and gossiping. For the first time in my life, I actually felt more like a normal woman than I ever had. Lunches with Lynda, shopping expeditions with Carmel almost every Monday morning to some obscure market she would find for us to hang out at, and babysitting Emily once a week made me feel whole again. And the best part of my life was spending time with Nate, who I had convinced into taking Chance into work with him on the days that I worked at the clinic. Yeah, he bitched at first, but he still bought Chance his own bed to sleep on in the corner of his office. On Sundays, Nate and I would go out for a drive. Well, I drove, and he white-knuckled himself to the seat. Not sure why, considering it was his idea in the first place. He said it was time I learned to drive American-style, and it would give me more freedom and the independence to get around whenever I needed instead of having to be chauffeured around everywhere. I had to admit, I was a little shocked that he was also learning to chill out and not worry so much about me. Well, just a little bit anyway. I did like his alpha protectiveness, especially in the bedroom. Life was good, at last.

Chapter Forty-five

Nate

As I pulled the SUV into the parking space at King Security, a loud bark came from the back seat. Turning, I was faced with a large, wet tongue as Chance tried to lick my face. Since it was a clinic day for Casey, it meant that it was a "take the mutt to work day" for me, and he always got excited as soon as we got here. Getting out, I opened the back door for him to excitedly jump out and turn around in circles before he instinctively walked over to the elevator and sat, waiting for me to press the button.

Everyone in the office loved the days I brought him into work, and I was pretty sure he did, too. I mean, so many pretty girls, stroking and patting you all day, feeding you treats, and taking you for a walks and a toilet break on their own breaks? Yeah, he had it made, and I had to admit I had grown attached to the mutt. As soon as I opened my office door, he went straight to his bed in the corner and curled up for his early morning, pre-snack time nap, and I went to turn on my computer. I had just sat down in my chair, when Paxton flung open the doors to my office and strode in to stand in front of my desk. He looked flustered and irritated. He wasn't wearing a jacket or tie, and his silk, button-down shirt sleeves were rolled up to his elbows, like he'd been up all night digging a ditch. Alarmed at his entrance, I stood.

"Paxton, what the fuck is wrong? You look like shit," I said impatiently.

"That's because I feel like shit. I just spent the last two hours at Portland PD." He sat, dropping down into the seat opposite me.

"What? What the hell for?"

Paxton ran both of his hands through his hair and down his face before taking in a deep breath.

"I got a call early this morning, asking me to go in and see a Detective Dillon. They couldn't tell me anything over the phone, and that scared the shit out of me. I thought something had happened to you. So, I pressed the point more until they assured me it had nothing to do with any of my family members or the business."

Walking around to the front of my desk, I leaned back against it, crossing my arms over my chest.

"And?"

"Peterson is dead," Paxton said.

"What?"

"He was found dead in his office last night. His throat had been slit from ear to ear."

Absently rubbing a hand across my chin, I tried to grasp what Paxton was telling me. Peterson was dead?

"So, what does that have to do with you?" I asked him.

"The last phone call he made was to my number."

"Why would he call you?" I asked, confused.

"I don't know. I never took a call from him, but apparently, he did call me, and it went to my voicemail."

"And did he leave a message?"

"Yes, two words: I tried."

"What the hell does that mean?" I said with frustration.

"I have no idea. I'm just glad I had an alibi."

"I fucking hope so."

"Of course, while he was getting his throat cut, I was at home with Lynda and Emily."

"Thank fuck for that," I breathed out with relief. "And you have more proof, not just Lynda's word right?"

"Yeah, video surveillance at home. It's date and time stamped."

"Good," I said, pinching the bridge of my nose with my thumb and finger. "So why would he be calling you?"

"I don't know. The last time I ever spoke to him was when you and Casey got back from Ashgabat."

Nodding, I walked around my desk and sat down. "Then we need to do some research," I said, flipping on my computer and hitting up Google for every news channel or information on the death of Peterson. We spent the whole day locked in my office, scouring the internet. I read so many reports on the killing that my eyes were starting to water. Paxton had called Lynda to see if everything was alright at home and let her know what had happened. I sent Casey a text, checking if she was okay and asking if she could text me when she left the clinic this afternoon. I was relieved when she sent me back a heart emoji. By 3 p.m., we were both mentally drained from trying to piece together what little bit of information we did have into something that made sense. Going to the bar, I pulled out two glasses and a bottle of single malt and brought it to the desk, pouring us each two fingers. I handed one to Paxton, and as he took the glass from me, it hit me like a ton of bricks.

"It's Casey."

"What?" Paxton said confused.

"The message he left on your voicemail. It has to be something to do with Casey," I said, mulling over the words in my head until it smacked me hard in the face. "'I tried,' Paxton, that's what he said. And the only thing that those words could mean is he tried to call off the sale."

Paxton's eyes grew wide with realization at the same time my phone pinged with a message from Casey: "Leaving now."

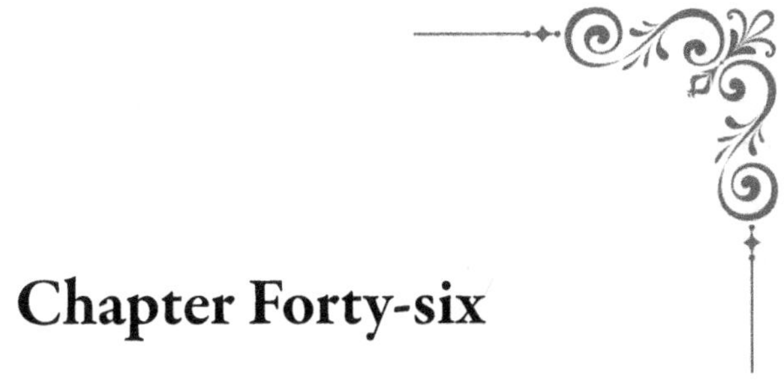

Chapter Forty-six

As I left the clinic, the best thing I had seen that day was the town car waiting at the curb and Nick leaning against it. I was so tired, I just wanted to curl up on Nate's couch in his office and sleep. It had been one long busy day. Nick opened the back door as I approached the car, "Hi, Nick," I said, but all I got was a silent nod, as usual. Sliding into the back seat, he closed the door and made his way around to the driver's side. Leaning my head back, I closed my eyes. It only took around ten minutes to get back to the penthouse, and I didn't intend on falling asleep for the short journey. But you know what they say about best intentions? Because when I opened my eyes and glanced out the window, it was pitch black outside. Rubbing my eyes furiously, trying to clear the sleepiness from them, I looked again, and there was nothing. No buildings, no cars, no lights, just blackness. I reached into my purse in search of my phone to see what the time was, but my purse was empty. Leaning forward on the chair, I knocked on the dark glass divider that separated me from Nick.

"Nick!" I called out. "Where are we?" When he didn't even flinch, I knocked on the glass again, this time harder, but he just ignored me and kept his head straight ahead. "Nick, talk to me. Where are we? Answer me!" I yelled and continued to pound my fist against the wall of glass. I screamed and yelled so much, the back of my throat was starting to sting and burn. I tried the door handle of the car. It shook slightly, but it was locked. Sitting back, I scanned the back seat, trying to find something, anything that I could use to help me get out of the back seat of this car. But there was nothing. What the fuck was going on? Could he not hear me through the glass? And where was my phone? Was I still asleep and dreaming? Trying to get my mind into some kind of order and clear my confusion, I tried to slow my breathing and pull myself together.

Nick was a good guy, wasn't he? He had worked for Nate for a long time, and Nate vetted all of his employees thoroughly, so what the hell was going on? Were we running to escape someone or something? Or was he running to someone?

"Nate will find me. He always does. He'll have some kind of tracker on the car or my phone or something. Just keep calm and stay strong. I can do this," I told myself, but could I do this? Whatever this was?

Chapter Forty-seven

N^{ate}

"Answer the fucking phone," I yelled as it went to Casey's voicemail once again. I smashed the iPhone onto the desk so hard I was sure the screen just shattered. The last text message I received from her was over three hours ago. I called the clinic, and they confirmed that she had left there around 3 p.m., and was picked up in a town car by her usual driver. Since then, my brain was in overdrive. Paxton alerted the local police and was down in the surveillance room, trying to locate the car or either one of their phones with the tracking devices we had in them.

Pacing back and forth in my office, I found myself standing in front of the wall of glass windows, looking out into the darkness of the night. She was out there somewhere, and I needed to find her. Hanging around here wasn't helping to cool the volcanic fury that I was trying so fucking hard to contain. This anger had been slowly building up all day, from trying to figure out the cryptic words that were left on Paxton's phone by Peterson to the realization of what those words actually meant. Picking up my phone with its now slightly cracked screen, I thumbed through my contacts and pressed dial on the number I needed. Within two rings, a chirpy, southern drawl came down the line. "Hey, buddy," Jax answered. I could barely hear him, and there was a lot of background noise. It sounded like he was at a bar or a party.

"Jax, it's hard to hear you," I said.

"Hang on, I'll take this outside," he said, then I heard him say, "I'll be right back, little lady, so keep my seat warm and my beer cold," followed by the sound of a door opening. The background noise became slightly muted.

"What's up, Nate?"

"Jax, I need you to come in," I said, sternly.

"What's going on?" he asked, his voice now deeper and serious.

"A lot. Peterson was found dead this morning, and Casey's gone missing. I think it might be Asferat." I heard his deep intake of air.

"I'm on my way," he said and hung up.

Looking down at my phone, my office door pushed open, and Paxton walked in. "Have you got anything?" I asked him anxiously.

"Casey's phone is off the radar, but the car and Nick's phone is still showing up."

"Where?" I asked impatiently, and Paxton spread a map out onto my desk and pointed to a spot on it, tapping it with his finger.

"There, on Mount Angeles Road, heading toward Olympic National Park."

"Washington?" I exclaimed, shocked at how far they had gotten in peak rush hour traffic.

"Looks that way. Have you tried calling Nick's phone again?" Paxton asked.

"Yeah, I tried a few times before, but there's no answer."

"Try him again, because that road has a bad reputation for cell drop out."

Picking up my phone, I dialed his number again. I was just about to cut the call before it rang out when he answered. "Nick? What the fuck are you doing?" I seethed down the phone line. I could hear him breathing, and after a short pause, I yelled, "Talk to me, you motherfucker."

"I wondered how long it would take you," Nick said.

"What the fuck are you doing?" My words were now coming out clipped and sharp.

"I'm making a financial decision in my favor. Nothing personal, Mr. King. It's just my new boss pays a lot more than you do."

"Whatever it is, I'll triple it," I said.

"Sorry, can't do that, I'm afraid. You see, my new boss isn't as understanding as you are, and if I try to stiff him now, well, let's just say I won't live long enough to reap any benefits from the paycheck," he said, laughing into the phone, which only enraged me more, but I decided to try a calmer approach.

"Nick, don't do this. You know Casey. She's a good person. Just turn around and bring her back. I'll pay you, then you can disappear, no questions asked."

"Nice try, but I know your reputation too well," he said, laughing again. Right at that moment, I was instantly done with being calm.

"Listen, you motherfucker, you have just made the biggest mistake of your life, because I'm coming for you, and when I get to you, you're dead." This time, I flung my phone across the room, and it smashed against the wall. Looking down at the tiny, shattered pieces, I closed my eyes against the pain that shot through my body before letting out a loud cry of anguish. "FUCK!" Heading back over to my desk, I grabbed my keys and a spare phone. Then, I pushed lightly at the wood on the bottom of the drawer, flipping it open. Reaching in, I pulled out the Glock I kept there and released the magazine, checking it before pushing it back into the butt of the gun. I push it into the waistband at the back of my jeans. Walking out of my office, I ignored the shout from Paxton as I got into the elevator, went down to the garage and slid into the Audi, slamming the door and firing the engine. "I'm coming, Casey. I'm coming."

The End........

.............for now

Coming Soon

Forever Free The final book in the Freedom Series
The Club - A Standalone Novel

For more information on Author J.Grayland you can follow on:

Twitter- https://twitter.com/ladyarcher1

Instagram- @ j.grayland_author_blog

Facebook- https://www.facebook.com/profile.php?id=100017500892338

Goodreads- https://www.goodreads.com/author/show/16842698.J_Gray

Website- https://www.ladyarcherbookblog.com

email- authorjgrayland@hotmail.com

Don't miss out!

Visit the website below and you can sign up to receive emails whenever J.Grayland publishes a new book. There's no charge and no obligation.

https://books2read.com/r/B-A-YZUJ-AXYYC

BOOKS 2 READ

Connecting independent readers to independent writers.